Moonlight

KEITH KNAPP

Outskirts Press, Inc.
Denver, Colorado

Outskirts Press, Inc.
http://www.outskirtspress.com

ISBN: 978-1-4327-1565-6

Library of Congress Control Number: 2007936796

Outskirts Press and the "OP" logo are trademarks belonging to Outskirts Press, Inc.

PRINTED IN THE UNITED STATES OF AMERICA

Special Thanks

Stephen May - Director of Public Works,
    Village of Westmont

Westmont Police Chief Randy Sticha

Gregory P. Harris for introducing me to
    The Big Board

And a very special thanks to Leslie. This book
    would not exist without you.

Visit the author at:
http://www.myspace.com/keithknapp

For my folks for always encouraging me to follow my dreams.

When The Lights Go Down In The City

1.

"Fuck."

The searing summer heat forced Jennifer Adams awake. A drop of fresh sweat swam down her neck. She could almost feel herself begin to stink, the kind of stink one only gets in the summer when not even the coldest, longest shower would suffice. Growing up, she had loved the months between May and September. Three months without school. Mr. Fatty the Ice Cream Man seemed to come around the corner just when she felt the sun was about to burn her brain to a crisp. Weekdays melted into weekends, and by the end of summer she couldn't tell a Monday from a Sunday.

That had been a quarter of a century ago. Back then she was a bright kid, head of her class, not a

1

care in the world. Jennifer was still a bright kid, although she was finding it harder and harder to refer to herself as a "kid" even though the majority of Westmont's town council still called her that. She thought she was probably the only mayor in the history of America to be called a "kid" while sitting behind her desk.

Her days of no cares in the world were far behind her. They were nothing more than distant memories. She found herself worrying about the town's rising debt more than if she had enough change in her pocket for a cherry flavored Popsicle. The decision between road construction on Quincy Avenue and building a new library had replaced the decision between chocolate and vanilla. But on this particular night, Jennifer was more concerned with her air conditioner than potholes and buildings.

Jennifer wasn't sure exactly when the power had gone out. It wasn't daylight yet, and she didn't bother trying to find her watch in the dark. The alarm clock next to her bed flashed 12:00 repeatedly — that was of no use at all. The power had come back on, but the flipped circuit-breaker wasn't allowing the air conditioner to return to life. In an hour or so, the house would be hotter than a sauna.

She glanced down at her husband of five years as she stood up from their bed. Stephen could sleep through a nuclear attack and probably not wake up until the fallout hit. There was no doubt he could fix whatever was wrong; the man had nearly run the town's power sub-station for the past two years all by himself, so it was a pretty safe bet that a simple flipped circuit would be no problem for him. But Stephen had pulled a double shift the day before and she figured the last thing he'd want would be to face the same troubles at home that he had been facing at work. Apparently they had been having problems with the grid for the past week, which was slowly driving the thirty-thousand plus residents of Westmont utterly bat-shit insane. Frequent outages and brown-outs were no way to spend a hot summer.

Slipping her robe on over her shoulders, she looked back at Stephen as he stirred in his sleep. She was tempted to wake him, but certainly the Mayor of Westmont could handle something as straightforward as a flipped circuit breaker.

She walked the walk of the barely awake out of the bedroom and down the hallway, stumbling in the dark until she found the door that led to the basement. She pulled it open, reached inside, and flipped the light switch. Light swam out from the basement, forcing Jennifer to squint her eyes until they adjusted. At least *something* in the house worked.

Once at the bottom of the stairs, she moved past the washer and dryer, past the central air conditioning unit which was as quiet as the rest of the house, past their mountain bikes (which had been used a total of two times) and faced the breaker board. The casing opened with a *squeak*, and she was confronted with twenty switches, all in varying positions. And, of course, all unmarked.

"Nice."

Jennifer started from the top and worked her way down, methodically moving from one to the next. The loud *CLICK* of each switch was almost deafening in the stillness of the echo-prone basement. When she got to the seventh one and flipped it back and forth, she heard the air conditioner next to the dryer pulse and hum back to life.

With a satisfied smile she closed the flap to the control panel and headed back upstairs to enjoy the cool air emanating from the vents. As she closed the basement door behind her, the whoosh of air from the vents shut off and the house was once again as quiet as the proverbial tomb. She opened the basement door, flipped the light switch back and forth. Nothing. The power had gone out.

"Fuck."

Stephen, so help me God, you better fix all this tomorrow or I'll have you fired.

Stephen slept soundlessly in the bedroom at the end of the hall, oblivious to his wife's silent threat.

Traffic had never been much of a problem in Westmont. Like most suburbs of Chicago, it housed a simple grid of streets, lined by either houses or small businesses. If you timed the lights right, you could make it from one end of town to the other in ten minutes flat.

Jennifer had been in her SUV for close to an hour since kissing Stephen goodbye that morning.

Evidently the traffic lights throughout the 'burb had been affected by the multiple power outages that had taken place over the course of the night. Sure, they were working now, but much like her alarm clock they all blink-blink-blinked red, bringing the cars on the road to an infant's crawl.

She was next in line at the cross-street and could see Westmont's one and only municipal building a block ahead. She caught the attention of the cop directing traffic, an older officer with the moniker of Gildy.

Gildy was pushing sixty and had been on the force since before Jennifer took office. Try as she might, all she could get out of anyone for his name was "Gildy." He had been called that for so long, no one could remember where the nickname had come from — or if it even *was* a nickname. Gildy liked it that way.

Gildy gave Jennifer a quick two-finger salute as he strode up to her SUV. "Mayor Adams. Runnin' a little late today, are we?"

Jennifer smiled. "There's no fooling you. Now I know why we give you all those plaques."

"And I thought that was just 'cause I'm old."

"It's that, too."

The impatient driver of a Nissan Stanza behind Jennifer blared his horn. Gildy leaned against the SUV's door, rolling his eyes at the sound. "Why don't you just go right ahead, Miss Mayor."

Jennifer slid the SUV into gear and gave the cop a reassuring smile. "Go easy on the guy," she said, nodding her head at the car behind her. "We've all had a tough couple of days."

"His day's about to get a little tougher," Gildy said as the Nissan popped its horn again. Gildy looked at the driver in the Nissan, then back up to the intersection where he watched the Mayor safely drive through the dead stoplights. The cop turned his attention back to the angry Nissan driver who rewarded Gildy's look with another honk of the horn.

Gildy held up a hand, keeping the irate driver at the intersection while he allowed the cross-traffic through. "Keep a lid on it, fella'. No one's goin' anywhere."

The municipal building was a flurry of activity, which was far from the norm on a Wednesday morning. Two village trustee members, Harding and Bryman, sped through the outer office, papers in hand, collars already damp with summer sweat. Bryman was the worse off of the two: sporting an extra fifty pounds, the humid summer heat was the man's worst enemy.

Jeffrey Harding had been a loyal trustee member of Westmont's political council since before Jennifer Adams even ran for the position of Mayor. He had no dreams or delusions of ever sitting in her seat one day — he knew he could do more behind the lines. Pulling strings and being the Master of Puppets were his strengths, and no one knew that better than Harding himself.

Scott Bryman never strayed far from Harding. He was the puppy dog to Harding's alpha dog status, which was exactly how they both liked it. Although Bryman himself was a genius with an IQ that hovered just over 160, he was the type of whiz kid that was still never sure of himself and found comfort in having others tell him what to do. It was his brilliance that brought the town out of debt two years ago following a hellish blizzard, and it was everyone's hope that this same brilliance would bring them out of the sky-rocketing debt that recent construction woes had caused.

Jennifer watched the two dash into the main meeting room as she walked up to her secretary's desk. Gloria Cortez greeted Jennifer with a smile. Gloria had graduated from Westmont High School a little over two years ago and had started taking business classes at the U of I. Those plans had undergone some modifications due to the baby that had been inside of her for the past seven-and-a-half months — classes at the university would have to take a back seat for awhile.

"Good morning, Mrs. Adams," Gloria said.

Jennifer placed her shoulder bag on Gloria's desk. "What's with Harding and Bryman?"

Gloria haphazardly adjusted papers, clearly frazzled by something. "They've been at it all morning. Trying to contact ComEd in Chicago."

"Any luck?" Jennifer asked.

"I don't know, they don't tell me anything. Harding's too busy looking important, and Bryman

7

is too busy making sure his nose is up Harding's ass." Gloria stopped herself and frowned. "Sorry."

"Never apologize for telling the truth."

A quick laugh replaced Gloria's frown as Harding and Bryman exited the meeting room and made their way back into their own office, each of them giving Jennifer a quick wave as they passed.

"The power's been off and on at the house since yesterday. It's driving me nuts," Jennifer said.

Gloria brought her paper shuffling duties to an end and looked up at her boss.

Jennifer returned the look with an inquisitive eye. "What have I missed?"

"You'd better get in there, Mrs. Adams," Gloria said.

For the second time since Jennifer had walked in, Harding and Bryman ran from their office back into the boardroom. Jennifer shouldered her bag and followed them in.

Every window to the boardroom was wide open, but no breeze came through to relieve any of the staff from the overpowering heat. It was like walking into a sauna without an air filter; the stench of human sweat and worry was as much a member of the committee today as any of the people.

Harding and Bryman sat at the far end of an old oak table in the center of the room. Malcolm Dwight, the one lawyer on the team, leaned back in his chair by a window. His head rested in the palms of his hands. The man was clearly beat.

"Okay, first thing's first: anyone have any idea what to do about the smell in here?" Jennifer announced as she walked in.

She was met with stagnant eyes. Apparently no one in the room was in the frame of mind for one of her mood-alleviating jokes.

"Okay, tough crowd," she said as she took her place at the head of the table. "Who wants to bring me up to speed?"

All eyes turned to Harding and Bryman, evidently the experts on the events of the day. Harding adjusted his bifocals, got the go-ahead nod from Bryman, and began.

"At roughly three o'clock yesterday afternoon, Commonwealth Edison started to experience odd power fluctuations. One minute everything would be fine, the next Chicago would roll into a brown-out as the suburbs — Downers Grove, Hinsdale, all of us — began to suck their power, putting a strain on the system."

"Tell us something we don't know," Malcolm said.

Harding ignored him. "This continued on throughout the night. Lights and power all over downtown ebbed and flowed, and while we can't get anyone to confirm it, I'd be willing to bet this could go on for some time. Maybe a week or more."

"Okay, so ComEd has a problem. What are they doing about it?" Jennifer asked.

"That's the thing, Jennifer. They're not sure what to do. As near as they can figure, a main power line was cut somewhere up North, which began this domino effect," Harding said. "At least that was the news last night."

Bryman sat up. "We haven't been able to reach them since."

"Where up North? Why don't they just call-"

Bryman cut her off. "Phones are down. They went inoperative this morning."

"That doesn't answer my question of *where*," Jennifer said.

Robert Goldman, the newest trustee on the board, spoke up: "Canada."

Jennifer looked from eye to eye, person to person, checking to make sure they weren't joking. "Canada?"

Malcolm leaned forward in his chair, placing his arms on the table. "Remember that blackout a few years back? Wiped out most of New York for a day?"

"Sure," Jennifer said.

"Same thing," Malcolm said.

Harding smiled. "Except different."

"How?" Jennifer asked.

It was now Goldman's turn to explain: "When New York went down, they were able to figure out in a matter of hours what had happened and fix it accordingly. But ComEd can't get in touch with anyone in Canada. Or New York. Or anywhere, for that matter. So suffice it to say, we're guessing here as to what's happening. Guessing."

"But if our guess is even close, once Chicago

goes down for good, so will we. *And* all the neighboring towns," Harding said.

Jennifer looked from Harding to Bryman, then back again. "Has anyone tried a cell phone? Maybe the calls could get routed through another tower."

Malcolm shook his head and leaned forward. "They're all down, too."

Finding that hard to believe, Jennifer reached into her bag and pulled out her cell.

The room watched as she flipped open the Motorola. The screen came to life, but she didn't get a single bar notifying her of service.

Bryman spoke as Jennifer held the phone in varying positions, trying to get a signal. "A number of people have heard reports that we're experiencing some sort of solar storm interference or some damn thing that's fucking with all the cell phones."

"And what, that messed with the air conditioner in the building, too?" Jennifer asked.

"No," Malcolm answered. "That just doesn't work anymore."

Gloria barged into the room before Jennifer could ask her next question. "Sorry to interrupt. The TV feed's back. They're getting something from New York."

Bryman turned to the small television behind him and flicked it on. The screen warmed up, showing a newscaster in a newsroom somewhere in Chicago.

"Well, Chicago's still up," Malcolm said.

Harding shushed him.

11

The newscaster, his friendly invite-me-into-your-home demeanor on vacation, addressed his television audience:

"...power in New York has been down for the past six hours now. Experts here tell us this is directly related to the problems we're having here in Chicago, but can offer no firm data on the cause or when power can be expected to return to normal. Chicago's power has continued to dance on and off, causing some mild havoc and confusion downtown as-"

The screen went to static.

Everyone exchanged troubled looks as Bryman flipped through the channels, trying to find another feed. He was met with white noise across the dial.

Malcolm rubbed his forehead, feeling a headache coming on. "Did Chicago just go-"

The TV and all the lights in the room shut off before Malcolm could finish. The electric hum of the ceiling fans stopped.

Jennifer looked up and watched as the fans leisurely slowed down their rotation. She was jerked out of her reverie when the screech of tires, followed by the sound of metal crunching against metal, came in from outside.

"Perfect."

When Gildy was fifteen he had run the fifty-meter dash in just under eight seconds. He was the talk of the high school for two weeks straight, and everyone was convinced that Nixa, Missouri would never be the same. He assumed his first place trophy still sat on the glass shelf in the den of his parents' house, collecting dust as his mother and father went into their eighty-eighth and ninetieth birthdays.

But that was forty-three years, two months and about seventy-thousand beers ago. Sure, he had kept in shape, but there's only so much one man can do to ward off Father Time and his wicked henchmen Sore Bones and Labored Breath. Gildy had noticed lately he wasn't all that he used to be. In fact, he felt he was a pale comparison to the man that had joined the Missouri State Troopers thirty-five years earlier. The hairline was the first to go, quickly followed by a small case of blurred vision and creaky knees. But he was still a damn good cop. No one ever second-guessed his ability to enforce the law or to continue to be an invaluable asset to the town of Westmont. Especially Gildy.

He was finally having the first second-guess of his career as he jumped out of the way of the oncoming Nissan Stanza. The driver, who had made it abundantly clear that he was not one prone to waiting in long lines at dead traffic lights, took it upon himself to veer out of his lane and race through the intersection. As Gildy saw the car speeding toward the intersection, making a mental note of the license plate (this asshole was getting a whopper of a ticket and a few nights in jail) the car suddenly swerved to the left and headed straight for Gildy.

When he was younger, Gildy would've been out

of the way long before the car came close to turning him into pulp. But now that his body had decided to not act quite so quickly to commands from the old noodle as it used to, he was just barely able to leap out of the way in time. He felt the bumper of the Nissan tap against his left knee just before he landed on the ground next to the front tire of a pickup truck.

Gildy watched as the Nissan tried to cut right, but it was too late. As the driver slammed on his brakes, the Nissan rammed head first into a Volvo on the opposite side of the street.

Gildy got to his feet, rubbing asphalt off his road-rashed hands, and limped toward the accident. He peered through the windshield of the Volvo, where the old woman who had been driving it looked more worried than injured. "You okay, ma'am?" he asked her.

The old woman pulled her eyes away from the hood of her car — which was now half as long as it used to be — and looked over at the cop. "Yes-I-he just-he just hit me."

"Anything broken? Anything hurt?"

The lady looked around the interior of her car, as if inspecting the automobile for damage instead of herself. "I'm alright," she finally replied. "I think I'm okay."

"Wait here," Gildy told the woman.

Relieved that the old lady was unharmed, Gildy limped stiffly over to the Nissan, favoring his left knee, and bent down to look at the driver. "What the hell did you think you were doin', kid?"

The kid looked from the old woman to Gildy and back again in mild surprise. Gildy recognized the boy as Eddie Miller, a troublemaker who had dropped out of high school his sophomore year three years ago and had been nothing but an annoyance to the townsfolk ever since.

"It just-" Eddie began.

Gildy scolded the boy. "Move your car to the side of the road, get it outta the way."

Eddie gave the cop a "fuck you" look as he stepped on the gas. The Nissan jolted forward half a foot — slamming into the Volvo again — then abruptly died.

Kid can't even drive a stick, Gildy thought.

Eddie turned the key in the ignition and got nothing in return. There was one barely audible click as the starter tried to turn the engine over, then it was silent. Eddie tried again, and this time didn't even get a click.

Gildy returned to Eddie's window. "Jesus Eddie, you gotta push in the clutch."

"I am."

"Quit screwing around and get this thing outta the way. You're ruining my morning."

"I'm not an idiot, you fucking jag off. And I ain't screwing around. The car is fucking dead."

"Mine, too," said the old woman who was leaning out of her Volvo.

Gildy took in a deep breath of frustration as he looked around. All across the intersection and up and down the street, people were getting out of their cars in puzzlement.

It was then that Gildy noticed just how quiet the morning had become. All up and down Cass Avenue and intersecting Naperville Road, none of the cars were idling. There wasn't even the sound of people *trying* to start their engines. Gildy glanced up at the traffic light, which had stopped flashing red and stared back at him with three dead eyes.

Jennifer Adams jogged towards what had obviously been the cause of the sounds she'd heard. Malcolm, Harding and Bryman followed close behind.

"What happened?" the Mayor asked.

Gildy broke his gaze from the stoplight. "I'm not too sure."

Malcolm frowned at the aging police officer. "What do you mean you're not sure? That kid obviously ran into the-"

Jennifer held a hand up as she looked down the block, trying to figure out what was missing from the scene. "No, that's not it."

Malcolm looked at her quizzically. "What do you mean that's not it?"

"The cars," Bryman noticed.

Jennifer looked to Gildy. "They're dead."

"All of them?" Malcolm asked.

Gildy ran a hand through his thinning hair. "Seems like it."

"Have some patrols put out on the major streets," Jennifer said to Gildy. "We need to get back to work and figure out what the hell's going on."

When they returned to the municipal building, Malcolm stayed outside to enjoy some fresh air and the newfound quietness that had blanketed Westmont. The secretary — he was pretty sure her name was Gloria — stood by the front entrance to the building, watching people attempt to start their cars, fiddle with cell phones and exchange glances that could only be interpreted as *what the hell just happened?*

Gloria looked at Malcolm. She had always thought the man used too much hair gel, and today was no exception. His hair was so slick it was probably permanently greased back. He seemed to have used twice his usual amount of Old Spice today, and her nostrils violently locked up at the scent.

She watched the lawyer fumble around in his sports coat for something. The jacket probably cost more than she made in a month, and she hated him for that. She hated him even more when she saw him pull out a pack of cigarettes and begin to light one up.

The inconsiderate asshole sucked in a lungful of cancer and blew it out into the world. At least it masked part of the Old Spice smell. Gloria instinctively touched her stomach. She threw mental slurs at him with her mind, convinced that if she yelled loud enough in her brain, the man would hear it and put out the cigarette. One thing Gloria hated was any kind of confrontation. Yelling at people with her mind was her way to avoid a direct altercation. It never worked, of course. She wasn't psychic and didn't believe in such things, but it at least stopped her from saying those slurs out loud. When she was done going through her rolodex of personal swear words in her head, she calmed herself down enough to actually speak with her mouth.

"Do you mind?"

"What?" Malcolm looked at her over his shoulder as another wave of smoke emanated from his nose. She shot lasers at him with her eyes, wished him dead, wanted to make him eat that fucking cigarette. There was a baby present, godammit. *Her* baby.

"I said, *do you mind?*"

"Look lady, we're outside, so-"

The man looked her up and down. His eyes finally landed on her pregnant stomach, and his expression changed from annoyed to even more annoyed.

Uh-oh. We got a real asshole here, Gloria thought.

Malcolm dropped the cigarette and stomped it out with a foot, making more of a production out of it than was really necessary. He looked at her again, using his smoking hand to make sure his hair was still slicked perfectly back (it was) and gave her a fake smile as he began to walk back into the building.

"I have a baby, you know. It's not healthy for it," she called after him.

Malcolm didn't slow down as he pulled the door open. "That's great."

Yep. He was certainly King of the Assholes.

Shaking her head, Gloria wondered how much longer she'd be able to put up with working with a man like Malcolm Dwight. She hoped she'd give birth and be on maternity leave before she smacked the guy in the head.

Gloria pulled her cell phone from her pocket. She flipped it open and was met with a blank screen. She tapped the MENU button. Nothing. The same went for SELECT, TALK and END. No matter what button she pressed, she couldn't get the phone to do a damn thing.

Just like the stop lights and the cars. Despite the fact that she was positive she had fully charged the battery just that morning, her cell phone was dead.

2.

eter Sampson shoved the last of the ham and
cheese sandwich into his mouth. He brushed the
crumbs off his lips as he chewed and swallowed,
staring at the blank tan walls of the Westmont ComEd substation break room.

Half a dozen tables that looked like they had
been bought at a yard sale were scattered about in a
haphazard fashion. Two vending machines had been
shoved to the side; one for sodas, and one presuma-
bly for sandwiches and snacks that was never filled.
Peter's eyes were locked on the soda machine,
which was begging him to buy a Coca-Cola from it,
when all the lights flickered. The vending machine
turned off, then on, then back off again.

The florescent lights above Peter did the same
dance, but eventually settled on half-power. Peter
had worked there long enough to know that when
the lights in the break room went on half power,

that meant the in-house backup generator had kicked on and Westmont was on the verge of a blackout — or was already in one. Which meant overtime.

Shit, he could use the money.

A flurry of activity passed by the open door. Three men blurred by, too quick for Peter to catch who they were. Not long after that, a short blast of an alarm went off. Above the door, a yellow light began to blink. Lunch was over.

Peter got to his feet and stretched as if he had just woken up from a nap. He combed his hair with his fingers and tossed out his empty Ziploc bag as he sauntered through the door into the hallway. The word "rushing" was not to be found in Peter Sampson's vocabulary.

"Lookie-out, Pete."

Peter turned just in time to avoid being run over by Zach McMillan, who raced down the hallway like his ass was on fire.

"Whoa whoa whoa there, Flash. What the hell is going on?" he asked the kid, who couldn't be a day over twenty.

Zach slowed down, but didn't stop. "Lights and alarms didn't tip it off for ya, huh? We got a failure." He gave Peter a smart-ass grin, and continued on his way.

Fuckin' prick Peter thought as he followed him. But he wasn't gonna run. No way in hell. He didn't get paid enough to run. Not even on overtime.

21

The Main Control Room was flooded with commotion. All seventeen employees on duty crowded into the room that was built to accommodate only ten people. Computer monitors nestled in the walls showed various areas of Westmont, its neighboring suburbs, and a few parts of the greater Chicago area. Some people barked orders while others took them. Confusion was in the air.

Peter was able to catch only fragments of conversations amidst all the hubbub.

"Generator's kicked on, but-"

"-over the town, I don't see-"

"-all at once? How is that even-"

Peter made his way through the madness to his station. He fell into his chair and began hitting keys on the keyboard. Power grids of Westmont popped up. Instead of the usual "everything is okay" yellow field he would get around each grid showing a small section of Westmont, they were all marked in red with an ominous "X" over each one.

And it was like that everywhere, on every screen.

Zach tapped on the keyboard at the station next to his. He took a quick glance over at Peter and saw the question marks in his eyes.

"The whole town went dead ten minutes ago," he offered.

Peter raised an eyebrow. "Bullshit, that's impossible. Some hacker is fuckin' around, playin' a prank with our system."

Zach turned to another monitor. "If it's a prank,

it's a damn good one."

Peter, still unbelieving, looked back to his screen then over to Zach. "This is impossible," Peter said. "There are safety measures, generators, the entire system is set up-"

"-so just this sorta thing doesn't happen, I know," Zach said. "I won't say that I understand it, only that we can fix it. No biggie. Maybe a transformer blew at the transmission station."

Zach turned his attention back to his monitor just in time to see the screen flicker, then die. The lights above them mimicked the screen and left the room in darkness. Seventeen groans filled the crowded control room. "And there goes the backup generator."

Peter jumped up from his chair and reached for the phone just beyond Zach. He picked it up and heard nothing when he put it up to his ear. Not even a dial tone. "The phones are down, too?"

"Looks like it," Zach said just as the room cycled itself back up. "And now the generator's up again."

"Maybe not for long," Peter said as he reached into his pocket for his cell phone. "Something's not right." He flipped it open, found Stephen Adams' emergency number, and hit TALK. As he looked at the small screen on the cell for acceptance of signal, all three signal-bars quickly disappeared and the phone shut itself off. Peter tried it again, but the screen remained as blank and expressionless as his own face looked at the moment.

Zach glanced at him. "Cell phone dead?"

Peter shoved the phone into his pocket. "Seems to be. Where's Stephen?"

"Beats me," Zach said.

Peter got to his feet and headed for the door.

"Where do you think you're going?"

"To find Stephen. We need to check out the backup generator," Peter said, and was out the door.

Peter found Stephen Adams standing in front of the door marked BACKUP GENERATOR ROOM with the ominous warning that HIGH VOLTAGE was just on the other side of it. The Big Man on Campus was trying to get the door open but wasn't having much luck with it.

"Great minds think alike," Peter said, approaching his boss.

Stephen struggled with the door in frustration. "Why won't these open?"

"Safety protocol. Power goes out, all the utility doors lock themselves magnetically," Peter said.

Stephen turned around. "Power's not out."

"Then the doors should open."

"But they don't. So what the hell's going on?"

"The control room is up and running again, so the backup must be on," said Peter. He looked back down the long and dark hallway behind them. "But all the lights here are out, which doesn't make any sense." The light from outside was enough for him to see the doors leading to various other rooms: the break room, the men's bathroom, the women's bathroom, and the janitor's closet. Making a bee-line for the closet, Peter motioned for Stephen to follow him.

The door to the janitor's closet opened easily. Inside it was as dark as the backs of their eyelids. Peter shoved a hand in a pocket and pulled out his Zippo. With one smooth gesture, he flicked it on.

The glow from the lighter created shadows that danced on the walls. Amidst a hundred different cleaning supplies, two vacuums and numerous mops, Peter found what he was looking for. He took two steps toward the back of the room and picked up a crowbar from a lower shelf. He gripped it in his right hand as he shut the Zippo closed with his left and brushed past Stephen.

"Why do we have a crowbar?" Stephen asked.

"In case we ever need to break open a door."

Stephen laughed and followed Peter to the backup generator room. Peter positioned the thin end of the crowbar in between the door and its frame. Placing his left hand on the butt of the crow-bar, he used all his body weight to force the tool as far into the crack as it would go. When it would go no further, he wrapped both his hands around it. Stephen moved next to Peter and situated his hands next to his co-worker's. They both locked their feet in place.

On a silent count of "three," the two men pulled with all their might. The tool creaked in protest. Something cracked on the door where the crowbar was wedged. Peter thought he could see the side of the door bend from the force of their efforts. But then again, the crowbar was bending, too. It was just a question of which would give first: the door or the crowbar.

Peter bit his lip and pulled with all his strength. Just as he felt his feet about to slip out from underneath him, something snapped.His feet slid out from below him. The two men fell backwards as the crowbar flew out of their hands and skidded across the hallway, bouncing along the linoleum. They both looked up at the door and saw that they had succeeded: the door now stood open a crack.

Peter got back to his feet. "Shit, I didn't think that would actually work."

"Neither did I," Stephen replied, rubbing what would soon become bruises on the heels of his hands.

Peter grabbed the handle and pulled the door open. Inside it was as dark as the janitor's closet, if not more so. Peter produced the Zippo again. The orange light allowed them to see a few feet into the room, enough to make out the dark shadow of the generator. They walked to it and studied the dials on the side. They all rested at ZERO.

"That's not possible," Stephen said.

Peter moved to the back of the machine to check the connections. All cords were accounted for and in place. To their naked eyes, it looked fine. Peter found the switch, which was still set to the ON position. He flicked it down to OFF, then back up again.

Nothing happened.

He did this three more times, all with the same result.

"How can we have even partial power if the backup isn't even on?" Peter asked.

"This is what I'm saying. We shouldn't have power."

"But we do."

"Partially."

Peter scratched his chin, puzzlement setting in. "This doesn't make any sense."

"Maybe something's up with the power plant itself, screwing with our transformers and buses out back," Stephen said.

"Anyone check those yet?"

Using the rear entrance of the substation, Peter and Stephen stepped out into what was essentially the back yard of the building. The yard was covered with a maze of metallic switch towers, head-high transformers, transmission wires leading out to the town, and the main distribution bus that regulated everything.

Stephen walked to the main transformer which was nestled close to the building. His knees cracked as he bent down to unhook the latches that kept it closed.

"Don't bother," Peter said.

"What?"

"Listen."

Stephen put his hands on his legs and listened. It didn't take long for him to figure out Peter's point.

He heard birds chirping from the nearby baseball field, a piece of newspaper from the neighboring street picked up by a breeze, and Peter's feet shuffle in the grass next to him. What he didn't hear was the hum of any of the machines that they were there to check.

Stephen got back to his feet. "It's gotta be the transmission grid. Or the power plant."

Peter's brow furrowed. "How could either of those have gone black with no warning, no calls from ComEd?"

"Maybe they had no warning themselves," Stephen said. "I heard on the news that some genius in Canada severed a power line up there. New York's been in and out of power all night. Maybe we're looking at a domino effect."

"You know as well as I do that's not possible," Peter said.

"It's not *likely,* but it's possible."

"Steve, the chances of that-"

"You got a better explanation?"

"What about that solar storm?"

"Could be. Find a phone that works, call NASA."

"All the phones are dead."

Stephen smiled. "You noticed that too, huh? Okay, so until we can get Neil Armstrong on the phone, this is *our* problem."

Peter shook his head in frustration and looked at his watch. He shook his wrist. Shook it again. The hands were stuck at eleven-thirty-seven; if his memory was correct, that was roughly the same time that the power went out.

"My watch is dead."

Stephen glanced down at his own. "So's mine."

"We need to find a way to get in contact with ComEd," Stephen said.

Peter looked at him silently for a moment. Then a grin lit up his face. "I have an idea."

Zach McMillan found Peter and Stephen huddled over something in the room next door to the backup generator. Peter had placed his Zippo on a desk that housed a tiny and obviously homemade battery-powered ham radio.

"There you guys are," Zach said, waving his flashlight between the two men. "I thought you said you'd be in the generator room."

Stephen didn't look away from the two wires he was stripping. "We were. Now we're in here."

"So what-"

Peter cut him off. "The backup is dead. And get that fucking light out of my face."

Zach sheepishly moved the beam away from Peter's head and toward the ceiling, where it briefly flickered off then on.

"What's the news out front? Any progress?" Stephen asked as he twisted the two wires together.

"We've lost all our monitors. We can't track anything. The only thing that works is Sammy's PSP, but that won't do us any good." Zach paused while he gave the ham radio a once-over. "What're you guys doin'?"

"I've been tinkering with this thing for the past year or so. It works. Usually," Peter said. "I'm hoping we can get in contact with Chicago. There're a couple guys who work at ComEd up there. We chat every now and then."

"You're aware of the Internet, right?" Zach asked.

Peter smirked, raising an eyebrow. "Sometimes I prefer the old fashioned ways."

"Ten bucks says it doesn't work," Zach said.

Peter flipped a switch on the back of the radio. "You're on."

Reluctantly, the machine sprang to life. The lights behind the dials glowed amber.

"Looks like you just won yourself ten bucks, Pete," Stephen said.

Peter was too deeply immersed in the radio to celebrate his winnings, turning knobs and trying to get a signal from somewhere, anywhere. The frequency dial hopped from side to side, eventually finding a home dead center in the middle of the display.

"Jammin'," Peter said, picking up the mike. "This is substation SS five-five-eight in Westmont. Anyone out there?"

He released the TALK button, and they all listened to the reply of static.

"Breaker breaker, this is ComEd substation SS five-five-eight in Westmont. Anyone copy? Charlie, you on up there? Over," Peter said.

Zach chuckled. "'Breaker breaker'?"

"That's what they say on TV," Peter said.

Stephen chimed in: "I think that's more of a trucker thing."

"Look, I-"

Before Peter could finish, a cacophony of voices and static erupted from the radio. He adjusted knobs and turned down the volume to reduce the feedback.

The dials spun haphazardly out of control, as if they were looking for a signal they couldn't find or that didn't exist. Bits and pieces of transmissions found their way through.

Crack.

"-stuck in the elevators in the Sears Tower, and-"

Crackle.

"-lost control of my truck on I-60. The entire freeway is a parking lot, no one's moving-"

Snap.

"-in Kansas City. My rig lost all steering, truck overturned in what I think is a corn field. But there's something else here."

The last voice came in the clearest. Peter spun knobs, doing his best to make the signal stronger.

"This is ComEd in Westmont, Illinois. I read you. What's happening? Over," Peter said to the mike.

They heard the trucker breathe a sigh of relief on the other end. *"Thank God I finally got some-one."*

"Where are you again? Did you say Kansas?"

"That's right. Kansas City. Everything, all the cars on the road. They just died," the trucker said.

Peter looked back at Stephen and Zach, who obviously couldn't make head nor tails of what the trucker was saying, either. Zach shrugged.

"Say again," Peter said. "You said all the cars died?"

"That's right, hoss."

Stephen shook his head. "He's drunk."

The radio snapped and crackled, threatening to go out at any minute.

The trucker went on: *"There's someone here. I think there's someone in my cab. I can't see him. I can only feel him."*

"Yeah, he's plastered," Zach said.

*"I don't-*crackle-*what he is-*pop-*telling me to-*hiss-*think he's in my head-"*

The radio produced a final snap of a sound, then shut itself off. The read-outs went from amber to gray as the machine whined itself down from life to death.

Peter squinted at the machine. "What the hell?"

Before Zach could move in to bring the glow of his flashlight to the radio, it flickered one more time, then it too died. Peter shook the device, slapping the bottom against the palm of his hand, all to no avail.

"Okay, now *this* doesn't work," he sighed.

3.

Lindsay Stone took a step back from the canvas, admiring the painting. The wilderness scene of the pond in her mind was coming along nicely. The water had just the right amount of ripple to it, the trees overhanging the pond were just the right height, and the wooden sign on the shore was perfect — even if she had yet to decide what should be written on it. But something inside her screamed it needed more. It needed more depth, maybe a brighter sky, maybe another bird in a tree or a duck bathing itself in the water. She wasn't certain what it needed, she just knew that whatever it was, it wasn't on the canvas or in her head.

She placed the brush down on the table next to her in between two bottles of sky-blue paint, a special shade her husband had found for her last Christmas. It was an obsession of Lindsay's to find just the right shade of blue for the sky, and in her seventeen years of painting, she had yet to find or make the right one. Richard had come close with this find, but it wasn't perfect. It wasn't the color she saw in her head.

Lindsay plopped herself down in the easy chair facing the painting and closed her eyes. She tried to relax, reminding herself that part of the reason she took the job as an art teacher at Amundsen High School was so she could have her summers free to pursue her painting. But not all art came easy to Lindsay, and sometimes the frustrations of not being happy with her work outweighed her desire to follow her dreams.

The sound of honking car horns pulled Lindsay out of her daze. She shook the thoughts from her head and stood up from the chair, moving toward their balcony door. She pulled open the blinds, letting the morning sun pour into the room. The honking got louder as she unlocked and opened the sliding door and stepped outside.

All the cars on North Sheridan Road, some twenty-two floors below her, had come to a dead stop. It looked like a rush hour traffic jam, but rarely had she seen one at this time of day. In the middle of the morning in Chicago, traffic usually never got *this* bad.

She looked to her right, up North Sheridan towards downtown. As far as she could see, on the intersecting roads and even on Lake Shore Drive itself, not one car was moving. Horns were blared as drivers exited their cars, stumbling about in uncertainty.

Perplexed, Lindsay stepped back into the apartment, picked up the television remote and clicked the ON button. Perhaps the news would offer her some insight into the accident, or whatever had caused the traffic jam. It was a welcome reprieve from trying to force herself to paint something that wasn't in her at the time.

When the TV didn't turn on, she tried hitting the button three more times, all with the same effect: nothing. Still holding the remote, she walked to the rear of the set to check the wires. Everything was still plugged in, and that's when it clicked with her that the power had gone out again. She had been so wrapped up in her painting that she hadn't noticed when the air conditioner shut down.

"Swell," she mumbled to herself as she dropped the remote back on their tan leather couch and walked over to the easel. Picking up her brush again, Lindsay returned to her task of finding that right shade of blue for the sky.

4.

Jennifer set the phone back in its cradle, frustrated. She rubbed her temples. Harding and Bryman stood behind her, having not strayed more than five feet from the Mayor since the fender-bender outside. Malcolm had sequestered himself in the far corner of the meeting room, absorbed with his cell phone, positive he could get it working again.

"Lines are down," Jennifer said. "Can't get through to ComEd, but we have to assume they're on top of this."

"Or just as much in the dark as we are," Bryman added. "Pun intended."

Harding crossed him arms. "On top of *what*, exactly, Mrs. Mayor? This isn't just a power failure. *Nothing* works. Cell phones are dead, cars aren't working, telephones are down."

Jennifer turned to the man, clearly fed up. "Do

you have a better explanation?"

"EMP."

"Of course," Bryman said.

"What?" Jennifer asked.

"He's right," Bryman said. "An EMP. Electro Magnetic Pulse. When a nuke goes off, it disperses a pulse, and everything that's electric," he snapped his fingers, "doesn't work anymore."

"A nuclear bomb." Jennifer tried the words on for size. They didn't fit. "Wouldn't we have seen an explosion, a mushroom cloud, fighter jets, *something?*"

"Not necessarily," Harding said. "They have bombs that can set off *just* an EMP. Then they attack when our pants are down."

Jennifer leaned against the table. "Alrighty, so where's this attack?"

Malcolm shut his cell phone closed in annoyance. "I can't get through to anyone. Fuckin' thing doesn't work at all, the piece of shit-"

"Enough, Malcolm," Jennifer said. "I'm really not in the mood for your bullshit right now."

Malcolm glared at the woman. If looks could kill, Jennifer Adams would have died ten times over on the spot.

"So, what's the, uh, plan?" Bryman asked. "What do we do?"

"Prepare for the worst," Harding said.

Malcolm began pacing the room, taking Harding's idea to its full extent. "Look, if this was just a blackout, no big deal. But it's not just a blackout.

Cells don't work, cars don't work. Hell, even my watch stopped. So we do what Harding said: prepare for the worst. It may not be a nuclear strike, but it sure as hell isn't just a power outage. It's some sort of attack."

The room fell silent. For the first time since they started working together, whether Jennifer liked it or not, she agreed with him.

Jennifer sighed. "We have to prepare for the worst."

5.

The Man stood in front of a small clothing store with the highly original name of "Big & Tall" in the center of town. It was proud to offer its line of clothes for the "BIG, TALL, AND EVERYONE IN BETWEEN!" according to the hand-written sign in the window.

The Man's jet black hair hung in front of his eyes. He brushed it away and caught a glimpse of his reflection in the display window. The vertical scar on his left cheek mocked him, reminding him of his painful past.

His eyes looked through the glass, past his reflection. He couldn't stand the sight of his own face. Not in a photo, not in a mirror. He'd rather cut off both legs with a rusty chainsaw than to have to look at that mug again. It was the face of his old life, his old self, his human self. That person had allowed himself to be hurt by others. He allowed that self to die a long, long time ago, and had felt better for it ever since. People didn't like him in his old life. His memory was fuzzy on a lot of events from that time, but that was one thing he remembered: no one liked him. Not even his parents.

Especially his parents.

Life had gotten a lot more tolerable since he had retired from the world of the living and was given this new job. It paid well. Shit, it paid *great*. It didn't pay in money, but in opportunity. Opportunity to change things, to make things the way he wanted. To make the world a better place.

His vacant black eyes sized up the dark trench coat in the window. It hung limply on a faceless male mannequin. It looked like crap on the display.

But it'd look perfect on him.

With a quick jolt from his elbow, the Man cracked the front window to the store. He straightened out his arm, pulled back a fist for a whopper of a punch, and let the window have it again. The glass shattered, sprinkling small button-sized pieces of glass across the floor of the display and the sidewalk at the Man's feet.

No alarms went off.

The Man stepped up through the window, kicking pieces of broken glass aside as he moved. Broken bits of window snapped and crackled underneath the dusty leather cowboy boots he wore. He pulled the black trench coat off the mannequin and slipped his arms into the sleeves. He adjusted the jacket on his shoulders. Tugged at the neck.

Pulled lightly at the accompanying belt. He was right — it was a perfect fit.

A stocky fat man in glasses poked his head through the rear curtain of the display. His forehead was drenched in sweat, and he looked like he had just come from a seven-course meal consisting of nothing but variations of ham.

"Just what do you think you're doing?" the fat man asked the stranger.

The Man in the Dark Coat looked down on the porky fellow, who looked back up at him, into those deep, black eyes that seemed to go on forever. Eternal blackness was in those eyes. Before the store-owner could utter anything remotely like a cry for help, the Man in the Dark Coat jumped down from the display and into the store, wrapped a hand around the man's neck, and squeezed until he heard something pop.

The store owner's body went limp, and the Man in the Dark Coat tossed it to the side. He grinned to himself, feeling fairly confident that the little pudgy man was only the first of many bodies that would be his to do with as he pleased in the days to come.

6.

Every seat in Westmont's Town Hall was full. Over one-hundred people were in attendance, and there were just as many outside. Night had fallen, but it hadn't brought any cool air with it; people waved magazines and papers in front of their faces, their only defense against a raging Mid-Western summer. The candles spread throughout the room for illumination didn't help matters much, either. The smell of smoke hung in the air.

Jennifer moved to stand behind the podium on the stage at the front of the hall. Harding, Bryman and Malcolm were in seats on either side of her. Police Chief Robert Hetaine sat near the edge of the stage. His uniform stuck to his body from sweat, making it cling to him like a second skin.

With no working microphone, Jennifer had to raise her voice to be heard. "Okay, settle down folks, settle down."

The murmur of questions and worries from her audience quickly died down, everyone eager to hear what the authorities had to tell them.

Jennifer looked over her now captive crowd. God she wished Stephen were here. One look in his supportive eyes was all the help she'd need to make the speech that she didn't want to make. But Stephen was still hard at work trying to sort out this whole mess, probably pulling a triple shift at the substation. That was Stephen as she had always known him — the man never gave up, even in the face of utter defeat. It made her uncomfortable that he wasn't here, that she couldn't talk to him and draw strength from him.

She took a deep breath and steeled herself.

"At approximately eleven-forty this morning, all power in Westmont was lost," she began. "Shortly after that, we lost all electronic equipment. I can assure you we are working on the situation, trying to get in touch with Commonwealth Edison in Chicago, and our own folks at the substation are doing everything they can to get us back up and running."

"Are we under attack?" asked a man in the front row.

The woman next to him, who was fanning herself with a crumpled *Time* magazine, stood up. "We heard it's like this all over. That it's not just here."

"And where did you hear that?" Jennifer wanted to know.

"Sully, my husband," she pointed to the grouchy looking man sitting next to her, "was in Downers

Grove when the power went out. He had to walk back, poor thing."

Sully rolled his eyes at his wife.

"Sully says the same thing happened over there," the woman concluded.

Jennifer groaned quietly and looked over at Harding. He nodded to her; *you gotta tell them.* She sucked in a breath. "The truth of the matter is, we don't know *what* is going on. We've heard the same reports as you. A main power line cut in Canada or a solar storm, and yes, we haven't ruled out the idea of some form of terrorist attack."

Gasps of worry and fright emanated from everyone in the room. Jennifer raised her hands in a calming gesture, but it did nothing. She raised her voice instead.

"But the chances of us actually being at war, at being under attack, I have to stress, are *highly improbable.* It's been nearly eight hours, and surely by now we would have had word from the military or government officials on the matter," Jennifer said.

"But our phones don't work. Nothing works," said another man. "Even if they wanted to tell us, they couldn't."

"Even so, it's highly unlikely-"

"But you don't know for sure," said the first man.

Sully's wife sat back down. "You don't know nothin' fer sure," she said to the Mayor.

Jennifer sighed. "No. We don't know for sure."

A sea of worry spread throughout the room.

Chief Hetaine stood up and walked to the podium, placing himself next to Jennifer.

"The entire police force is on tactical alert," Hetaine began. "So far, there is nothing to suggest anything more sinister than a simple power outage, despite the oddities some of you may have noticed. I suggest everyone just stay calm and stay in your homes until this thing blows over. Westmont is a nice town. A small town. And it's my home. So I'll say this once: any signs of looting or immoral behavior will be dealt with quickly and efficiently." He said this last part looking at the rear of the hall, where Eddie Miller stood, hands in his pockets.

"*Very* efficiently," Hetaine repeated for the boy's benefit.

Jennifer patted Hetaine on the shoulder. "Thanks, Robert," she whispered to him.

"Just be careful of what you say. You nearly had me shitting in my pants a few minutes ago," he whispered back.

"Noted." She turned her attention back to the townsfolk. "You all heard Chief Hetaine. Go home, get some rest, get a good night's sleep, and I'm sure things will be back to normal by tomorrow morning."

"What if it isn't?" asked Sully's wife.

"Then I'm wrong and we'll all go to the Taste of Chicago on my bill. How's that?" Jennifer said. "Now everyone go home, and be good. Watch out for one another."

Jennifer stepped away from the podium, signaling to the room that her speech was done and the meeting was over. Harding and Bryman moved to her side as the townsfolk began to file out of the hall.

Malcolm approached her from behind. "You call that preparing for the worst?"

"Yes. If something else is going on, something we don't know about, I don't think we need the entire town going ape-shit before we can figure it out and deal with it. You'll find that sometimes you have to hope for the best while preparing for the worst. I'm hoping that everyone can stay calm until then," she said. "I'm going home."

Jennifer knelt by a chair and picked up her bag. She gave a slight nod to Hetaine as she walked out. Hetaine smiled back to her as he made his way to Malcolm, Harding and Bryman.

"Cut 'er some slack," he said to Malcolm.

"Hey, I just call 'em like I see 'em. People deserve to know the truth, don't you think, Chief?"

"Yes, I do. But we don't know what the truth is. You'd do best to remember that before you send my town into a panic," Hetaine said.

The chief followed Jennifer out the side entrance, leaving Malcolm, Harding and Bryman alone on the small stage. Malcolm looked out over the now empty hall.

"Adams is in over her head. We need someone that can lead us right now, not someone that tells everyone to go home, jerk one out and sleep it off," Malcolm said. "For all we know, they could be planning an attack *right now*. Planes could be flying over New York, L.A., on their way here. And she wants everyone to get a good night's rest and be nice to one another."

Malcolm turned away from Harding and Bry-man and stared at the exit Jennifer had used. His eyes turned into slits, and for the briefest of moments, Harding could have sworn the whites of Malcolm's eyes had gone black.

"I want you two to keep your eyes and ears open," Malcolm said. "You hear anything out of the ordinary, you come to me, not her, understand?"

"But Mr. Dwight-"

Malcolm cut off Bryman with a snarl. "Just do it," he growled. He then stormed off the platform, leaving Harding and Bryan alone on the stage, wondering just what the hell had gotten into Malcolm.

At the rear of the hall, just to the right of the front doors, a man in a trench coat watched Malcolm Dwight leave the stage in a fury of anger.

The Man in the Dark Coat smiled.

7.

*L*indsay.

The china dish shattered on the kitchen floor, eliciting a tiny shriek from Lindsay. She put one hand to her chest, the other to her head, and tried to calm herself down. She carefully stepped over the broken plate, which had been part of a beautiful wedding gift set from Richard's parents, and peered into the dining room from the kitchen. The light from the candles she had found in the hall closet and positioned around the apartment provided just enough illumination to allow her to see down the hallway to the front door and spot any potential intruder.

"Richard?"

Lindsay was met only with silence; she was still all alone. But she had sworn she heard a voice. She was sure of it. She looked down at her paint covered hands and saw that they were shaking.

As she moved into the dining room, the front door clicked open, and Lindsay jumped with another tiny shriek. She spun around to see a very tired and haggard looking Richard Stone walk in and close the door behind him. Their eyes locked, and she could tell he could see the alarm in her face.

He dropped his briefcase and quickly marched over to his wife. "Jesus, baby. Something wrong?" He wrapped his arms around her, kissing her on the forehead.

"You startled me is all."

Richard ran his hands through her scarlet hair, bringing the locks to a makeshift ponytail behind her neck. "Yeah, everyone seems a little bit jumpy today."

Lindsay gave him a peck on the lips before pulling away and returning to the kitchen, the voice she had thought she had heard forgotten. Richard followed her and his eyes found the broken china on the floor.

"What happened?" he asked her.

Lindsay pulled a small broom and dust pan from the kitchen closet. "Slipped outta my hands while I was drying it. Not only am I jumpy, but I'm a klutz, too," she said, beginning to sweep up the remains of the plate. "What's going on out there?"

Richard leaned against the wall. "No one knows. They say the blackout covers the whole city."

"What about all the cars? I don't think any of them have moved since this morning."

"No one seems to know anything about that, either," he said.

Lindsay dumped the plate debris into the trash. As she put the dust pan and broom back into the closet next to the garbage can, she looked over to her husband. They had been together long enough for her to not have to say out loud what she was feeling.

"Don't be scared," he said, moving closer to his wife.

"But all this... I mean the power goes out, fine... but that business with the cars — *all* the cars..."

"It's not just the cars," said Richard, opening the refrigerator door and grabbing a lukewarm Miller Lite. "Everything electrical is fried."

Lindsay stared at him blankly. "What does that mean?"

Richard twisted the cap off the beer and took a swig. "I'm not sure."

"Something big has happened, I can feel it," she said.

Richard laughed. "You're being paranoid."

"No," she said, stepping her voice up a notch. "Something's not right, something doesn't *feel* right."

"You're starting to sound like one of my patients."

"That's not funny."

Richard placed his half-empty beer bottle on the counter and took her hands in his own. "I'm sorry, hon. Look, I'm sure there's nothing to worry about.

If something bad had happened, we'd know about it by now. Tomorrow morning the power will come back and everything will be back to normal. You'll see. It'll be fine."

Lindsay stumbled to find her words. What Richard said was probably true — she was no doubt overreacting — but deep in her soul she knew something was wrong. "You're right, I'm sorry. It's just been a long day, and with the heat-"

Richard stopped her from talking by bringing his mouth to her lips and kissing her. He stroked her hair as her hands found their way out of his and around his back. Their tongues danced with each other as Richard began to unbutton Lindsay's paint-stained over-shirt.

Richard broke away from the kiss. "Maybe if we get you out of this," he pulled at her shirt, "you'll start to feel better."

Lindsay gave him a smile, the smile that had won his heart and his loins over ten years ago. She finished unfastening the shirt, exposing her bare breasts to her husband.

"You're right," she said. "I'm starting to feel a little better already."

As was his habit — and the habit of most men — Richard had dozed off shortly after their love-making. He pulled his eyes open, hoping that Lindsay would understand that the three mile walk from his office downtown where he had practiced psychotherapy for the past five years had taken its toll on him.

He rolled over to give her a kiss, and instead of his wife, he found he was about to plant a wet one on her pillow.

"Lin-baby?"

In the darkness of their bedroom, Richard couldn't see three inches in front of his face. He rubbed his eyes with his fingers and looked around. He saw a soft amber glow coming from the living room.

A grin came to his face as he realized Lindsay had given in to her after-sex habit just as he had. While Richard was prone to passing out, Lindsay usually found herself full of energy and vigor after sex and would return to whatever painting she was working on. Neither of them took the other's actions personally — it was just the way things were.

He swung his legs out from under the sheets, pulled on his boxers, and made his way out of the bedroom.

Five candles lit up the living room enough for Richard to see that his wife wasn't there. His intuition had been right — it certainly appeared she had been working on her painting — but the brush had been placed back in the water jar, the paints covered up for the night.

The curtains in front of the balcony caught a breeze, catching his attention and allowing him to see outside. Lindsay stood out on the balcony in her nightgown, alone, smoking a cigarette.

Richard stepped out to join her, gently placing a hand on her shoulder. She didn't jump or spin out of alarm, but simply turned to face him.

Her face looked weary, with bags under her eyes, giving the impression that she hadn't slept in days.

"You okay?" he asked her.

"I'm fine," she answered, exhaling smoke from her mouth. "Just a little headache, is all."

"Usually that's the kind of thing a man hears *before* sex, not after it."

Lindsay tried to laugh at the joke, but all she could manage was a half-smile.

"Is there something else bothering you, baby? Is there something else you want to talk about?"

She turned away from him and looked out over the balcony, down across North Sheridan Road. Less than five blocks away, she could see Lake Michigan reflect the light from the almost full moon in the heavens.

"It's beautiful, isn't it?" she said, her eyes mesmerized by the view. "Without all that city light, you can see forever."

"It is," Richard agreed, worried at her quick and sudden effort at changing the subject.

She took her final drag from the cigarette and smashed it out against the railing. She dropped it, watched it fall to the street below, then turned around and headed back inside. "I'm gonna try and get some sleep."

Lindsay slid back into the apartment and walked

into the bedroom without so much as a glance at her painting. Richard then knew for sure something was wrong. Lindsay always looked at her works in progress when she passed them. She didn't like anyone to know that — she felt it somewhat egotistical for an artist to admire their own work — but he had caught her doing it on more than one occasion, and found it endearing. And he understood it.

She was, after all, one helluva painter.

Richard stepped back into the apartment, blowing out candles as he made his way back into the bedroom. When he got to the flame by Lindsay's painting, he stopped to appreciate the work himself.

His eyes widened as he saw a painting that resembled nothing like anything Lindsay had ever painted before. While all her usual elements were there — a pond, trees, forest animals (the woman had a love for nature) — it was the changes to the scenery that troubled the doctor.

Instead of a bright blue, the sky appeared to be a dark, almost blood red. The trees had been reshaped to thin skeletons of what he remembered them being that morning, and the duck in the pond and the two birds in the sky were gone. Lindsay had also finally found the words to paint on the little sign on the shore: *No more room.*

Lindsay pulled the sheets up to her chin. Regardless of how hot it was in the apartment, she wanted to cover up. To disappear underneath those sheets, to hide forever.

She rolled onto her side and brought her knees up, her mind drifting back to the lovemaking from earlier that night. She didn't want to think about it, but her brain wasn't giving her much choice.

As their passion had heightened, the volume of the Voice in her head had grown with it. She knew now that it was the same voice she had heard earlier, that her mind must have been playing the same tricks on her then as it had during sex.

As she closed her eyes, giving it her all to force herself to fall asleep, she could still hear the deep male voice echo in her head.

Lindsay.

Lindsay.

Lindsay.

8.

Peter Sampson sat at the end of a long oak table, the kind used for meetings that were usually mandatory and boring. Peter rubbed his eyes, pushing himself to stay awake on what was now the twelfth hour of his work day. Nine others had grouped themselves into the room: seven technicians, Zach McMillan, and a charming fellow by the name of Andrew Brimington, who was probably the biggest prick of a Head Supervisor Peter had come across in his sixteen years of being a working man. No matter the job — pizza delivery guy, data entry man or the six months he spent as a cashier at Home Depot — Peter Sampson and supervisors just didn't mix well.

Two of the technicians had located a handful of candles that were kept stashed away for emergencies, which no one would argue this now qualified as. The candles sat in the center of the table, giving the room an even drearier look than any of them wanted. Shadows waltzed across the walls, never in one place for more than a few seconds. The constant motion threatened to bring up Peter's ham and cheese sandwich, but he was able to keep it at bay.

Everyone's eyes turned to the door as Stephen Adams swung into the room like a whirlwind.

Andrew eyeballed him. "So nice of you to join us."

"Sorry," Stephen said as he found a seat next to Peter. "But I thought working on the problem might be a little more productive than talking about it."

Andrew placed his hands palms down on the table and stood, as if he were addressing a platoon of Marines about to go into battle. The man was exhausted and worn out. His gray hair glowed orange from the candles, and the wrinkles on his fifty-seven year old face grew deep like the Grand Canyon.

Andrew wiped a bead of sweat off his chin. "So no one has an explanation."

Mumbles of "no" and "not me" mixed with some shrugging shoulders swam through the room. Andrew rolled his eyes in annoyance. It was obvious the man had called the meeting to get some answers, and not the negative ones he was receiving. Andrew was a man who didn't like to hear negative things.

Head Supervisors tended to be that way, Peter thought.

Andrew cleared his throat. "You're telling me the power, the whole system, just flickered out. No warning. Not grid-by-grid. Nothing broke. It just-"

"Stopped working," Peter finished for him.

Andrew repeated the phrase. "Stopped working. Stopped working," as if saying it a few more times would make it easier to swallow. He moved away from the table and turned his back to the room. He pulled at his blue dress shirt, which was soaked to the pits with sweat.

"Stopped working," he said again.

Peter leaned back in his chair. "That's right. We can sit in here all day and night and go 'round the room telling each other what happened shouldn't've happened, or we can just accept that what couldn't've happen *did*. Instead of figuring out what happened, maybe we should be trying to think of what we should do about it. Like Stephen said: we need to *do* something, not *talk* about it."

Stephen looked at his friend with a cocked eyebrow. "You're about to get fired," he whispered.

"I know," Peter whispered back, immediately regretting what he had said to the Head Supervisor.

Andrew eyeballed Peter. Peter looked away, ready to hear a string of expletives that would make the most liberal of nuns burst into flames.

Instead, Andrew said, "Pete's right. Everybody take a second break. If you wanna take off, go home, that's your prerogative. You've all been here today long enough, but I'd appreciate it if you'd all stay. If not, be here tomorrow as close to eight as you can."

Everyone in the room gasped in unison. They

had all been certain that what Peter had just said, no matter how logical it was, would be the cause of the gnarliest, darn-tootinest swear-fest this side of a Quentin Tarantino movie.

Not wanting to ruin the old man's good mood, Peter was the first to stand and head for the door. Stephen followed. But before Peter could cross the threshold, Andrew cleared his throat, causing Peter to pause and turn. He knew the throat-clearing was for him.

"Peter, a moment."

Stephen slapped a hand on Peter's shoulder. "Nice working with you."

Stephen exited the room, leaving Peter alone with Andrew. He stared at his employee silently, arms folded across his chest, a fresh bead of sweat dripping down his forehead.

"Show me this generator that doesn't work."

Like a general surveying the battlefield before ordering an attack, the Man in the Dark Coat had been examining the streets of Westmont, touching the minds of those he could. It was a gift he had been born with, a gift he had always had.

When he had taken over the body that he now used, some twenty-five years ago, Thomas Manning had been a thin and frail boy struggling to make it through high school alive. The boy had been easy to seduce and had allowed him into his mind almost without having to be asked. The Man in the Dark Coat had joined with the boy, and they had been together ever since.

The kid was scared of everything — even his parents. Upon further discussions with Thomas, the Man in the Dark Coat discovered he wasn't so much afraid as he was ashamed. He felt like he was letting his parents down, every step of the way, every day of his life. He wasn't the football player his father had wanted, and he wasn't the genius his mother had hoped for. Touching the parents' minds, they discovered together that it was a valid theory; Thomas Manning's parents were ashamed of their own son.

So the Man in the Dark Coat dealt with them, just like he now had to deal with the people of Westmont and those beyond, bringing them about to his way.

The New Way.

After twenty-five years of waiting, the world was finally ready for a change. It just didn't know it, yet.

There was an itch in the back of the Man in the Dark Coat's mind. Small at first, but he knew within a minute it'd be a full-blown headache. Something needed his attention. This was how it started — always an itch at first. He hated the itch more than the migraine that followed, but that was just the way it was, just the way it worked. He couldn't do anything about the itch in his brain other than tolerate it. He had to — he had no other choice. However, the pain... when it came, it came big and strong.

Along with the pain, came information.

The itch went away.

And the pain began.

Stopped working.

That's right.

The Man in the Dark Coat closed his eyes. They rolled back, as if to stare at the gray matter inside his skull to find the solution to an unsolvable problem. Without realizing it (he never did) his hands slowly raised themselves palm-up, facing the darkening sky. He listened harder. He knew the voices.

He knew all the voices.

Pete's right. Everybody take a break.

The assholes at the power plant.

He knew they'd eventually figure out something more was wrong than just their precious power shutting down, but their swiftness of it surprised him. He could sense in their voices, in their thoughts, that they knew something was up. That something wasn't totally kosher about today.

They were smarter than he had given them credit for. He'd have to remind himself in the future to give these beings more credit than he felt they deserved.

Peter, a moment.

Nice working with you.

Show me this generator that doesn't work.

His eyes snapped open with an almost audible *pop*, and he about-faced and trucked halfway down the block. To his left was an abandoned house. Deserted for who knew what reason, it had obviously seen its fair share of vandals. Rocks and beer bottles littered the lawn. Most of the windows were broken. The unmistakable aroma of shit and piss came from somewhere inside. It was perfect, as if it had been waiting for him.

Just for him.

With a smile and a nod to whomever had provided him with this temporary sanctuary to do the immediate task at hand, the Man in the Dark Coat walked through the yard and up the rickety wooden steps of the house. Once inside, he could get down to business.

Once inside, he could start the war.

Andrew knelt in front of the technological monster that was the backup power generator. In its ten years of operation, it had never once suffered an illness. For it to just *go off* like this, in Andrew's mind, was an impossibility.

Andrew flipped the same switches Peter had. He walked around to the back of the machine, and with Peter holding his now very necessary Zippo lighter above Andrew's head, inspected the same display panel Peter had. With a "Harumph," Andrew grabbed a flashlight that sat on the second shelf of the utility case next to them, and toggled the on/off switch back and forth. And, like Zach (Peter was growing annoyed of watching his boss do the same exact things they had already done an hour ago) got no results.

"Nothing works," Andrew said.

Peter rolled his eyes. *No shit.*

Andrew stood up, keeping the flashlight in his hand in case it decided to start working. He looked around the room, absent mindedly flipping the switch of the flashlight on and off, on and off, on and off. His eyes followed a metal tube up the side of the wall, where it disappeared into the ceiling. He handed Peter the flashlight. "Give me a boost."

Curious as to his boss' plan, Peter placed the flashlight back on the shelf and put his Zippo next to it, leaving it open and ignited. Andrew raised his arms up and grabbed hold of the metal tube. He lifted a leg, at which point Peter knelt down behind him, cupping his hand under Andrew's foot. Andrew took a step up using Peter's hand, and together they managed to hoist him up to within reaching distance of the ceiling. Once there, Andrew pushed up on one of the fiberboard tiles and shoved it away into the depths of the space above. Placing one foot on a computer desk — being careful not to trample all over the keyboard and mouse — and the other on Peter's shoulder, Andrew moved even higher, poking his head through the hole he had made.

As soon as he was up there, Andrew discovered he was as blind as the proverbial bat. He couldn't see the wires that the metal tubing held secure along the wall and up to the ceiling, where they then traveled the length of the building. "Hand me your lighter," he ordered.

"You steady?"

Andrew lifted his two-hundred pound frame off

of him (much to Peter's delight) and moved further up. He was now in the ceiling up to his torso, legs dangling. The sound of him grabbing something followed by a grunt let Peter know the man had found purchase on something up there.

"The A/C vent goes right by here. It'll hold," Andrew said, his voice sounding a mile away.

Peter moved away and grabbed the Zippo from the shelf, turning it off. As he handed it up to his supervisor (would it really be so bad if the air conditioning vent *didn't* hold?) he thought he heard something *click* behind him. Once Andrew had the lighter, Peter turned his attention behind him toward the source of the noise, which had come from somewhere in the vicinity of the backup generator.

As Andrew grumbled and griped with the wires above, Peter knelt down to the generator. He listened more than looked, trying to pin-point the source.

There.

There it was again.

From the other side of it. No.

Right in front of him.

No.

Dammit if it didn't sound like the sound was moving all around the *inside* of the generator.

Before he could put any more thought into what it was (a mouse? A rat? A big, furry, disease-ridden rat?) the lights behind the dials flickered on, and the generator hummed to life.

Peter stumbled backwards, not at all prepared

for it to snap back on like it just had. Smiling, he yelled "You did it!" up to Andrew.

"Whurpt?" Andrew said from somewhere in the ceiling.

The room lit up with a florescent glow, bright as day. The computers in the room came back on as well, one by one. The generator hummed quietly, as if nothing had ever been wrong.

"You did it!" Peter repeated. "It's back on!"

Andrew let himself drop from the ceiling. He landed with a thump and a grunt, then looked around in mild amazement as the room cycled itself back to life.

"I didn't do anything yet," he said to Peter.

The drone of the generator grew, and the machine began to emanate a high pitched squeal that both men knew wasn't a natural sound for it. They looked at one another as the florescent lights above them became brighter and brighter, growing with intensity along with the high pitched squeal.

They florescent lights arced with electricity and began to explode, marking a path from the door to the rear of the room.

Right where Peter and Andrew were standing.

The two men ducked, shielding their heads. Andrew squinted his eyes tightly shut as shards of glass and loose coating powder rained down around them.

The light sockets above crackled with electricity as the whine of the generator intensified, now more of an animalistic growl than a hum. Peter found himself looking at the dials on the side of the machine, which were dancing wildly to-and-fro. Read-out lights on the generator began their own little waltz, doing a tango to their own little tune.

Behind them, the computers began to rumble their own rumble of a noise before they, too, began to explode. Like the lights, they burst one-by-one around the room, sending fragments of glass, plastic and the occasional microchip their way.

Peter watched the flashlight fall from the shelf. It turned on and off like the lights and the computers, all by itself. It finally settled for ON, growing brighter and brighter with each passing second. The plastic around the bulb began to warp from the heat. Peter knew that wasn't possible — flashlight bulbs like these just didn't get that hot — but there it was, happening right in front of them.

Their attention was drawn again to the backup generator. It's snarl had turned into a sort of whine-yell, like it was trying to talk, trying to tell them something. They both got to their feet, ready to run the fastest forty-yard dash in history out of the room before the thing blew apart.

Then they heard a new sound, and despite the oddity, it seemed like the generator had figured out how to tell them what it wanted. They stopped. They couldn't help it. When something like a power generator starts talking, you're apt to listen. And listen they did. Very carefully.

STAY AWAY.

It was the last thing either of them heard before

the power generator exploded.

His arms fell back to his sides and his eyes opened. His lips, which had curled into a menacing sneer, slowly turned into a smile.

"Stay away, motherfuckers," the Man in the Dark Coat said. "Stay away."

9.

John Whitley was not a man a mother would allow to watch her children while she paid the parking meter. Whether that was an actual truth or not was still up for debate; no one had ever asked John to watch their kids. To John that didn't matter: no one hated John Whitley more than John Whitley. He reminded himself of this fact as he scratched his unshaven face.

The universe had seen fit to withdraw its power once again from Westmont Village. Third fucking time in less than a week. It was no coincidence that John was on the final leg of his novel, his first in almost three years. It was just his luck that as he got close to finishing it, some unforeseen event would sweep in out of nowhere and fuck it all up.

From the blue haze of the moon outside, John figured it was somewhere around ten o'clock. It had been almost two days since the power had started playing its game of off-then-on-then-off-again. When it had first gone out, John had welcomed the silence. All his work had been saved to his laptop, so there was no fear of losing anything he'd written and there was nothing quite like a break you were forced to take. But now it was getting downright annoying — he had work to do.

He swiped the frayed hair from his eyes and drew his attention back to the monitor in front of him. A blank screen stared back, the tiny flames from three candles behind him flickering on its screen. John let out a sigh and puffed on a cigarette, one of those nasty kinds kids would get at the discount store because they were cheap. Hell, he liked them. The fact that they were cheap was just an added bonus.

He took the final drag and tossed the butt into an overflowing ashtray as he leaned back in his chair. This was not the life he had envisioned for himself. The town was right, but the house was all wrong. He had envisioned a grand, lovely, much-too-big house bought from selling the movie rights to his books — of which he had so far sold only one, which had been turned into a less than stellar made for TV flick starring some guy from a cancelled sitcom and an actress on the final legs of her career. He and Tracey would grow old together, maybe have a kid or two, and he'd continue to write books and teach the occasional seminar at local colleges before he retired and died in obscurity, probably from lung cancer.

Instead, he rented a small two-bedroom house, Hollywood no longer wanted anything to do with his books, and Tracey would not be growing old with him. But at least he had gotten the town right. Westmont had been his home since he was two years old, and he was pretty sure he'd die there. This was the life he had been given.

Or chosen.

That would be Tracey's voice. In his head, never quite as silent as he'd like. She would always argue his theory that Fate was in control, not him. And certainly not God. God had lost this *hombré* as a partner when He saw fit to take Tracey away from him. If He truly works in Mysterious Ways, John wanted no part of it. No sir, no how.

But right now he didn't have time to wax philosophic with creepy voices in his head. He had a book to finish, a rent check to clear, and another pack of smokes to suck down.

As he reached for the notepad next to the monitor, his fingers grazed the revolver that lay beside it. Tracey had hated, detested, downright despised the thing, but John had insisted on it. Even in such a peaceful town as Westmont, he knew you just couldn't trust folk. Now more than ever he was glad he had held onto it. He heard rumors from a few of his neighbors of some locals that had gotten rather antsy since the outage. A of couple houses had been broken into, and John thought he had heard a car accident or two around the time the power went out for good. Nothing to write home about, but it was more action than the town had seen in all his years there.

He moved his fingers away from the gun to the pen lying on the notepad. He could finish the last chapter longhand (which he hadn't done since college) and type it up in the computer later. He poised the pen in his right hand, brought the tip to the yellow legal pad, then-

-nothing.

His mind was a complete blank. Although he had the ending of the book in his head — he'd had the ending for months — none of the words were coming to him. It was like trying to search a computer for a file you thought you had saved, only to find out that nope, you hadn't. It's gone. In place of that file in his head was a giant white space.

A giant white space waiting to be filled with something.

He swiped up his pack of smokes. Lit one up.

"Fucking perfect."

He ran his thumb across the Zippo, feeling the rough edges of the engraving on it. *JPW*. A wedding gift from Tracey. He tossed it back on the desk and sucked in another lungful of cancer.

"Just fucking perfect."

Don't swear.

Tracey again. She had been dead for years, and the woman could still haunt him from the grave about his swearing. But hell, he loved her for it. That was part of the reason he married her. She always cared for his well-being, be it smoking, drinking, or in this case swearing (she always thought that very ungentlemanly of him) but had never pushed it. She was a Big Believer in things "happening for a reason," and knew that John Peter Whitley could only be the person that John Peter Whitley wanted to be. Right now, John Peter Whitley wanted to smoke and swear.

If he hadn't been so intent on driving her voice out of his head so he could enjoy bringing himself ten minutes closer to death, he might have noticed that when Tracey talked to him, a small part of that gigantic white space went away.

10.

The building rumbled and shook, and a booming shake went through the floor. The five hard-working employees of Commonwealth Edison that had decided to hang around, taking a short break in the lunch room, looked up at one another from their snacks of Doritos and Cokes in alarm and puzzlement.

The first thought to spring to Stephen's mind was "earthquake." Growing up in Northridge, California had conditioned Stephen for such a knee-jerk reaction. When his brain reminded him that he was in Illinois now, he became fairly certain that it wasn't an earthquake.

"That was the generator," he said.

The man sitting next to him (Stephen thought his name was Paul) shot up, followed by Zach. The other two — an older woman whose name escaped Stephen at the moment and one of the electrical technicians — stopped eating and stared up at the three.

"Come on," Stephen said as he grabbed a hanging fire extinguisher and ran out the door.

Stephen covered his mouth and nose with the sleeve of his shirt, which had already begun to turn yellow from the smoke. His eyes burned. His tear ducts couldn't produce enough tears to keep his eyes from stinging madly. Whatever had exploded in the back hadn't caught anything on fire yet, but the smoke was over-powering. He knew he should wait it out for the firemen. But no alarms had gone off, and even if they had, something told Stephen their fire trucks were about as useful as his cell phone right now.

He looked behind him to see his co-workers following him, hunched over on the ground, getting as far away from the smoke crawling along the ceiling as they could. Zach had secured a second fire extinguisher, and Paul had located one of the med-kits peppered throughout the station. He could only make out the blurry shapes of the other two, but they were there.

Zach jerked his head forward. "The generator room!"

Crawling on his hands and knees, Stephen wished he had watched *Backdraft* a few more times. Through the smoke, he was able to see at most five feet in any direction.

"Peter! Andrew!"

Stephen moved forward, careful to keep his head down while trying to keep his eyes up. It was proving to be an almost impossible task.

When they came to the meeting room, Stephen was out of breath and coughing hard. Zach bumped into him from behind, and Stephen could hear the kid's labored breathing. The black smoke was now mere inches above their heads, and it wouldn't be much longer before the entire hallway was covered in the stuff from top to bottom. Stephen thought if they went any further, they might not be able to see (or breathe) to make it back out of the substation.

The path out of the building, back the way they had come, wasn't there anymore. Where the floor, the walls, and vacant air had been there now danced smoke as thick as mud. Stephen turned the other way — further into the depths of the building — and discovered that while there was smoke there, too, there didn't seem to be as much of it. As if the smoke wanted them to go that way.

"Just keep going," Paul shouted, seeing the distress in Stephen's eyes. "We can make it out the back!"

Propping himself up on the heels of his hands, Stephen tossed his shirt aside, took in what breath he could (which wasn't very much) and lead the group through the smoke.

The smoke steered Stephen, Paul, Zach and the other two, all crawling on their hands and knees, into the backup generator room. It seemed to guide them, to push them, to *force* them in that direction.

The room was a shambles; bits and pieces of things everywhere, but they were so far gone and damaged and burnt, they couldn't even begin to guess what some of the objects might have once been. The generator had blown up, that much was obvious. The explosion had done so much destruction that there was really nothing left in the room to burn. Smoke seemed to come from everywhere and swam out the door and through the vents, finding every nook and cranny that it could to move about.

As Stephen was about to call out for Peter and Andrew again, he caught his breath and stopped. Against the wall was Andrew Brimington. Actually, *against* the wall wasn't quite right; more like *through* the wall. Andrew's head had taken the brunt of the impact, probably being blown backwards from the blast. Both the wall and Andrew's head were cracked open, and what was left of his head was now stuck halfway through the wall. His right arm was gone, and Stephen didn't see it anywhere.

Peter hadn't been as lucky; his body had been sliced in two by one of the metal coverings to the generator. It slit him horizontally, right at the torso. The lower half of his body had landed in a far corner, while his torso rested on what was left of a computer table next to Stephen.

"Oh my dear Lord, what happened?" asked the woman.

Stephen turned around, still on his hands and

knees. "They're dead. Let's get out of here while we still can."

The woman and the tech backed up as Paul and Zach turned around and began to move back down the hallway. Stephen paused, taking one last look at Peter before he followed them, when Peter's eyes snapped open. Stephen let out a hoarse scream and skirted away, pushing Paul into Zach.

Paul turned around to see Peter's eyes open and staring at Stephen. The man who they thought was dead tried to talk, but his throat had been burned in the blast, leaving him forever speechless.

Stephen shook his head and told himself he'd deal with this trauma later. Nothing a little psycho-analysis couldn't handle. He moved back toward Peter with the idea to grab him and carry him out. As fucked up and unbelievable up as it was, the man was still alive. When he reached for Peter's arm, which hung off the side of the table, Peter seemed to try and sit up. He couldn't, of course, but there was the very good chance Peter didn't know his legs were twenty feet away from him on the other side of the room.

He stared Stephen straight in the eyes, the kind of stare that tells someone they mean business. He tried to talk again, with no success.

"Save it, we're gettin' you outta here," Stephen told him. He turned to Paul. "Help me with him."

Peter grabbed for Stephen's collar, attempting to pull him closer. All he ended up doing was dragging his upper body across the table, so that he was now two inches from Stephen's face. He tried talking again. This time three separate gargles came out of his mouth. They might have been words, but Stephen couldn't be sure.

Then Peter looked across the room and smiled. Stephen followed his friend's gaze. As a second burst of fire from another, although smaller, explosion from what remained of the power generator came their way, shooting through the doorway and covering Paul and the rest in flames, Stephen thought he had figured out what Peter had said. Even though it made no sense.

Stephen put his arms up in front of his face as Peter's words echoed in his brain:

No more room.

11.

Malcolm Dwight stepped into the darkness of his office. While everyone else had decided to head home after the town meeting, Malcolm instead opted to head back to work. He felt drawn back to the municipal building with the kind of feeling that he had forgotten something.

He flipped the light switch out of habit, and laughed at his own forgetfulness when he heard the *click* of the switch but no lights came on. There was enough light sprinkling through the window behind his desk from the almost full moon outside for him to see by, and that was good enough for him. He preferred it darker, anyway.

He sat in his swivel chair and noticed a small envelope on his desk that he didn't remember being there before. Scrawled across it in chicken-scratch handwriting was the name *Malcolm*. He didn't recognize it as being the handwriting of anyone in the office.

Ripping it open, he found a single sheet of paper with the same, almost unreadable handwriting on it. He tilted it toward the window, letting the light of the moon bounce off the paper.

Malcolm,
I can help you get what you want. Jennifer Adams can be removed. They will go to the high school. I will meet you there.
We have much to discuss.

That was all it said. No signature, no salutation. Just a cryptic message from an anonymous stranger. Malcolm crumpled up the paper into a wad and let it rest in his clenched fist. He had never had any desire to rid Westmont of Jennifer Adams, but the letter implied otherwise. And the more he thought about it, the better the idea sounded. Adams was weak, timid, and not at all the kind of leader a town needed in a crisis such as the one they were facing now.

Malcolm was positive he could do a better job.

What the high school had to do with anything he couldn't even begin to guess. He'd just have to go there himself, meet his secret admirer, and get some answers to his questions. Things were getting stranger by the hour, it seemed. Things were changing.

Malcolm embraced change.

12.

Police Officer Heather Steinman stood at the back of the balmy room, head in her hands, awaiting the arrival of Chief Heteine. Her eyes moved between the other uniformed officers that had assembled in the room. The majority of the small force that served and protected the village, all forty-four sworn-in officers, had been ordered by word of mouth (since all communication was down except for old fashioned gabbin') to report to the police station. Like every other place in town, the roll-call room was dimly lit with candles.

That sense of safety and security, even though she knew it was bogus, had been ripped from her. Now the candles weren't annoying, they were downright depressing and also served as a reminder that her TiVo had most likely missed all the shows she had it scheduled to record.

Heather was not the daring type. Never had

been. She came from a family of cops, and felt obliged — perhaps even forced — into becoming one herself. Being a cop was almost a Steinman family business, going back five generations. Her father would have been proud of her.

When Heather was twenty-two, a mere three months before graduating from college in Michigan, Officer Joseph Steinman had been involved in a minor and not very exciting traffic accident. His patrol car had been hit by a slightly inebriated driver at the stoplight on Burlington Avenue, just in front of the train tracks that went through town. The accident wasn't severe, and was considered nothing more than a fender-bender.

At the time of impact, her father's head had smacked into the door frame. The jolt to his skull ruptured an aneurism in his brain, killing him in a matter of seconds. He never knew what hit him.

Heather signed up for the academy one month later. She had graduated at almost the head of her class, throwing herself into her studies, and had been patrolling the mean streets of Westmont, Illinois ever since.

Which was a good three weeks ago.

They had partnered her with an aging patrol officer that went by the name of Gildy. That's all she ever knew him as, and that was all that was printed on his name tag. Gildy was a man destined to walk the streets wearing blue for the rest of his life, and from what Heather had gathered, he was every bit as right with that as rain. He felt he could do more good walking the streets with his knowledge and expertise than he could by being a detective behind a desk, or barking orders from behind a captain's badge. He reminded her of the character Sean Connery had played in *The Untouchables*, without the sexy Scottish accent or the history of being suave super-spy James Bond. Heather had taken to him immediately, despite the lack of an accent. Hell, after all the man had known her father.

"No dozin'. Chief sees ya', you'll be pullin' traffic duty for a week," a voice said behind her.

Heather turned to see Gildy smiling down at her. The man was almost six feet, and towered over Heather's five-foot-five frame.

"I doubt any of us will be pulling traffic duty," she said. "Speaking of which, I heard you saw some action yesterday morning."

Gildy took off his cap and ran a hand over his balding head. "Most action I've seen since nineteen-eighty-nine, when the line went around the block for that first *Batman* flick, the one with Michael Keaton," Gildy said. "I think some kid cut in line, some other kid threw a tantrum. Had to call their parents."

Heather tilted her head at him. "The movie theater called the cops for *that?*"

"Not at all. I was behind them in line."

Heather stifled a chuckle as Chief Heteine walked into the room. The officers snapped to attention as Heteine took off his hat and casually waved it at them: sit down, cool it.

He stood behind the podium at the front of the room, unbuttoning the top two buttons of his shirt. A candle had been placed on either side of the stand. Heteine glared at the tiny flames with utter hatred, as if those two things were the source of all his woes, the reason he was putting on weight, and the cause of cancer in the world.

Heather saw his look, and knew just how the man felt.

Heteine inhaled a deep breath and began. "I've just returned from a meeting with Mayor Adams. As you've all probably guessed by now, we will be on tactical alert immediately and indefinitely."

Groans came from some of the cops, which were quickly silenced by others. This was their job, they had a duty. Both Heather and Gildy knew this and kept silent.

"I know, I know, it's not gonna be fun. I'm hardly looking forward to it myself, and I'm pretty sure my wife is gonna kill me, which would be a favor, putting me out of my misery, but I'll be out there with you," he said. "Sleep in shifts, we have the facilities here for that. Four hours off, here, sleeping, twenty on until this is over. Vests are mandatory, riot gear is being prepped."

Heather nodded at Heteine, getting his attention. He pointed to her. "Go."

"Sarge, excuse me for asking, but *riot gear?*"

Heteine's eyes moved over the room, looking from cop to cop. They all stared at him with that very same question in their eyes.

"It's just a precaution. There have been reports — *reports*, mind you — of some looting and violence up in Chicago. And you've no doubt heard about some of the trouble we've seen here." Hetaine paused. "I don't want what happened at Jack's Big & Tall store to be a sign of things to come. People are no doubt getting a bit antsy, and doing some really stupid things. So until this thing blows over, we have to hope for the best, but be prepared for the worst."

Gildy raised a hand, eager as a seven year old in grade school that's dying to ask a question he know will stump the teacher.

Heteine pointed at Gildy. "Go."

"Sarge, what if it *doesn't* blow over?"

"Power should be back within a day or so. They're working on it day and night, so just hang in there," Heteine replied.

Gildy raised his hand again. Without waiting to be called upon, he started talking: "But it's not just the power, it's everything. Is ComEd gonna fix all the cars, too?"

"Gildy," Heteine said, "I'm just telling you what the Mayor told me which is what ComEd told her."

Hetaine paused for a second, glancing over his troops. A look of strength was in their eyes, but also looks of worry, of confusion.

The chief leaned forward on the podium. "Okay, look. I don't know what's going on anymore than you do. Yes, that's what the Mayor told me, and she's a smart gal, but I'd bet dollars to donuts she

85

has no idea when anything's gonna be fixed more than my cat at home does. Westmont is a small town. A nice town, and I happen to like it. A lot. I'd like to die here an old man of natural causes. Go out there, make your presence known. That should be enough."

"And if it's not?" came a voice from somewhere in the middle of the group, a cop who obviously wished to remain anonymous.

Hetaine looked at the group, but at no one in particular. He gathered in the sight of his troops, wanting more than anything to give them an answer but knowing that he didn't have one for them.

13.

The woman held her hands out to him. Reaching for something. Was it him? No. She wasn't reaching for anything, really. She was pleading. Begging for her life. She was in pain.

John reached out for her, but it was too late. The woman, he recognized her now, Tracey, fell deeper into nothingness. As she drifted away, her eyes filled with blood. Her mouth opened, showing thousands of dollars worth of dental work going down the drain as her teeth rotted and fell out of her head.

This is all your fault.

The sun crashed through a sliver of an opening in the drapes. John usually kept them shut; he found the outside world a distraction to his writing. The man had dug deeper and deeper into himself since Tracey died. Sometimes the hole he dug became so deep he couldn't see through the window no matter how open he kept the drapes. Which was pretty much the way he wanted it.

He had fallen asleep on the couch sometime after midnight. He looked at the Winnie the Pooh clock (Tracey's purchase, not his) hanging in the kitchen, which still read 11:40. He looked down to his watch, which was now nothing more than a gray mirror strapped to his wrist with the word CASIO above it.

John could feel the heat from the outside trying to get into his house. He sat up on the couch, his shirt soaked in nightmare-produced sweat. He'd had them off and on for the past year, and could never remember more than flashes of images, only bits and pieces of what had happened in them. Tracey was always in there somewhere, lurking about, but the memory was gone faster than he could recall it. John figured that was just as well; something told him that if he could remember them in full detail he'd complete his journey to crazy and end up in Batshit Insane, Illinois.

John forced himself up and made his way to his desk. He grabbed his pack of Pall Mall's and made to shake one out. The small pack gave him a few bits of tobacco and nothing more. Somehow over the course of the night, he had managed to finish off the last of his cigarettes.

He snatched his keys and wallet from inside the top desk drawer and strode toward the front door, a man on a mission for a fresh pack of coffin nails.

John was greeted with a blast of Midwest summer air as he stepped outside. The air was still and muggy. It was already eighty-five degrees, and he knew it would only get worse. He locked the door behind him and headed down the front walk toward Pauley's Liquor, which stood two blocks away and was his main source of smokes, soda, and the occasional late-night junk-food binge.

John didn't notice the kid, no more than nineteen years old, hiding in the bushes that separated John's yard from his neighbor's.

Eddie Miller's eyes stayed fixed on the man, a gangly thin guy in need of a haircut, as he locked his front door and headed down the block. Eddie had taken what Chief Heteine told the town, had told *him*, personally. Shit, Heteine had been *looking right at him*. How could he not take it personally?

It WAS personal, buddy. Don't you forget that.

Eddie looked around for the culprit of the Voice, but saw no one. It wasn't the first time this week he'd heard that voice, a strong, booming, rumble of a voice, when he was all alone. At first he thought it was his subconscious being a little louder than usual. But now he was beginning to think differently. This voice, whatever it was, seemed to be telling him things to do. Giving him ideas. It was egging him on to be the bad boy, the *really* bad boy, he knew deep down he honestly was. It was encouraging Eddie to be his true self.

Whatever it was, it didn't matter. He didn't care. He agreed with the Voice every single time he'd heard it. So no harm, no foul.

When the homeowner was out of sight, Eddie slipped out from behind the bushes marking the property line. He scooted around the side of the house, giving the two windows he passed on the way a try. They were locked tighter than a Preacher's daughter, so the back door it was.

When he reached the back yard — which looked as though it hadn't seen a lawnmower in months — he ducked into the shadows the house offered from the morning sun. The window next to his head was locked, but now that he couldn't be seen by any nosey neighbors on the street, a locked window was nothing more than a mild annoyance.

Use your shirt. Break it.

He pulled off his Chicago Cubs over-shirt and wrapped it around his right hand. It took two hard punches, but the glass finally gave and shattered. After wiping out the remaining shards in the window-sill, Eddie reached in and unlatched the lock. Up went the window, and in went Eddie.

"Johnny-boy, I was wondering when you'd show up."

Pauley Smitrovich was a stout man well into his fifties who carried himself like a seventy-year old. John had always assumed it had to do with the fact that the man inhaled half the cigarettes he brought into his small store. The writer reminded himself that he most likely smoked just as much as Pauley, and made a mental note that he'd have to quit soon or end up looking just like the pudgy store owner one day.

John let the door shut behind him. The top of it slapped against a small silver bell which *dinged* every time somebody entered or left. It was a sound John had grown accustomed to, one that made this place feel as much like home as his house down the block.

"Hey there, Pauley." John took a quick survey of the establishment and found most of the shelves had been swept clean. There wasn't much left, at least nothing much of what John wanted or needed.

"Sold out of almost damn near everythin'," Pauley said before John could ask. "Bunch'a folk come in yesterday, wiped me clean. They were freaked, man. Panicky."

"Is that so?"

"That be so. Tell me, wha'd'ya make of all this?"

John shrugged. Until now, he hadn't made much of it at all. The power went out. Big fuckin' whoop. The power went out all the time — with nearly every household cranking their air conditioners to full blast for three solid months, it had simply become part of the Chicago summer season.

"I'm not sure, Pauley. You?"

"I'll tell you what I think, but you ain't gonna like it. No one does," he said with a grin.

"Hit me."

"Aliens," Pauley said matter-of-factly.

"Aliens," John repeated.

91

"Aliens. You know man, they come down, their planet's all fucked up, they're outta room or whatever, so they want our planet, but it's not the way they want it, so they change things, get rid of us, trying to make it their own," Pauley explained. "Like, what'cha call it. Terra-farming."

"Terra-forming," John corrected.

"Yeah, that's the thing."

John laughed. "I think you've seen one too many episodes of *The X-Files*."

"Shit man, I've never watched that fucking show. That one guy, The Monotone my wife call's 'im, can't act for shit. But if this is the kind of thing they put on that show, then they probably know all about it," Pauley said.

"Who? The producers?"

"The government."

"Ah. The truth is out there and all that, huh?"

"There ain't no truth out anywhere, Johnny. Not out there, not in here. They don't want us to know the truth, because *there is no truth.*"

"A space nut *and* a conspiracy nut, Pauley? This is a side of you I didn't know about," John said. "Really, I didn't have you pegged for either."

"Neither did I, until yesterday."

John was afraid to ask, but he did anyway. "What happened yesterday?"

Pauley shot John a disbelieving stare. "You really do get all lost in your house with yer writin' don't'cha?"

John simply shrugged at the man. His "shut-in"

status in Westmont had become near legendary since his wife had died. No one saw much hide nor hair of the writer except for Pauley, and that was twice a week at most.

The storeowner shook his head. "You really need to get out more."

"I like my privacy."

"Anyway," Pauley said, "these two girls come in. You know, the punk kind with colored shit in their hair and the jewelry crap in their eyebrows an' noses. They come in every other day 'cause they know I'm the only guy in town'll sell 'em smokes. They were good kids. *Were.*

"They waltz right up to the counter, right where you're standin' now, an' start mouthin' off at me. No 'hello' or nothin'. They spat out strong words, tough words, like they was tryin' to get me all riled up. They was actin' really strange, too. Their eyes were different, like the color was all gone or some fuckin' thing. They kept dartin' about, like they was expectin' someone to come in at any second.

"So they both reach into their purses, and get this, each of these kids had a Glock, man. Where do kids get guns like that? Fucking Glocks! So I pulled out this."

Pauley reached underneath the counter and produced a double-barreled shotgun. He held it in both hands lovingly.

"Jesus Pauley, where the hell'd you get that?"

"I've always had it, my man. It's the kind of thing you don't advertise to your customers. Might turn some people off," Pauley said, running his eyes up and down the firearm. "So I pull this out, and they wet their pants like they was back in grade school. Then they high-tailed it outta here."

Pauley caressed the shotgun absentmindedly as he went on. "And I'm not the only one. Dana up at the Stop N' Chat said some couple up an' robbed her while she was out front handin' out all the ice cream before it melted. Can you imagine that? Nice lady just tryin' to be nice to some kids, then some assholes rob 'er.

"An' Jack, down over at that Big N' Tall clothin' store he thinks is the bee's knees? You heard about 'im, right?"

From John's look, Pauley could tell that John had not heard about the events in the clothing store.

"Some nut job broke in, broad daylight, stole a coat an' broke Jack's neck," Pauley said. "Prolly killed the poor bastard instantly."

"Jesus."

"I'm telling' ya', Johnny — I don't know if it's the heat or what, but people sure are turnin' into assholes real quick around here."

John hadn't realized that he had taken two steps back when Pauley brought the shotgun out for show-and-tell. He moved back to the counter and rested his hands on the glass above the lottery tickets.

"That thing loaded?" John asked.

"Hell no. I don't have no shells. Friggin' thing prolly doesn't work anyway. But it did the trick," he laughed. "You shoulda seen those two girls run, Johnny. You shoulda seen 'em! Put *that* in your book."

Pauley shoved the gun back under the counter.

"That's a really beautiful story," John said with a wry grin.

"Thanks," Pauley said as he grabbed a full brown paper sack from the shelf behind him. "When I saw everybody was clearin' me out, I put some things aside fer ya'."

He placed the bag on the counter between John's hands. John peered inside and found a fresh carton of Pall Mall's, a couple of notepads, and a six-pack of Coke.

"Notepads?" John asked.

"Hell, you're a writer. There ain't no power. Figured you might need somethin' to write on."

"Alien nut, conspiracy nut and psychic," John said. "How much?"

Pauley smiled. "On the house, my friend."

"Come on, Pauley, you know I can't do that."

"Don't make me pull out the shotgun again. I'll do it."

John gave him a quick smile and a laugh. "Then who would you complain to every day?"

"Now get outta here and finish up that book. I'd hate for somethin' as stupid as a power failure to delay my reading of the next John Whitley novel," Pauley said, then pointed to the carton of cigs. "Just don't smoke 'em all at once; that's all I got left. I can't be certain, but I'm bettin' I won't see any shipments soon."

"I'm sure the power will be back before I make my way through all these."

"I dunno, John," Pauley said. Then he blinked his eyes. When he opened them again, John thought the man's iris' had lost their usual blue-ish tint. They had turned completely black. Dark, deep, and black. "I don't think it's comin' back. I don't think *anything's* comin' back."

John backed away toward the front door. He was not easily freaked out by the little ticks people sometimes exhibited, but right now — well, Pauley was freaking him out. The man's eyes just weren't normal. "Um, okay, sounds great."

Pauley shook his head and blinked his eyes a few times. The dark blackness of his iris' was gone, and he looked at John with blue eyes.

John pulled open the door. The tiny silver bell gave out a tiny silver *ding*. "Okay, then. I'll catch you later, Pauley."

The bell gave off two more *dings* as John walked out the door and headed back to the sanctuary of his home.

"I hope so, Johnny," Pauley said after him. "I hope so."

14.

"Where do you think you're going?"

Lindsay looked up from the bed, where she had been packing a change of clothes. She picked up the backpack and slid out of the bedroom, not looking back at her husband. "I have to know if Amy's alright."

Lindsay's sister lived in Downers Grove, almost twenty-five miles from downtown Chicago. Amy Ryder was a twenty-seven year old paraplegic who had never been able to walk and was prone to bad mood swings when the slightest thing went wrong. When they were children, Lindsay remembered the times when her wheelchair would lock up (this was before they had been able to afford to buy her one of those fancy electronic ones) and Amy would make her sister wait on her hand and foot, slurs coming out of her mouth as quickly as they came to her mind. Medications and psychoanalysis never seemed to help Amy; in fact, she seemed to refuse any and all help, unless the mood fit her. Although Amy was five years Lindsay's senior, she acted more like a younger sibling than an older one.

Lindsay was certain her sister would need her. She figured the past few days would've put Amy in a black hole of a mood, probably somewhere between depression and suicide, and whatever lay beyond. Their parents had both died ten years ago, and Lindsay was all Amy had left.

Richard followed his wife into the kitchen, where she grabbed three bottles of water from the no longer cold refrigerator.

"I'm sure she's fine," he told her.

"You don't know that."

Richard took her by the arm. "That's a full day's walk, babe. She's fine. And if she's not, I'm sure her friends are looking out for her."

Lindsay pulled her arm away and walked into the living room. "She doesn't have any friends. You know that."

"Yeah," he said. "But going all the way to Downers Grove is insane."

"I can't just sit here and wonder if she's okay or not," Lindsay said, slowly turning around. "I'm not gonna sit around all day, waiting for the power to come back, waiting for *everything* to come back, not knowing if she's alright or not. You say going to Downers Grove is insane. I say sitting here and doing nothing is just as crazy."

Richard held his wife's look. From her steady-as-a-rock glare, he knew she wouldn't budge on the matter. When Lindsay had made up her mind about something, it stayed that way.

"How do you plan on getting there?" he asked.

Lindsay shrugged. "Our bikes are still in the storage room, right?"

"Should be."

"Then I figure I'll bike as far as I can." Lindsay ran through the route in her head. "Probably until I hit I-88."

"And then...?"

"I don't know. If the same thing happened to all the cars there as here, if the road's blocked," she said, "I'll walk."

They stared at one another for a moment, sizing up the ending of the argument.

"Are you coming?" Lindsay asked him.

Richard grabbed his set of keys from the kitchen counter. "Well I sure as hell ain't lettin' you go alone."

Negotiating the twenty-two flights down to the first floor proved more difficult than either of them thought. Even with the single candle Richard carried in a holder down the steps, Lindsay was constantly unsure of her footing. She hated the feeling of not knowing if she was on the last step of a flight of stairs or not, and doing it twenty-one times in a row was almost maddening. The flickering of the candle wasn't as much help as she'd hope it would be.

The odd noises they heard coming from various floors only made a bad situation worse. They silently wondered if they should turn back to their apartment and bolt the door when they heard a man who sounded like he was crying for his mother on the fifteenth floor. Or stop off on the twelfth, where they couldn't decide if someone was laughing hysterically or yelling in pain — or both. When they got to the tenth floor, they picked up their pace when they clearly made out a series of gunshots from at least three different kinds of guns.

They came across an elderly man who had curled himself into a ball in the corner of the landing between the third and forth floors. The man's hands shook, trying to hide his crying face.

Richard paused and handed the candle to Lindsay. "Sir, are you okay, are you hurt?"

The old man slowly lifted his head to reveal eyes of black in a tear-soaked face. Richard thought his own eyes were playing tricks on him, but when Lindsay moved the candle closer, he saw both of the man's eyes appeared to be giant pupils. No color, no whites.

Just blackness.

Richard stepped back. "Jesus."

The old man leapt to his feet, much faster then he should have been able to. He seized Richard by the collar and gasped out a breath of air full of meatloaf and liquor. Lindsay yelped, and the old man looked over at her.

"They're all dead," he slurred, sounding half

drunk. "All dead. No more-"

Richard shoved the elderly and clearly insane gentleman back into the corner, grabbed Lindsay, and pushed her ahead of him. He side-stepped the stranger as he followed Lindsay down to the third floor. The old man curled back into himself and sat down, muttering.

"No more room... No more room... No more room..."

Richard and Lindsay fell through the doorway leading into the first floor, and they both slammed it shut behind them.

"What the hell was *that* all about?" Lindsay asked.

Richard took the keys out of his pocket. "You tell me."

Lindsay looked at her husband with puzzled eyes.

"It's the same thing you wrote on the sign," he said, "in the painting, by the pond."

She continued to give him a blank stare. "I did?"

"Yeah, last night," Richard said as they approached the storage unit. "After we, you know, were done, you were working on your painting. You wrote 'no more room' on that little sign."

"I don't remember that. Are you sure?"

Richard unlocked the door to the storage unit. "Positive. It made about as much sense in the painting as it did coming out of that guy's mouth."

"Weird."

Richard was still looking at Lindsay over his shoulder when he pulled the door open. The only warning he had was Lindsay's quick scream as two teenage boys jumped from the storage unit and knocked him to the ground. The bigger one had the doctor pinned to the floor with his knees. Richard stared up at the boy.

His eyes were just like the old man's. Black, dark, and lifeless.

15.

The mayor took a sip from her lukewarm bottle of Evian water. She felt haggard, finished, and looked twice as worse. Her eyes scanned over to Harding and Bryman, seated to her right. The fans overhead no longer gave the meeting room the impression of a breeze. The windows were open, but that did little to rescue the politicians from the summer heat.

Malcolm sat at the far end of the table, mesmerized by the small stack of reports in front of him. Try as she might, Jennifer couldn't bring herself to look the man in the eyes. It hadn't gone unnoticed by her that the lawyer had been acting differently toward her ever since the town meeting. She caught him on more than one occasion scowling at her, as if he wanted her dead and gone. He had become silent. Moody.

And his eyes. There was something about his

eyes that just wasn't quite right.

The four of them (actually three — Malcolm hadn't uttered one word since the meeting began) had been going over reports given to Jennifer by Chief Hetaine. The reports told the tale of a town moving in a direction that none of them wanted to see it go in. Despite their pleadings with the citizens, people had seen fit to begin looting the business district. One incident had even turned to physical violence — a clothing store owner attacked and killed in his own place of business — and that was one more than the mayor of Westmont wanted to hear about. Something had to be done quickly before matters escalated and it turned into a situation none of them where ready to handle.

She had said to prepare for the worst. She hadn't counted on the worst actually happening, or that it would come about so quickly.

Jennifer closed her eyes and ran a hand through her hair. Sweat slicked the blonde locks on her head back, making her look ten years younger.

"At least we're not downtown," Malcolm said, breaking not only his own silence, but the silence in the room. "That place has gotta be one big massive shitball right about now."

"Okay," Jennifer said, digging into her reserves of strength. "So we need to find a way to get some sort of communication back up and running. We have to try and get the people together, let them know that this kind of activity will *not* be tolerated."

"Isn't that what the town meeting was for?"

Harding asked. "I thought Hetaine put the force on tactical alert."

"It obviously had little effect," said Malcolm.

Jennifer ignored the comment. "If people saw that we were at least *trying* to do something, it would help. People need a voice to listen to, to let them know everything's gonna be okay. And we need to reach the whole town, not just the select few who decide to come to another town meeting."

Bryman leaned in. "Before things get out of hand."

"Things are already out of hand," Malcolm noted.

Jennifer gave him a grim smile. "Maybe things won't get *more* out of hand if we give them some hope."

Malcolm rolled his eyes. "Giving people hope won't solve anything."

"But it would be a start," came a voice from the doorway. Everyone turned to look at Gloria, who stood in the doorway, arms folded above her stomach.

"Honey, you're not even on the committee, so why don't you go back out there and-"

"That's enough," Jennifer said, cutting Malcolm off. "You're both right. It won't solve anything, but it'd be a start."

"It'd be a waste of time," Malcolm said, "Besides, we have no way of communicating with the entire town."

The room went silent. No matter how good her

intentions were, Jennifer simply had no way to talk to the entire town now that the TV and radios, or any kind of technology, was kaput.

Gloria's eyes lit up. "Yes we do."

Everyone turned to look at her.

"The high school," she said.

Malcolm's ears pricked up. "Excuse me," he said. "Did you say the high school?"

Gloria walked further into the room and rested herself against the table. With the extra weight in her womb, she could only stand for so long before her back started to ache and throb.

"I worked on the school newspaper my sophomore year. They have an old printing machine, a Gestetner mimeograph I think they called it," said Gloria. "It's really cool. We had this one teacher, Mr. Tydell who wouldn't have anything to do with compu-"

"Does it still work?" Jennifer asked, cutting her off.

Gloria shrugged her shoulders. "Beats me. We never used it."

Malcolm stood and slowly made his way to Gloria. "If we can get it working, we can open up at least *some* sort of line of communication with everyone."

"I thought you said it was a waste of time, Malcolm," Harding said.

Malcolm shot Harding down with his eyes. It was a look that made Harding quiver in his loafers and his heart skip a beat. A look he'd never seen from Malcolm before. A look of pure hate.

Jennifer caught the glare and got to her feet. "Okay, easy guys. We don't need to start making enemies." She motioned to Malcolm and Gloria. "You two head for the high school, see if that printer still works. If it does, I don't know, I'm sure between the two of you you'll think of something good and political to put on there. Harding, Bryman, I want you two to stay here and keep an eye on things from this end."

"What about you?" Gloria asked.

Jennifer reached into her pocket for her cell phone. She looked at it one more time, maybe hoping to see a tiny bar pop up for service. When it remained dead, she tossed it on the mahogany table where it landed with a *ker-thunk*.

"I'm gonna head on over to the substation and find out why I haven't heard from Stephen."

16.

Eddie shoved the book on top of the dresser to the side, a beaten hardcover novel titled *Into the Darkness* by some guy named John Whitley. He had never heard of the man, but that didn't surprise him — Eddie never had been much of a reader. *X-Men* comics and *Playboys* were as far as he wanted to take it. He opened the top drawer of the dresser. What looked like the glimmer of a gold watch sparkled up at him with a wink *(Take me! Take me!)* when he heard keys rattle at the front door. The man who owned the house was home.

First the car broke down, then Heteine crawled up his ass, and now something as simple and painless as a little breaking-and-entering during a blackout had been fucked up. The kid just couldn't get a break.

Eddie quickly shut the drawer and aimed himself at the bedroom door. He heard the front door click shut, followed by the unmistakable sounds of a doorknob being locked and a deadbolt being thrown.

He ran for the window and tried to pry it open. The damn thing had been painted shut, so that wasn't an option. He could break the glass, but by the time that little mission was accomplished, whoever had just come home would surely have heard the glass being shattered, and would be in the room in a matter of seconds.

There was no two ways about it: Eddie was trapped.

John took the bag from Pauley's Liquor to the kitchen and set it down on the counter. He pulled out the carton of cigarettes, and as he placed it on top of the refrigerator, something on the floor caught the rays of sunlight and bounced them up to his eyes.

His knees cracked as he knelt down. Shards of broken glass lay sprawled across the linoleum floor. John glanced up to see the broken window.

This was certainly not the way he had left his beautiful home.

In all his years in Westmont, not once had his house been broken into. He had never been mugged. His car had never even been keyed. It was the kind of town where you could sleep soundly at night with the front door unlocked and the windows wide open.

Then John's brain made the appropriate conclusion: whoever was responsible for the broken glass could very well still be in the house.

Feeling like he was being watched, John immediately whirled around. But the coast was clear. Or at least as far as he could see, which was just past the kitchen door. He stood up (knees cracking again, this time seeming as loud as a gunshot) and moved to the kitchen doorway. He poked his head through and looked into the living room.

Empty.

And still on his desk, seemingly untouched, was his revolver. Whoever was robbing him either hadn't been in the living room, was a complete idiot, or had something much bigger than a revolver.

John moved quickly and quietly through the living room, swiped the revolver off the desk, and turned around. Much to his relief, he still seemed to be all alone. But he knew he wasn't. He just *knew* it.

He told himself the smart thing to do would be to consider himself lucky he hadn't been attacked by anyone, run like hell out the front door and make a bee-line for the police station. But John was angry. He felt violated, hell, he'd *been* violated. Some asshole actually had the nerve to break into *his* house while he went out for smokes.

There was a reason John Whitley hated people.

His house wasn't large by any means. He'd already been through the kitchen and the living room, which left the bathroom and his bedroom up for inspection. John closed his eyes and listened. The only sound he heard was coming from him, from his racing heart and his breath going in and out and in and out of his mouth.

John held the gun in both hands and walked toward the bedroom.

Eddie flattened himself against the wall and held his breath. Hiding behind the bedroom door, he figured his only chance of escape was the element of surprise. He hadn't thought to bring a gun with him, and was kicking himself for that now.

Slowly bringing his leg up, careful not to let his knee touch the door, Eddie reached under his right pants cuff. His fingers found the handle of the small hunting knife nestled in a sheath around his ankle. He pulled the blade out and silently let his leg back down.

His ears perked up as he heard someone move through the living room. Then all was silent. Eddie closed his eyes, listening for any further noises to come from the living room. Something went *creak*, the kind of creak a floor makes when a person steps on a loose board.

The knuckles on the hand holding the knife turned white as every muscle in Eddie's body tensed up.

The floor beneath John's left foot creaked as he walked toward the bedroom. John froze immediately, swearing at himself. He knew this house like the back of his hand, and should've remembered that the floor had squeaked there since the day he and Tracey moved in.

He could punish himself later about that. Chances were the person or persons in his home, if they were still there, had heard him. Any possibility of catching the intruder unaware was gone. He readied the gun and sprinted toward the bedroom.

Eddie heard the footsteps in the living room grow heavy and move more quickly shortly after the floor groaned. Whoever it was, they were coming toward him. Fast. Eddie brought the knife up to eye-level, ready for attack.

The man that barged into the bedroom looked to his left first, away from Eddie. Seizing the only stroke of good luck he'd had today, Eddie pushed violently at the bedroom door. It swung on its hinges and slammed into the doorjamb, just missing the man.

The homeowner turned around in shock. Eddie got a whiff of surprise himself when he saw the man whose house he had broken into was holding a revolver.

Kill him.

Before the man with the gun could pull the trigger, Eddie ducked and swiped at the man's leg with his knife. There was a tearing sound as the man's jeans ripped, then his skin. The blade went in deep, and gave a long, nasty cut.

The man screamed, followed by a loud *BAM* and a brief flash of light as the gun went off. Something smashed into Eddie's stomach, forcing him to fall back and drop the knife.

John fired three more shots without even thinking about it.

BAM.

BAM.

BAM.

The first two shots missed their mark entirely, hitting the closet door behind the thief, splintering the wood. The third slug hit its mark.

The bullet entered the man's stomach an inch above where the first shot had landed and exited from his back, forming a third hole in the closet door. Blood churned out of the two wounds as the robber pressed his hands against the wound and fell limply to the ground.

"You shot me."

John stood above the now motionless intruder. Blood seeped into the carpet. John looked down at himself, and saw his shirt was covered with blood, too, as were his hands. He dropped the gun, more worried now about his appearance than about protecting himself.

His left leg gave out underneath him. Blood oozed out of the fresh knife wound. John put his hands over it, pushing down hard with pressure to try and slow the bleeding.

But the blood just kept continuing to stream out of his leg, swimming through his fingers and onto the floor where it mixed with the robber's own.

17.

The second teenage boy made a bee-line for Lindsay. Using all his strength, Richard grabbed the one on top of him by the shoulders and violently shoved the attacker off of him. The kid tumbled off of Richard, smacking into the second boy's legs. Both teenagers crumbled to the ground, their legs twisting together.

"Come on!" Lindsay yelled, reaching a hand out to Richard. He took it, and she hoisted him back to his feet. Abandoning their bikes in the storage unit, the two bolted for the door at the end of the hallway, which lead to an adjoining alley. Richard forced the door open with an arm, and they ran outside into the daylight.

Realizing they had no way to lock the door once they got outside, all Richard and Lindsay could do was run as fast as they could. At the end of the alley they were met with a small local tavern which sat on the connecting Foster Avenue.

Lindsay looked behind them to see the two Changed Boys blast out of the apartment building and into the alley. Luckily for Richard and Lindsay, they looked the opposite way from the direction the Stone's had run.

Lindsay pushed Richard to move faster. "Into the bar!" she said in a whisper-yell.

Before they could be spotted, Richard and Lindsay swung around the corner towards the bar. Spinning into the moldy alcove, Richard pushed on the door. It didn't yield. He cupped a hand around his eyes and looked through the small amber window set in the entrance. Inside, it was dark and empty.

"Closed," he said, turning to Lindsay.

Frantic for escape before the two boys figured out which way they had gone, Lindsay looked up and down the block. To their east was North Sheridan Avenue, and Lake Michigan beyond. To the west was another bar, a grocery store, a video store, and stairs leading up to the elevated train tracks.

"We're taking the el," she said, then pulled Richard out of the alcove and made way for the train station.

Richard and Lindsay pushed through the unlocked doors to the station, which were badly in need of a paint job. Finding no one manning the turnstiles, they hurtled over the railing and ran up the stairs, two at a time.

At the top of the flight of stairs, a decrepit looking homeless man stirred in his sleep as the two ran past him. He put out his hand, making to ask for a donation for his cause — which was probably some form of booze — but by the time he did, Richard and Lindsay were well past him.

The saloon-style doors swung on their hinges behind them as they came to the edge of the wooden platform. From this height, they were able to look out over the horizon, towards the suburbs and where they wanted to be. The tracks ran north to south, and Richard thought that by following the tracks south towards the city, they'd be able to find an exit to a nearby tollway they could then use to get to Downers Grove.

Richard lowered himself off the platform and onto the dead tracks. He turned around, assisting his wife with the three foot drop. When her footing was secure, Lindsay leaned over and peered down to the street. Their pursuers were nowhere to be seen, but she did spot a middle-aged man exiting the video store carrying an arm-full of DVDs.

"Now what do you suppose he plans to watch those on?" she said to Richard.

Richard grinned. "We'll let him figure that one out. Come on, let's get moving."

Lindsay took him by the hand, and they began walking towards Chicago.

"Did you see their eyes?" she asked.

"Couldn't miss 'em," said Richard.

She gave her husband a troubled and worried look. "What was wrong with them?"

Richard shook his head. "I'm not sure, baby. Probably just strung-out on something, maybe had a long night."

They continued on their way. With each step, Lindsay thought she heard the Voice in her head getting slightly louder. It was more calming, this time. More caring. And the volume wasn't as cranked up as it had been before, but it was there, just barely, calling out to her.

Lindsay.

Lindsay.

Lindsay.

18.

Malcolm and Gloria walked between the cars that had stalled in the middle of Cass Avenue. People were still out on the street, and that was a good sign. The bad sign was most of them seemed to be a few cards shy of a full deck.

A small boy stood in the middle of the street, eyes aimed to the sky. He looked like he was listening to something — or listening *for* something — and he was gonna stay right where he was until he heard it.

An elderly man exited the shoe store half a block ahead of them, and he definitely appeared to be hearing something. He kept on repeating "I know, I will, I know, I will" over and over again. He walked down the block, away from Malcolm and Gloria. They could still hear his mantra that he knew and that he would as he turned right at the next corner, moving out of sight.

Gloria felt that she was witnessing the beginnings of a society breaking down. For whatever reason, possibly a combination of the sweltering summer temperature and the loss of all power, the people of Westmont were not taking things lightly. The broken glass on the sidewalks were sure signs of lootings. But signs of lootings did nothing to prepare them for the zombie-like behavior of the townsfolk now.

Malcolm gripped Gloria's arm tighter as he told her to stay close to him.

"What's wrong with everyone?" she asked, more to herself than to Malcolm.

He didn't answer. His attention had been drawn across the street, where a man wearing a trench coat was staring at them. Malcolm stared back, positive he had seen the stranger somewhere before. The Man in the Dark Coat held his gaze, and then simply, elegantly, he smiled.

Malcolm slowed his pace, not able to take his eyes off the man across the street.

"What? What is it?" Gloria asked.

"That guy. Looks familiar."

Gloria followed his eyes to the Man in the Dark Coat. "There're lots of people in town, you know. You've probably met half of them at sometime or another."

"I know. He just-"

Before Malcolm could finish his sentence with the words *looks wrong*, a lone brick sailed past their heads and crashed through the front window of the electronics store behind them. Three kids, none of them more than fifteen, pushed Malcolm and Gloria out of the way as they jumped through the window of the store. Yelps and screams of delight and victory could be heard from them inside as they found their own private stash of XBoxes, DVD players and iPods.

"I think we need to find somewhere safe," Gloria suggested. "Let's get to the high school."

He nodded in agreement. "No argument here."

Malcolm led them down an alley that would allow them to cut through the busy streets, hopefully avoiding the majority of the people.

The Man in the Dark Coat watched the three prepubescent boys kick the remaining glass from the windowsill of the electronics store. The boys had been bored, itching for something to do, just standing by their bikes watching the adults of the world act more like children than the people who told them when to go to bed.

All it took was a little push to turn the kids from spectators to players. He had leaned down to the mop-haired red head of the trio and simply said: "That store. Do it." The three of them had looked at one another, and without so much as a second thought, they had proceeded to break apart the window of the store with a brick. Kids were fun, and always easy to talk into doing what he wanted done. Especially if he knew they'd have a good time doing it. Kids would be kids.

As the teenagers entered the store, he noticed the man who had caught his gaze lead the pregnant girl away from the street and down an alley. Malcolm was right on schedule, the Man in the Dark Coat knew, even if Malcolm didn't know it himself. Then there was the girl. The girl troubled him.

She was the first person the Man in the Dark Coat had come across that he couldn't read. Her mind was a vacant field of white to him, and that really pissed him off. He knew that there would be some that he couldn't see, some that he would have no control over. But that did nothing to prepare him for the feeling of uncertainty the girl created in him.

And he hated, fucking cut-off-your-balls *hated* the fact he had even an ounce of uncertainty.

But Malcolm Dwight was coming along well, and wasn't one of those that he couldn't see. Malcolm's mind was a wide open pasture to the Man in the Dark Coat.

19.

Jennifer approached the substation in fear. Over the past hour since she had left the municipal building, the Mayor had gone over any and every explanation that seemed plausible for her not hearing from her husband since yesterday. From the mundane idea that he was simply too busy to get word to her how things were going, to the horrific notion that whoever owned the gun she had heard half an hour ago from behind her had friends that decided to loot the substation, killing everyone inside.

While the last idea was certainly ludicrous, Jennifer knew that it was now not totally out of the question. The first time she had heard live gunfire was thirty minutes ago, and that was enough to spook her plenty.

The front doors were unlocked. Upon pulling them open, she was bombarded with the smell of burning plastic and wood. Inside it was dark and dingy, but she could see well enough to conclude that something had burned up the inside of the station.

"Oh, Jesus," she said as she ran inside.

The door closed on its spring hinges behind her, cutting off most of the ventilation and locking her inside with the horrible smell. She found herself in the main hallway, where she'd been plenty of times before. To either side of her were various offices, a break room, bathrooms, and the janitor's closet. Directly in front of her, all the way in the back of the building, was the station's backup generator room, where she could tell the fire and smoke had originated from. The doorway was blackened and charred. It looked brittle, as if it would fall apart from the slightest touch.

She slowly moved deeper into the building, coming closer and closer to the room in question.

"Stephen?" she called out in a tentative whisper. No one answered.

Jennifer moved past the break room, past the meeting room, past the janitor's closet. The closer she got to the generator room, the less she was liking the looks of things. She could make out specks of blood mixed in with burnt chunks of paint on the walls.

She stepped on something, and like a shot of espresso directly into her chest, Jennifer's heart skipped several beats. She moved her foot off of the object and bent down. As she was about to pick it up, she stopped herself.

She had stepped on what was unmistakably someone's pinky finger. She hoped and prayed to God that it wasn't Stephen's, but there was no way to tell for sure.

She put a hand to her mouth, helping her lips stay closed so vomit wouldn't spray all over the floor. She slowly backed up, confident that whatever was in that back room, she didn't want to see it, didn't want a part of it, no way, no fucking how.

Jennifer ran out of ComEd Substation SS-558 on Cass Avenue, her hand still over her quivering lips. The edges of her jawbone began to ache and twitch, and when she had made it twenty feet from the building, the mayor of Westmont let her lunch fly out of her mouth and onto the sidewalk.

She fell to her knees, wiping the fresh vomit off her lips. She kept her eyes closed, tears streaming down her cheeks when she decided she had to make her way to the high school. Her only hope of salvation was finding the others and getting out of this now hellish town.

20.

John leaned against the bathroom sink, seconds away from fainting. A cigarette dangled from his mouth, the smoke threatening to drift into his eyes and blind him. He hadn't been able to pull his pants off over the slash in his leg — the sharp jabs of pain the fabric caused against the wound proved too much for him to handle. He found the pair of scissors he kept in the drawer next to the sink and cut the jeans just below his thigh. He caught a glimpse of himself in the mirror, one long pants leg, one short. It would've been comical had the pain not been so great and had he not just shot and killed a man.

As a rule, he carried no alcohol in the house. Rule number one of A.A. was to keep the evil drink (and anything else one might ingest to escape reality) away. Not even rubbing alcohol, most types of mouthwash, and hell, he had been surprised to learn that there were even some toothpastes with alcohol as an added bonus ingredient.

He grabbed the towel hanging on the door and carefully wrapped it around his leg. He didn't want to, but he had no choice but to look at the cut while he did this. His entire left leg was covered in blood, and it looked like the knife had severed some muscle tissue. He was no doctor, but it didn't take one to know he'd need stitches. Lots and lots of stitches.

The towel went around his leg twice. He held his breath, counted to three, then grabbed either end of the towel and pulled tightly. Sweat poured down his face as there was a final sharp pierce of pain before his leg at last went numb. He tied the ends of the towel together and let out his breath. The worst of it was over.

He picked up the fresh pair of loose-fitting jeans off the toilet seat he had brought in with him, and very slowly and very carefully, pulled them on one leg at a time. Once he had tied the string together at his waist, it didn't seem so bad. At least he looked fairly normal and wouldn't draw any suspicious looks on his way to the hospital. Then the cops would probably become involved, but John didn't think there'd be any serious trouble. It was, after all, self-defense.

As John moved out of the bathroom, he paused. Somewhere in the distance two quick *pops* from a gun went off. From the sheer startling volume of the blasts, John thought the shooter was perhaps three, four blocks away at the most.

He now found himself with a dilemma: stay inside his house with the dead guy and risk loosing too much blood, or venture out into the world and hope no one aimed a gun at him.

John limped past the bedroom, unable to keep his eyes away from the dead body on the floor. The thief lay in a pool of blood, both his and John's.

Favoring his sliced leg, John hobbled towards the front door. He figured taking his chances out there were better than sitting in his living room and bleeding to death. He dropped his cigarette in the ash tray and picked up his keys as he passed his desk. It was only seven blocks to the local hospital. John prayed he wouldn't pass out before he got there.

Sunlight blinded the writer as he stumbled outside. He put up a hand to shield his eyes, but it did no good. The sun was relentless in the summer, and in its current position, John figured it was around noon. His shadow was directly below him, the sun beating down straight on his head, unyielding. It was gonna be one hell of a long walk.

He made it to the sidewalk without incident. Once he reached the boundary of his lawn, however, his energy drained and dizziness kicked in. A spinning world began to take over. The edges of the trees and the buildings became fuzzy, like a drunk cameraman trying to rack the focus on a camera and missing the sweet spot every time.

A ruckus across the street brought everything back into sharp detail, and his world stopped spinning.

Two kids came running out of Pauley's liquor

store. One of them turned their head briefly in John's direction, and he could make out the ponytail and heavily made-up features of a teenage girl. The other one had shorter blonde hair with a bright streak of red in it. Both of them had jewelry in just about every place one could think of to put jewelry on one's face. They were laughing, running, almost skipping, having the time of their fucking lives until Pauley came barreling out of his store, shotgun in hand.

The essence of "pissed off" was etched across the store owner's face. He hoisted the shotgun up to his shoulder.

"I told you kids ya'd get som'a this if ya' came back!" Pauley shouted, then let loose with two blasts from the gun. Apparently Pauley had found some ammo.

The first shot hit the blond girl with the streak of red. She caught it behind the kneecap, and the lower half of her leg bent forward with a *crack* John could hear from his front lawn. The second discharge landed square in the back of the second girl, the one with the ponytail. The force of the gunfire punched the girl forward, making her trip over her own feet. She landed face first on the cement. The skin on her right cheek was scratched and torn by the road. Neither of the girls had had time to even scream.

John watched all this without understanding, without being able to do anything other than raise a hand. Before he could purse his lips together to form a word, he felt his eyes grow heavy, and darkness overcame him.

21.

Off in the distance, Heather heard glass breaking, as if someone had smashed through a
store window. Usually if she were to hear such a
thing, it was her sworn duty to run to the scene to
aid and protect the innocent and arrest the not-so-
innocent. But today, right now, things were far from
usual.

The truth of the matter was that she was hearing
glass break everywhere. She had a feeling she'd be
hearing it in her dreams for months. People had begun to loot stores, which she found more disap-
pointing than angering. She had grown up here, and
to see it turn to violence like this tore her up inside.
She could imagine something like this happening
downtown, but not in a suburb. Not in her home-
town. Westmont had always been a peaceful place,
and for it to gear itself up for a riot like this so
quickly just didn't seem normal.

Then again, not much that had happened in the past two days could qualify as "normal." What had she expected people to do? Everything they had grown accustomed to over the past hundred years had been taken away in the blink of an eye. Maybe a riot wasn't the best way to deal with it, but it sure seemed a great way to let off some steam. Yes, Heather was disappointed. But not surprised.

Her eyes focused on the reason her and Gildy had come to the corner of Adams and Norfolk; a madman standing on top of the hood of a Volvo, yelling obscenities mixed with wild animalistic growls. He held a baseball bat above his head, the rays of the sun bouncing off the shiny aluminum. He swung it down on the front windshield, creating a spider's web crack in its center. Then he gave out another fierce yell, the kind Heather had only heard on the Discovery Channel from predators in the wild.

She looked over to Gildy, who stood next to her in the opening of an alley. "This guy's lost it," she said.

"No doubt."

Heather tugged at her bullet proof vest, unable to get a secure and comfortable fit from it. Wiping sweat from her brow, she pulled her gun.

Gildy stepped out of the alley and onto the sidewalk. "Alright. Let's go have us a talk."

Heather followed her partner out into the street, which was crowded with dead cars. They squeezed between a station wagon and a pick-up truck, all the while keeping their eyes on the man who had a beef with the Volvo.

Heather heard another pane of glass break and shot a glance to the electronics store across the street. Three teenage boys jumped into the store, clearly having the time of their lives.

"One asshole at a time," Gildy said, keeping his eyes trained on the baseball bat-wielding lunatic.

Heather knew Gildy was right. All around them, she could see the fabric of society begin to break down. The kids in the store were only a part of it, and they didn't seem to wield any immediate danger.

But the guy on the car with the baseball bat, he was a problem.

The man took another Babe Ruth-style swing at the windshield, and this time it shattered, sending spirals of broken glass in every direction.

Heather was grateful that the majority of the folks on this particular block seemed to have decided to either stay inside and lock their doors or just plain leave. Except for the three kids who were now inside the electronics store, the street was left to herself, Gildy and the slugger.

Aiming her Beretta at the clouds, Heather let off two quick shots.

The slugger looked up from his handy work. Upon seeing the cops, he let the aluminum bat fall out of his hand and began backing up, his feet creating shoe-shaped dents in the hood. Heather and Gildy broke into a run, making it to the Volvo's trunk just as the man jumped off the hood and landed on the concrete. Without wasting any more time, the slugger turned-tail and scurried in the opposite direction.

Heather ran around the driver's side as Gildy bolted around the passenger's. They caught up to the rioter at the same time, Heather grabbing his left arm while Gildy grabbed his right. Together they jerked the man back. He lost his balance and fell backwards, forcing the two cops to hold him up by his arms.

He let out another of his Discovery Channel yells as Gildy spun him around and pulled out the cuffs from his belt. He tightened a cuff around the man's left wrist, closing it severely enough to put a damper on his circulation.

"Easy there, pal. Inning's over, take a break," Gildy said, forcing the man to his knees.

He looked up at Gildy. He didn't say anything, didn't utter another scream or even a whimper. He just looked up at the elderly police officer, and smiled.

That's when Gildy noticed the man's eyes. They were vacant and looked fake, more like marbles than eyeballs. The color of the iris' was gone, as was the whites of the eyes themselves. Top to bottom, the man's eyes had gone completely black.

"Jesus, Heather. Take a look at this."

Heather leaned down to inspect the baseball fan's eyes when the sound of a shotgun firing in the distance gave them all a jolt. Before Gildy could secure the handcuff to the car's bumper, the slugger seized the opportunity the distraction gave him and violently pulled his hand away. The man jumped to his feet with an energy that surprised the cop.

Another boom from a shotgun was heard, not more than a block or two away. "Dammit," Gildy said. "Okay, fuck it, forget him. He dropped his bat, anyway."

The two officers raced towards the sound of the shotgun blasts.

22.

The commuter train sat half on the tracks, half off. The front three cars — those furthest from Richard and Lindsay — had dropped off the elevated rail at the juncture of a sharp turn. They remained connected to the other five silver cars, hanging over the edge, a giant train-ladder to the ground.

"Must've lost control when the power went out," Richard said.

They stepped off the right-most track and onto the middle one, walking around the crashed train. They were both tall enough to see through the windows, and what they saw was anything but comforting.

There were no more passengers inside, but the remains of a violent accident were more than noticeable. Vertical handrails had been ripped from their housings and lay sprawled across the floor.

Seats were dented and cracked. Most alarming of all was the sight of blood.

More blood than either of them thought a train wreck such as this could have caused. The floor was covered with the stuff.

As they walked on, they both noticed more than a few cracked windows with sprays of blood in the center of the cracks — making them both think the cracks were caused by people's heads.

Lindsay looked away. "What happened here?"

"Whatever it was, it's not good," said Richard. He looked ahead of them to the next stop, and pointed. "Let's get off here. We should be close enough to the tollway by now."

"Music to my ears."

They spotted a group of six others who had decided to take the walking route as they approached I-83. Hundreds of cars could be seen stopped in their tracks, abandoned by motorists on their way to or from work, running their late morning errands or embarking on a family vacation that was suddenly cut short. The long stretch of interstate that was now the world's largest parking lot greeted Richard and Lindsay with little hope.

Richard put up a hand for a friendly wave, and two members of the group returned his salutation. The man in the lead, one of the wavers, sported a three-piece suit and a briefcase. His blue silk tie was undone and hung lazily around his neck. The waver next to him wore a similar suit, but carried no briefcase. Behind them was what Lindsay assumed was a small family — a mother and father walking on either side of a little girl no more than eight or nine years old, who held both their hands. To the left of the father walked a man in a Chevron jumpsuit, no doubt a truck driver of some sort.

"Where you guys headin'?" asked the first waver when they were close enough to hold a conversation.

"Downers Grove," answered Richard.

Lindsay smiled at the little girl, who did not return the gesture. She seemed shaken and afraid. It wasn't surprising — they had come from what was undoubtedly the worst traffic jam in history. The small child certainly had to be exhausted and more than a little freaked out by all of this.

"Downers Grove. That's a long walk," said the truck driver.

Richard smiled. "It's not like we can drive."

The father moved next to the man with the briefcase, keeping his daughter and wife close to him. "Are you coming from Chicago? What's it like?"

Richard bowed his head. "I wouldn't recommend going there, if I were you."

"Well, you ain't," snapped the truck driver. "I'd recommend you not walk down the interstate, but that's just me."

"Why not?" asked Lindsay.

"People aren't normal," said the mother. "There was a cop car behind us when it happened. When we decided to group up and walk back, the cop... he, well..."

"He attacked us," the father finished for her.

Richard's eyes widened in disbelief. "He *attacked* you?"

The mother nodded her head.

The truck driver stepped forward and raised his hand up. It wasn't until then that Richard and Lindsay noticed the man was carrying a crowbar, which was speckled with blood on the business end. "I had to take care of him," he said, as if it was a warning.

"Easy there, big guy," Richard said, putting up his hands. "We're not like that. We were attacked, too, in our own building."

The man with the briefcase stepped forward. "Did you see their eyes? Where they-"

Richard nodded his head before the man could finish. "Black as night."

"Then it's like this everywhere," said the second suit wearing man.

"At least downtown it is," said Lindsay. Then, with her eyes locked on the trucker's crowbar, she whispered to Richard, "Come on, let's go."

Richard nodded.

"We don't want to lose any more daylight," Richard said to the group. "You guys be careful."

"You, too," said the man with the briefcase.

The group moved around Richard and Lindsay. Lindsay pulled her eyes away from the bloody crowbar and over to the little girl. She limped, and there was blood and dirt freckled throughout her fragile-looking blonde hair. The child turned to look back at Lindsay, as if she could sense her stare. Then, without uttering a sound, the kid mouthed the words "no more room."

Shaken, Lindsay turned her attention back to Richard.

"Let's keep moving," he said. "We still got a long ways to go."

23.

Malcolm and Gloria considered themselves lucky to have found an open window that lead to the arts and crafts room of Westmont High School — the rest of the building seemed to be locked up tight for the summer. The window was small; barely big enough for Malcolm to fit through. There was no way in hell Gloria would be able to make it through the opening in her condition, so Malcolm had had to go in alone, drop himself to the floor, and let her in through the front doors.

The school was deserted and smelled of erasers and floor polish. As dead as the building was, it looked like someone had been in every week or so to keep it in tip-top condition for the kids coming back in September. Gloria didn't give the lockers or classrooms a second look; they were all things she had hoped to never see again, and yet here she was passing Mr. Haggerty's office door.

For Malcolm it was a different experience entirely. Thirty-two years had passed since he had set eyes on these walls. What amazed him the most was how much the place hadn't changed. Sure, they had repainted, using the same beige-and-purple color scheme. The lockers were the same ones that were there when Malcolm had pantsed Jimmy Shaleman his sophomore year, the same lockers that where there when he got a week's worth of detention for clogging all the boy's toilets with feminine hygiene products, the same lockers that where there when Samantha Browning told him she'd had a crush on him since the seventh grade.

He let his fingers slide along the cool metal of the lockers, trying to see if he could remember which one had been his. He couldn't; those memories were long gone by now, replaced with eight years of law school and thousands of cans of Heineken's.

They turned down a hallway that Gloria knew would lead them to the gym. Through there they would be able to cut across the center of the school to the newspaper office, where according to Gloria, an old newspaper printing press was kept.

Malcolm reached into his pocket for a cigarette. He lit one up, this time being sure to blow the smoke away from Gloria. She looked at him as if to say *What did I tell you about that?*

"Sorry. I've always wanted to smoke in these halls."

Gloria shook her head at him, scolding him by

rolling her eyes, but at the same time a slight smile found its way to her lips. Boys will be boys.

"You have that down good," he said.

"What?"

"The mother-look. Haven't seen that since I was seven."

"I probably got it from my mother."

"You got that look a lot, huh?"

"No," she answered. "My dad did."

"But not anymore?" he asked.

"Not since he left, no," she said.

They walked in silence for a few steps, Gloria quickening her pace so she'd be ahead of Malcolm. Malcolm took another drag and let it out slowly as they came to a set of doors. Above them was a sign that read GYMNASIUM. To Malcolm they looked half as big as when he last saw them. The doors no longer towered over him with the fear of gym class, communal showers, and an always shouting P.E. coach. Now they were just plain old doors. Gloria pulled one of them open and stepped in ahead of Malcolm.

The gym, like the rest of the school, was dark and abandoned. There was a foreboding nature about it. Gloria shivered, rubbing her arms with her hands. Malcolm knew how she felt. There was something about the school that was a little off, as if the building didn't want them there.

Gloria pointed to the other side of the gym. "We just cut straight through to the other side, head on through those doors, and the newspaper office will be on our left."

"Hey, I'm sorry about your father."

"You didn't make him ditch out on us," Gloria said.

"I know. I'm just sorry, that's all."

"My dad was an asshole. Grade-A, top-of-the-class-with-honors, capital-A Asshole. Him ditching mom was the best thing that ever happened to her," she said.

Once through the second set of doors, they came to another hallway, identical to the first. Gloria led them to the third door on the left, which had the words WESTMONT HIGH SCHOOL NEWSPAPER stenciled in bold block letters on it.

Malcolm flicked his lighter on and moved ahead of Gloria. "Probably shoulda picked up a lantern."

Gloria gave him a fake smile as she opened the door with one hand and stepped inside.

24.

Jennifer Adams was a block away from the municipal building when she lost it again. She fell to the ground, her kneecaps smacking into the sidewalk with a sound that was sure to be followed by bruises the next day. Her blonde hair, usually immaculately groomed, now dirty and greasy from the soot in the substation, fell in front of her face. Her lips quivered. Her hands shook. What she saw at the substation couldn't have been real. Could it?

The stars had just begun to show themselves in the darkening sky. Usually around this time people were getting home from work, sitting down to dinner and yapping with one another about their days. But not tonight. Even though she couldn't see anyone, she could hear them.

The sound of a window crashing a few blocks away. What she was pretty sure were gunshots came from somewhere behind her, but not close

143

enough for her to see what was happening to provoke gunplay in Westmont. She had heard gunshots throughout her journey to and from the substation, and although she hated to admit it, she was getting used to it.

She was a block away from her office, kneeling on the sidewalk in her torn and grimy suit, wondering just what the hell was happening to her quiet little town. Two days ago it had been one of the safest places to live in the country. Now nothing worked and her husband could be dead.

Before more images of what the wreckage of the substation could re-enter her mind, Jennifer forced herself back to her feet and took the final steps to her office building. She found the front door locked, and used her keys to get in. None of the windows had been broken, and it looked like the municipal building had been left untouched. So far.

Jennifer closed and locked the door behind her. She found her way to her office, discovering the building to be empty. Malcolm and Gloria would probably be at the high school by now, getting the printing machine ready to return communication to Westmont. Harding and Bryman had no doubt joined them.

She sat behind her desk and laughed. What good would something printed on a newspaper do *now?* She had the sinking suspicion most of the people in Westmont wouldn't give a shit; they didn't seem to be giving a shit about much of anything else. But they were out of options until the power came back.

And even then, when things finally returned to normal, Jennifer wondered if *she'd* give a shit about anything. She kept on trying to tell herself that Stephen was probably still alive, out there somewhere, looking for her just like she was looking for him.

Wiping away a tear that had gone down her cheek un-noticed, she scribbled a quick note to Stephen, telling him she was at the high school. There was certainly the chance her husband would come here looking for her. If he did, telling him she was safe at the high school seemed the smartest way to ensure their reunion.

When she was done, she put the pen back in the drawer and placed the letter in the center of her desk. She didn't know if she'd ever seen Stephen again, let alone this office. Everything she was doing she felt like she was doing for the last time. Which again, was preposterous, this was just a power outage.

Where nothing worked.

Not even cars.

And people had apparently gone insane.

Okay, so it's more than just a power outage, she thought. Whatever this *was*, she was doing no good sulking about it at her desk. She needed to get to the high school, bring as many people together as she could. Then they could decide what the next step should be.

She grabbed the letter off her desk along with the tape dispenser. She could tape it to the front door, where Stephen would be sure to see it. As she moved around her desk, her legs gave out from under her and she found herself on the floor. Her throat was tight with sadness, and the tears began. They just came and came, everything she had been holding inside came out all at once.

Jennifer Adams cried.

She cried for a very long time.

25.

The police station was a cacophony of commotion. From his desk in the lobby, Chief Hetaine watched two patrol officers escort a very disgruntled and handcuffed old woman into the back. She looked out of place in the station; round-rimmed John Lennon style glasses, a shawl over her shoulders, and a purse circa 1975 gave the impression that this was a lady that wouldn't hurt a fly if it took a shit in her soup.

As they passed Hetaine, he heard a long line of expletives fall out of her mouth at a breakneck speed. Upon closer inspection, he noticed there were droplets of blood across her shawl, apparently from a head wound she had suffered. Her Lennon glasses were broken, with one lens cracked and the other nowhere to be seen.

"What'd she do?" Hetaine asked one of the passing officers.

"No more room!" cackled the old woman.

"Assault, if you can believe that," said the first one. "And she keeps on saying that."

"No more room!" she said again, as if to prove the officer right.

Hetaine raised an eyebrow. "Who'd she attack?"

"Us," said the second with a tinge of embarrassment in his voice. He quickly whisked her away into the back while the crazy old loon chanted *no more room, no more room* the entire way.

Hetaine shook his head as he watched the three move down the hallway to the holding cells, which were filling up quickly. The day had started nice enough, he thought, a few complaints from local merchants on some break-ins, peppered with questions about what would be done about everyone's cars sitting in the roads, was about all he'd had to deal with.

But over the past few hours, violence had seemed to have found a new home in Westmont. The old woman was just the most recent of many citizens who had begun to act bizarre, not at all like the nice and pleasant small suburban families that they were. Hetaine was sure that the tactical alert would be enough, that the mere sight of his officers out there on the streets in bullet-proof vests would be enough to keep people in line.

Apparently, he decided, he was wrong. Way fucking wrong.

Prepare for the worst. Hope for the best. With no way to communicate with anyone, it looked like this was as good as things were going to get.

The front door opened again. Hetaine looked up to see the next civilian to be brought in.

A lone man entered the police station, looking as out of place as could be in a trench coat in the middle of summer. It swayed behind him in a gust of a breeze from the doors as they closed.

The Man in the Dark Coat scanned the station, looking for someone.

"Can I help you?" Hetaine asked the man.

"Possibly," said the Man in the Dark Coat. "I'm looking for some friends of mine."

"Well, we got a good portion of the town locked up in back," Hetaine snorted. "Looking for anyone in particular?"

The Man in the Dark Coat gave the chief a slow grin. "No," he said. "The ones in back will do for now."

The New Way

26.

The front bumper of the Winnebago was kissing the rear bumper of the car in front of it, a Honda Hybrid. They had been on the tollway for upwards of four hours now, and fellow walkers were few and far between. It seemed most people who had been caught in traffic when their cars died had seemed fit to leave the interstate a long time ago. Which was fine by Richard — most of the people they had run into since leaving their apartment hadn't been the most friendly of folk.

Lindsay rubbed her head and squinted her eyes even though the sun had begun to set over an hour ago. She had felt the onset of a migraine coming her way — the kind where it feels like there's ice-picks being shoved into your eye sockets — not long after they arrived on the interstate and met the first group of walkers.

Richard pulled open the side door to the Winnebago, hoping that the owners had left some aspirin or ibuprofin inside. He also hoped there wasn't a Changed Person lurking around in there, just waiting for some idiot to open the door and peek inside.

The interior of the Winnebago was dark, and upon first sight there did not seem to be anyone in the vehicle. Richard stepped in, reaching a hand behind him for Lindsay to take.

"Hello?" he said to the motor home. "Anyone here?"

After ten seconds of silence, Richard was sold on the idea that it was empty and pulled his wife inside.

He was pleased to discover that there appeared to be no signs of violence here like they had seen in the commuter train. He moved to the kitchen area, which consisted of nothing more than a hot plate and a small basin sink. Above the sink where a group of cabinets, held closed by safety latches.

He unlatched the first cabinet and found himself looking at boxes of Hamburger Helper and macaroni and cheese. The second cabinet was where the travelers had decided to keep their Tupperware, which was still neatly arranged and stacked according to size.

Lindsay watched her husband open up the third cabinet where they had hit the pharmacy jackpot. Aspirin, ibuprofin, Pepto Bismol, Extra Strength Excedrin; if it relieved pain, reduced fever or calmed upset stomachs, it was here.

"Thank God," she said, pushing Richard out of her way and letting go of his hand. The pain in her head had grown by the second over the past couple of hours, and she was fairly sure if she didn't throw some pain killers at it now, the veins in her forehead would burst open. Which, when she thought about it, wouldn't be such a bad thing — at least then the unbearable pressure in her head would probably go away.

She grabbed the green bottle of Excedrin, twisted off the child-proof cap, and poured five into her mouth.

"Hey, easy does it," said Richard.

Ignoring him, Lindsay turned the faucet on and shoveled handfuls of water into her mouth, swallowing the pills. The cool water felt good going down her throat, and she immediately began to feel like her old self again. She turned the water off as Richard put a hand on her back.

"Easy, babe. You're gonna make yourself sick, taking that much."

Still bending over the sink, she said, "I don't think I could feel worse than I already do."

"That bad, huh?"

She nodded her head. Yes, the headache was *that* bad. But what she was neglecting to tell her husband was that the headache was accompanied by a voice — the same voice she had heard in their apartment — and was getting to be so loud she could hardly concentrate on anything else. What made it even more maddening was the Voice wasn't

153

changing it's tune. It just kept saying her name over and over again: *Lindsay, Lindsay, Lindsay, Lindsay.* She'd pay anything just to hear the fucking thing say something, *anything,* else.

Richard put a hand to her head, feeling for a temperature. From the look on his face, Lindsay gathered her forehead felt warmer to him than a cool 98.6. He looked at her with worried eyes.

"Maybe we should stay here for awhile," he said.

Lindsay straightened herself up, stretching and cracking her back. She twisted her neck from side-to-side, feeling bones and tendons loosen and pop. Just that little bit gave her a small dosage of relief. And she was confident as soon as the meds hit her system, she'd be right as rain.

"No," she said. "I want to keep moving, get there as soon as we can."

"Alright," Richard said, "but you just say the word, and we'll pull over, find a motel room, maybe watch some porn on the pay-per-view."

Lindsay smiled. "You're a funny guy. I knew there was a reason I married you."

Richard smiled back. "It certainly wasn't for my good looks."

Taking his hand again, Lindsay followed Richard out of the Winnebago. Her headache was, in fact, subsiding remarkably quickly.

But the Voice was still there. Still calling her name. And, as she had wished, it was beginning to finally change its tune.

Lindsay.
Lindsay.
Lindsay.
Kill your husband.

27.

Heather and Gildy had found the man lying unconscious on the sidewalk. Whoever had fired
the shotgun was nowhere to be seen, so they turned
their attention to the wounded man on the ground.
While it was clear that the man's injury had not
come from a gun but rather a blade, the cut on his
leg was severe enough to require stitches. Together
they had carried John Whitley to the police station,
avoiding the busier sections of town.

They found the police station deserted upon
their return. The place had been turned upside
down, and there wasn't an officer in sight. The
blood on the floor and the bullet holes in the walls
told Heather and Gildy all they needed to know: in
the short amount of time that they had been gone,
the riot had escalated and found its way inside the
police station. And now all the police officers were
gone, along with the rioters, to God knows where.

Even more disturbing were the twenty empty holding cells in the back. They had all been forced open, without a key, and any prisoners that had been in there were long gone.

On the wall above Chief Hetaine's desk was a map of Westmont. It now sat crooked on the wall, frayed on all corners. Written in the center of the map in red (Heather hoped it wasn't blood, but she had the feeling with the way things were going that it was) were the words: "NO MORE ROOM!"

Concerned, Gildy shut and locked the door behind them, blocking it with one of the benches sitting in the corner. He kept his gun in his hand and his eyes wide open.

Heather pushed the sharp pointed edge of the needle through John's skin. Starting from the bottom of the gash, she worked her way up as quickly as she could before he awoke. The needle successfully made its way through the skin, and Heather pulled the other side of the cut towards the needle, beginning to close the gap. The dead silence in the police station made the sound of the needle going through John's skin overpowering; the only sound seemed to be the sliding of the thread through this man's leg.

Heather began her fourth stitch. Pulling the thread tight when it was through, she looked at John's eyes. They were closed and he looked peaceful, as if in a beautiful dream world.

* * *

Wake up.

I want him out of my house. Our house.

He already is. You're not at home anymore.

Please, take me home.

You need to wake up, hon. You can't give up. Not yet.

I want to be alone. No, not alone. I want to be with you.

You ARE with me, baby. You are.

You don't know what it's been like.

Yes, I do. I've been there every step of the way. You know that.

It's not the same.

It's all we have.

I've been holding on for so long, Trace. I don't know how much longer I can do it. I'm tired. So fucking tired.

You have to open your eyes, hon. Now.

I can't.

For me, baby. There's not much time. Open them for me.

John snapped his head up from the floor and was out of his daze, out of the conversation. Talking to Tracey calmed him when things got tough, when his heart raced, when he felt like killing the next person he saw. He knew they were just his own voices in his head, calling back on memories from their marriage.

But there was something different about it this time. Her words were — the only way he could put it — more alive.

His head was swimming with pain and confusion. There was a kid. Someone had broken into his home. Had he shot the kid? He was pretty sure he had. And Pauley. An image of the fat liquor store owner chasing two girls down the street with a shotgun came to mind. He was pretty sure Pauley had shot the two girls, too.

John was on his back. He could feel the cold hard cement through his shirt. He wasn't outside anymore. Someone had brought him indoors.

"Well lookie who's awake."

John gazed up with blurry eyes at the female cop who had spoken. "Where am I?"

"Police station," came a male voice from behind him. "What happened, buddy?"

John tried to sit up, but Heather kept him down. "I'm not sure," he said. "I was in my bathroom, then... he shot those girls. Jesus. He killed those two girls."

Heather and Gildy exchanged looks. John's lack of details was unsettling.

"Who shot what girls?" Gildy asked.

"Pauley. He was mad. I don't mean pissed off, well he was that, too, but I mean crazy-mad, not himself," John said. His eyes scissored between the two cops. "Are they okay, the girls?"

"We didn't see any girls," Heather answered. "We heard the shots and were kinda hopin' you knew what happened."

"You know about as much as I do," John said. He lifted his hands to massage his tight and stressed neck. It was then that he noticed some extra weight around his wrists — the weight of a pair of hand-cuffs.

Heather and Gildy towered over John, arms crossed.

"Waitaminute, you don't think *I* had anything to do with that, do you?"

"We'd be idiots if we thought otherwise, pal," Gildy said. "We heard two shots, and by the time we got there, the only person around was you."

John ran through the facts in his head. While he knew they were wrong — he knew what he had seen — he also knew that what the cops were telling him was the only logical explanation they could have come upon. The more he thought about it, the more he didn't blame the cops for cuffing him. If the roles had been reversed, he'd probably have done the same thing himself.

Heather squatted down next to him, resting her elbows on her knees. Her bullet-proof vest rose up on her torso, and she had to un-velcro the bottom strap to be more comfortable.

John glanced past Heather to a window behind an officer's desk. The sunlight was gone, and he was able to make out a few stars in the night sky.

"Jesus, how long was I out?"

"Five, six hours," Heather said.

John's eyes moved over the floor of the police

station. Chairs had been tossed to the side like toothpicks and blood was splattered all over the flooring. He was pretty sure he saw a tooth next to Heather's right foot. Sure signs of a brutal fight if John had ever seen them.

"What happened here?"

Heather ignored his question and locked eyes with John. "You said there were two girls."

"Yes."

"And where are they now?"

"If they weren't lying in the street when you found me, I don't have a fucking clue." John's eyes danced around the police station again. "Where're all the cops?"

Gildy moved to the other side of the writer, so that John was now book-ended by the cops. "Same place as the two girls. We have no fucking clue. This Pauley guy. Who's that?"

John put up his hands. "Whoa, just slow down there, Ponch. Kinda been through a lot here. Gimme a little time."

Gildy slammed John's hands down into his lap and grabbed him by the collar. "I don't know that you deserve anymore time, shit-bird."

John pulled his head back from Gildy's, doing his best to not inhale one atom more of the cop's ancient breath. He turned to Heather. "Is this guy serious?"

Heather rolled her eyes over to her partner. "Ease up, Gildy."

Gildy released John. "Answer the question.

161

Who's Pauley?"

"He owns the liquor store down the street from me. Look, I know how this looks, but you gotta believe me. I didn't do anything," John said. He wasn't pleading — he knew there was no point of that. It just made him feel better to say his peace.

Gildy hoisted John up by the arms, jerking the man to his feet. "The way things are right now, you won't mind if we choose to not believe you."

"I didn't do anything," John said one last time as he was escorted to the rear of the police station, where he assumed he would shortly be finding himself behind bars.

28.

Eddie sucked in a breath, his first in what felt like hours. His eyes snapped open, wide. The air was alive with a tinge of cigarette smoke. He breathed it in, relishing the slight taste of nicotine, tar and smoke.

A man had woken him up, but he was gone. The man was tall, wore some sort of long coat, and Eddie knew that this man had been his best friend forever. It didn't matter that he couldn't recall the man's name. What mattered was that he was awake and had business to do. He had to help this Man in the Dark Coat.

He lifted himself up and rested on his elbows, taking in his surroundings. From what he could make out in the gloom of the early night, he was in a bedroom that wasn't his and that he didn't re-member entering.

Get up.

Eddie obeyed the Voice. It was the Voice of the man who had woken him up, his best friend forever, whatever his name might be. He dusted himself off. His hands ran over the holes in his body, which looked like they had come from gunshots. But there was no pain and he wasn't bleeding.

You have a new job.

Eddie made his way into the kitchen, leaving footprints of blood on the carpet. Once at the sink, he picked up a glass from the nearby drying rack and filled it with water. He downed it all in one gulp, letting the water swim down his throat and enter his belly. He did this three more times before he began to feel more like himself again.

I need some help. You're the man for it.

Fuckin-A I am.

Go to the police station.

He turned away from the sink, dropping the glass on the floor. He didn't notice it smash to the ground or the crunching of the broken glass under his feet as he walked out of the kitchen. His mind was elsewhere. Like his friend had said, he had a new job and he was the man for it. There wasn't time to be tidy.

He made a straight line for the front door. As Eddie walked outside and headed for the police station, he wondered just how much this new job paid.

29.

A *kah-bang* echoed throughout the station as Gildy slammed the cell door shut. John rested his head against the bars, the coolness of the metal alleviating at least some of the massive headache he felt coming on.

Gildy walked past two desks just out of John's reach over to Heather, who leaned against the jail cell across from the writer's.

The cops were fatigued and worn, John noticed, as if they had been through hell and back and were about to return there shortly. Both of their uniforms were soaked to the pits with sweat, and John thought he saw some blood on Heather's left sleeve.

The back room, like the front of the station, was a shambles. Papers and reports littered the floor, and there was the unmistakable markings of bullet holes in all the walls. Heather lifted a chair that looked like it had been tossed across the room by the Incredible Hulk and placed it right. Gildy sifted through papers on someone's desk. Droplets of blood were on the pages.

"You guys sure throw a helluva party," John said.

Gildy didn't look up from the blood-splattered pages. "Shut up."

"Look, whatever's going on, do you really think locking me up in here will do anyone any good? Look at this place. It's not safe here," John said. Then he looked from his cell to all the others. All the other *empty* cells.

"Say, am I the only bad guy here?" he asked.

Heather reached to her holster and pulled her Beretta. Every muscle in John's body tightened.

Holy shit, she's gonna shoot me, John thought.

Instead of firing, Heather placed the firearm on the desk next to her. "It's not safe anywhere."

John walked to the other side of his cage, moving closer to Gildy. "I promise I won't run."

Gildy raised an eyebrow. "Excuse me?"

John had never been keen on using what little fame he had gathered over the years as a novelist, but if there was ever a time to use it, it was now. "Look, maybe you've heard of me. My name's John Whitley. I'm a writer."

"Your parents must be proud," said Gildy.

"Come on. I'm famous. They even made a mini-series out of one of my books, maybe you saw it, *Into the Darkness*."

Gildy laughed. "You wrote that?"

John returned his comment with a defensive

grin. "The book. Not the mini-series."

"Well, I hope for your sake the book was better, 'cause the mini-series sucked."

John moved away from the bars and sat down on the cot in the rear of the cell. He put his head in his hands. "Yeah, I wasn't a big fan of it, either."

Heather walked to John's cell, her arms crossed, her face frozen in a contemplative stare. "So John. You were lying on the sidewalk. Unconscious. Cut up. What happened."

John looked up from the floor. "I thought you guys didn't care."

"Might as well tell us how ya' got there while we figure out what to do with ya'," Gildy said.

John ran his fingers through his hair, going over the facts of the day in his mind. "Okay. It's kinda fuzzy, but I'll give it a go. I go out for some smokes — to Pauley's store, you know, the guy who shot the two girls you think I shot — and when I get back, some asshole is going through my shit in my bedroom. We got into it, and I had to shoot him. Go back to my place if you don't believe me. Right in the bedroom. A dead guy. Still has the knife in his hand, I bet."

Gildy shook his head. "A knife?"

John shot a glace at the cop. "Yes, a knife. Hence the knife cut on my leg."

"And this is the guy who gave you that slice?" Heather said.

"You sure don't miss much, do you?" John replied.

The two cops scowled at him, not amused.

"Sorry, it's been one of those days," John said. "He was just a kid, maybe eighteen, nineteen. He was crazy, didn't seem right. Like Pauley, just kinda not all there. And his eyes..."

Gildy lifted his head. "What about his eyes?"

"They were gone. All black."

30.

Jennifer.

The mayor snapped her head around, looking behind her in every direction. It was getting late, and most people had probably holed themselves up in their homes for the evening. Perhaps the majority of the people had actually taken her advice to mind and stayed indoors; people were sitting in their beds right now, reading a book with a loved one or doing what came naturally. It made sense to her; none of the stores were open, all of the restaurants were closed, so really, what was there to do? She hadn't been a bit surprised at the near emptiness of the streets.

Not to mention that the occasional shout-out from some nutball or a series of gunshots going off in the distance would be enough to keep any sane person locked up tight in their home. What that said about her — a lone woman walking down the street at night and hearing those very things — she didn't want to know.

When she heard her name called out, it was enough to startle her away from her visions of what may or may not have happened to her husband. She truly wanted to believe that none of the blood — nor the pinky finger — belonged to Stephen. But she knew there was no way she could be sure of that fact.

The street behind her was vacant. The blue light of the rising moon reflected off the sidewalk and automobiles, basking the block in a cooling and re-freshing shade of azure. On any other night, the silence and calming light would have been pleasant. A beautiful evening to take your loved one out for a walk.

Jennifer forgot about the voice that had called her name and proceeded on her way toward the high school. She had no idea what she would do once she got there. Printing out upbeat sounding flyers for the town seemed insane at this point, and was probably utterly useless. She was beginning to think a better plan might be to just forget that altogether and head out of town. She wasn't sure where they should go, but with every step she was feeling more and more like Westmont was not the place to be.

She crossed the street, needing to step around an abandoned Ford truck that had stalled in the cross-walk. Directly in front of her was her grocery store of choice, Jewel. She figured she was about a mile away from the high school when she heard the

Voice again. This time it was proceeded by an itch at the back of her skull, like somebody was poking at her with a very small needle.

Jennifer.

She whirled around again for the second time since her walk began. Like before, she found herself all alone on the street.

"Hello? Anyone there?" she asked, the sound of her tiny voice almost deafening in the middle of the dark silence.

She waited for a full minute, holding her breath, listening for a reply. When one didn't come, she thought the best thing to do was to shrug it off as stress-related. This was, after all, turning out to be one hell of a stress-filled week.

She continued on her way, hoping that the others would all be there by the time she got to the school, and then they could leave this town.

The man who used to be Stephen Adams watched his wife cross the street. As Jennifer paused to look at the grocery store, Stephen quickly and quietly made his way across the intersection, stopping at the Ford truck. He bent over, kneeling down to hide behind the vehicle, keeping it between himself and his wife.

She started up again, and Stephen began to move away from the truck. Before he could move much further, he saw her stop again and turn in his direction. He froze, holding his breath. Had she seen him?

The Voice returned and told him that no, Jennifer hadn't seen her husband crouching behind the Ford. She was simply confused at the new state of things, but would come around eventually. And if she didn't, the Voice continued, it was Stephen's job to make sure she did.

He watched his wife pick up her pace again. When she was almost a block away, Stephen shuffled out from behind the truck and continued his silent pursuit. For better or worse, 'til death did they part, Stephen Adams would be with his wife again.

31.

Gloria found two old coffee cans (which seemed to be every high school's method for storing small objects) and placed some torn up newspaper in them. Malcolm lit them both with his lighter. With only one copy of the *Westmont Herald* located for fuel, they knew the small bonfires wouldn't last more than an hour. They'd need to find more paper, both for the fire and for the printing machine, of which there didn't seem to be any nearby.

The machine itself stood in a corner, hulking and dark, a relic from long ago. It was no bigger than a standard typewriter, not that either of them had seen one of those machines in years. It looked to Malcolm more like a deli-slicer than a printing press, with a handle on one side he assumed was for rolling the paper through and a tray in the front for the finished copies.

"Don't suppose you know how to work it?"

Malcolm asked.

Gloria headed to a wall cabinet, opened it and peered inside. "I'm afraid not," she said over her shoulder. "I'm hoping there's some sorta manual in here." She moved objects in the cabinet this way and that, clearly not finding what she was looking for.

"Great," he said as Gloria continued her search. The rest of the room contained a few stools, a couple of small desks, and that was it. "Why'd you work on the paper?"

Gloria's head was deep inside the cabinet. "What?"

"Why'd you work on the paper? Dreams of being Lois Lane?"

She backed out of the cabinet, dusting her hands off on her skirt. "More like Lois Lame," she answered. "Turns out my nose for news was about as sensitive as your smoking etiquette."

"No reason to be harsh," said Malcolm. "I was just trying to make conversation."

"Pardon me, but you've been less than a gentleman. And that's not only around me, but around the Mayor, as well," she said, stepping closer to the man, clearly not intimidated at all.

"It's politics," he argued.

"It's rude."

Malcolm stepped away from her and snorted. "Sounds like your sense of politics is about as sensitive as your nose for news."

Gloria stared daggers at Malcolm as he turned

away and started out of the room. "Well now you're just being an asshole."

"You keep looking for that manual, I'm gonna go find some more paper," he said, and was gone.

Gloria watched the lawyer leave, wondering why she got stuck with the biggest asshole in the state.

The Man in the Dark Coat knew he had once been in a building like this — or rather, the body of Thomas Manning had. Memories from most of Manning's childhood were blurred, nothing more than shadows of the past. The force that took over his body thought this might have been the very high school Thomas Manning had attended until he had found him, but he couldn't be sure. It didn't matter.

The scent of Malcolm was easy enough to follow. The man had been sweating, and the aroma of Old Spice was pungent in the air. Not to mention that the psychic connection he shared with the lawyer grew stronger the closer he got.

But the woman was different. He could smell her perfume (she didn't use much, but it was there) the gel she used in her hair, and beneath all that, he could smell *her*. He didn't know why, but pregnant women seemed to give off a scent like no others. It was the scent of life. Of new beginnings. Of innocence.

It was a scent he hated.

What he hated even more was that he couldn't sense her like he could the others. He knew there would be a handful of souls he'd be blind to, but he hadn't prepared himself for just how strange and annoying a feeling it would be to not feel someone he knew was there. The girl wasn't like the others he couldn't see. Minds that were blocked to him showed up as black blotches in his head, as if he had rubbed his eyes too hard for too long and was left with only that dizzying red-black haze that would move across his vision.

The girl, however, was an empty whiteness. And every time he tried to look at that whiteness, it would blind him.

The rest of the town had been easy. A push here. A suggestion there. Sometimes he even *liked* getting down-and-dirty, as with that pudgy fuck in the clothing store. But deep down he was a very impatient man, and the mystery of the girl and the others he couldn't see was getting on his nerves.

He came to two tall doors marked GYMNASIUM. The scent was stronger, and he could feel that beyond the two doors it would be stronger still.

Allowing himself that grin again, the grin that told him play time was near, the Man in the Dark Coat cracked his knuckles and entered the gymnasium, eager to finally meet this girl his mind couldn't see.

32.

"Tell me more about the eyes," Gildy said as he unlocked the cell door.

John watched the door swing open with a squeak. He looked up at the cop, unsure of just what the man's motivations might be.

Gildy held John's look, serious. "I've seen the same thing."

The cop moved out of John's way, giving him ample room to exit the cell. Heather walked into the room, boxes of magazines for their firearms in her hands. She looked like she was preparing for a war, and from what John and seen before he passed out, he thought she might not be too far off. Her eyes were determined yet far away. Focused, but else-where. As if she was fully aware of what she was doing, and didn't like it one little bit.

John didn't blame her.

He pulled his eyes away from Heather and her

growing arsenal. "They were just black, all the color was gone." He paced to the other side of the room, contemplating the day's actions. "You know, I think Pauley might have been like that, too. Just for a second, when I was in the store. Before he went, you know, psycho."

Heather stacked the boxes of ammo on a desk and looked up at the two. "Just for a second?"

"Real quick, like a flash more than anything. I thought I was just over-tired." He turned back to Gildy. "You said you saw it, too?"

"The guy we were trying to arrest before we came after you," said Gildy. "This fucking guy was having at it baseball-style with a car."

"Lovely."

As Heather moved into the adjoining room, which John suspected was some sort of armory, he couldn't help but take notice of how well the uniform fit her. Even though shadows ruled in the room, he could still make out the slope of her back into her buttocks, and the way the holster, now with the Beretta back in it, rested at the side of her right hip.

He pushed these thoughts out of his head as Heather disappeared into the armory and he saw Tracey appear in the doorjamb. He hadn't seen his wife since the day she died, when he got to watch her last breath escape through her bloody lips. But there she was, in the clothes he saw her in last: blue jeans faded from wear, a yellow blouse, and her fa-

178

vorite pair of Nike's. All basic attire, all looked great on her. Her hair was still slicked back in a strict pony-tail, just like it had been the day she died.

John gave himself a classic eye-rub and head-shake, the kind he had seen in countless movies.

When he was done, his dead wife still stood before him.

Tracey?

Hey, baby.

You're dead.

Yes, I am.

Am I going crazy?

You always were a little crazy, but no.

Then what's going on?

In time.

I don't know what to do, I don't know what you want me to do.

I want you to be happy.

Not without you. We've been over that.

Tears formed in John's eyes.

I'm so sorry, Trace. The whole thing. All my fault.

It was an accident.

His dead wife moved out of the doorjamb and past John. He watched her, mesmerized, as she stopped at the end of the hallway of cells and looked down at Gildy, who was rummaging through the ammo Heather had brought out.

Gildy took no notice of her. Apparently John was the only one with enough damaged brain cells

179

that could see her.

No it wasn't. I should've kept it in control, I should've-

It's not important now.

Tears made his vision blurry. He quickly wiped them away, not wanting to lose sight of Tracey even for a second.

Why are you here?

To help you. You have a big job ahead of you. You all do.

The conversation was cut short as Tracey's face was replaced with another. John couldn't identify the person at first — it was too dark to make out anything beyond shadows.

His mind's eye image of Tracey disappeared as the man lifted a gun from his side — a revolver. John thought it looked suspiciously like *his* revolver. The person — a kid by the looks of him — aimed John's gun at Heather, who was returning from the armory.

"LOOK OUT!!!" John yelled.

Heather snapped her head up and spotted the intruder. In less than a second, the boxes of ammo were on the floor and her Beretta was in her hand and the trigger was being pulled.

Gildy moved away from the desk and already had his own gun drawn. Together, the two cops let out three shots each. The kid ended up with three bullets in his torso, one between his left eye and nose, one just above his collar bone, and the final shot from Heather landed in the kid's mouth.

The guy went down, bone and blood leaving a trail in the air where he had been standing. He hit the ground with a *thump*, landing face first on the cement floor. His nose *cracked* as it bashed against the tile and folded across the kid's face.

John fell to the floor himself. He scurried away like a crab to the far side of the room. The whole while, all he could think of to say was "shit-shit-shit-shit-shit."

Heather moved past him, keeping her gun aimed at the man's head.

John let out a breath. "Holy-shit-Jesus-fuckin-Christ-what-the-hell-just-happened?!"

Gildy stood on the other side of the kid. Sharing a silent nod with Heather, Gildy used his foot to turn the teenager over onto his back. The kid still held the revolver in his right hand.

"Eddie, you stupid idiot," Gildy said.

"You know him?" Heather asked as she kicked the gun out of Eddie's hand with a foot.

"Eddie Miller. His father runs the pizza place by my house."

John found the strength to get to his feet. Still shaking, he wiped sweat and tears from his face. He walked over to the desk they were using to stack their ammo, getting as close to the incident as he was able to without getting sick. Five feet from the dead body seemed to be about it. Any closer, he was pretty sure there would be some bona-fide collector's item John Whitley vomit on the floor.

181

"Fuck me."

"Excuse me?" Heather asked.

"That's the guy," John said.

Heather and Gildy stared at John.

"Excuse me?" Heather repeated.

"That's the guy I told you about. I came home, and he was robbing my house. We fought, and that's when... that's when he stabbed me, and I shot him," John said.

Gildy eyeballed John. "I thought you said he was dead."

"He sure looked it when I left."

Gildy smiled and gave the writer a short laugh. "Well, if he wasn't before, he sure as fuck is now."

"No, no, no, I shot him three times. This dude was fucking *dead*," John said. Then his eyes spotted the revolver laying on the floor, next to Heather's foot. "And that's my gun."

Heather and Gildy let their gun-hands rest at their sides. Still alert, they both bent down to inspect the body. Gildy touched the young man's chin, and Eddie's nose fell off of his face.

"Jesus," Gildy slurred.

Heather leaned in closer, as if something wasn't quite right, as if something was bothering her besides the fact that their new writer friend was convinced he had already shot and killed Eddie Miller once today. Then she saw it, and immediately knew why things didn't seem right.

"He's still alive," she said.

"What?" from Gildy.

Gildy looked closer, and he saw it, too. The pulse of blood was still moving through Eddie's neck. It wasn't the push of blood making it's final run from the body to the outside world — it pumped, with a beat and a rhythmic purpose. Eddie's chest moved up and down in breath. It was slow, but it was there.

Gildy, ever so carefully, turned what was left of Eddie's head to the side. The exit wound exposed itself to the cop. Oozing out of the hole, not looking anything like it did in the movies, were small chunks of Eddie's brain. The muscle in his head slipped past a strand of skin and fell to the floor with a *plop*. Blood slid down and around the gray matter, pooling on the ground. A portion of bone held onto his skull for one more second, then fell to the ground with the rest of the head-slop.

"No way in hell should he be alive," Gildy said.

Heather and Gildy looked at each other again, sharing another one of their silent conversations. After a nod from Gildy, Heather pulled out her handcuffs from the back of her belt. As she reached for Eddie's hands, Gildy took two fingers and slowly pried open the boy's eye that didn't have a bullet through it.

A colorless black eye stared out at him. Gildy looked over to John, who could see the black eye just fine from where he was.

John tried to smile, doing his best to make light of a terribly bad situation. "Told ya'."

* * *

The Man in the Dark Coat was at center court when he heard the gunshot and his head snapped back, as if had taken the bullet himself. He almost fell, but managed to quickly shake off the bolt from out of the blue and remain on his feet. His head hurt — a massive onslaught of a migraine had begun. He rubbed his temples and slowed his breathing, which had quickened to almost hyperventilation speeds, and listened.

Shit-shit-shit-shit-shit.

Holy-shit-Jesus-fuckin-Christ-what-the-hell-just-happened?!

Eddie, you stupid kid.

You know him?

Eddie Miller. His father runs the pizza place by my house.

His connection to Eddie Miller was still alive and well, but muffled and confused at the moment. He had become so involved, so excited, in the prospect of meeting the pregnant girl he couldn't see that he had let his guard down. It would take some time for him to properly re-connect with the kid.

He's still alive.

Excuse me?

The Man in the Dark Coat reached out with his mind and tried to touch the two people talking. The first one that spoke — a woman — he couldn't see. But the second one — a man — yes, he could make him out. He sensed a third person in the room, but he was as blind to the Man in the Dark Coat as the woman was.

But he didn't think that would matter. The other man, the man he could sense — he now knew Gildy was his name — was a cop. From Gildy's mind, he pulled that the woman was his partner. Gildy didn't seem to know the other man in the room too well, but he knew name was John Whitley and that he was a writer of some sort.

The Man in the Dark Coat would worry about them later. Right now, he knew he could touch Gildy. He could make him hear the Voice. And through him, he just might be able to dispose of his partner and the writer.

Eddie Miller's head was milky with pain. The room spun and spun, like he was in a dryer that just wouldn't fucking stop spinning. His vision was somehow impaired. He couldn't seem to make things out as well as he used to. Just a day ago he had had 20/20 vision. Now everything was a big blur coated in red.

As consciousness slowly came back to him, he was able to start making things out again. Or at least take some good guesses. Vertical lines were in front of him, but they didn't seem to stay still. Whether that was the lines, the room, or his head, he couldn't be sure. He looked to his right, and he was close enough to a gray brick wall to figure out that it was a gray brick wall.

His vision found the lines again, and they

seemed to come into sharper focus, as if someone was adjusting the controls on a very big TV. Just beyond the lines he could make out two... no, three people. Just standing there, watching him, and occasionally speaking to each other. No... they weren't speaking to each other, they were speaking to *him*.

As the mumblings of their voices started to sound less like mumblings and more like words, the lines came into better focus. Now he knew where he was. Should've recognized it from the get-go.

He was in a jail cell.

Which meant that the people that were talking to him were most likely cops. He fuckin' hated cops.

"Can you hear me?"

It was a female voice. He looked at the blurry figure that had spoken and tried to speak himself. All that came out was a garbled "Mruph-il-uck."

"Can you hear us? You okay?" A man's voice.

"That's a stupid question." The female again.

Eddie fought hard to find his words. They were in there, in his head, but he was having a hell of a time getting them to come out.

"I- I- uh- fuck, yeah. I can hear you," Eddie tried to say, but it came out, "Uh- uh- uh- fuugh, yiiih. Ih khun hur you."

A monster of a headache was starting to take form. He attempted to rub his temples but found he couldn't move his hands. Something cold and metallic was holding them behind his back.

"Who are you?" Eddie asked, the words coming more easily, now.

Handcuffs. That's what was holding his wrists together. Yep, he was in jail alright.

"I'm Officer Steinman. This is Officer Gildy. That's John," she said. "He says you broke into his house and stabbed him."

Eddie looked from her to Gildy, then to the other man who stood far back from them, leaning against another cell.

"Who the fuck is John?" Eddie asked.

"You've been in an accident. How do you feel?" Gildy asked.

"Like I've been in an accident," Eddie said.

"Do you remember anything?" Gildy asked.

"Stop asking so many damn questions. You're making my head hurt," Eddie said, amazed he was able to get the words out coherently enough. At least he *hoped* he was being coherent. He was pretty sure he was; his strength seemed to be coming back, now.

"What's the last thing you remember?" Heather asked.

Eddie ignored her and looked down at his lap. It was covered in something dark and wet. There was a tint of red to the stuff on him, and it didn't take long for him to realize it was blood. It was smeared all over his skin, his legs, his shirt. He was drenched in the shit.

Gildy moved away from the bars. The kid in the cell, the kid that had apparently died twice today, looked up at him with a peculiar expression that

187

combined anger and utter confusion.

"I think I need to go to the hospital," Eddie slurred.

Gildy ignored him. "This is the strangest shit I've ever seen."

"No argument here," John agreed.

Heather put a hand to her chin and stared hard at Eddie. The kid seemed to be solely focused on Gildy. He just gazed at the cop drunkenly, his head moving side-to-side, as if he heard a song only he could hear.

"So, Mr. Miller," she said, "care to tell us what happened?"

"If I knew, I'd tell ya', lady."

Heather leaned in closer. "You know you should be dead, right?"

Eddie smiled. "Dead. Alive. It makes no difference anymore."

"And just what the hell is that supposed to mean?" Gildy asked, a stern pop to his voice.

"Fuck off."

"Listen here you little dumbfuck-"

Heather put up a hand, cutting her partner off; *easy, big fella.*

Eddie just kept on looking at Gildy with that one eye of his. They couldn't find his other one, not that any of them had looked all that hard. Eddie didn't seem to mind so much. He could see well enough. He closed his eyes, as if he was trying to hear something again. Then: "No more room."

Heather, Gildy and John exchanged glances.

"No more room?" John asked.

"No more room. That's all he wants me to say right now," Eddie replied.

"That's all *who* wants you to say?" Heather asked.

"Him."

John put his head in his hands, tried to stifle a laugh. A small giggle escaped, and Eddie looked his way. "What's so funny?"

"This whole thing is so ridiculous. I mean, I was scared there for a second. Fucking terrified. Now I'm sure I'm just having a flashback," John said. Then, to the cops: "I did a lot of acid in college."

"Good for you," Gildy said.

John approached the cop and pointed at his chest. "Look, man. I didn't ask to come along on this ride, so why don't you just-"

"Why don't I just *what?*" Gildy said, moving closer to him, pushing his chest into John's finger, forcing him to back away.

Before Heather could break them up from possibly one of the stupidest verbal fights she'd heard, Eddie sucked in a lurid breath and began to laugh.

The three of them froze and looked at Eddie. His mouth was wide open, showcasing a mouthful of bloody gums. Only three teeth remained. His tongue was mostly still there, and shook back and forth with laughter.

"Jesus," John said, all signs of his own chuckle long gone.

Then Eddie abruptly stopped laughing. "Not Jesus, you idiot," he said. "You think if your Almighty Savior, that good little man who died for your sins, you think if he came back from the dead that everything would be hunky-dory, life would be grand, famine would disappear, and you'd all float up to the sky playing fucking harps?"

He stopped, possibly to suck in another breath, more likely for dramatic purposes. Eddie was turning out to be quite the showman.

"If that carpenter of yours *were* to come back, you think he'd be happy?" Eddie continued. "He gets whipped silly, dragged across the desert, and nailed to a cross. All for what? I think if he came back, he'd be pretty fuckin' pissed, don't you?"

Gildy started for the cell. "Why you blasphemous motherfucker."

Heather stopped him. Gildy was fuming, the veins pulsing in his neck, his skin now a vibrant red, which was a far cry from the pasty white it usually was.

"Easy, partner," she said, "He's just trying to get a rise out you."

"It's working," Gildy returned.

"Forget this clown," Heather said. "Let's finish stocking up and get rollin'."

"Rolling?" John asked. "Wait, we can't leave." The thought of Tracey standing in the doorway, telling him that people needed his help, came to his mind. "Where are we going?"

Gildy moved away from Eddie's cell and started stuffing boxes of ammunition into a duffle bag.

"We're getting the fuck outta Westmont."

Not yet.

"Not yet what?" Gildy asked John.

John and Heather exchanged puzzled glances.

"Why can't we leave yet?" Gildy asked.

"He didn't say anything, Gildy," Heather remarked with an air of worry in her voice.

"Sure he did."

No he didn't, Gildy.

This time Gildy had been looking directly at John and Heather when he heard the Voice. What he heard he hadn't heard through his ears. It had been a voice in his head.

The Man in the Dark Coat's eyes opened and his arms fell back to his sides. Now that his reconnection with Eddie Miller and his soon-to-be new recruit Gildy Clarkson was well underway, the Man in the Dark Coat could get back to the task at hand. He aimed himself towards the exit of the gymnasium, eager to meet the lawyer face-to-face, and to finally get his eyes on the pregnant girl he couldn't see.

33.

The row of tollbooths stood half a mile away from Richard and Lindsay Stone. The moonlight reflected off the glass windows, giving the state's means of paying for the upkeep of the freeway more serenity than it probably deserved.

As was the case everywhere else, cars were stalled across the road, both before and after the booths. A few had been caught in the midst of paying their toll when the outage hit and sat next to the coin collectors, forever waiting for the comforting *ding* telling them that the state had their seventy-five cents and it was okay to move on.

Richard and Lindsay kept to the right side of the road, ensuring that they would be able to see all lanes of traffic. They had seen only one other group of walkers since the Winnebago — a father and son team heading in the opposite direction who seemed just as wary about the Stones as they were about them.

"How's your head?" Richard asked Lindsay.

She kept her eyes straight, squinting at the glass booth enclosures ahead of them, looking for a sign of other walkers. "It's a little better."

Richard looked over to his wife. He knew her well enough to tell she was either lying or hiding something. The full truth was not in her voice. She caught his glance, and looked sheepishly away.

Before he could ask, she said, "I've been hearing a voice."

Richard stopped walking and hastened his breath, listening. "From where? Behind us?"

"No," she said, then pointed to her forehead. "Up here."

"You hear something in your head...?" he asked.

"Some*one*, not some*thing*."

He took her by the hand and began walking toward the tollbooths again. "What's it saying?"

"He just keeps saying my name. Over and over again."

She looked over to him, worry written across her face. "Before you ask, no, I don't recognize the voice."

They were five car lengths from the tollbooth when they heard something fall and break. It startled them both — it was the first sound that hadn't come from either of them in well over two hours. The something that fell sounded like it rolled back and forth on the ground, until it finally settled into place. All was quiet once again.

And there was no mistaking that the sound came

from the tollbooth directly in front of them.

They had both seen enough horror movies in their lives to know the smart thing to do would be to *not* move in for inspection. Whatever it was, it was probably left better all alone in the tollbooth.

They moved horizontally across the four lanes until they came to the median. Feeling that they were far enough away from the source of the sound, they proceeded onward, keeping their eyes glued to the tollbooth where the noise originated from.

"Did you-" Lindsay started.

Richard held up a finger. "Shh."

The tollbooth attendant stood up in his little glass cubicle and scratched his head. He looked confused as he inspected what appeared to be a broken half of a coffee mug in his hand. The other half was no doubt the cause of the noise that they had heard.

"Keep moving," Richard whispered.

They crossed the threshold of the booth, and as they passed the basket where millions of coins had been dropped the attendant yelled out to them.

"Seventy-five cents!"

Richard and Lindsay stared at one another, neither of them sure how to react to the request.

"Is he serious?" Lindsay finally asked.

Before Richard could answer, a set of fingers crawled up the window in the booth next to them. The nails were bloody and broken, as if they had just spent a day punching hides of beef in a frozen locker ala Rocky Balboa. The fingers were attached to an equally bloody arm.

The owner of the arm stood up in the booth and dusted off the button-up shirt of his tan uniform, repeating his co-worker's wish for "Seventy-five cents!"

Richard smirked at the man. "You're kidding, right?"

The attendant opened his eyes, which were as black as the eyes of the teenage boys they had seen in their apartment. The changed person looked at Richard — at least that's what he appeared to do, it was hard to tell without pupils — and smiled.

"No more room," he said. "And that will be seventy-five cents."

Richard pushed Lindsay ahead of him and past the gated tollbooth. She jogged around a parked Saturn while Richard glanced behind them.

Neither of the attendants — there seemed to be only the two — jumped out of their booths to offer pursuit, as Richard had been sure they would. Instead they simply stared at the couple through the glass, smiling at them with those black eyes of theirs.

"Seventy-five cents!" said the first again.

Richard swung his head forward again, making sure to keep his wife ahead of him. They sprinted into a run, moving around and between the stalled cars while the attendants repeated over and over again their demand for seventy-five cents.

*　　*　　*

Lindsay's eyes darted back and forth, quickly inspecting the windows of each car they approached, expecting a changed person to spring out at them from a front seat. She looked behind her at Richard, who kept on a hand on her shoulder, incessantly pushing her to run faster and faster. She didn't need any motivation from him to make her legs pump as fast as they could, her muscles already burning.

Richard's eyes moved to the side of the road, and he pointed. "Take that exit!"

She followed his gaze to the off ramp four lanes away. Taking his cue, she moved around a rusting semi, banging her knee on its bumper. She ignored the sharp jolt of pain as they made their way across the four lanes to the exit, gaining speed with each step, as if just getting off the freeway would make everything alright.

As they came to the off ramp, Lindsay looked behind them again at the two attendants. They both still stood in their booths, but had given up trying to get their toll money from the Stones. They remained motionless, and although she couldn't be certain, she felt as though they were grinning at them, uttering the three words that continued to make no sense to her:

No more room.

34.

The reflection from the small fire in the coffee cans shimmered in Gloria's eyes. Now that she had the chance to be alone, her emotions could finally be let free. She had gotten into the habit of keeping things close to the chest whenever somebody she didn't know that well was around. Even if it was just a shaky breath or a case of puffy eyes, Gloria didn't like anyone seeing her this way.

She wiped a tear off her cheek and rested her head in her hands, wondering what the future held for Gloria Cortez and her unborn child. The past seven months had been more Hell than Heaven for her, but she had slowly come to believe that her pregnancy was a blessing and not the curse she had originally dubbed it. That didn't stop the pain of the past from punching her when it wanted, though.

The baby inside of her gave out a kick. The child (she didn't want to know the sex — she liked surprises, and besides, it really didn't matter) had been doing that more and more the closer she got to her delivery date. Which, according to her doctor, was in a scant forty-three days.

Gloria put a hand to her belly, comforting the unborn child. "It's alright. Mommy's just having a bad week, is all." She rolled her eyes at her own comment. "More like a bad year."

Footsteps approached from outside and shook her depression away. Despite her best efforts, another tear had found its way down her cheek. She wiped it away as the door opened behind her.

"I was wondering if you got lost on your way back," she said, turning around. "Did you find any-"

Malcolm was not the man walking through the door. This man was taller, dirtier, younger, and wore a trench coat.

The man put up his hands. "Whoa, sorry there, ma'am. I saw the light from outside, figured there'd be people in here. It's damn peculiar out there, and I'd rather not walk the three miles back to my pad," he said, walking deeper into the room.

The tone of his voice had an immediate calming effect on Gloria, and her breathing slowed. Her eyes stayed fixed on the stranger, and it didn't take long for him to figure out it was fear in her eyes.

"I apologize, ma'am. I'm a little scared myself. I tend to go off at the mouth when I'm like that. I'll leave if-"

"No, no, it's okay," she said. "I'm sorry. It's just been, you know..."

"One of those days?"

Gloria nodded.

"I know the feeling. I'm Thomas Manning." He put out a hand.

She took it. "Gloria. There's a guy somewhere out there, Malcolm. He's trying to find something more for the fire." She pointed to the coffee cans.

"No one thought to bring a lantern, huh?" Thomas asked.

"Guess not," she said. "Why, you got one?"

Thomas sat down on a stool next to her, swiping the trench coat he wore behind him so he wouldn't sit on it. "Nope. Didn't think to bring one. Never had much use for one, until now."

Gloria eyed the man's coat. "Kinda warm for a coat like that, isn't it?"

"Heat's never really bothered me. It's the cold that does. Thin blood, I suppose."

Gloria let her chin fall to her neck, hiding her eyes from the new arrival. Thomas continued to look at her, trying to read what this girl was all about, and was coming up empty.

"So, what do you make of all this?" he asked.

"Search me," she said.

"Peculiar. Damn peculiar. Everything just up and breaking like that."

Gloria nodded politely. Thomas went on: "You think it's everything?"

"What do you mean?"

"I mean all the cars don't work. My watch died on me. I don't see any lights *anywhere*. I got

199

twenty-twenty vision, Miss, I can see pretty far," Thomas said. "I think this might have happened everywhere. To everything."

"What do you mean *everywhere?*" she asked.

"Well Miss, if it was just us, just Westmont, we'd see the lights from Chicago. But there ain't none. And the sky: nothin' but stars." He took a breath. "You think all the planes up in the air shut down, too?"

Gloria looked at him. From her expression it was clear she hadn't considered that. "Jesus, I hope not."

"Me, too. But I think that's just what happened. Lights, watches, cars, no reason the planes wouldn't fall right out of the sky. And hospitals, old men with pacemakers," he said, letting Gloria's mind fill in the gaps.

Gloria finally looked back up at Thomas. "I think you're pushing it there, mister."

Thomas laughed. "I'd like to agree with you. Then I just look at my watch or remember how no one's car would start back up a few days ago. If those things don't work, chances are nothing else works, either."

"I hope to God you're wrong."

"I'm sure you do."

35.

Eddie stared at the silver chain that connected his right wrist with his left one. He knew he wasn't in this thing alone — the friend that owned the Voice was always with him — but he also knew he had to discover his own means of escape. He couldn't depend on his new friend for everything. Some things you just had to do on your own.

He looked up to see the female cop with her back to him, shoving something into a backpack. The ancient cop named Gildy walked out of the room and into another. He didn't see the writer anywhere.

Shifting his attention back to the handcuffs, he knew the first step to getting out of the cell would be to rid himself of their hindrance. The rings of the cuffs were tight around his wrists, and there was no way he'd be able to wiggle out of them. The thought of gnawing off a hand came to mind — a length he'd certainly be willing to go to for his new friend — but he realized if that were even possible, it would take hours.

Then it came to him.

Gritting his teeth, Eddie took his left hand in his right one, creating a vice. With all his might, he squeezed his right hand into a fist, closing it tighter and tighter, until he heard the bone in his left thumb pop.

Put down the box.

The Voice was loud in Gildy's head, the loudest thing he'd ever heard. He winced in alarm, but didn't drop the box of ammunition he held in his arms. He froze and tried to regain his composure, his mind playing back an echo of the Voice in his head.

He was still standing as motionless as a statue when Heather came into the back room. Walking around him, she said, "Is that the C-4 you guys confiscated awhile back?"

Gildy's mind went back to the memory of six months ago, when a group of high school kids had somehow managed to get their hands on three pounds of the explosives. They claimed they had gotten it off the Internet, and no one questioned them; these days, getting something like that on the ol' Information Super Highway wasn't entirely out of the question. When the local police had researched the website, they weren't a bit surprised to find the domain name was no longer in use. It was then up to the military and the FBI to sort through the mess, and while they had been assured that an investigation was, in fact, underway, no officials had yet come to claim the C-4.

PUT DOWN THE BOX.

This time the Voice was too powerful to ignore. Gildy dropped the box, and it landed in a clutter on the floor. Heather jumped, hoping to God it wasn't the C-4.

"Gildy, you okay?" Heather asked.

He slowly turned around, his face a blank canvas of an expression. He said nothing, as if he had been struck mute. Even in the darkness, Heather could see the change.

In a matter of seconds, the blackness of the cop's pupils grew outward.

Heather stared at his eyes. Those dark, black eyes, as expressionless as his face.

"No more room," he said as he took her by the arms and threw her into the cell area.

The sound of something hard and metallic scraping against the floor snapped John out of his nap. He quickly scanned the room, confusion clouding his mind, the kind that takes over during those first few seconds when one wakes up in an unfamiliar place.

The scraping sound had come from the hallway leading to the jail cells. He shook his head to clear it and pushed himself up from the chair, banging his knee on the officer's desk he had dozed off at. He thought he heard a rustling coming from the cells, and what might or might not have been somebody grumbling.

You have to leave here, John.

Talking to Tracey from time to time, as he'd done since the day she died, was nothing new to John. As real as the conversations seemed, he knew it was just electrical current in his brain, his psyche's way of dealing with her death and at his own possible cause of it. But until yesterday — about the time the power what kaput — they had merely been memories of conversations. Sometimes he'd use his memory of her to help him in troubled times, often repeating to himself *what would Tracey do, what would Tracey do* over and over in his head until he got a grasp on what kind of advice she would've given him had she still been alive.

But now she was offering advice, orders even, without him "asking" her.

These weren't memories.

Now, Johnny. Leave now. He is going to shoot all of you.

Something fell and crashed onto the floor. John ignored the voice (there'd be plenty of time later, he thought, to punch out the details of just how crazy he was) and ran into the hallway.

Heather was cowering on the floor, her back against the bars of Eddie's cell. Gildy stood over her, zombie-like, and moved toward her like a man on a mission. A man on a mission to seriously fuck up this woman.

Eddie's right arm reached through the bars and grabbed Heather by the throat. She was jerked back with a *gack*, the wind knocked out of her.

Heather's eyes were blurred with tears and alarm. Her hands instinctively went up to the arm around her throat, but Eddie only squeezed tighter. Gildy stepped closer to her and reached for his holster, pulling his gun. Heather tried to talk, but Eddie was making sure she wasn't gonna get so much as a whimper out.

To John's amazement, she pulled her own weapon and aimed it at her partner. She tried to talk again, prompting Eddie to force her neck even tighter against the bars.

John looked to the table where the cops had collected their ammunition and found a gun — he thought it was a Beretta — laying next to three cans of mace. Moving quickly, he seized the gun in his hands. From this angle, John was pretty sure he could nail Eddie though the bars.

"Hey!" John yelled.

Eddie's head spun to face John, and the two locked eyes. John noticed that the handcuffs were still on Eddie's right wrist, the left clasp of it dangling below his pinky. The kid's left arm hung limply at his side, the thumb broken and smashed into itself. He had broken his own hand to squirm out of the cuffs.

The report from the shot echoed in the small hallway, causing John to cringe as his ear drums pulsated in pain. Eddie's head flew back, blood spraying the back of the cell. While Eddie had been having his staring contest with John, Heather had turned her gun away from Gildy and shot Eddie through the bars.

The kid's arm fell back into the cell with him, and Heather quickly ducked out of the way, covering her own pounding eardrums as Gildy let loose with two shots. He missed Heather, the shots landing in the wall behind Eddie.

John watched as Heather rolled onto her back and let two of her own bullets fly at Gildy. The first shot went over his head, but the second bullet made contact with Gildy's chest, smacking into the man's bullet proof vest. Gildy fell back and slumped against the cell opposite Eddie's.

Heather had her gun aimed at Gildy, and it shook in her hands. Gildy was like the others. Like John's friend in the liquor store, and the slugger in the street, and the prisoner in the cell behind her. Gildy had somehow, someway, become one of these changed people.

"Gildy, no," Heather said through sobs that were becoming harder and harder to hold back.

Her partner's eyes snapped open. They were still the dark black they had been before. This time they were accompanied by a look of pure and utter hatred.

"You will like the New Way," he said to her, "because there is no more room."

He aimed his gun at her again, leaving Heather no choice. Closing her eyes, she emptied her magazine into the man that used to be her partner.

As John looked in on Eddie, Tracey started in on him again. *Leave, get out of here, please, baby. You and the cop, go to the high school. You have to go there NOW.*

Entranced by Tracey's words, John barely heard the shots coming from Heather's gun and entering Gildy's body.

Tracey's voice became louder in John's head. *You can't stay here. LEAVE HERE NOW!!!*

John shook his head clear of his wife's words. Heather stood in front of the cell Gildy's body now lay in, her gun still pointed at the dead man on the floor. John reached out a hand to cover Heather's, slowly pushing her gun down.

"I'm sorry," he told her.

"He was like the kid," she mumbled. "His eyes. Oh, God, his *eyes*. They were just like the kid's. Oh-God-what-the-fuck-is-*going-on-HERE?!*"

Heather stared into the cell at Gildy. She slowly pushed John's hand away from her gun and released the magazine. Grabbing a fresh one from the table, she reloaded and pulled back the chamber. Without so much as batting an eye, she walked over to Eddie's cell and emptied the magazine into the already dead juvenile. Each shot sounded more angry than the last. John didn't try to stop her.

When her magazine was empty, Heather let the

gun fall from her hand. She stood motionless in front of the locked cell, staring at the dead body of Eddie Miller, who now had more lead in him than blood.

"Come on," John said to Heather, grabbing her hand and snapping her out of her murderous daze. "We need to lock up your partner and get movin'."

Heather broke his gaze and looked down at Gildy. "What?"

John slid Gildy's cell door shut and heard the lock click. He shook it a few times, testing it to make sure it was tight. "You saw that kid get up once today. I've seen it twice. And each time, he seemed to be in a worse mood. I'm not taking any chances your partner here wakes up even more pissed, too."

Heather backed away from John and the cell and grabbed one of the backpacks of ammunition, sliding the remaining ammo clips and mace cans into the open bag. She zipped it up and handed it to John while she shouldered the other. John followed her out the back door.

Once outside, Heather made sure the door was locked tight. Side by side, they moved onto the empty sidewalk. The streets were deserted, the only sound was that of the breeze playing with the useless power lines above them.

"Which way is the high school?" John asked.

Heather pointed to their right. As they began walking, Heather asked, "Why the high school?"

"My dead wife told me to go there," he said

matter-of-factly.

"Oh."

She was still in a daze, and she was fairly certain she'd never come out of it. She had known Gildy for only a few weeks, but shooting someone — especially a man that had known her father — hadn't been high on her list of things to do before she died.

"You don't believe me, do you?" John asked.

"What?"

"The dead wife thing."

"Oh," she said. "I don't know. I don't care. Whatever you say."

They walked in silence for a few steps, neither of them sure what to say next. Finally, John broke the silence. "I think it might be safe to assume that something more is going on here than just a power outage."

"I've seen enough today that I'd be apt to agree with you," Heather said.

John looked down at the sidewalk, watching his blood-stained Reeboks step-step-step. "Do the words 'no more room' mean anything to you?"

"No. You?"

John shook his head. "The kid said it, it was on the wall in there..."

"And Gildy said it," Heather added. "But it doesn't mean anything to me."

"Well, it seems to mean something to a lot of folks around here," John said.

Heather looked over to ask what he meant by

such a cryptic statement when she saw what he was talking about. Spray painted against the side of the police station in big red block letters were the words "No More Room."

The same thing had been painted on the doors of the fire station across the street. The same words were written in soap on five of the cars in the street beside them. A very old school kind of prank, Heather thought.

"Maybe the whole town has gone completely and utterly fucking bonkers," Heather said, then paused, eyeing the writer. "And I'm not ruling you out of that equation, either."

John smiled. "Nor I you."

36.

Malcolm carried two bundles of newspapers in his arms as he made his way past the half-court line in the gym. Memories of phys-ed floated through his mind. He and his old friends would come to this very court every Wednesday and Thursday after school to shoot some hoops and shoot the shit. They weren't very good at the game and none of them ever made the high school basketball team, but that didn't matter too much Malcolm and his friends.

As he exited the gym and approached the door to the newspaper office, Malcolm thought he heard voices, although he couldn't make out any exact words. One voice belonged to Gloria, and the other... the other one sounded familiar. Malcolm concentrated on the male voice coming from the room, and soon enough, he had it.

It was the same Voice he had heard in his

211

head earlier.

Drop the papers, Malcolm.

Unable to refuse the order, Malcolm put the papers down on the floor. He didn't want to, he tried to stop himself, but it was as if he was a prisoner in his own body, merely watching his actions as if they were taking place before him on a TV.

Go into the coach's office.

The lawyer did a one-eighty and marched back through the gym to Mr. Grover's office, which sat directly next to the boy's locker room. He had no trouble remembering where it was — he had been there a lot back in the day. Not to be scolded, but because all the students loved and looked up to the man. There was many a day when Malcolm would enter Grove's office (everyone called him "Grove," even the teachers) and the coach would offer Malcolm advice on everything from his future in college to girls. Usually it was about girls.

He tried the knob, confident it would be locked, but to his amazement it opened easily. He stepped in and halted in front of old Grove's desk.

Upper right-hand drawer.

Without hesitation, Malcolm walked around the desk and opened the upper right-hand drawer. Grove had always kept it locked, but like the door, this was unlocked, as well.

In the back.

Malcolm reached in until his hand tapped against the rear of the drawer. His fingers fell on something six or seven inches in length and made out of metal.

Take it.

He grabbed the object and pulled it out. The metal he had felt was the handle to a switchblade. Malcolm pressed the button on the side of the handle and the blade flicked out with a *swish* of a sound. The sharp blade stared up at Malcolm.

Put it in the back of your pants.

He closed the knife and did as he was instructed.

Now come back.

Malcolm shook his head, snapping out of his delirium. He looked at his surroundings, surprised that he had somehow managed to end up in Grove's office. He rubbed his temples, feeling a headache coming on. Maybe that's why he had come in here — for some aspirin or ibuprofen. Although he could never remember getting a headache bad enough to cause him to black out, that must've been what had happened. After all, Grove's desk drawer was open.

There were no pain relievers in the open drawer. He searched the others until he found a bottle of generic ibuprofen and took hold of it. He tossed two in his mouth and swallowed them dry.

As he made his way out of the office, something glimmered on one of Grove's shelves at eye level. He took the hand-held gas lantern off the shelf, confident it would do the job better than a bundle of newspapers and some empty coffee cans. Score one for Grove for being prepared.

37.

Cass Avenue was, for the most part, deserted. John figured it was around four o'clock in the morning, and Westmont was always asleep at this time. Every town was asleep at this time. But Westmont felt more than merely asleep. The sound of the occasional car, air conditioners, the hum of electricity that signaled civilization — all that was gone. He hadn't noticed it until now, but he heard no planes, no helicopters — nothing.

It truly was dead quiet.

Not being one for uncomfortable silences — of which this situation was in spades — Heather decided to ask John about his dead wife. After a few false starts and what seemed like some painful reflecting on bad memories, John spoke.

"My wife died about three years ago. It was my fault. I didn't handle it so well."

"What happened?" she asked.

John smiled at the good part of the memory. "I had just made my first big sale. It wasn't going hardcover, it was straight to paperback, but it was more money than Tracey or I had ever seen.

"My new publisher threw a big shindig at The Drake downtown. My agent was there, a few of the more prominent store owners from Chicago showed up. My agent was really busting her ass to sell the book. And me. Shit, apparently Oprah was supposed to be there, but I never saw her."

Heather smiled. "Wow, Oprah, huh?"

"They wanted me to do interviews right before and after the book hit. Guess it was a slow week for Oprah. The movie rights were already sold." John smirked. "Movie rights are pretty cheap if no one's ever heard of you before."

They turned a corner and continued walking.

"I had been sober for almost five years. Tracey cured me of that. She cured me of a lot of things, but that was the big one. But that night, that night..." John trailed off, lost in the memory.

"It was too much, huh?" Heather offered.

"Yeah," John said, a bit surprised at her almost immediate grasp of what was going through his mind three years ago.

"My father was an alcoholic."

John nodded his head — she knew what it could be like. "Then you've probably heard the stories. We can snap when things get really low, or when they get really high. And man, they were *really high* that night.

215

"I told Tracey I was gonna allow myself one drink, just for that night, and for her to watch me. I hadn't been to a meeting in years, hadn't felt the need for it. Fucking things were depressing as hell, anyway. Everything was fine, so I figured one drink couldn't hurt. She frowned on it. She had quite the frown, would make you stop taking shits if that's what she wanted, but I think the bug of the night had gotten to her, too, and she let me. She let me."

They came to an intersection. Neither bothered to look both ways before crossing the street. John continued.

"What she didn't know, or had forgotten, is what terrific actors and liars alcoholics are. What she didn't know is when I casually mentioned I wanted one drink, I had already downed seven shots of whiskey. I think part of me was hoping she'd smell it on my breath, fuck, you could smell it from Downers Grove I had hit it so hard, but she didn't. Or at least didn't say anything."

Heather made to reach out and touch John's shoulder comfortingly, but thought better of it and let her hand fall back to her side.

"When we left, I was plastered two ways to Sunday," John said. "My acting chops had returned tenfold, and she thought I was only buzzed. I convinced her I was alright, that maybe not only tonight did we celebrate my first sale, but maybe I had beaten the big bad alcohol monster once and for all."

John paused, ran a hand through his graying hair.

"On the drive home, I lost control on I-95 and plowed into the median. Can't remember if I swerved to avoid something, blacked out for a sec... It's all a blur now. We spun around a few times, I'm not sure how many — I was spinning the entire night — and just as the car was settling down, a semi smashed into us, on Tracey's side of the car."

"God."

"The driver of the semi was fine. I was fine, and there were no other cars involved. Tracey, she lived for maybe two, three minutes tops. I couldn't move her from the car, her legs were broken in more places than I could count. And she just stared at me, stared at me with these vacant eyes, and all I could say was 'I'm sorry' over and over again."

John stopped walking. He rubbed his temples, doing his best to keep his emotions in check.

"Soon after that, I started to hear her. First in my dreams, then when I was awake. Nothing big. You know, things she used to say. Keep the kitchen clean, eat all your peas, shit like that. I figured 'Okay, great John, now you have this to haunt you the rest of your life. Good job.'

"I thought over time she'd eventually go away, or I'd get over it, I dunno, something. But her little visits became more and more frequent. I had gone back to drinking halfway through my second novel, and on one drunken night, I said to myself what the hell, let's talk back to her and see what flies.

"She talked back, but I knew they were only pieces of conversations we had had in the past.

She'd reply to me the way I thought she would, nothing more. Every night I'd tell her how sorry I was, that the whole mess was my fault, that I was such a shit, and shit needs to be punished before it's finally flushed down the toilet. She would listen to me. I could feel her listening to me, and she'd offer her advice, you know, memories of the same advice she'd given me during our entire marriage.

"That all changed yesterday."

"What happened?" Heather asked.

"She knew what was happening. It wasn't a memory of her anymore, it was..."

"Like she was really there."

John nodded. "She was. I saw her. I'm not drunk now, you've been with me all day and night. Tonight, she told me I, we, have a job to do. And that-"

Heather cut him off. "And that we needed to go to the high school."

"Yeah," John said. "Crazy, huh?"

"Fucking insane."

They picked up their pace again, walking a little bit closer to one another than they had been before. Heather put a consoling hand on John's shoulder as they continued on their way towards Westmont High School.

38.

"Malcolm, this is Thomas Manning. He owns a bookstore over on Quincy. Thomas, this is Malcolm Dwight."

Malcolm stood unmoving in the doorway, oblivious to the words coming out of Gloria's mouth. He stared at the stranger who called himself Thomas Manning with knowing eyes.

"Good to meet ya'," Thomas said, stretching out a hand for a shake. Malcolm walked over and slowly took Thomas Manning's hand in his own, placing the coach's lantern on the ground. "Gloria here's told me a lot about you. Well, as much as she knows, anyway," Thomas laughed.

Malcolm held onto the man's hand. The Voice. He couldn't believe it, but he was shaking the hand of the man with the Voice.

"I see you did one better than paper," Gloria said, motioning at the lantern as Malcolm and Thomas released their grip.

Malcolm looked at Thomas, dazed. Thomas held his look, knowing that Malcolm was relishing the moment of being allowed to meet the owner of the Voice.

"Yeah," Malcolm finally said, looking down to Gloria. "Figure this way there's less of a chance of us burning the school down."

"Good man, Malcolm. Please, have a seat," Thomas said.

Malcolm sat across from Gloria, the still burning coffee cans between them. "So, Thomas. You own a bookstore?"

"Sure do. Ever been to Books Period on Quincy?"

"Can't say that I have," Malcolm replied. "I'm not much of a reader. I get enough of that from law books."

"It's my home away from home. Which is right below the bookstore itself, so I'm always at home, and I'm always at work. Except for right now, of course."

Malcolm grinned. "Of course."

The three sat in silence for a few moments, until Gloria's stomach let loose with a rumble that could've been heard from the high school's baseball field.

Thomas raised an eyebrow. "Someone's hungry."

Gloria patted her belly. "Now that you mention it, I'm ravished. With everything that's been going

220

on, I guess I hadn't noticed how hungry the two of us were getting."

"Dear child, in your condition, that's something you must notice," Thomas said, standing. "Don't you agree, Malcolm?"

"Yes."

"Point me in the direction of the cafeteria, and I'll see what I can find," said Thomas.

"That's really very kind of you," Gloria said. "It's through the gym to your right."

"I'll go," said Malcolm, making to get to his feet. Thomas held out a hand, motioning for Malcolm to stay put. "Nonsense. You stay here and keep her company. I'm sure she's heard enough of my ramblings for one night."

The Man in the Dark Coat shoved his hands in his pockets and made for the door. When he got to the doorjamb, he shot Malcolm a quick glance. The two locked eyes. Malcolm gave him a look filled with questions, an obedient soldier awaiting orders. Thomas smiled, and before moving into the hallway and out of sight, Malcolm heard five words from him in his head:

Don't kill her. Not yet.

39.

Eddie Miller pulled himself up from the floor of the cell, which was sticky with his own blood and spit. Unless he had lost count, this was the third time he'd woken up in this condition in just as many days.

Gildy lay crumpled on the floor in the cell across from him. He looked dead, as dead as they come, but lately that saying didn't seem to hold much weight.

"Hehhhy, cuhp," Eddie mumbled out the left side of this mouth. His right side didn't seem to work that well anymore. He felt around the inside of his mouth with his tongue and discovered that his right cheek was no longer there. His tongue slipped through the hole, in between stringy lines of flesh.

Eddic tried again, enunciating as best he could. "Hey, cuhp." He thought that was about as good as it was going to get.

Gildy didn't move.

"Cuhp, wahk uhp." Again, Eddie had to punch his enunciation. "Wake up."

His world was dark. There was a sporadic flash of light as he tried to open his eyes. They'd open for a second or two, then shut again of their own accord. The occasional blurry image of someone or something from his past swam in front of him each time his eyes opened then closed. His tenth birthday party, when his parents finally got him that bike he had been clamoring about all summer. There was his mom on the day of his graduation from the academy, his dad standing right next to her, as proud as a father could be. There he was meeting his new partner, Heather Steinman.

Then everything got bright, too bright, forcing Gildy to squint his eyes shut. When he opened them again, his vision quickly adjusted to the room. As dark as it was, Gildy thought he could make out a cot and some bars.

He shook his head as if waking up from a deep, long sleep. Or possibly a coma. A coma that had changed him.

"Thurre yuh guh, pihg. Yuh goht eht," a voice said.

Gildy lifted himself up and leaned against the bars of the cell. He let himself wake up and get accustomed to his surroundings. Gildy always was a bit grumpy when he first awoke, and this was no exception.

223

"Kehs. Yuh guht the kehs, man?"

That voice again.

Gildy's eyes focused on the image directly in front of him: a man standing in the cell across from his own. He knew this man, but couldn't remember from where. He couldn't remember why he was in a jail cell, either. He certainly didn't recall being put in there.

"Duhn't look sho confushed, et'll all come back," the boy in the cell across from his said. He had some sort of speech impediment, but seemed to be doing his damnedest to get over it. "You goht the keys, ur whut?"

Gildy fished around in his pockets, eventually producing a set of keys on a chain attached to his belt. The kid smiled as Gildy got to his feet and inspected the shiny objects in his hand. His brow furrowed as his fingers felt each key one by one, all seven of them. His eyes went up to the kid's — Eddie was his name, he remembered now — as if he was asking him what the fuck he was supposed to actually *do* with the keys now that he had them.

"Christ, youh're dumber than uh dog weth uh luhbuhtuhmy. Open the fuckin' shell door" Eddie said.

Gildy tried to decipher Eddie's words. It took almost a full minute, but he was finally able to lock onto what Eddie meant: the kid wanted him to unlock the cell doors.

Eddie reached out with his good hand to beckon the cop over. "C'mon, sharp sshtuff. Lemme outta here."

224

Gildy shook the cobwebs of recent death from his head and walked to his cell door. Reaching through the bars, he was eventually able to find the appropriate key and let himself out. Moving over to Eddie's cell, he slipped the key into the hole. Eddie slid the door open forcefully, pushing Gildy out of the way.

The kid began to move down the hallway when he turned around and noticed Gildy still standing where he had left him, staring blankly at the gray brick wall.

"Let's go. Bossh wahnts ush over at the high shchool."

Gildy followed Eddie out of the hallway. They quickly moved to the front door, Eddie as excited as a kid. Gildy, however, was emotionless. His braincells had begun to fire more brightly with each passing second. He understood that Eddie wanted him to follow him, although he wasn't sure why. But a Voice, deep in the back of his head, told him that he needed to be at that high school, too.

40.

Heather spotted her old high school up ahead, a block away at the apex of a small hill. Memories flooded in as she realized they were taking almost the same exact route she used to take to school every day when she was a kid. She smiled at the bits and pieces of her childhood that moved through her mind as they got closer.

Across the street from the high school was a house Heather remembered quite well and very fondly. Every day after school she would go to that house to baby-sit the two Brunswick boys. If it weren't for their babysitter, the two boys would have been latchkey kids. Their parents usually didn't return home until well after eight o'clock. Heather and the Brunswick boys, Harold and Jimmy, would fill those hours with video games, a healthy dose of MTV (when they used to actually play music videos) and participating in epic battles for galactic domination by either the heroic Rebels or the evil Empire, starring a cast of dozens of action figures. She was of course always Princess Leia.

John caught her grinning to herself. "What's so funny?"

"I used to baby-sit the two kids that lived in that house over there," Heather said, pointing to the two-story green home with the immaculate lawn across the street.

John adjusted the backpack on his shoulder. "You went to Westmont High, too?"

"Four of the worst years of my life," she answered.

John smiled. "High school didn't agree with you, huh?"

"Did it agree with anybody?"

"I was a nerdy bookworm," John laughed. "I've tried to block out most of those years."

Before they could continue down memory lane, John felt a weight push down on him, as if he was being forced to the ground. It was nothing spectacular nor entirely tangible. He just felt... *heavy.*

John looked at Heather.

"I feel it, too," she said.

Heather's hand found the gun holstered to her side. She pulled it out, nodding to John to do the same. "I think we need to be careful."

John clicked the safety off on his Beretta. "No argument here. I got that nervous feeling, you know, when they say you have butterflies in your stomach."

"Me, too. Feels like a whole bunch of 'em. Thousands," Heather said.

"Millions."

They slowly and carefully approached the front doors of the school. In the reflection of the glass, they could see the sun peeking over the horizon. John looked at the mirror image of himself staring back at him in the glass. His hair was a mess, he hadn't shaved in days and his clothes looked like something he pulled out of a dumpster ten years ago. He'd looked better.

"Ready?" Heather asked.

"No."

Heather pulled the handle on the door. The door swung open easily enough — it was unlocked.

"At least we didn't have to break in," John said.

"That's a pretty hefty misdemeanor in this town," Heather replied.

The two gave each other their best reassuring looks (which weren't very reassuring at all) then walked into the high school, guns ready, nerves shot, eyes wide open.

41.

The Man in the Dark Coat walked through the cafeteria with two armloads of food he had scavenged from the kitchen. Finding the crackers and Prego soup hadn't been difficult. What had been difficult was accepting the fact that he wasn't all-powerful yet. Try as he might with the pregnant girl, he just couldn't read her. Her mind was as empty as a cloudless sky to him, showing up as a blank spot in the canvas of his mind. Even with the extra strength he'd gathered from Eddie Miller, Malcolm Dwight, and countless other souls that were now his to do with as he pleased, the girl remained invisible. As were the two people in the police station.

But those two people were gone. When he had reconnected with Eddie Miller and been able to fully join with Gildy after the brief messiness at the station, the other two — John and Heather — were gone. The Man in the Dark Coat had a feeling that they might be on their way to this very place, although he couldn't think of a reason why that would be. He certainly wasn't calling them to the high school, that much he knew for sure. If they came, so be it. They could be dealt with.

All the blank spots could be dealt with.

He wasn't sure if these "invisible ones" should simply be killed, or if he could find a use for them. Perhaps they represented a greater value to the New World than those he was able to join with and control. Which was why, he told himself, it was vital to learn as much about them as possible. Learning was ever so important.

Something squeaked behind him. He looked around and saw only the folded up lunch tables and chairs. Nothing else. He listened intently, opening his ears to the sounds of the room. At first all he heard was his own breathing. Closing his eyes, he blocked the sounds his body made and concentrated on the air and the space around him. What sounded like a cockroach scurried across the floor behind him.

Just below the sound of the roach, he could hear someone breathing. No... there were two of them. Two separate bodies were in the room with him. Hiding. Their breaths were shallow; they were *trying* to hide, but he could hear the anxiety in each inhale, the fright in each exhale. A man and a woman.

Thomas smiled to himself with a tiny "who cares" shrug and continued on his way back to Malcolm and Gloria. Two more of those he couldn't see had shown up, proving his premonition correct. It made things all that much easier.

Now he didn't have to go looking for them.

Heather had wanted to talk to the man in the trench coat that was walking through the cafeteria. Surprised that there had actually been someone in the high school, Heather was eager for information that the man might possess.

John disagreed. He couldn't say why — he wasn't sure of the reasons himself. He just knew that the man they saw didn't feel right, that he was out of place. He thought the weight both of them had felt outside a few minutes earlier was a kind of warning against this man in the coat. Plus he was wearing a trench coat in the middle of the summer, which was downright weird.

John and Heather both stopped breathing when John's tennis shoe squeaked on the linoleum. They became as motionless as statues and held their collective breath for as long as they could, which wasn't very long. If there was one thing John was learning about being afraid, it was that it made holding your breath nearly impossible. Twenty years of being a smoker probably didn't help matters either.

They watched the man stop dead in his tracks. They were terrified he'd turn around and see them, but he didn't. After a few seconds, the man simply shrugged and went on his way with his crackers and cans of soup.

When the door closed behind the man in the trench coat, John turned to Heather. "You know him?"

"Never seen him before. You?"

"What makes you think I'd know him?"

"What makes you think *I'd* know him?"

"You're a cop, don't you all, I don't know, aren't you supposed to know everybody in town?" John asked, the words sounding even more stupid to him as they came out of his mouth.

Heather got to her feet. "Let's follow him and see what's what."

The two made their way for the exit of the cafeteria, following the Man in the Dark Coat's footsteps. John was extra careful to not let his shoes squeak again.

42.

Malcolm itched at the knife concealed in the back of his pants. He knew he was supposed to keep it hidden, but damn if it wasn't uncomfortable.

Gloria had dozed off in the corner, away from the morning light that was cascading through the one window. He watched her sleep, her breath going in and out of her lungs in a smooth, rhythmic fashion. He imagined the child inside her was asleep, as well. Peaceful.

But something was different. Something inside was telling Malcolm that the girl and her child were a threat. A threat to what, he had no idea. He assumed that was what the knife was for, but his mind was getting more and more foggy by the second, as if old information was being pushed out and his brain was waiting for new information to be put in. A memory dump. His instincts told him to wait.

That's all. Just wait.

Gloria stirred in her sleep. Her legs twitched, and her right arm moved out in front of her face, as if she was shielding herself from something. She moaned something unintelligible, then calmed back down. At the same time, Malcolm wanted to both comfort her and slice her throat open. He knew that wasn't him, that wasn't how he was brought up. Thou shalt not kill and all.

But that didn't stop the thought from being there.

The man who called himself Thomas Manning entered the room, bundles of food for their stomachs in his arms. Thomas smiled at Malcolm, then as he was about to speak, he noticed Gloria sleeping in the corner. He silently put the food down and talked in a whisper:

"Don't wanna wake her just yet." Thomas looked at Malcolm, studied him. "Something wrong, chief?"

Malcolm searched for words, but they were hard to find.

"It's okay. I know what ails ya'. You just have to trust me that this is all for the better. When this is all over, I think I have a good spot for you. Good job, pays well, no benefits, but I don't think you'll be needing any," Thomas said.

Finally, after much struggling, Malcolm found his words: "I don't understand what's happening."

"You don't need to," Thomas said. "Just be confident in the fact that I know what's right, and the world will be a better place for it. You don't need to think anymore. I'll take care of that for you."

"My head... it hurts, it feels... it feels like it's not all there."

Thomas started to laugh, then quickly stopped himself before it became a cackle that could awaken the girl. "You chose law as a profession. I think it's safe to assume your head wasn't all there to begin with."

"I want to understand. But I can't," Malcolm whispered.

Thomas lifted a hand and opened it, palm up. He closed his eyes as he balled his fingers into a fist. He squeezed his hand tight. Knuckles cracked.

"You're resisting me, Malcolm. Why are you resisting me?"

Malcolm's eyes closed and his head wobbled back, as if his neck had become a slinky.

"Just let me in, let me take control, let me be the boss. For once in your fucking life, let someone else be the boss," Thomas said. He dug deeper into Malcolm's mind, searching for the flaw that was preventing him from making the lawyer a good little soldier.

His fist tightened more, his knuckles cracking again."Ah, there it is. The girl. Yes, yes, we all care very much for the girl. But you seem to care a little *too* much for her. Is that it?"

Malcolm's eyes opened. "I don't know. I don't want to, I want to do what you say, but..."

Thomas opened his own eyes. He stared at the

man, and for a moment it was just the two of them in the room. Thomas smiled, a solution coming to him.

"It's okay, buddy. Don't feel bad. I didn't want to do this just yet, but it's probably for your own good. It's a shame. I think I could've learned something from her.

"Take out the knife."

Malcolm reached behind him and took the blade out of his pocket and pressed the button. *Snick.*

Put it up to her neck.

Malcolm walked over to Gloria and did as instructed.

The only way to learn about life is through death. Cut her.

The edge of the blade touched Gloria's neck.

"Whatever you're doin', pal, just stop it right now."

Malcolm's eyes snapped open. Thomas spun around to see a female cop and a man standing in the doorway. The woman was the idiotically brave one that spoke. She held a gun, aimed directly at Malcolm's head.

Thomas grinned at the woman. "I thought I heard something in the cafeteria."

"Shut it," she said to Thomas. "You, in the suit. Drop the knife."

Thomas took a step toward her. Heather kept the gun on Malcolm, whose eyes darted back and forth between the cop and Thomas.

Behind Heather, John brought up his gun and

trained it on Thomas, who took another step toward the two.

"Hey, he's the one with the knife," Thomas said, pointing to Malcolm.

"You're not exactly doing anything to help," John said.

Malcolm looked down at the blade, still poised at the girl's throat. He pulled it away and let it fall to his side.

Thomas frowned at Malcolm. "You disappoint me, Malcolm. I really thought you were better than all this."

John and Heather watched as the Man in the Dark Coat's eyes rolled into the back of his head. His palms raised themselves into the air, and the whites of his eyes turned black.

Put the knife to your neck.

Malcolm brought the knife up to his throat.

That's when things clicked with John. "He's doing this," he said to Heather. "He has something to do with all of this."

"What makes you say that?" Thomas asked.

"I can feel it," John answered.

Thomas laughed, this time not holding it back, and the laughter came strong and loud. Gloria stirred, the Man in the Dark Coat's laughter pulling her out of her nap.

"You can *feel* it?" Thomas laughed.

John kept serious. "I don't know how I know. I just do."

Thomas curled his hands into fists behind his

back. He stared at John, trying to get a read on him.

"Hm. Yes. Just like the girl. You're standing right in front of me, yet I can't read you at all."

"Enough," Heather said.

Gloria got to her feet, rubbing sleep from her eyes. Her eyes widened in alarm as she took in the situation she had woken up to. "Malcolm? Who are these people? What's going on?"

Heather's gun hand shook. Not from some mystical power that Thomas held, but because she was scared.

John put out his hand and lowered Heather's gun.

"Don't. He's like the others. It won't do anything," John said.

"What-?"

"It's him. *He's* doing this," John said. "He's why we're here."

"Hey, you're the geniuses that got everything and everyone so addicted to energy that when it was gone, so was a big part of you," Thomas said. "You're the species that shot yourselves in the foot, not me."

John squinted at Thomas. "You're doing all this?"

"No," Thomas said, "I'm just helping things along."

"What is it you want from us?" John asked.

"Let evolution take its course. Let the world become how it was supposed to be from the get-go," Thomas said. "And I'm afraid there's no room for either of you in that world. Malcolm."

Malcolm jumped, the knife still ready for action in his hand. He sprung at Heather as John leapt out of the way. Heather let loose two rounds from her gun at Malcolm. Gloria let out a cry as the first one pierced his shoulder, forcing the knife out of his hand. The second bullet landed in Malcolm's upper thigh, bringing him to his knees. As soon as the rounds were out of her gun, she swiveled the muzzle over to Thomas.

"You and your friend are coming with us, now. You're under arrest," Heather ordered.

John heard Tracey's voice in his head loud and clear:

The girl.

John's eyes moved from Thomas to Gloria, who had backed herself into a corner, frightened beyond belief after waking up to a roomful of violence and weirdness a hundred times worse than any nightmare she'd ever had.

Thomas spoke to Heather, "I'm not going with you anywhere. You can't arrest me; your laws don't apply to me."

"Oh my God," Gloria let out in a barely audible whisper. Her eyes were locked on Malcolm.

John and Heather followed her gaze to Malcolm's body on the floor. He stood back up, the effects of the gunshots seeming to have worn off. Blood poured out of both wounds. His eyes were dark and bloodshot. The eyes of evil.

John was suddenly pulled from behind by someone just outside the room. The force of being jerked to the side caused John to release three rounds from his Beretta. His gun had still been trained on the Man in the Dark Coat, and each and every bullet hit its mark.

Gloria shrieked as bullets entered Thomas' chest, stomach and right leg. But Thomas just stood there, unflinching. He let the bullets hit him, welcoming them.

Before Heather could turn around to see who had nabbed John, an arm wrapped itself around her throat. She was able to turn just enough to get a look at the appendage around John's throat — an arm that had a mangled and broken hand attached to it. She looked behind John's head to see Eddie Miller's one remaining eye wink at her. The owner of the arm holding her had to be Gildy. Her former partner was now threatening to crush her windpipe.

"G-Gildy," she managed to get out.

Gildy remained silent as he grabbed Heather's gun from her trembling hands, tossed it across the room away from everyone else, then looked to Thomas for direction.

But Thomas' attention had been taken away from the main action. His eyes were focused on a dark corner of the room. In the middle of that darkness, a small speck of a circle formed a few feet above the ground. It glowed yellow with a hint of the calming amber of the setting sun.

John turned to face the corner in question. Eddie

let him — he was just as transfixed on whatever was going on there as John. Everyone was. Everyone except for Gloria, who stood with her back against the far wall, her eyes shut tight and her lips pursed into an violent frown.

Heather was the only one who caught the oddity of Gloria's state. She didn't have time to try and decipher what Gloria was doing — or what was being done to her — as the circle-speck grew bigger, and was soon four feet in circumference. It held that size and shape, hovering in mid-air, unassuming.

Thomas' eyes were slits, staring at the thing with complete and utter hatred. Whatever it was, he knew its purpose and didn't like it. Not a bit.

He quickly turned to Eddie and Gildy, along with their captives. His voice was deep and angry. John thought he heard a touch of fright in there, as well. "You two finish your job here." He closed his eyes again and brought his hands up. His feet rose from the ground, producing an inch of air between his dark leather cowboy boots and the floor.

Before Heather or John could even try and comprehend what was happening, Thomas vanished. There wasn't anything magical about it. No smack of energy like on *Star Trek*, no portal to another dimension opened up behind him. He simply disappeared.

Across the room, Gloria exhaled a grunt as she fell back to the ground, her legs limp, her eyes still closed. By the time her hands hit the floor to brace herself, the yellow speck that had been growing in the corner of the room faded away just as quickly and quietly as Thomas Manning had.

Eddie smiled out of the still working corner of his mouth as he grabbed the gun from John and dropped it to the floor. "Okay, writer. Write yer-shelf outta 'dish one."

43.

Jennifer crouched at the far end of the hallway. A few doors ahead of her she had heard yelling, followed by gunshots, some mumbled speaking, and now everything had gone eerily silent. She thought she had heard Gloria's voice coming from the newspaper room, but it was faint.

She was frozen, but not with fear. In fact, she was amazed to discover that she wasn't afraid at all — the thought of her missing (and possibly dead) husband had numbed all emotions. She was frozen because she couldn't think of what to do. She was the mayor, and had no idea how to help these people.

Footsteps approached her from another hallway, but the echo-prone walls of the high school made it impossible to tell which direction they were coming from. She looked ahead of her. Behind her. Not another soul in sight.

Still spooked by the massacre at the substation, Jennifer stood up and found the nearest unlocked door — a janitor's closet directly next to her — and quickly moved inside. Leaving the door open a crack, she peered out with one eye, waiting for the person to appear.

The dark shadow of a man turned the corner. Jennifer couldn't make out any details, but his clothes looked ragged, worn, as if he had gotten them from a dumpster. The man was making his way for the newspaper room. Jennifer slid back from the door an inch, and cringed when her shoe scratched against the floor. She swore at herself, praying that it wasn't as loud as she thought it was.

The man stopped. Listened. He slowly turned his head in the direction of the closet. Apparently the acoustics of the hallway did nothing to keep her location a secret.

Jennifer shuffled forward, careful to be as quiet as the proverbial mouse, to peek through the crack of the open door. She was shocked and relieved to be looking at the face of her husband through the opening of the door.

She pushed it open and ran into his arms.

"Stephen! Oh, Stephen, thank God, I saw what happened, I thought you were-" she stopped herself.

Her husband stared down at her silently. His clothes were ragged and torn. Messy. No, it was more than that. It looked to Jennifer like his clothes had been burnt. As was his face, which now that she was closer, resembled more of an overcooked mask of Stephen Adams than anything else. Black and red, his eyes stared into hers. As he smiled, the skin around his lips cracked and fresh blood ran down his chin.

"Hi, honey," he said. "So good to see you."

Eddie let go of John and pushed him into Malcolm. Malcolm caught John and spun him around so that he faced Eddie, Heather and Gildy.

"Jesus," John said. "No offense, but you are all some ugly motherfuckers."

Malcolm kicked the back of John's left leg, and down he went. Malcolm kneeled behind him and tightened his arm around John's throat.

"There's no more room for you here," Malcolm growled.

"Any way you could be a little more specific, pal?" John asked through choked breaths.

Malcolm brought his mouth next to John's ear. "You either join us or spend the rest of your existence in oblivion."

John tried to look back at the man. "That clears a lot up."

Malcolm punched John in the kidney. John winced in pain and pushed his chest out. Every muscle in his back screamed in agony. He tried to wiggle free from Malcolm's unyielding grip, but it felt like someone had just rammed a fork into his back, and there was only so much wiggling he could do.

Heather was able to get John's attention with

her eyes. She was staring at something just to John's left, trying to get him to look at the floor. He followed her eye-line and took a quick glance to his left. Laying no more than six inches from where he stood was the knife Malcolm had been holding before he was shot.

Gildy caught on to his partner's ploy before John could. His eyes found John's. He gave the writer a quick subtle nod. *Go ahead, do it*, it said.

"Gildy, please," Heather said, trying to look behind her. "Let us go. I don't know what that guy did to you, but this *is not you.*"

Her words were true. Gildy knew that. Even as he moved her away from him, holding onto her hair so she couldn't run and ripping the backpack off of her shoulders, he knew this woman was his friend. The last thing he wanted to do was to hurt her. He wanted to help her, even as he dropped the backpack of extra weapons and ammunition to the floor. His body wouldn't obey his commands to let her go, as if there was an uncontrollable need to kill her. As if his life depended on it. She was right, this *wasn't* him. But there was nothing he could do to stop it. Whatever was happening to him, whatever force had taken control of his mind and body, it had made killing a primary instinct. Gildy had been reprogrammed, and there was nothing he could do to change that.

Heather reached behind Gildy for his gun. She pulled it out of his holster before he could stop her and pushed him away with an elbow. She lost some hair as Gildy did his best to hold onto her. The sound of hair being torn from her skull was still playing in her mind when Gildy struck her hard in the chin and her head rocked back like her neck was nothing more than a Slinky. Gildy promptly reached for her gun arm. Heather managed to pull it away from him in time, but her grip on the gun faltered, and the firearm was sent flying across the room toward the pregnant girl in the corner.

John took advantage of the commotion, snatching the knife as Gildy's gun flew from Heather's hand toward the girl. It landed by her feet with a metallic *thud*.

"Pick it-" Heather started. Her words were cut short by Gildy's hand wrapping around her mouth.

Malcolm turned his head in time to see Gloria go for the gun. John took this opportunity to jam the knife into Malcolm's skull, where it made a deep crevasse in his forehead.

Gloria screamed as Malcolm fell backwards. Terrified, she picked up the gun and aimed it at Eddie. The weapon was way too big for her and shook in her hands. It looked like an over-sized novelty gun in between her petite fingers.

Heather opened her mouth, and when two of Gildy's fingers slipped between her teeth, she chomped down hard. Several layers of skin remained in Heather's mouth as Gildy instinctively recoiled, pulling his hand away. He pushed Heather to the ground, grabbing his bleeding hand.

"*Shoot him!*" Heather yelled as she landed on her knees.

Eddie moved toward Gloria. She kept the gun on him — or tried to, anyway — and pulled the trigger.

Click.

Eddie was closer now, no more than ten feet away. She pulled the trigger again.

Click.

And again.

Click.

"The safety!" John roared. "On the side!"

Gloria had no idea what he was talking about, but she looked at the side of the gun anyway. She found a small switch there and flicked it, then pulled the trigger again. Her arms flew up into the air from the recoil as the gun went off with a *BAM*.

It was a lucky shot, landing in Eddie's abdomen. He doubled over in pain as blood poured out of his new bullet wound.

Eddie looked up at Gloria, his hands pressed hard against his stomach. He smiled at her, pulling his hands away to let the blood flow. It dripped down to his already blood-soaked pants and pooled onto the floor.

Heather looked behind her at her former partner. The shell of the man she had known stood in the doorway, his eyes darting back and forth between the occupants of the room. Heather couldn't be sure, but she thought she saw confusion in those black eyes. And something else: concern.

John swung his backpack over his shoulder and unzipped the top. Reaching in, he pulled out a can of mace. He jumped between Gloria and Eddie and drenched the thrice-dead-guy's face with the stuff.

Eddie went down hard and fast as the mace soaked into all the cuts and slices on his head. It seeped into his open eye socket, causing a hellish scream to exit the kid's mouth. Even if he couldn't be killed, John was relieved to see that he could still experience pain. Lots of it.

As Eddie's face made a sizzling sound like that of a steak being cooked, Gildy stopped watching and acted. He pushed Heather further into the room. She stumbled with a moan and landed on her face next to Malcolm, who still had the knife sticking out of his head. Her cheek skidded across the floor, ripping skin away.

Heather turned around in time to watch Gildy leap at Eddie, and they both went down. Gildy reached under Eddie's arms and put him in a good ol' fashioned half nelson. Then he turned the kid toward Gloria, giving her a good, clean shot.

"Do it!" John yelled.

Gloria shot the gun again, three more times. The first bullet missed entirely, splintering the wood in the far upper corner of the room. The second shot landed in Eddie's head. The third landed in Gildy's shoulder, sending both men down backwards, Eddie on top of Gildy.

Malcolm reached for Heather, who was getting

to her feet. As he made to grab her by the arms, she put a palm up to the handle of the blade in his head. She shoved at it hard and heard something inside his head *crack* as the knife went further into his skull. Malcolm staggered back, cringing in pain. Heather's hands remained on the handle to the switchblade and as Malcolm moved backward, the blade silently slipped out of his forehead.

John ran to Gloria and took her by the hand. He tried to pull the gun away from her with his other, but she held onto the weapon for dear life, and wasn't about to let it go.

"Okay, fine, keep the gun," he said. "Let's just get the hell outta here."

Jennifer forced Stephen's head away from her own. She wasn't sure what death smelled like, but she was fairly confident it was close to the rotting odor coming out of Stephen's mouth. He had her pinned to the floor, his knees burrowing into her shoulders.

As Jennifer dug a finger into his left eye, three people fell out of the newspaper room two doors down. Jennifer had been too preoccupied with her own situation to notice the volume of the mayhem coming from the room. The sudden appearance of the three people into the hallway caused both her and her husband to halt their marital dispute.

The woman of the trio, a cop, shut the door with a swift kick from her leg. "What the fuck was *that* all about?" she asked as she closed the switchblade.

The three paused and stood frozen in the hall-way, staring down at the couple on the floor.

A look of recognition came to Gloria's face. "Mayor Adams?"

The mention of her name snapped Jennifer out of her shock. She *had* heard Gloria earlier, after all. Shaking off the quick sense of relief she felt know-ing that she was now no longer alone, Jennifer grabbed her husband, a hand on either side of his head. Using her legs for leverage, Mayor Adams rolled Stephen off of her. He fell to the side reluc-tantly, his head smacking into the ground. Jennifer scampered to her feet as Stephen shook dizziness away.

The cop passed the knife to the man next to her and reached for her holster. Finding it empty, she held out her hand to Gloria. "The gun."

"W-what?" she stuttered, looking as lost as dazed and Stephen.

"For the love of shit," the man with them said. He slid the switchblade into a back pocket, took the gun from Gloria and slapped it into the cop's wait-ing hand.

In one swift, slick motion, the officer released the spent magazine. It clanked on the floor as she slid in a fresh one and pulled and released the slide, giving the Beretta a round in the chamber.

"Step to the side, Mrs. Mayor," she ordered Jennifer.

"What the hell are you doing?" Jennifer yelled as she approached the trio, waving her arms in front

of the cop.

The man grabbed Jennifer by the arms, pulling her out of the cop's line of fire. "Get outta the way!"

Stephen got to his feet, rubbing blood off his chin. He glared at his wife. "You fuckin' bitch."

Jennifer watched as the cop's finger began to tighten around the trigger.

The mayor fought and kicked at John. He held her tight, but she moved with vicious power. She wasn't gonna stop until he let her go.

"No, don't, don't shoot him, he's my husband! Don't kill him!" she pleaded.

Stephen was walking toward them now, looking like a man who had been to hell and back. And if this man had been dead like Eddie, just maybe he *had* been to hell.

"DON'T KILL MY HUSBAND!"

"I don't think that'll be a problem," Heather said as she pulled the trigger three times, *BamBam-Bam.*

Jennifer was frantic. "Noooooooo!"

The back of her husband's head blew wide open, popping like a balloon. Bones in his neck cracked. His body fell limp to the ground, empty of life, and he stopped calling his wife a bitch.

"What the hell did you just do?" Jennifer yelled at them. Then to John: "Why did you hold me back?! *What the hell is going on?!?!*"

"Your husband's dead, Mayor Adams," John

said calmly.

"No shit! She just shot him!" Jennifer squirmed out of John's grasp and reeled back a fist to pummel Heather's face with.

Heather put up a hand and caught the mayor's closed hand before it could make contact. "He was dead before then."

Gloria screamed at them, "Come on, fuck it, talk about this shit later and let's just *get the fucking hell out of here!*"

The four ran down the hallway, John keeping Jennifer in front of him so she wouldn't lag behind. The woman kept looking behind them at the man she claimed was her husband, and John couldn't blame her. If that fella was the guy she had traded wedding vows with, there was no doubt in John's mind that she had just gotten an unhealthy dose of terror and a subscription to Nightmares for Life.

"Take a left up here," Gloria said.

"Where are we going?" Heather asked.

John: "Front door?"

"You better fucking believe it," Gloria said.

"Stephen-oh-dear-all-mighty-God-Stephen," Jennifer chanted, more to herself and to God than to the three of her new companions. John was pretty sure if he didn't continue to nudge her in the back and keep her moving, the mayor would faint and drop right then and there.

They came to the bank of doors John and Heather had gone through less than an hour before.

A thin sheet of metal and some glass was all that remained between them and freedom from the craziness of the high school.

Jennifer was the first to the exit, John practically smashing her against the glass. It shuddered in its frame. Both her and John put their hands on the horizontal release and shoved hard. They were rewarded with absolutely nothing — the door didn't budge an inch.

John looked down and saw the security latch on the floor. He knelt to the ground, wrapped his index finger around the silver hook, and pulled.

"John, John, *come on*," Heather begged.

Jennifer looked down at the man that had held her back from saving her husband, and saw her opportunity to let her anger take its proper course. She kicked him in the side of his face, sending him falling backwards.

Jennifer turned back toward the hallway, tears streaming down her face, her throat tight and raw with sorrow. Her breath caught as her eyes focused on the man approaching them.

Stephen Adams slowly made his way back to his wife. He had one hand braced against the wall, leaving a smeary blood trail on the beige paint that grew longer with each step. His other hand moved up to his head, as if to slick his hair back. As his hand went over what remained of his hair, a chunk of his skull fell to the ground.

And that's when Jennifer Adams fainted, right then and there.

John rubbed his jaw, staring at the dead man walking towards them.

Heather still had her gun drawn, but she was pretty sure it wouldn't do much good. "He came to faster than Eddie."

Gloria's eyes ping-ponged between Heather and Stephen. "Eddie?"

"We'll talk about it later," Heather said as she raised her gun and fired off five more shots at Stephen. The bullets landed where she wanted them to — even under such strange stress as this, she was still a good shot — landing in his torso and head. Stephen fell back to the ground, lifeless. "Hurry it up, John. Before he wakes up again."

John pulled at the latch. "I'm trying." It still wasn't moving. "Come on, dammit," he muttered under his breath. Then, as if his words were a magical spell, the latch released and the door was unlocked.

"There!" he exclaimed, jumping back to his feet.

Before they could think about pushing the door open, the latch re-locked itself. John bent back down to pull the latch up again, but this time it wouldn't move.

Heather put a shoulder into the exit, and Gloria joined her. John snapped back to his feet, and together the three of them: a police officer, a pregnant girl and a recovered alcoholic writer, pushed and shoved and heaved on a door that refused to open. The glass splintered in its frame as they all banged into the door again and again.

Gloria glanced up and looked through the now broken glass. She put up a hand, stopping their assault on the door. "Look."

Across the street from the high school, in the small playground of the neighboring junior high, twenty or so citizens from Westmont milled about aimlessly. John thought one of them looked like Pauley, the nice man who had kept Pall Mall's in stock for him.

"Jesus," John said. "What the hell's wrong with them?"

The one that looked like Pauley swung his head around in John's direction, as if he had heard him. Pauley motioned to the two people next to him, a man in a blood-covered business suit and a teenage girl who couldn't've been more than thirteen years old.

Soon all twenty-something people in the playground were staring at the four in the high school.

"Jesus, he heard you," Heather said.

"That's impossible," said Gloria.

John snorted. "So's coming back from the dead."

As the group outside crossed the street, everything seemed to go dark, as if the rising sun itself was disappearing from the morning sky.

It wasn't just the sun — it was everything. As if the iris of a camera was slowly being turned to let in less light, the outside began to disappear.

The clouds in the sky were the first to go, followed by the tops of the trees behind the playground. John looked left out the window, to the house Heather had said she had once baby-sat two kids, and saw it fade away into darkness.

He altered his focus from the house to the glass in the door itself, and realized it wasn't the outside that was disappearing into another realm, but that something was moving and covering up the windows. No, not covering up the windows; the glass itself was *changing*. It was as if the molecules of the glass were being altered, obscuring the outside, making the windows not windows anymore but big rectangular plates of black obsidian.

In less time than it took to take in what was happening, they couldn't see outside anymore.

John looked to Heather. "Just what the hell is going on, here?"

"We can figure that out later," Heather told him. Then, to Gloria: "There a place in here where we'll be safe?"

"I highly doubt it," she answered.

"How 'bout a place to hide?" John asked.

Gloria thought, running over her four years in the building for a possible safe haven. She found one and smiled. "Follow me."

Gloria turned and headed back to the heart of the school. Heather holstered her weapon and motioned for John to pick up Jennifer's feet. Heather took her by the shoulders, and together they followed Gloria to a place they hoped no living dead lunatics would go.

257

As they made their way down another hallway, John looked behind them at Stephen. Before they turned the corner, John thought he saw the half of the man's head that was still attached to his body move.

44.

J ennifer awoke to find herself surrounded by tubas kept safe in their cases, what appeared to be a drum set underneath a tarp, and shelves and shelves of books on everything from Mozart to *The Complete Idiot's Guide to Playing the Guitar*.

"Take it easy there, Mrs. Mayor. You took a nasty fall back there."

She rubbed her eyes and let them focus on the man kneeling above her. "Where the hell am I?"

"Music room of the high school," the man above her answered.

Jennifer squinted, trying to focus on the scraggly man in need of a shower. "And who the hell are you?"

"Name's John Whitley. Despite the circumstances, it's a pleasure to meet you."

Several torches, each made of two legs from a wooden stool wrapped together with pieces of old

Westmont High School band uniforms, illuminated the room. Jennifer looked past John to see her secretarial aide sitting next to the cop that had shot her husband. They each sat on a stool, watching John pad the cut on her head with a trombone player's coat.

Jennifer grabbed the coat from John's hand and took over dabbing duties. She looked at the blood smeared on the jacket. Deciding it wasn't enough to warrant any further worry, she let the coat fall to the floor. "Somebody better tell me what the hell just happened, or I'm gonna go crazy."

John helped her sit up straight. "Easy."

"Fuck you and your easy. What's happening?"

John snapped his head back. This was not the kind of attitude he had been expecting from the town's mayor. "We're not too sure."

"Give it a shot. You two," she said, pointing to John and Heather, "you seem to know something."

Gloria added: "Yeah, a little enlightenment would help. You, old guy," she said to John, "what was all that about her husband being already dead?"

John and Heather exchanged looks. John nodded to Heather: *Go ahead, you try and explain this*.

"It looks like it's the same thing that happened to your friend in there," John said.

"Malcolm," Gloria offered.

"It's the same thing that happened to Malcolm, the same thing that happened to my partner, the same thing that happened to our prisoner," Heather said.

John exhaled. "And the same thing that seems to be happening to everyone else."

"Care to elaborate?" Jennifer asked.

John went into detail about his incident with Pauley at the liquor store and the hoodlum kid Eddie Miller. He told them about their eyes, the dark black voids that they had become. Together, John and Heather described the experience in the police station to the two women, and how as far as they could figure people in Westmont seemed to be changing. The dead weren't staying dead anymore. They ended their tale to Jennifer with visions of the stranger in the trench coat, and how he seemed to exhibit some control over the others... and then he simply vanished.

After a full minute of silence, Jennifer lifted herself up to her feet. "Are we talking about zombies here?"

John stifled a laugh. "I guess that's one way to put it."

"No, that's not right," Heather interjected. "These people — some of them seem to change before they die. Zombies don't change until after they become zombies."

"In movies," John said.

"Right. In movies," Heather agreed.

"So it's like they're turning into zombies before they really die and turn into zombies," Gloria said.

"Something like that," said John. "And they seem to have no problem listening to that man, that wacko in the coat."

Jennifer shot a look at John. "That's certainly a lot to swallow."

He cocked an eyebrow. "Tell me about it."

Gloria lifted her head. "He said his name was Thomas Manning."

"Who?" John asked.

"The man in there," Gloria answered. "The one that disappeared. He said his name was Thomas Manning."

Heather and Jennifer shook their heads; they had never heard of the guy. John's eyes, however, wandered the floor, as if he was searching for something.

"Thomas Manning," he said to himself, just above a whisper.

"That name mean something to you?" Heather asked.

"I don't know. It sounds familiar."

Jennifer laughed. "Maybe you two went to high school together."

"Maybe," John said.

Jennifer crossed her arms and paced the room. She felt like she was in the middle of a debate in the meeting room of the municipal building, but instead of trying to decide the best way to run for re-election, they were debating the possibility of dead people coming back to life.

"And why are we in the music room?" she asked. "Correct me if I'm wrong, but I would think the smart thing to do would be to, you know, run as far away from here as possible."

"That was the plan," John said, moving across the room to the covered drum set. "But then we got locked in the school."

"And how did *that* happen?" Jennifer wanted to know.

"That was after you passed out," John said.

Gloria's bottom lip shivered. "It just happened. We can't get out, and we can't stay up there." She started to tear up. "You saw your husband, Mrs. Adams. Oh, God, I'm so sorry, but you saw him, what where we supposed to do?"

Gloria folded her arms protectively across her chest, doing her best to hold in her tears and failing. Jennifer's own eyes had begun to water up at the mention of Stephen. She walked over to Gloria and wrapped her arms around her. She wasn't sure about John and Heather, but she knew she could trust Gloria. Jennifer had come to almost love the child, and to see her like this broke her heart.

"It's okay," Jennifer said to her, her own grief gone for the moment. "It's okay."

"I'm so sorry," Gloria said with a shaky voice.

Jennifer held the girl's head back, peering into her eyes. "What about Harding, Bryman, any of the others?"

"I haven't seen them since we left your office," answered Gloria.

Heather cleared her throat. "Everyone's been acting strange since the power went out. You all have to admit you've noticed that."

Jennifer and Gloria nodded.

"The town turned into a riot scene in just a few days," Jennifer said.

"What does this have to do with, uh, the undead up there?" Gloria asked, wiping her tears away.

"I'm not sure, but it has to be connected somehow. It's too weird not to be," said John. "And that guy up there. He's certainly not from around here."

"No shit," said Heather.

"Disappears into a yellow portal. Not something you see every day," John said. "Comforting."

Heather looked over to Gloria. "I'm not so sure that was him."

John gave Heather a quizzical look.

"He seemed... afraid of it," Heather finally said.

There was a long silence, the kind of silence that follows after you just told someone their best friend, or maybe their husband, has just died.

"That man up there," Heather said to Jennifer, breaking the silence. "He was your husband?"

"Yeah. But I- he never- I don't know what's happening. Some of what you said, I mean, I think I saw some of it."

"What do you mean?" John asked.

"Stephen works — worked — at the power station. And when I didn't hear from him, I went there, and everyone was gone, just gone," Jennifer said. "There was blood everywhere, the building was just burnt. Torn apart. I didn't see Stephen, so I thought he had made it out somehow. I guess he made it out, but... there was blood *everywhere*. The smell. You can't imagine the smell."

Heather put a hand on Jennifer's shoulder. "I'm sorry."

John stood from his stool. He shuffled to the wall and leaned against it, deep in thought. He did the same thing when he was stuck in a chapter in one of his books, when he had no idea where to take the story next. Instead of letting ideas come to him, like he had been taught, he had gotten into the habit of forcing an idea to come his way — good or bad — in order to continue.

"Whatever happened to Gildy happened to her husband. And I think this Thomas Manning guy has something to do with it," said John. He looked from the mayor to the pregnant girl to the cop. He was starting to think of Heather as a friend, possibly his first friend besides Pauley (who had obviously bought himself a first class ticket to the Nut Farm) since Tracey died.

Heather caught his look. "Something on your mind, John?"

"I think we should cut our losses and head to Chicago," he said.

"No way in hell. I'm not going back out there, nu-uh," Gloria said.

"I think that would be a tremendously bad idea," said Heather.

Jennifer looked from John to Heather. "Why?"

Heather was stern. "We've seen a town of thirty-thousand practically fall apart. In just a *few days*. A city of eight million could potentially be much, much worse. Chicago's not that far away.

Not to mention the dozens of suburbs that surround us." She paused, taking in a breath. "We head the opposite direction. We can go through Downers Grove and-"

Jennifer held up a hand. "What makes you think this has happened in Chicago?"

"What makes you think it *hasn't?*" Heather slammed back.

Jennifer rested her weary head in her hands. The cop had a valid point.

Heather continued. "If we assume what's happened here has happened elsewhere, we should head towards less densely populated areas. I don't think we should take any chances in Chicago. People that *should* be dead aren't, and the people still alive don't seem to be mentally well."

"Except us," John said.

"Except us," Heather repeated.

"So the question is," John said, "what makes *us* so special?"

Gloria raised her hand, as if she were in a classroom. She didn't wait to be called on — she just wanted everyone's attention. She looked at Heather. "The other cop up there, the one that attacked you. He's your partner?"

Heather nodded.

"You said the same thing that happened to everyone else, you know, whatever happened to make them all weird, you said that happened to your partner," Gloria said.

Heather nodded again.

"Okay," Gloria went on, "then if everyone else went crazy, why didn't he?"

"He did," John said.

"But he helped us," Heather pointed out. "He could have killed us, but he didn't."

"You're right," John said. "As nuts as he was, he helped us at the end."

"If Gildy was willing to help us, maybe he's also willing to tell us what's going on," said Heather.

John turned his head toward her. "So what do we do now?"

Heather stood. "We go ask him."

45.

It was an hour before sunrise when Richard and Lindsay Stone walked past a sign welcoming them to the Village of Westmont. They had lost all sense of time around the town limits of Berwyn, and Richard found himself in mild shock at the sight of the sun peeking over the horizon.

Since leaving the freeway, they discovered that their best defense against the changed people was to simply ignore them. They found that if they kept their eyes on their feet and continued walking as if everything was right with the world, the changed people would eventually give up trying to talk to them. Like the two in the tollbooths, who had seemed intent only on getting their toll money and nothing else. As if they were wild animals, only prone to violence when provoked. Perhaps the changed people were just as scared of Richard and Lindsay as they were of them.

Then, Richard reminded his wife, there were the others, the ones in their apartment building. The two teenagers there had attacked them for no reason, unlike the old man in the el station or the tollbooth attendants. Richard thought there was a rhyme and a reason behind their varying attitudes, but he couldn't quite wrap his mind around it yet. Some of the people were violent. Others just seemed to be a few sticks shy of a full pack of gum.

Richard turned to his wife. "How's your head?"

"It hurts. It fucking hurts."

"Can you still hear it?"

Lindsay listened for a moment, her head cocked like a dog that doesn't understand its master. "No, not right now."

"At least there's that," he said. Richard was frightened for his wife. He did all he could to convince her that no one was talking to her, that there was no magical fairy or demon in her head, but sometimes she could be as stubborn as her sister.

Richard assumed it was stress-related and that it would all pass like a bad dream once things got back to normal. That was his hope. But he could tell by looking in his wife's eyes, those blue-green eyes that he fell in love with three years ago, that things would be getting worse before they got better. They were bloodshot from more than just lack of sleep. There was something else going on in there, something she wasn't telling him.

They were now two blocks into Westmont. Lindsay slipped off her backpack. She plopped it on the ground and plopped herself right next to it.

"Why are you stopping?"

"Because I'm fucking tired," she said.

Taking off his own pack, which was mostly water bottles and the few first-aid supplies they had found in the abandoned motor home, he swung his head around to look at her. "You didn't used to swear this much."

"You try feeling like this for twenty-four hours straight, see how well *your* Christian morals hold up."

He sat down next to her and moved to brush the hair away from her eyes. She withdrew violently, as if scared and annoyed with him at the same time. Her eyes burned into his.

"Hey, hey, easy cowgirl. We're in this thing together, you know."

She put her head in her hands, rubbed her temples. "You can help by shutting the fuck up and giving me some more pills."

"I think you've had enough. Take anymore, you're apt to get sick."

"I already *am* sick and I don't fucking care just *give me something for this pain in my head.*"

Richard recoiled from her verbal attack, her worst yet. Her recent attitude was the exact opposite of her usually happy-go-lucky-Church-on-Sundays demeanor.

As he reached into his pack for the ibuprofen they had taken from the Winnebago, she said, "I'm sorry, Richie. I'm just not feelin' so hot, you know?"

He pulled out the bottle and shook three into his

hand. "I know. Here."

She took the pills from him and washed them down with a water bottle from her own pack.

"Thanks."

"Listen, how 'bout we move on for a bit more, find a place to take a breather. You look like you could use the rest." He wanted to hug her and make everything okay again, but knew it was in his own best interest to keep his hands to himself for the time being. If he wanted to keep his ability to speak and his nuts intact, that was.

"Yeah, okay, that'd be fine I guess," she answered, sounding as enthusiastic as if he had offered to give her a free root canal.

Richard stood up and slid the straps of his backpack over his shoulders. "Maybe we'll get lucky and some regular folk here will have a store open or something."

"I doubt it."

Richard put out a hand to help Lindsay up. She looked at it, took it, and allowed him to bring her to her feet. She picked up her own pack and began to slide it over her shoulders.

"Let me carry that for you," Richard said, reaching for one of the straps.

Lindsay snapped her arm away from him and bore a hole into his skull with her eyes. "*I can carry it.*"

She swung the other strap over her shoulder and silently marched ahead of him. Richard watched her for a few steps, worried, then caught up with her. When he returned to her side, he slyly stuck his hand in hers. To his surprise, she took it instead of recoiling from his touch. There was still a part of his old Lindsay in there somewhere.

They walked further into the town. Lindsay pressed her fingers into Richard's hand. He gripped her back tightly, not wanting to ever let go. It felt like a safe haven to both of them.

"I don't know what I ever did to deserve you," she said.

"I think you were drunk when I asked you out. That might have something to do with it."

"I'm being serious, Richie. I've been such a bitch these past two days," she said.

Richard grinned. "Really. I hadn't noticed."

Lindsay rolled her eyes. "You're right. Maybe I was just drunk," she said, and began to laugh quietly. Richard joined her, and they shared their first happy moment since they had left Chicago. For a couple of seconds, things felt normal again.

She hadn't smiled — truly smiled — since the shit hit the fan and they had left Chicago. And now, there it was. A true bona fide she's-really-happy smile.

Richard hoped they would find a way to help her keep that smile. But as he looked at her, he felt that hope might be far-fetched. While her face was her face, lips curled into a smile, her nose crinkling a little bit from the grin, her eyes were still dark and bloodshot. Nearly black.

Almost as black as those of the changed people they had come across.

46.

John was able to find the little boy's room without too much trouble from Gloria's directions. Three hallway lengths down from the band room, John pushed the door open to the boy's bathroom and stepped inside.

His stool-torch lit up the linoleum like a firecracker, and the flame bounced off the mirror, adding extra light. He carefully placed the torch in one of the sinks, making sure the business end was securely propped up from the basin.

Taking a look at himself in the mirror, he was immediately reminded of his years of drinking. Deep, dark bags had formed under his eyes. His hair stuck out every which way, and there were drops and smears of blood across his shirt. He turned the faucet handle with the notion to clean up, only to find no water coming out of the spigot. With no power to pump water into the building, they were left with no indoor plumbing.

"Fucking great."

After relieving himself, John went back again to the sink and raised his injured leg up to the basin. He rolled up the cuff to inspect Eddie Miller's handy work. He hadn't noticed until just now — really the first quiet moment he'd had in a awhile — that the pain had been down-converted to a mild itching. He unwrapped the bandage, exposing the amateur stitch job of a cop.

Blood had dried over the stitches and stuck to the bandages. He knew he shouldn't touch it — not without any kind of antiseptic — but he couldn't help himself. Besides, the pain was mostly gone, anyway.

John picked at the scabs that had formed and wiped away what remained of the blood on his leg. Instead of the nasty gash he had expected to see, all that was left were the stitches. No cut, no bruising. Just five stitches in his leg for seemingly no reason. It had completely healed.

He searched his mind, engaging in a quick self-analysis to make sure that he was awake, that he wasn't hallucinating, or that he hadn't gotten plastered at some point and was in the middle of a blackout. Everything in the ol' noggin seemed fine, he thought. He hadn't gone crazy, it seemed that his leg had miraculously healed.

At least he hoped he hadn't gone crazy.

Rolling the cuff back down over the stitches, John decided to hold off on telling the others about this tiny little miracle. On the off-chance that his mind had taken a leave of absence, he didn't want to look like a total nut in front of all these strangers.

Ensuring that she had a full magazine in her gun, Heather slid the weapon into her holster. "Watch over her. She's been through a lot."

"Hey, I'm fine," Gloria protested.

Heather looked hard into Gloria's wide eyes. "I was talking to you."

Jennifer's brow furrowed. "Hey, I'm fine, too."

"Then why don't you two just watch over one another."

The door to the room swung open. Heather instinctively pulled her gun out and aimed it at the man coming through the door.

"Easy!" John said. "It's just me."

Heather relaxed her grip on the gun and placed it back in the holster. "Sorry. Just a bit jumpy, I guess."

John walked over to Heather, who handed him a clip for his "new" Beretta, one of two extras they had crammed into the backpacks before leaving the police station.

John stuck the extra clip in his back pocket, next to the gun that stuck out of his pants. He swung his backpack full of extra ammunition and mace cans over a shoulder, keeping his torch in his right hand as if it were a weapon and not a source of illumination.

"I still think this is a bad idea," Jennifer said.

Gloria nodded. "I'd have to agree. It's a suicide mission."

John smiled at her. "You'll get no argument from me. This will go down as one of the more stupid things I've done in my life."

"Then why go?" Gloria asked. "The music room is sound proof. We're safe here. No one can hear us as long as we keep that door closed."

Heather grabbed a torch of her own and stared at the flame. "We're not safe anywhere unless we find out what this Thomas Manning guy is really doing and what he *can* do."

"You ready?" Heather asked John.

"No," he said.

"Neither am I. Let's go."

Their torches lit the hallway more than John was comfortable with. The walls were smeared with blood, as if somebody had dipped their hands in red paint and run up and down the hallway, arms outstretched. Which for all he knew was exactly what these crazies had done. The floor was just as bad with footprints. He tried to look away, to avert his eyes from the blood marks. But no matter where he looked, the dark red goop was in his line of sight. Neither of them could think of where so much blood could have come from, and neither of them really cared to find out.

They came to a corner where a set of bloody footprints marked a path both to and from the newspaper room. The room where Gildy had saved them. The room where the strange man had risen into the air and vanished. The room where things had gone from bad to completely fucking insane.

Heather stopped them and peered around the turn.

It was even worse around the bend, if that was possible. The walls were more red than beige. Heather wondered if the human body even *had* that much blood in it. But besides the blood (which would be enough to turn her around on most days) the coast was clear.

She squinted down the hallway at the front doors. A pool of blood had collected where the mayor's husband had fallen. His body was gone, and whether that was a good thing or a bad thing, Heather couldn't be sure.

She waved John to follow. He moved the Beretta from his left hand to his right, taking no more than a two second glance at the place on the floor where Stephen Adams used to be. Both his palms were sweatier than they'd ever been in his life, worse than his wedding day, and he was having trouble keeping a secure grip on the handle. Heather seemed to be doing fine with hers, but she was a pro, John told himself. She could probably do this kind of thing in her sleep — she was a cop. He was just a writer.

As they moved closer to the newspaper room, they noticed that the door was open a crack. An orange yellow glow emanated from the doorway, accompanied by the snap and crackle of fire. The two made their way to the room, trying to be careful not to step in the blood. Avoiding it was an impossibility. Heather stopped them again just outside the door and peeked in.

The antique printer had been set aflame, and burned crazily in the corner. Maybe a little "fuck you" from the Man in the Dark Coat's cohorts. The room was full of the scent of smoke. Something foul was just underneath that stench, something neither of them could identify. John thought it might be the smell of burning flesh and hair.

Heather entered the room, John two steps behind her. She looked to her left and stopped abruptly, her breath stuck in her throat.

"What-" John started, then he saw it, too.

Gildy's body had been torn to shreds. Portions of him were spread about the room in a haphazard fashion. His right arm lay crumpled in a corner. A shoe, still with his left foot in it, sat by one of the coffee cans they had used for light, which had since lost its flame.

They didn't see the rest of him, but they were pretty sure they had found the source of all the blood. Apparently they hadn't taken Gildy's traitorous act lightly.

"Holy Jesus," John said.

Heather walked deeper into the room. She stepped in something, something that squished under the heel of her boot. She didn't have to look down to know that, whatever it was she had stepped in, it no doubt used to be part of Gildy.

She spotted her partner's torso at the far end of the room, opposite the flaming printing machine. She was relieved to see his head was still attached to it. Not that it mattered, but at least they had left the man with *that*.

She moved closer, fighting tears. "Oh, Gildy."

She bent down to look at his face, one last look before they moved on, one last quick good-bye.

"I'm so sor-" she gasped as Gildy's eyes opened. "Shit!" she yelled, and fell back.

John jumped back himself, instinctively aiming his gun at the ripped apart cop.

"No!" Heather screamed, putting her hand up in front of John's weapon.

Gildy's eyes tracked Heather's movement knowingly. He opened his mouth as if to speak, but no words came out.

"He's not dead," she said. "He's still not dead."

Gildy moved his mouth again, and it became obvious he was trying to tell her something. Heather inched closer, no longer thinking about the blood on the floor, or the bits and pieces of flesh that had become stuck to her shoes. She watched his mouth move, straining her ears to pick up what he was trying to say.

"N-nnoooo mooooore. R-room."

Heather moved her head closer to Gildy's. "No more room?"

"No more." He was able to get the words out of his mouth, but it was an obvious struggle.

John looked back at the printing machine, making sure the fire wasn't crawling their way. Luckily, it seemed confined to the machine. "Great. This again. What does that mean?"

Heather spoke softly to Gildy. "No more room *where*, Gildy?"

Gildy pursed his lips together to form another word. Muscles had been torn out of his neck, making his ability to speak a near impossibility. But with some apparently painful effort, he was able to get the word out.

"Hell."

"No more room in Hell?" John asked.

Heather swung around to look at John. He was staring straight at her, the same look of disbelief in his eyes that must have been in hers.

"They run out of cots down there or something?" John joked.

"I think we're talking about a serious over-population problem down there," Heather said.

John eyeballed her. "Don't tell me you're actually buying this."

Heather ignored him, keeping her attention on her partner. "Why haven't *we* changed?"

Gildy's eyes volleyed back and forth between the two until he was finally able to push another word out of his mouth. "Innnuhsssssssssssssttttttts."

Heather brought her face close to her friend's, watching Gildy's eyes examine her. She could tell he knew he didn't get the word out right, and he tried again.

"Iiiinnnuhhh-sonce."

Heather ran the syllables through her head. "Innocence?"

Gildy did his best to nod, enough to let Heather know she had hit the nail on the head.

"Innocence?" John asked. "I don't get it."

Gildy looked to John. "You," he said. Then he looked back to Heather. "You. Innocence."

Gildy strained to get out more words. It was clearly painful for him.

"I can't see him like this anymore," she told John.

"Burn me," Gildy said matter-of-factly.

Heather's eyes drooped in sorrow. "No, Gildy. I can't."

Using all his strength in a move that seemed to cause him an incredible amount of pain, Gildy reached up and seized Heather by the collar with his left arm. He brought his face inches from hers. "He can see you through me."

"Who?" John asked.

"The asshole in the trench coat," Heather answered for him.

Gildy nodded. He released his partner and she stood, her eyes never leaving his. "Okay, Gildy. Okay."

"Wait," John said. "What's the point of that if he can't die? I mean, if he's already dead. I don't know what I mean."

Heather spoke through sobs. "Maybe if... he's damaged enough... burnt enough... he can't see anything. Can't hear anything." She looked back at

281

John, biting her lip. "And that man in the coat won't be able to see us."

"We should get him to a hospital," said John.

"You saw what it's like out there," she said. "There's nothing they can do. Nothing anyone can do. It's better this way." She looked down at Gildy. "It's what he wants."

As much as John didn't like the idea of burning Gildy alive (or dead) he had to admit to himself that Heather was right. Even if they could break out of the high school and get the man to a hospital, there'd be no telling what state of mind the people there would be in, or if they'd even be able to help Gildy. John looked into Gildy's eyes, and while he still saw the man behind the blackness, he could tell that that man was gone.

"Burn me now," Gildy rasped. "While his control over me is still weak."

Gildy watched Heather step in front of John and bring the torch in front of her face. What could only pass for a smile came to his lips. A smile of sincerity, the smile Heather had grown to know and love despite the short span of their partnership.

Gildy closed his eyes for the last time as Heather brought the fire above Gildy's chest. His silver police badge was still attached to his uniform. She reached out, carefully took off the badge, and lit his shirt on fire. She then dropped the torch quickly, as if she couldn't get it out of her hand fast enough.

Turning around, she heard the fire grow behind

her as it ate up what was left of her former partner. She walked past John silently, and was out of the room.

"Sorry, buddy," John said, then followed Heather out.

The flames continued to engulf the cop who had only been known as Gildy and would probably only be remembered as that. His lips curled further into a smile, and soon the flames engulfed that, too.

47.

Lindsay spotted the black smoke coming from the window of the high school before Richard did. She crossed the street, and Richard had the feeling that she didn't care if he followed her or not. He jogged to catch up with his wife, who placed herself to the right of the window. Richard stood to her left, watching Lindsay stare through the window.

Her eyes swept over the inside to see a room swallowed up by smoke. It appeared that the conflagration was winding itself down, and had been confined to just the one room. She couldn't make out much more than that.

"Probably vandals," Lindsay said.

"They could still be in there."

"No, I don't think so," she was eager to say.

"No way, bad idea."

Lindsay paused, listening. Richard mimicked

her, straining his own ears to hear what she heard. Nothing but the slight breeze of the morning and his own breath came to his ears. He found himself wondering if Lindsay was hearing the Voice again.

"You can wait outside if you want," she said as she began to walk around to the front of the building.

Bring him in with you.

The Voice broke its connection with her as Lindsay turned to face her husband. "I'd feel better if you came in with me, though."

"It could be dangerous in there."

"It's dangerous out here."

"There could be other walkers in there." Richard said. "The bad kind."

Lindsay turned around and moved toward the school again. "Then you'd better come in and protect me."

She could feel his eyes staring at the back of her head as she moved. By the time she had taken three steps, she heard Richard begin to follow her, and a smile came to her face.

"You're hearing the Voice again," Richard said, a statement, not a question.

Lindsay didn't break her stride. "Don't be ridiculous."

They reached the front door, which was open a crack. The glass in the window of the door was split down the center, but still held in place.

Lindsay reached for the handle and pulled the

door open without a worry. She walked in as if nothing was wrong with the world, and Richard followed.

With their backs to the doors, neither of them noticed the silky black substance crawl out from the grass and begin to cover the school again.

48.

nnocence?"

John nodded. "That's what he said."

Jennifer pulled off her suit coat and placed it on a stool. She tugged at her blouse, trying to give her body some ventilation from the heat. The room had grown stuffy, and she wasn't sure how much longer she could handle being cooped up in the band room of a high school. "Innocent of what? It doesn't make any sense."

John got off his stool. A weather-proof lamp that Jennifer and Gloria had found sat next to him, giving them steady light and making things seem a bit more normal. None of them missed the constant flickering of the fire from the torches. "Now tell them the really creepy part," John said to Heather.

Jennifer and Gloria stared at Heather as the cop tried to find the words to make what she was about to say sound less insane that it sounded in her head.

She was unsuccessful with that, so she simply blurted it out. "Gildy said the man in the trench coat could see us through him."

Silence engulfed the room. Gloria and Jennifer exchanged glances, then brought their attention back to Heather and John.

"Excuse me?" Jennifer asked.

"Don't ask me," said John. "You now know as much as I do."

Jennifer shook her head. "This is all a bit weird."

"If you want weird, take a look at *this*." Propping his injured leg up on the stool, John rolled up the cuff to reveal Heather's stitch-work. The stitches were still there — all seven of them — but the cut itself was gone.

John rubbed his hand over what used to be a wound.

Heather stared at it in awe. "What happened?"

John shrugged. "You got me. I went to redress it, and, well, you see what I see. I didn't say anything 'cause it seemed too weird. Figured my mind was playing tricks on me. Then I thought about that bundle of joy with his magic show, and this didn't seem so weird anymore." He rolled the cuff back down over his leg. "It's as if-"

"Someone's watching over us," Gloria finished for him.

Jennifer's eyes volleyed between John and Gloria, trying to grasp the weight of what they were saying. "What, you mean like God?"

"I don't believe in God," John said.

Gloria's eyes widened. "How can you not believe in God?"

John held her look. "How *can* you believe in him?"

"I have faith."

John snorted. "Faith? You have faith in a being that lets us war with one another, one that allows famine and suffering and deadly diseases contracted by the very act that we use to procreate?"

Gloria held his stare.

"And this God," John continued, "this same God that sees fit to do... whatever the hell it is that's happening. Believe in that? No thanks."

Jennifer and Heather exchanged quick glances with one another — they were staying out of this one.

"He's testing us," said Gloria.

"Don't give me that line. If he's truly out there, I've had enough testing done on my life. And now this. Are you telling me that all this is some sort of test from your God?"

Gloria bit her lip. "He's not *my* God, He's *our* God, and I don't know. But it's not about knowing, it's about feeling. And faith. It gives me hope."

John took in a breath, slowly exhaled. "Look, I'm not trying to knock your faith, kid. I just find it hard to believe that someone who created everything and gave us life would fuck with us so much."

"Okay, enough of the philosophy class," Heather butted in. "Regardless of beliefs, John, you have to admit, something sure seems to be keeping the four of us out of the funny farm."

"Because of innocence?" Jennifer asked. "Do you really think the four of us are truly completely innocent? Everyone has broken the law at some point or another in their life."

"I think they're talking about sin," said Gloria.

"And your sins can be wiped away," Heather said. "Forgiven."

John looked over at the cop. "Don't you have to pray for that? To have your sins abolished?"

"I haven't prayed or gone to church since I was a little girl," Heather said. "But maybe our sins, the sins of the four of us, were wiped clean because of who we are." She looked at John. "Living amends."

John nodded in understanding. From the look of puzzlement on the faces of Gloria and Jennifer, he knew neither of them had had the pleasure of dealing with an alcoholic.

"In A.A. there's a thing called 'living amends'. Two of the twelve steps have us make a list of people we have wronged, then make amends to them unless, you know, the person just doesn't want to ever talk to you again or might shove a knife up your ass for something you did ten years ago. In such cases, we do a 'living amend,' meaning we don't do that bad shit anymore," John explained.

"If our sins were wiped clean because of who we are, then who *are* we?" Jennifer asked. "What makes us so special?"

Heather looked at each of them as she talked.

"You watch over the town, with only people's best interests in mind," she said to the mayor. Then to Gloria: "You're about to become a new mom, you're bringing a new life into the world."

"And you're a cop," John said, "protecting and serving the public. But what about me?"

"I think yours is different, John. You blame yourself for your wife's death," Heather said.

"What's that got to do with anything?" he asked.

"Your guilt has kept your soul clean. You said it yourself that you apologize to her and ask her for-giveness for your mistake every day," Heather said.

John let Heather's words sink in. Try as he might to find the bullshit in what Heather was say-ing, it all somehow made some sort of sense to him. "And he can't touch the innocent."

"Apparently not," Heather said. "But besides us, there sure seem to be a lot of sinners in the world."

"No shit," John said, sitting back down on his stool. "If this man out there is able to take control of the sinners of the world, well hell, that's just about everybody, ain't it?"

Jennifer said, "So what do we do now? Sit here for the rest of our lives, wait for the rest of the world to go crazy?"

"Right now, I don't think we have much of a choice," said Heather. "We seem to be trapped in here."

John gave her a grim smile. "Then we need to find a way out."

49.

Richard and Lindsay walked past row after row of lockers, their footsteps clip-clapping away on the linoleum floor. They could just make out the faint smacking of the dying fire.

"The room we saw should be right up ahead," Lindsay said.

"Great."

They turned the corner and came to the hallway of blood. The two stopped dead in their tracks.

Lindsay choked on her breath. "Jesus Christ."

"What the hell happened here?" Richard asked out loud, not expecting an answer from Lindsay. But he got an answer anyway, and it came from behind.

"Had ourshelfs a lil' party," Eddie Miller said. "Now it loosh like we get to have ourshelfs uhnother."

Richard and Lindsay swung around, coming

face to face with a kid covered in blood and a man in a business suit with a giant vertical gash in his forehead. Behind them stood — barely stood — a man in what remained of a ComEd uniform. Most of his head was gone, and it looked like he might have spent some time in the fire they had come to examine.

Malcolm Dwight stared at the two new arrivals, eyeing them up and down, sizing them up. He stayed behind Eddie as the kid with a mashed hand and the attitude to go with it licked his lips at the newbies.

Before she could scream, Lindsay was grabbed by Eddie and tossed halfway down the hall. His mangled hand left a blood stain on her shirt that would never wash out. The strap from Lindsay's backpack slid off her arm as she slammed into a locker.

Richard shouted a loud "HEY!" as he back-handed Eddie. The boy was violently forced into the closed lockers to their left. The metal crinkled and cracked, and the echo of the impact sounded like it could've come from the Grand Canyon.

Don't kill them. Hurt them.

Malcolm heard the Voice loud and clear, and proceeded to obey his newest order. He lunged at Richard, both men hitting the ground with force. The wind was knocked out of Richard's lungs, and for a few seconds he couldn't breathe. Malcolm dug his knee deep into Richard's chest.

Stephen Adams took two steps toward them, attempting to join the fight, but succeeded in only tripping over his own two feet. His body had become so garbled, it made something as simple as walking a chore.

Eddie shook wooziness from his head and pulled himself up, using a locker handle for support. His eyes found Lindsay, and he smiled. "Husband's not very bright," he told her.

Between white-hot bolts of pain, Richard looked over Malcolm's shoulder to see Eddie standing at full height, shoulders bent, ready to attack his wife like a bull. He looked back behind them to see the man in the ComEd uniform try and pull himself back up and fail.

Lindsay got to her feet, leaving her backpack on the floor. "Please, don't, whatever you're doing, whatever you want, just please don't," she pleaded with Eddie.

Let them go. She'll take care of the others.

Malcolm looked up at Eddie. Eddie gave him a small nod, and Malcolm released his prisoner.

Richard pushed the dead-looking man off of him and sprang to his feet, turned, and ran toward Lindsay. It felt like something had cracked in his chest from Malcolm's knee, but he'd have to worry about that later. Lindsay held her hand out to him, and the two ran, ran like hell, down the hallway.

"He can see them through her," Malcolm said. "I saw what she saw. In my head. From *him*."

"Me, too," Eddie said.

Malcolm's lips bent into a smile, which wasn't

much of one now that his lips had been torn in two places from being shot in the head. "There's lots to be done."

"Losh to beh done," Eddie repeated. "But not here. Shuh womun will tache care of the onesh shere."

The two beings that used to be men casually walked to where Stephen was again trying to pick himself up. They each grabbed an arm, hoisting the man to his feet.

The three moved to the front doors of the high school. The darkness that covered the doors dripped away, revealing the gray morning light outside. The doors swung open of their own accord and Eddie and Malcolm walked out, dragging Stephen with them. As they walked down the path leading away from the high school, the doors closed and were once again was covered with the black nothingness, and the latches re-locked themselves.

Richard winced with each running stride he took. The thumping of their sneakers atop the linoleum was a dead giveaway. They might as well just yell *here we are over here, assholes!*

They turned left around a corner. The next hallway to their left, if Lindsay's memory served, would be the one soaked in blood. If they could stay ahead of the freaks that had attacked them, they'd be able to loop around, go back the way they came, and right out the front door before their attackers realized they had simply gone in a circle.

Lindsay stopped running. She cocked her head to the side, listening.

"What-is-it?" Richard asked quickly, all one word. "Come on, we have to move, have to get outta here."

Lindsay *shh'd* him.

Richard caught his breath. "What, is it the Voice? Are you hearing the Voice again?"

"Shut up," she said, putting up a hand. "It's not that. I think there're others in here."

Richard was frantic to get moving again. "Yeah, those three psychos back there, now *come on!*"

"No, it's not them," Lindsay spat out. She looked up to a door just beyond the hallway of blood with the word MUSIC ROOM stenciled on it. "There are people in there."

Go to them.

"They're probably in there for a good reason," she told Richard as she began walking to the door. "They might need help."

"So do we."

Lindsay stopped and listened again. "Strength in numbers, Richie. We can probably help each other."

"What if they're like the others?" Richard asked.

"What if they're not?"

"Thomas Manning is controlling their minds. Maybe controlling all of this," said John. "Everything's leading back to him."

"I find that rather hard to believe," Gloria said

to John.

"You saw a man disappear into thin air, and another get up off the ground after he was shot in the head. If that's not proof things are a little off, I don't know what is," John said.

"Let's say you're right, and this guy, this Thomas Manning, has something to do with it. So what?" Jennifer said.

Heather moved toward the mayor, all business. "No more room." She paused for effect, looking at each of them. "What if what Gildy said is true, that there's no more room in Hell?"

Gloria stood up from her stool and stretched. "Then we're in a lot of trouble."

"He's taking people from the town and changing them somehow, making them violent, evil," said John. "Taking them before they die, before their time."

Gloria pointed her eyes at John. "You buy *this*, but not God."

"I've *seen* this shit, sister."

"We're talking about Hell on Earth?" Jennifer scoffed.

"It's only a matter of time before he gets to everyone and we're the only ones left," said John. "All the hiding in the world won't do dick for us then."

"If we stay here, we die. If we try to do something, try to stop this thing, we at least have a chance," Heather said.

Jennifer asked, "So how do we stop him?"

"I have no idea," John said.

Jennifer stood and paced the room. She absent-mindedly picked at some dried blood on the arm of her shirt.

"We could start by looking for him," Heather said.

"How're we gonna look for a man that can disappear whenever he wants to?" John asked.

"This is insane," Jennifer noted. "If the choice is between staying here and looking for this nut-job, my vote is to stay here. Besides, we don't even know where to begin to start looking."

"I do," Gloria said.

All eyes turned to Gloria. "We go to where he works. He said it's his home away from home," she said.

"Where does he work?" Heather asked.

"He owns Books Period on Quincy," Gloria said.

"He told you this?" John asked.

"Yeah," Gloria said, smiling. "He's his own biggest fan."

Jennifer put her head in her hands, massaging her temples and craving a nice big bottle of extra strength Excedrin. Leaving the debate of politics for the debate of Hell on Earth was giving her a migraine.

All this was not only too much for her to handle, but it was downright ludicrous. She had grown up agnostic and didn't believe in Heaven and Hell. She had left open the possibility of believing in God, but she hadn't seen any proof yet.

She also knew that just sitting in the music room of the high school was an invitation for trouble. Despite her remarks to wait it out for help, deep in her gut she knew they couldn't do that. A voice inside of her told her that just wasn't the way the Mayor of Westmont should do things.

"Let's vote on it," she said.

"What?" John asked.

"We live in a democratic world, Mr. Whitley. We should try and keep it that way. Now, who here thinks we should go to the bookstore and look for this guy?" Jennifer asked.

John, Heather and Gloria raised their hands in unison.

"I don't think there's much of a point in asking who's against it," Jennifer said. "But I'd like to go on the record saying this whole thing is a waste of time. If you want to leave, we should head towards Chicago. At least there there'll be others, more people, more chances, more help."

"Or more people like the ones up there," John added.

Heather looked at Jennifer. "If he's not at the bookstore, then we'll do your plan, we'll go to Chicago."

Jennifer nodded. "Fair enough."

Their conversation was cut short by a *KNOCK-KNOCK-KNOCK* at the door.

50.

Heather pulled her gun and aimed it at the door. John followed her example and drew his weapon. "Great. They're knocking now."

"Please, let us in," came a faint female voice from the other side.

"We're not like the others," said a male voice.

The gun wavered in John's hand.

"Let them in," Heather said.

"Are you fucking crazy?" John said. "What if they're like your partner, or her husband? What if they're changed?"

"What if they're *not?*" Heather asked in return. "Look, if they turn out to be psychos like the others, we fire away and hope we can make it past them."

"That's the worst plan I've ever heard," John said.

"John, we're gonna have to leave here sooner or later, and it might as well be sooner before more of them show up," Heather said.

John stared long and hard at the cop. At that moment, he wished he could have one of those silent conversations with her like she seemed to have with Gildy. While terror swam through every bone in his body, he also knew Heather was just being the voice of reason. The longer they camped out in the music room of the high school, the greater the chances were that they could eventually end up facing an army of changed people right outside that door.

"Okay," John said. He walked to the door and put his hand on the doorknob, looked back at Heather. "Ready?"

"No," Heather said.

Bringing his gun up to eye level, John opened the door.

Lindsay and Richard were greeted with the business end of a Beretta when the door finally swung open. Another person in the room, a cop by the looks of her, had one on them as well. Richard pushed Lindsay behind him and put his hands up.

"Whoa, whoa, whoa," he said to the man with the gun. "We don't want any trouble."

"Neither do we," said the man. He looked over Richard's shoulder to see Lindsay's wide eyes staring at him. They were the eyes of a frightened child, of someone who had seen more in their life (or the past few days) than they could handle.

She caught his look. "Please don't leave us out here."

"How do I know you're not like the others?"

"Look at my eyes," Richard said.

Richard held the man's gaze, letting him take a good, long look at his eyes which were a little bloodshot, but they didn't showcase the black nothingness that the changed people's did.

The man looked back at the cop. She nodded her head in approval, that the couple seemed legit.

"One sign of either of you being completely bonkers like everyone else, we'll do what we have to," said the man as he lowered the Beretta.

"Ditto," Richard said.

The man pulled the door open the rest of the way, allowing Richard and Lindsay entrance to their safe haven.

The two groups exchanged stories of their experiences since the power outage. Richard reluctantly agreed with John's theory that somehow people were dead but not dead. In what had quickly become an insane world, it seemed the only sane option. He told John of the few walkers they had run into during the course of their journey from Chicago, and that the ones with normal eyes seemed scared out of their wits. The others, the changed ones, didn't seem to be violent across the board, as their encounter with the two attendants at the tollbooths had proved. Richard ended his tale with the three changed people in the hallway who had mysteriously let them go after attacking them.

Jennifer's hand quivered in her lap at the

thought of one of those three changed people possibly being Stephen. "Did one of them," she started, then abruptly stopped herself. She wanted to inquire about Stephen, but didn't want to know the answer.

"Did one of them what?" Richard asked.

"Nothing," Jennifer finally said. "Never mind."

"Wait, I missed something," John said. "How did you two get into the school?"

"That's a good question," Heather said, rubbing an index finger on her gun. "The school was blocked off. The doors were locked."

Lindsay looked to Richard. "We just walked in," she said. "The door was open."

"That's not possible," Heather said. "He locked the doors and jammed the windows hours ago."

"Who?" Lindsay asked.

John ignored her and turned to Heather. "They let them go."

"Shit," Heather said, realizing what John was getting at. "He let you in. He wanted you in here."

"Who?" Lindsay repeated.

Jennifer said, "You wouldn't believe us. I hardly believe us myself."

"Try me," Richard said.

John sucked in a breath, ready to be ridiculed once again in his life for having the over-active imagination of an alcoholic author.

"There's a man, but he's not a man. I don't think he's human. He's big. Brooding. And he wears-"

Lindsay cut him off. "A trench coat."

303

"You've seen him," Heather said.

Lindsay looked at her husband with the same look John just had: she was about to say something that would make the others in the room think she was ready for the big padded room in Joliet.

"No," she said. "I mean, not in real life. In my head. Actually, come to think of it, I've never seen him, in my head, that is. I don't know how I know, but I know he wears a trench coat." She took in and exhaled a shaky breath. "Which really makes no sense in the middle of summer."

John shot a look to Richard, who shrugged. "She's said she's been hearing a voice since-"

"The power went out," Jennifer said.

Richard nodded. "About then, yeah."

John turned to Heather. "He's gotten to her, but not completely. Not yet. Not like that kid or the others."

A light bulb popped on in Gloria's head. "Maybe he's not as compatible with some people as others. Like, it takes him more work to get in there."

"The more innocent you are, the more difficult it is for him to get in," said John. "Is that what you're saying?"

Richard stood up, holding up his hands in mock surrender. He paced to the other side of the room, passing a trombone case and the covered drum set. He had put up with Lindsay's stories — that's all they had been to him up until then — about the Voice in her head. But now these people, these complete strangers, seemed to be on a wavelength all their own.

They were corroborating Lindsay's psychosis, making matters worse before he could try and make them better.

Richard seemed to stare at all of them at once. "You mean to tell me this guy is *real?*"

"We met him," Gloria said. "He wasn't very nice."

"Well that's a relief," Lindsay said. "I thought I was going crazy."

"What was he saying to you?" John wanted to know.

Lindsay put her head in her hands. She avoided her husband's gaze and looked anywhere in the room but at him.

"Tell me," Richard said.

The room was silent, awaiting Lindsay's answer.

She slowly looked up at Richard, her lips shaking. "I told you. Mostly it just said my name."

Jennifer watched the woman admit to hearing the Voice and what it had been saying to her. While she certainly wasn't ready to come forth about her own infrequent visits from a voice, she at least felt some relief of not being all alone in the situation.

"There's more," Richard said to his wife.

"I'm not lying to you."

"I didn't say anything about lying," said Richard. "I said there was more. There's more you're not telling us."

Lindsay held her breath, then let it out at a snail's pace. "It told me to kill you."

Richard stared unbelievingly at his wife. In all their years together, they had never held a secret from one another. For this being their first, it sure was a doozy. "Why didn't you tell me?"

"What was I supposed to say? 'Hey honey, my head hurts, are we there yet? By the way, someone keeps telling me to kill you?'"

"No secrets, babe," said Richard. "I could've helped."

Silence blanketed the room as Richard turned away from Lindsay, obviously hurt. She put out a hand, resting it on his shoulder. She laid it there lightly, expecting him to violently shrug it off any second.

Instead, he put his own hand on top of hers, and gently patted it.

John reached into a pocket and pulled out his pack of Pall Mall's. Flipping open the top, he saw he had only two left. He scanned the room, his eyes landing on the girl's curved stomach.

John closed his pack of cigarettes and shoved them back into his pocket. "What is this, some sort of mass-psychosis?"

"It rarely happens. Not to this extreme, at least. Maybe more of a mass-delusion. But yeah, it could be." He looked to Lindsay. "We're dealing with something not really in the textbooks here."

"What are you, some sorta psychiatrist?" John asked.

"Yes," Richard said as he stood, placing his hands in the pockets of his worn jeans. "An idea, or a fear, can grow from one person and move on to the next, and the next, and so on, to the point that the majority of a select group can be perceived as believing or thinking the same thing in a given amount of time. It's related to the idea of Primary Perception, that all life is connected and intertwined."

"Laymen's terms, doc. We're not all shrinks here," Gloria said.

Richard shuffled the coins in his pockets, searching through his memory for a way to break it down for the group. "In Milan, around 1630, pestilence and plague swept through the country. A journalist reported a prediction that the Devil had come to town, and would poison the town's water supply."

"Slow news day," Jennifer interjected.

Richard went on, ignoring the comment. "The story spread, and soon enough people believed that their crops had been poisoned, along with the water. They began to execute those they thought responsible. A pharmacist named Mora had some unknown potions and chemicals in his home, so he was accused of being in league with the Devil.

"He eventually confessed, after a good bout of torture, to working with the Devil and poisoning the city. He named other accomplices, and soon enough person after person came forward admitting to cooperating with the Devil. They were judged, found guilty, and executed.

"Even after that, people still came forward, believing they were employed by the Devil to bring about the downfall of mankind. Through fear alone, people believed that they were either being poisoned, or employed by Satan to do his bidding."

John looked at Richard with skepticism. "Are you saying that this guy might not exist? That he's a figment of everyone's imagination?"

"Bullshit," Gloria said. "We saw the guy. He floated and vanished." She looked up at Richard, who was now standing behind his wife, his hands on her shoulders. "And there was never any prediction that the Devil was gonna come to Westmont and make us all nuts."

"He never said he was the Devil," Heather pointed out.

"What happened to the town? After all those people were killed?" Jennifer asked.

Richard folded him arms across his chest. "Nothing. There was no poison, the Devil never came forward and wiped out the town. People just believed it was happening, and that was enough to make it happen."

"Like Orson Welles with the *War of the Worlds*," John added.

Richard smiled. "Exactly. You get one guy out there with a brilliant hoax, eventually he can turn it into an epidemic."

Heather looked over to John, worried. "Except that this time there seems to be some truth to the hoax."

"Then we really need to find this guy," said John.

"Before we venture into this man's arms, we should try and find out as much about him as we can," Richard said. "Does anyone here know anything about him we haven't already discussed?"

"I know where he works," Gloria said sheepishly, knowing the information was of little use at the moment.

"Right," said Richard. "And we've already established we can't get out of the school just yet, but it's a start. Anything else? Anything practical?"

John folded his arms. "I don't know anything off the top of my head, but his name was familiar. There was something about him."

"So the next thing to do," Richard said, "would be to find out who our Orson Welles wannabe really is."

51.

After a quick excursion to the front and side doors of the high school, where they discovered that the black nothingness was still keeping the doors locked tight and they weren't moving for anybody, they decided that John, Gloria and Jennifer would make an expedition to the school's library — their only instant source of information. This decision was met with displeasure from Jennifer and Lindsay; Jennifer thought it best they stay together as a group and Lindsay now wanting nothing more than to find a way out of the high school and get to her sister in Downers Grove.

Gloria was the voice of reason, suggesting it best to split up: one group for information, the other for supplies. No food was found in the band room, and Gloria was eating for two. With seemingly no way out of the high school, she thought their energies would be better spent on unraveling what was hopefully an elaborate hoax by Thomas Manning and finding food, rather than trying to bust through whatever was covering the school and keeping them locked in.

How that could be part of a hoax — along with the undead attacking them and Thomas Manning levitating and disappearing — was a question Gloria wasn't sure she wanted an answer to. Deep down she knew there was something more than a practical joke going on in Westmont, and maybe the entire world.

John and Heather silently determined that there was the very good chance Lindsay couldn't be trusted; an eye needed to be kept on her. And they could tell by looking at her husband that he had his doubts, too. If even half of what they thought about this man in the trench coat was true, there would be no way to tell if or when he were to take control of Lindsay. Not wanting to seem obvious about their new fear, they had to trust that Richard Stone was a smart enough man to know when his wife had gone completely over the edge.

John pushed the door to the library open with the toe of his sneaker, half expecting it to be locked. It swung open easily.

The gas-lamp didn't provide them with much light, only enough to see ten, fifteen feet in front of them at the most. Like the rest of the high school, the room was deserted. Nothing scurried, not even a mouse. John looked at the skylight above, which no longer gave a window to the heavens. The same black nothingness that covered the windows to all the doors covered the skylight, as well.

Tables scattered about the room for studying were empty, and for the first time since the power went out, Jennifer felt a sense of utter loneliness. The sight of those seven vacant wooden tables where kids would learn, cram for a test, or plan how they were going to ditch seventh period didn't sit well with her. Yes, they would be unoccupied at this time of day and year regardless of what was going on outside; it was the thought of where all those kids where *now*, what horrors they had seen or were experiencing at that very moment, that made her visibly shudder.

"So where do we start?" Jennifer asked, her voice quivering.

"That's a good question," Gloria said, turning to John. "What exactly is it we're looking for?"

"His name," he said.

"Uh-huh. Okay. Like a book he wrote or something? He didn't strike me as the writerly type," Gloria joked.

John smiled back at her, pushing her further into the library with a hand. "No, but I'm fairly convinced he's here, in our town, for a reason. He has some history with it, he was born here, I don't know. If I could just place where I've heard his name before..."

John moved behind one of the two front counters, leaving the lamp on a center table to give them all equal (albeit shitty) light. "Look for phone books, year books, town history, that sorta thing," he said.

"Cool, we'll just give him a call, tell him he's creepin' us out," Gloria said, giving John a smile and a wink.

He smiled back, hoping that they would be even half that lucky.

Heather led the group down the hallway that had taken her and John from the gym to the newspaper room, her hand never leaving the sidearm strapped to her belt. Lindsay carried a second gas-lamp behind Heather, while Richard brought up the rear.

"We can cut through the gym," Heather said. "The cafeteria's just on the other side."

"I take it you went here," Richard said.

Ahead of them Heather could see the two oak doors that opened up into the gymnasium. "Four of the worst years of my life."

Richard looked at the cop, an eyebrow raised. "Really. Usually people tend to look back on their high school days as some of the happiest moments of their lives."

"Are you charging me by the hour for this, or just trying to make polite conversation?"

"A little bit of both. You'll know when you get the bill."

They reached the doors to the gym. Heather brandished her weapon, prepared to enter. "We move straight across, single file, quickly and quietly."

Heather had the very nervous and unpleasant feeling that *he* was there, the Man in the Dark Coat, always with them, watching their every move. Heather could feel it in the back of her head, stronger now that Lindsay was here. Despite what Gildy had told them, Heather wasn't fully convinced their "innocence" could keep Thomas Manning from getting inside their minds forever. Once he connected with Lindsay, who appeared every bit the nice and innocent type as Heather did, how much longer until he could connect with the rest of them?

Heather pushed the door open with the tip of her gun. She moved in silently, her fear-laden breath making more noise than her shoes on the floor.

Richard looked back at his wife. The expression on her face mirrored his own.

They were scared shitless.

As Lindsay crossed the threshold, she thought she heard something snap and pop behind her. She quickly swung her head around, peering back into the dark hallway behind them.

Richard grabbed her arm, making her jump. "What is it?"

The Voice told Lindsay to ignore what she had heard, so she did. "Nothing. I'm just a little freaked, is all."

"You and me both, babe," Richard said.

Lindsay followed her husband and the cop into the gym, the sound of whatever it was forgotten.

52.

The name "Thomas Manning" was not found in any of the phone books John had located underneath the front counter. This didn't shock him; he had a sinking suspicion that Thomas Manning would not be in anything published recently, but rather in something out of Westmont's past. The name was familiar to him, but it was a vague memory, a blurry one, as if it were something out of his own past, as well.

He boosted himself up on the counter, letting his legs dangle down. Reaching into his pocket, he pulled out his pack of Pall Mall's along with his lighter. He eyeballed his two remaining cancer sticks, then looked over to the row of books Gloria had ventured down. Convincing himself that she was far enough away for the second-hand smoke to not cause any harm other than a foul smell, he shook out one of the cigarettes. With one swift motion — a move he had mastered during his twenty-plus years of smoking — John opened the Zippo, flicked it to life, lit the Pall Mall, and shut the lighter. He inhaled deeply, his first cigarette in hours.

The acrid smell of the cheap cigarette smoke quickly overpowered the smell of books in the room. John was distraught by that; ever since he could remember, he had loved the smell of books. He wasn't sure what it was. While part of it was the scent of the paper, there was just something different about the way a printed paperback affected his nose compared to a blank sheet of Kinko's copy paper. As much as he enjoyed that smell, his need for nicotine and tar won out.

The Zippo sat in his hand, his fingers moving it back and forth in his palm. The soft golden glow from the gas-lamp caught his engraved initials in the lighter. *J.P.W.* John Patrick Whitley. Tracey joked when she had given him the lighter that if he should ever suffer amnesia like the main character from his first book *Into the Darkness*, he'd at least have the benefit of knowing what his initials were.

He wished she were here right now. She might not have all the answers, but she always gave him a sense of hope. The days and weeks after her death, John felt the hope in his heart slipping away. The hope that one day he'd get over her. The hope that one night he'd get a good night's rest. The hope that the world really wasn't as shitty a place as he thought.

But without Tracey around, all John's inner-hope was lost. Without her, the world *was* a shitty place. In fact, lately it had become much, much worse. Just by looking into Tracey's eyes, he'd known that not *everyone* in the world was a complete asshole. But she'd been quiet for awhile, now. Ever since he had entered the high school.

He made the connection quickly and easily. Not only were they being kept in here against their will by unseen methods, but Tracey was no longer around to give him sage advice from the grave. Quite possibly whatever was darkening the windows was also blocking Tracey from him, jamming their signal.

John felt even more alone now. Helpless.

For a self-proclaimed atheist, John was starting to believe (against his own better judgment) that there might be powers in the universe greater than him and science.

The computers were nothing more than paper-weights now, so Gloria wasn't able to look through their files for Thomas Manning's name. Luckily, though, it appeared that someone who worked in the library was as much of a pack-rat as she was. Gloria had never thrown away one magazine she'd bought or one letter she'd received in her life, and someone in the library had never thrown away a single copy of the *Westmont Herald*. Box after box of back issues of the town's paper sat on and in front of shelves in the rear of the room.

Gloria suspected the culprit was Mrs. Brewer, the petite librarian who had worked at the high school since as far back as Gloria's mother's first year there, and undoubtedly before then. Mrs. Brewer had the knack for remembering every student that had ever graced the halls, so it was really too bad she wasn't here. If the man in the trench coat had some connection to the high school, Mrs. Brewer would know about it. But the librarian wasn't around, and Gloria found herself wondering what the elderly lady had been up to for the past two days. Was she in town? Had she become one of the walkers like Richard and Lindsay? Or had she become one of the changed people?

Gloria shook those thoughts from her head. Asking herself questions that she didn't know the answers to was a sure-fire way to go insane a little bit faster than she already was.

Her protruding abdomen made it impossible for her to bend over and pick up even one box, so one of the others would need to help her bring them out into the reading area, where there was more light. As she was about to call out John's name for his assistance, she felt her child wake up and kick. She had gotten used to this, but it still startled her even this late in her pregnancy. Edginess had taken over Gloria's mind, and she was finding that the slightest thing — even as something as natural as her unborn child kicking her — was unsettling.

She patted her stomach. She could sense with the connection she had with the growing life in her body that the child was upset. And something else, something that caused a tightness in her chest and a quick hot-flash across her brow. She wasn't sure how she knew it, but she did.

Her child was scared.

Jennifer took it upon herself to go through the old high school yearbooks. With no idea of where to start looking for the name "Thomas Manning," — their descriptions of the man's age ranged from the mid-twenties to early forties, however the hell *that* was possible — she decided to simply start from the most recent year and worked her way backwards.

The light from the lamp was enough for her to make out the dates on the spines and the names of the students in the indexes. She had made it as far back as 1983 with still no results, not even a relative or someone else with the same last name, which was odd since Manning wasn't all that unique a family name.

She was quickly coming to the conclusion that John Whitley (she could now smell the smoke coming from the man's cigarette) was mistaken about Thomas Manning's connection with Westmont. There was no record of him in the library, and she seriously doubted there would be. For all they knew, "Thomas Manning" wasn't even his real name.

She paused as she grabbed the 1982 yearbook. Her eyes glazed over as her mind went back to the events of Stephen's attack. His face distorted, blood

319

dripping off his chin. The bullets entering his body.

Take care of the cop, and I can bring him back to you.

Jennifer wasn't ready to admit to herself, let alone the others, that she, like Lindsay, had been hearing a Voice. The idea alone was preposterous, and there was no way in hell she was going to let herself accept the fact that someone was talking to her in her mind.

She squinted her eyes shut, willing the images of her husband and the sound of the Voice out of her head. She repeated to herself *it's not real, it's not real, it's not real* until she could hear herself think again, and the echo of the Voice went away.

She focused on the scent of John's cigarette to help bring her back to reality. Looking to her right into the reading area, Jennifer spotted John sitting on the counter, smoking a cigarette, lost in thought.

"There's no smoking in here, you know."

Startled, John turned to look at her. "You gonna tell on me?"

Jennifer placed the 1982 yearbook back on the shelf and stood. "We're not gonna find anything, I hope you know."

"Why do you say that?"

Jennifer folded her arms and leaned against the book case, keeping herself in the shadows so John couldn't see her puffy about-to-cry eyes. "I've already gone back to nineteen-eighty-three. I don't think this guy went here."

John took the final drag from his cigarette and

stomped it out on the floor. "Go back further."

"What?"

"I don't think we're dealing with someone normal. He may look twenty-five, but I have a feeling he's older than that," John said.

"You and your feelings."

"Humor me. You got anything better to do?"

"Yeah. Head for Chicago."

John slid off the counter and walked to Jennifer. "You heard what they said about downtown. If you wanna go, I think you'd be making the journey by yourself. Once you find a way out of the school, of course."

"Fine then," she said. She reached for the next yearbook in line, 1982, and tossed it to John. He caught it in his right hand, never breaking Jennifer's stare. "You're helping me."

53.

Heather, Richard and Lindsay had made it to half-court without incident. Richard glanced over at his wife, who had been continuously looking behind her since they had entered the gym. "Something wrong?"

"That's kind of a stupid question, babe," she answered.

"You keep looking back there," he said. Then, with a hint of trepidation: "Are you hearing the Voice again?"

Lindsay seemed sidetracked, but still answered the question. "Please stop asking me that. I just feel like we're being watched. Or like we missed something back there. I don't know."

"We probably *are* being watched," Heather shot back at them.

"So this guy you saw, you think he's the same one that my wife's been hearing?"

"I'm not an expert on the subject, but it sounds like it, yeah," Heather said. "He seems to be able to control people, no reason to think he can't talk to them, too."

"But how can he do that?" Lindsay pleaded, almost cried. "It's just not possible. I want him out of my head."

Richard put an arm around her shoulders.

"It's like I'm constantly being mentally raped," Lindsay whispered.

Heather gave Lindsay a sorrowful look. "I'm not trying to pretend I know what's going on, only trying to grapple with what I've seen. Whoever this guy is, *whatever* this guy is, he's not human."

"Then what is he?" Richard asked.

"Not sure," Heather said, moving her eyes forward. "But he ain't from around here, that much is for certain."

Something fell from the top of the bleachers to their right, which had been folded up into the wall to make room for some friendly summer basketball fun. They all turned in unison to watch the something drop and hit the ground, then fly back up with almost as much force. It plunged back to the ground, then bounced again, the echo reverberating off the polished floors.

"What the hell?" Richard said as the object rebounded off the floor and headed their way. He put up his hands and caught the basketball like a pro. He twirled it in his palms, smirking almost playfully at his wife.

"Spaulding. Brand new. Haven't held one of these in years," he said. "Think I can make the shot from here?"

As Richard lifted his arm to toss the ball into a hoop, Heather spotted movement behind him, something that made her eyes widen.

"We have to get out of here," she said, grabbing Richard's throwing arm. "We're not alone."

"What?"

The cop was already pulling him toward the exit as the ball fell from his hand and rolled down the court.

Lindsay followed Heather's eye-line. At the top of the folded up bleachers on the other side of the court, dozens — perhaps hundreds — of Spaulding basketballs began to fall. Soon enough, the noise of basketballs bouncing on the court floor was almost deafening, as if a dozen teams had suddenly started practice.

They were still a good fifty feet from the exit when the balls began to pick up velocity and aim themselves straight for the trio.

54.

John held the lighter in his hands. He flipped the lid open, closed. Open. Closed. Each time with a little *clink* of a sound.

"That's a nice lighter," Gloria said as she walked back into the reading area, brushing dust off her hands.

"Thanks," John said, ceasing his compulsive opening and closing of the device as Gloria eyes the initials stenciled on it.

"J.P.K. That you?"

"Yep. John Patrick Whitley."

The name rang like a little chime in Gloria's head. "Sounds like an assassin's name. Wait, I've heard that name before."

John smiled to himself, not giving her any help.

"*Into the Darkness*," Gloria said, proud to have located the title in her head.

"You found me out."

Gloria smiled a big grin. "Cool. I loved that book." She paused, looked up at him with hound dog eyes. "Not so much the mini-series, though."

John laughed.

"So what happened to you?"

John recoiled from the remark.

"Sorry, that came out wrong," Gloria said. "I mean, where have you been? That book was what, two years ago?"

"Three," John corrected. "And I've been here," he said, motioning to their surroundings. "In Westmont."

Gloria looked at him, now with star-truck eyes. "How come you never wrote another book?"

"I did," John admitted. "No one liked it. Sophomore Slump, my agent called it. I guess no one wanted to read about the personal lives of farmers in Vermont."

"I'll admit," Gloria said, "that doesn't exactly sound like a page-turner."

"Lots of folks out there would agree with you."

"Sheesh, John Whitley. In the flesh. I'm surprised I didn't recognize you sooner."

John began to open and close the lighter again, not realizing he was doing it. It felt good in his hand. Warm. "Well, there wasn't a picture of me on the book, was there? I wanted people to buy the book, not be turned off by the geek on the back cover."

"Funny."

"I thought so."

"You'll have to autograph one for me sometime."

"Sure," he said. "So, find anything?"

Gloria leaned against the counter, taking the weight of her child off her back. "Some boxes of newspapers, nothing more. You'll have to bring them out here. I'm hardly in the condition for it."

John snapped the lighter closed and shoved it in his pocket. "Lead the way."

He followed her down the aisle of books leading to the stacks of boxes. Out of instinct and a born love for books, John found himself reading their spines. It was still fairly dark, but he was able to gather from titles such as *A Flower for Rose* and *Love of All Times* that they were in the middle of the romance section. Something about that struck him as funny; a high school library with a section devoted to romance.

"I didn't realize kids today were into this kinda shit," he said.

"Hm?"

"Romance. I always thought little old ladies who lived in Florida read books like *A Flower for Rose*. Not teenagers in the mid-west," John explained.

"This section gave me hope," Gloria said.

John stopped. "You actually *read* this stuff?"

Gloria swung around on a heel and put a finger up to John's face. "Hey, not all good books are about spaceships and worm holes."

"It was a black hole, actually."

Gloria turned back around and headed for the end of the aisle. "Whatever."

"What did these give you hope for?"

Gloria sighed. "That the world wasn't this shitty place where men were assholes and women didn't care."

"Careful, you're starting to sound like me."

"In that case I'll be sure to book a session with the doctor back there when we get outta this dump," Gloria said.

They came to the stack of newspapers and boxes Gloria had been aiming them at. John leaned down to inspect them. "So did it work? These books give you hope?"

"As much as they could. Then this happened," she said, rubbing her belly. "And romance had very little to do with this. I just hope I don't fuck it up."

"What do you mean?"

Gloria stopped. "You have any kids, John?"

"None that I know of."

Gloria twirled a lock of her hair with her fingers, making her look more like the child she really was than the mother she would soon become. "This is my first. And I hate to admit it, but I'm scared outta my mind. Anything this Thomas Manning guy can do is nothing compared to the thought of being the sole person responsible for another living being."

"Hey, if all those other assholes out there can do it, I'm sure you can, too, kiddo" John said with a reassuring smile.

"Easy for you to say, old man. It's just... you know, I realize all this kid's gonna have is me. How can that possibly be enough?"

John hesitated, then decided to ask. "What about the father?"

Gloria's eyes fell to the floor. Her pupils traced the lines of the tiles up and down, right to left.

"I'm sorry," said John. "It's really none of my business."

"No, it's cool," she said. "Let's just say I'm the only thing this kid's gonna have."

"The kid'll be lucky to have you."

"We'll see about that," Gloria said sharply.

John picked up one of the boxes of newspapers. "Old man?"

Gloria stepped in front of him, a smile slowly returning to her face. "Maybe you didn't notice, but you got some nasty grays at your temples."

John grinned at her joke as she led the way back through the aisle of love, mischief, and men baring their over-pumped chests to the world and into the reading area of the library.

John dumped the box on the table with the lantern and took off the lid with one hand, his other absent-mindedly going to his temples, as if he could feel the gray with his fingertips. Dust mites and spider webs danced in the air, causing both of them to cough and cover their mouths. Gloria waved her hand in front of her face, only making the flying dust move about even more.

"Sorry," John said.

"Not your fault," Gloria said through spurts of filth and grime that tasted like Lemon Pledge and old dirt. "She may not have thrown anything away, but she sure sucked ass at keeping things clean."

Gloria pulled out the top copy of the *Westmont Herald*, which was crusted with age. The pages were yellow and brittle, but still legible.

The date read August 29, 1968, and it proudly showcased the headline *Bell Strikers to Vote on Proposed Pact.*

"Now *there's* your page-turner," John remarked with a smirk.

"So what exactly is it we're looking for?"

John reached into the box and grabbed the next newspaper on the stack. "We'll know when we see it."

"I was afraid you were gonna say-"

A falling yearbook fell down from above, cutting Gloria off. It landed in the middle of the desk with a *SLAM* causing both of them to jump. Gloria put a hand to her mouth to muffle a squeak of surprise and looked up to see Jennifer standing above her.

"Jesus, lady! You nearly gave me *and* my kid a heart attack!"

"Yeah, I think I wet my pants a little on that one, too," John said.

Then they looked down at the yearbook Jennifer had brought out, which was open to a page of mostly smiling seniors.

"Nineteen-seventy-seven," Jennifer said.

John and Gloria looked at the faces of kids from 1977 and found the one marked Thomas Manning. To their surprise, little Tommy Manning looked like a normal, happy kid, cowlick and all. The only thing drawing away from the kid's happiness was a scar on his left cheek.

"Holy shit," John uttered. "I remember now. I didn't recognize him back there, but this is the dude."

Below Thomas Manning's name were the words

HE WILL BE MISSED.

John's stomach rolled over. His chest felt tight, and he suddenly found it difficult to breathe. "We had a couple of the same classes. He disappeared just before graduation."

Gloria looked at him with wide eyes. "So what happened to him?"

John went over the name in his head again and again. Thomas Manning. Tommy Manning. How could he have forgotten?

He looked over at Gloria. "It must've been two weeks before graduation. It was all over the papers." He looked up at Jennifer. "You don't remember this?"

"I didn't move here until nineteen-eighty. And I was eight years old in nineteen-seventy-seven," Jennifer said.

John ignored the roundabout backhand on his age. "Anyway, two weeks before graduation, this kid's family, his entire family — mother, father, I think he might've had a kid sister — were murdered in their home. Tommy never came back to school. At first everyone thought he had been killed, too."

"But he wasn't?" Gloria asked.

"They never found a body," John said, the memories coming back more quickly now. "Then there was an investigation into the murders and his disappearance. Shit. 'The Manning Killings.' That's what the papers called them.

"So they have one group of cops trying to figure out who killed the Manning's, and another group trying to find the kid. A few months into the investigation they realize that all the evidence is pointing to Thomas Manning being the killer. So then they only had one guy to look for."

Gloria sat back in her chair. "Whoa. He offed his whole *family?*"

John stared again at the picture of the boy from 1977. "That was the consensus. They interviewed all of us at the school a few weeks after graduation. You know, trying to find out if any of us knew where he was, or why he'd do it, that kinda shit.

"But none of us really knew him. He was quiet, kept to himself, didn't have any friends. The kind of kid you forget about five minutes after you meet him."

"Like they say," Jennifer said, "it's always the quiet ones."

"Wait," John said, snapping his head up from the yearbook. "You hear that?"

The two women froze. They cocked their heads like dogs, listening.

"No, I don't-" Jennifer started, then she heard it. They all heard it.

Somewhere outside, beyond the walls of the school and the windows they could no longer see through, yelling, screaming, pain-induced sounds could be heard. They were more like sounds of animals being tortured than human voices, but they knew that they were human none-the-less.

"Jesus," Gloria said, moving closer to the wall. "What's going on out there?"

John stood, holding up a finger for them to be quiet.

Someone outside, and from the sound of it someone relatively close to the school, was in what could only be the worst pain of their life. A scream that sent chills down all their spines blasted through the wall as if it were made of paper.

Then everything became silent again.

The three looked at one another, holding their collective breath, waiting to see if any more sounds of anguish would come through the walls.

"That can't be good," Jennifer said.

John reached into his pocket and gripped his talisman of a lighter tightly. "Let's just be glad that whatever's happening is happening out there and not in here."

"Sure," said Gloria. "But how long until whatever's out there makes it's way in here?"

55.

Although Heather had her gun drawn, and it would no doubt be easy to pick off the basketballs that were bouncing their way, the idea itself seemed absurd.

She ducked a ball that had aimed itself at her head while Lindsay managed to skirt another that was moving toward her feet. What caught their attention was that the balls were rolling *too* fast, as if someone or something very strong had heaved them at them. They seemed to have a mind of their own.

Richard caught one and tossed it into the air. It connected with another ball that was coming down on them, deflecting it away. It was almost humorous, more unreal than the freaks that had attacked them.

One smashed into Lindsay's right arm, and with a *snap* the woman spun around and fell. "What the hell is *this* all about?"

"Beats me, let's just get the hell out of here," Heather said.

Richard and Heather helped Lindsay to her feet. The trio made their way for the exit as more of the Spauldings dropped from above, most of them landing so hard the rebound shot them back up to the ceiling. Heather dodged another as it ricocheted off the floor and flew at her head. It missed her and kept on its way, smashing into the glass backboard across the court. It shattered, spraying thousands of tiny pieces of glass on the floor.

Lindsay stopped to watch the basketball fly over the cop's head, wondering where all these balls where coming from, and didn't notice a second ball barreling straight at her. It made contact with her abdomen and sent her sailing back with a "Whoomph!" as all the air left her lungs. She landed a good ten feet away from where she had stood.

Richard moved quickly and fiercely. It was obvious to Heather that the man was no stranger to the court. He jumped over a ball that looked to be clocking in at a good twenty miles-per-hour and put up his left hand, ready to deflect another ball that was on a destination for Lindsay's head.

Heather saw it before Richard did; another basketball, coming from the opposite direction and just as fast, right for Richard's outstretched arm. As the ball flying toward Lindsay made contact with Richard's hand, the second ball picked up speed and slammed into his elbow.

His arm bent backwards at the joint, and he

yelled out a cry in pain that made Heather's ears cringe. Lindsay must have gotten her air back by then — she let out a scream as loud as her husband's.

The basketballs that had broken Richard's arm fell to the ground and rolled away on their own.

With Heather's attention drawn away, another ball came from behind her and smacked into her gun-hand, sending the firearm soaring across the court. The gun landed at the half-court line.

Richard fell to his knees, trying to hold onto his broken arm. It was bent completely backwards at the joint, so that now his palm was behind him. The slightest touch sent sharp knife-piercing howls of pain that ran all the way up his arm. All he could do was let it hang, let it hurt.

Heather evaded two basketballs that were coming from either direction at her head and hit the ground. Using her momentum, she was able to skid most of the way to center court. She thanked God for the freshly polished wood floor as she pushed the remaining two feet using her toes, and her fingers found the grip of her gun.

Turning over onto her back, with no other well-rounded ideas coming to her, Heather began to blindly fire at the basketballs.

John slid his Zippo back into his pocket. The warmth of the metal and the connection he felt to Tracey with it seemed almost magical, but he knew it was nothing more than an old sentimental keepsake, bringing tears to an aging man's eyes. Maybe Gloria was right. Maybe he *was* getting old.

A short loud burst echoed from somewhere in the high school. It was followed by a man's scream in pain, and three more quick pops.

John was already up and halfway to the library doors by the time Jennifer and Gloria realized that what they had heard were gunshots, and the man screaming in pain was Richard Stone.

Lindsay cradled her husband's upper body in her arms as more basketballs made their appearance onto the court. Richard lay on the ground, his head in Lindsay's lap, and was no doubt in unqualified torture. Tears streamed down either side of his face. His jaw was clenched so tight that Lindsay was certain his teeth would crack apart. Richard didn't let the fact that his teeth were locked together stop him from screaming — that came through loud and clear. Her ears cried out in a pain of their own from his banshee-yell.

"Stop it, STOP IT, *STOP IT!!!*" she roared.

Heather looked back at the two, firing off another shot. Her bullets were hitting their marks — there were so many balls it was almost impossible for her to miss — but she knew it was doing no good. They were multiplying, breeding from somewhere. She knew there was no way in hell a high school could have *this* many basketballs — she estimated there to be somewhere in the neighborhood of three-hundred by now — and she couldn't spare the ammo.

"Get him up."

Lindsay propped Richard up. The movement caused Richard pain, unbelievable pain, but he didn't let that be a reason to start with the screaming again. She helped him to his feet, pushing up on his butt. She stood up herself and wrapped an arm around his waist. They both looked at Heather for the next order.

Heather nodded toward the exit.

Lindsay swung her head around and saw the two towering doors twenty feet away. A short run. It didn't appear to be much of a problem, except for the obstacles that were flying in front of them. They were gonna have to take some hits to get out of the gym.

Sweat pouring down her face, Lindsay jumped into a full run, dragging Richard with her. Heather brought up the rear, emptying her spent magazine when they were fifteen feet from the doors. She didn't bother to re-load; getting out of the room had become more important than firing at the basket-balls. She slid the gun back into her holster and ran full force behind the not-so-happy couple, pushing them with her hands.

Ten feet from salvation, a basketball found Lindsay's legs. She tripped over her own feet, sending her and Richard spiraling to the ground. Richard went down with a "GUH!" and managed to turn himself so that when he smacked into the floor, he landed on his good arm.

Lindsay's head hit the ground, producing a *smack* that cut through the cacophony of the bouncing basketballs. Her left arm reached out toward the door, only two feet from her reach.

As if beckoning her wish to get the fuck outta Dodge, the doors opened and a set of hands reached in and grabbed her outreached palm. As they began to pull her out, she took hold of Richard's collar, ensuring he'd be dragged with her.

When Richard's feet passed the threshold, Heather jumped forward, two Spauldings missing her ankles by inches. She tucked and rolled through the exit, slamming into the wall of the adjoining hallway as someone quickly closed and locked the gymnasium doors behind her.

She looked up to see John making sure the locks would hold (they would) and peer into the gym through the small glass window. Jennifer and Gloria bent down to attend to Richard and Lindsay.

John backed away from the doors as the basketballs tried to crack the glass. "Now there's something you don't see every day."

Heather took a quick peek into the gym through the slanted window as a basketball rebounded from the glass. "Let's move. I'd rather not stick around to see if they can pick locks."

56.

The doors to the swimming pool were locked with a chain that criss-crossed itself into a figure-eight, kept in place by a Schlage padlock. Closing one eye, John took aim on the lock. He was too focused to hear Heather say "Wait, don't," and he fired his gun.

His aim was good, the bullet landing dead center in the middle of the security device. The lock jumped and bounced from the force of the shot, finally settling back into place in its original position.

Heather watched with a knowing eye as John strolled up to the doors to pull the chains off. He held the lock in his palm. It was warped and bent, but still did its job of keeping the doors locked and secure. He looked back at Heather.

The cop smiled. "You've seen one too many movies."

John walked back to the group in defeat as

Heather took aim on the doors. Instead of aiming for the lock, she fired off three quick bursts at the chains themselves.

The wood of the doors splintered as the chains exploded into shrapnel. When the echo died, it was Heather's turn to stroll up to the doors. She pulled the broken chain out through the now deformed door handles, letting it fall to the ground with a metal *clank* that reverberated throughout the halls.

Heather looked over her shoulder at John. "You'd need a shotgun to blast through one of these things."

John shrugged his shoulders. "Learn something new every day."

Heather pushed the doors open, allowing the group to look in on the unlit room, the light from their two lamps doing little to showcase the square-footage of the area. John was the first to enter, having silently been chosen as leader for this part of their excursion by the others. He took the lamp from Gloria, who looked ready to face an army. John figured that was a good thing. At least *one* of them appeared ready for whatever lay ahead.

Gloria followed John, gripping his free hand with both of hers. Toughness aside, the girl was shaking. Apparently she didn't have as much of her shit together as John thought. And could he blame her? Finding Heather and the Stone's fending off sports equipment was more than enough to drive anyone over the edge.

Lindsay and Heather carried Richard in by the

upper arms. The man mumbled something that sounded like "where are we?" but came out "whuuuur ur eee?" Jennifer was last to enter, a look of solemn determination on her face as she put their second lamp down on the ground to shut and lock the doors behind them.

Gloria pulled at John's hand. "Careful."

He looked down to notice his next step would have taken him into the pool. He pulled his sneakered foot away from the edge and looked back at Gloria. "Thanks."

"Don't mention it."

Heather and Lindsay took Richard to a bench against the wall. They laid him down on his back, careful to keep his twisted and broken arm as immobile as possible. Lindsay stroked his sweat-soaked hair with a hand. His eyes closed, and what might have been a smile from the knowing touch of her hand came to his face.

"It'll be okay, honey. It'll be okay."

"We have to do something about his arm," Heather said.

"We can't, not like this," Lindsay said.

Jennifer approached them. "If you don't, it could set that way. He'll never be able to use it again."

Lindsay looked up at her.

"I broke my arm when I was ten," Jennifer said. "Bent all the way back, like his. The doctors had to break it again to set it straight."

"Not on your fucking life," Lindsay declared.

Heather leaned in close to Richard and opened

one of his eyes with a finger. "Bring that lamp over here," she said to Jennifer.

"What the fuck do you think you're doing?!" came from Lindsay.

Ignoring her, Jennifer held the lamp above Richard's head. His open eye, courtesy of Heather, stared blankly at the ceiling. The pupil didn't contract from the light, and he didn't try to shut it. The man was out cold.

As Heather inspected Richard's eyes and felt for a pulse, Jennifer swung her eyes over to Heather's head. She stared daggers at the cop, the woman who had shot her husband, despite what he had become. The Voice played in her head like a broken record.

Take care of the cop, and I can bring him back to you.

Take care of the cop, and I can bring him back to you.

Take care of the cop, and I can bring him back to you.

She tried to wish the Voice away. She screamed in her mind, as loud as she could, a powerful banshee yell that only she could hear. But the Voice wasn't going away, and the idea to take care of the cop so she could have Stephen back was seeming like a better and better idea.

Not here, though. And not now. When the time was right, she would know it. She also knew she couldn't take the cop alone. Her eyes moved over to Lindsay.

"He's passed out from the pain," Heather said. "We do it now, he might not feel it until he comes to."

"No. No-fucking-way-in-hell. Get away from my husband. Now."

Heather held Lindsay's stare. "Have you heard the Voice lately, Mrs. Stone?"

This garnered the attention of John and Gloria. Lindsay looked from the cop, to the mayor, to the writer, to the pregnant girl.

"What are you saying?" Lindsay asked.

"She may not know it," John said.

"Yeah," Gloria agreed. "What if he can, you know, talk to her, or control her, or whatever he does, and she doesn't know it?"

Lindsay went to stand up. "This is ridiculous. I'm *me.*"

Moving away from her husband was all Jennifer needed to get the answer she wanted. She took Lindsay by the shoulders and spun her around — not violently, just forcefully enough to let the woman know she meant business.

"I agree. That's what I thought, too. But I've been going over it. Stephen, that's my husband, or was... he wasn't right at the end, Lindsay. And I don't think he knew it." She looked over to Heather, then back again. "And this cop here, she probably saved my life. She knows what she's talking about."

"Let go of me."

"You just stepped away from the man you love while someone you just met told you she wants to break his arm," Jennifer said.

Gloria half-smiled. "Doesn't sound like a sane choice to me."

"I'm not the crazy one here, *you're* all the fuckin' psychos," Lindsay uttered.

John nodded to Heather. "Do it."

Before Lindsay could put up any more of a dispute, Heather took Richard's deformed arm by the wrist in one hand and secured her other hand just below his armpit. She pulled the arm as straight as she could (which wasn't very straight) before bringing her hand out from under his arm.

"NO!!!" Lindsay yelled.

But Heather was already in a crouching position. With all her weight, she used her forearm to push on Richard's broken elbow. The limb gave with a *crack* and they all heard muscles and tendons rip and tear.

Gloria looked away, sickened.

Heather felt around Richard's shoulder, then nodded to herself. "It's dislocated, too."

"FOR GOD'S SAKE YOU STUPID CUNT, GET YOUR HANDS OFF MY HUSBAND!!!"

As her words bounced off the walls and trailed into oblivion, Jennifer seized Lindsay even tighter, seeming to pull the wind and any further slurs out of her. She gave the distraught woman a stare. A stare that seemed to say *I know what you're going through, and there's something we can do about it.*

"Get her out of here," John said.

Lindsay shot butcher knives at him with her

345

eyes. "You fucking asshole, what right do you have to-"

"Is this enough?" he said, holding the Beretta up to her. He didn't aim it at her, not directly, just in her general direction.

"You're all crazy," she said, but stopped fighting. She let Jennifer take her around the swimming pool. Gloria watched as the light from the lantern moved away from them towards what looked like a locker room. The light entered the room, walked down a few steps, and was gone.

"Thank Christ," Gloria said.

"I wasn't really gonna shoot her, you know," John said.

"Hell, you might've been doin' us all a favor if you had," Heather said. She waved at John. "Need your help."

He walked over to Heather and knelt down. "What can I do?"

"I'm gonna sit 'im up. You hold his back up, I'll pass you his arm. Take his hand, pull it as hard as you can, like he's hugging himself. When you hear a 'pop,' you're done. Ready?"

"No."

Heather took Richard's hand and gently pulled it up to his chest.

"So what happened in there? With the basketballs, I mean." John asked.

Heather passed him Richard's hand. "Wish I knew."

John took hold of Richard's arm by the wrist. "It

looked, well, weird."

"The fucking things just came out of nowhere," she said.

"I don't think he wants us to just stay here, anymore," John said.

"What *do* you think?"

"I think he wants us gone, out of the way. Before we heard your shots, there were all these crazy screams coming from outside. Whatever he's been doing, I think he's almost done, and he'll soon be turning his attention back to us."

"That's comforting," Heather said. "Okay, go ahead and pull."

John gritted his teeth — he was not looking forward to the popping sound Heather had described — and pulled Richard's shoulder back into its socket.

"Sit."

Lindsay parked herself on the wooden bench between the two rows of metallic lockers. She watched Jennifer set the storm lantern down on the floor. The woman stood over her, arms crossed.

"You think I'm crazy," Lindsay said to her. "I can see it in your eyes. You think I'm turning, like the others."

"I don't think that at all," said Jennifer, then she kneeled down in front of her. "In fact, I'm on your side."

Lindsay was taken aback by the comment. "What? Then why did you let her *do that?*"

Jennifer's eyes flashed blackness for a second, then returned to their normal pale sky blue. "Because the time isn't right. Not yet. We need to work together."

Lindsay stood up from the bench and took two steps back from the mayor. "You're like them. You're one of them. The changed people."

"You've heard him, too, Lindsay. So don't be afraid or act surprised. You're on your way there, too," Jennifer said. Then her eyes changed back to black, and stayed that way.

Lindsay backed further away. Her eyes found a path around the mayor to the door that led up to the swimming pool where the others were. Where safety was. Lindsay knew that even though Jennifer was right — she had certainly heard the Voice — she still had her wits about her.

Lindsay made a bold dash around the mayor, but Jennifer was fast and relentless. Before Lindsay could scream for help, Jennifer lunged at the woman and wrapped one hand around her mouth and the other around her chest, stopping her instantly. They crashed into the lockers, Lindsay pushing with all her might to get the crazy woman off of her.

57.

Heather had fashioned a make-shift sling for Richard out of John's button-up, leaving the writer in a Metallica t-shirt that looked like it had been in its fair share of mosh pits over the years. Richard hadn't woken during the procedure, which both Heather and John had been thankful for. It would hurt like hell when he woke up, but the shrink was lucky — he had missed the worst of it.

John looked over to Gloria, who sat on the far side of the room, her bare feet dangling in the cool water of the swimming pool. A saddened, cloudy-day look had come to her face. John wanted to walk over and put his arms around the kid, tell her everything was gonna be alright. But not only did he not believe that himself, he knew the girl's look. He'd had the same one himself for over three years, and a big part of that look meant to stay the fuck away.

He pulled out the last Pall Mall from his pack

along with his Zippo. As he smoked his last cigarette, he brought Heather up to date on their discovery in the library. The history lesson of Thomas Manning proved to bring up more questions than answers.

"So he murders his family, disappears for thirty years, then comes back to town with the power to control people," Heather said, trying to make it sound less preposterous than it really was.

"Apparently," John said, blowing out a puff of smoke. "But what if..." He shook the crazy idea from his head.

"What if what?"

"You'll think I'm insane."

"There's really no stopping that, John. You talk to your dead wife."

John smiled. "Yeah, guess I do."

"So spill it."

John filled his lungs with smoke and let it out slowly. "We've seen Eddie Miller, Gildy, Jennifer's husband, all come back from the dead. What if this Thomas Manning guy is really dead, too? And whatever he's become is more than whatever he was before, like Eddie and the others?"

Heather rolled Gildy's badge, still partly covered with the dead cop's blood, in her hands. John hadn't noticed, but he thought she might have been playing with it since they had finished doctoring with Richard.

"Or," she said, "what if Thomas Manning isn't Thomas Manning."

"Huh?"

"You said it yourself. Maybe some other force took control of Thomas Manning." An epiphany came to Heather. "And what if that force is the force that killed Thomas Manning's parents?"

John shook his head. "Are you trying to say he's possessed?"

"Just a theory, hot-shot. If Thomas Manning was a real kid, and you said he was, he went to this school, then I'd say something changed him back then like it's changing everyone else now," Heather explained.

John flicked part of the ash from his cigarette onto the floor, thinking. "And what, he waits thirty years? What's he been doing since then?"

"Maybe the same shit he's doing now. You gotta admit, John, the world keeps getting worse and worse."

John took his final drag and let the cigarette fall to the tile floor. Suddenly, two loud slams came from the locker room Jennifer and Lindsay had entered.

John turned to Gloria. "Stay with Richard."

Lindsay tried to catch her breath as Jennifer lifted her up off the floor and slammed her hard against a row of lockers again. They shook in their foundation. She looked down at those dark and evil eyes and saw the love of death in them.

She kicked out with both her knees, hitting Jennifer in the stomach. The mayor released her grip on Lindsay's shirt and stumbled back. Lindsay fell, her

351

arms stopping her descent an inch before her face hit the ground. Down on the floor, she looked over to the bottom of the row of lockers.

Their connection to the tiles was flimsy, at best. The screws linking them to the foundation where old and rusted after years of shower water, sweat, and God knows what else. With Jennifer still clutching her stomach, Lindsay quickly crawled away on her hands and knees, moving behind the row of lockers. She struggled to get back to her feet, everything above her neck crying out in pain.

Lindsay got to the end of the row just in time to see Jennifer pop out from the other side. Lindsay shrieked in surprise. The mayor blocked her escape route, and inched closer to the woman.

"The New Way is the only way, Lindsay. You have to see that," she growled.

Jennifer kept moving closer, forcing Lindsay to walk backwards. They moved down the aisle until Lindsay's butt came in contact with one of the many sinks perpendicular to the lockers.

Jennifer grinned. "No more room."

Lindsay looked behind her at the sink and the mirror above, realizing that Jennifer's saying had an even more immediate meaning; there was no where left for Lindsay to go.

"Excuse me, Mrs. Mayor?"

Jennifer spun around to see Heather standing in the doorway, gun raised. John stood to her side, his gun also poised at her head.

"That's no way to treat a voter," Heather said as

the mayor began to move away from Lindsay and toward the two intruders. Heather stared at Jennifer's eyes, and saw that at some point within the last half hour, they had lost Jennifer Adams to Thomas Manning.

With Jennifer's attraction on the cop, Lindsay made a break for it, running down the row of sinks and back into the first aisle of lockers. Once there, she jumped on top of the bench and gave the lockers a shove with her shoulder. They rocked forward — she could hear the screws giving way — then they rocked back, the lockers settling in place.

With one final push of adrenaline combined with muscle power and pure fear, Lindsay was able to rock them forward once more. This time she heard the screws crack and break, and the lockers came tumbling town, right on top of the changed Jennifer Adams.

The Mayor of Westmont let out a grunt as the lockers — ten of them connected together side-by-side — slammed into her.

Walking back around the row with trepidation, Lindsay was both shocked and pleased to see that the lockers had done their job. Jennifer now lay smashed between them and the bench, her face staring up at the ceiling. Her back was bent the wrong way, forcing the woman into a reverse right-angle.

Lindsay let out a cry as blood shot from Jennifer's mouth and into the air as the lockers settled into their new place.

John and Heather re-holstered their weapons and approached the Mayor of Westmont. Heather bent down over the body and felt for a pulse even though she had a feeling she wouldn't find one.

She was right. Jennifer Adams was as dead as they got.

Lindsay looked down at the cop. "Her eyes, they went all... she was... one of them," she stammered.

"I know, I saw," said Heather. She closed her own eyes and let her hand rest on the dead woman's throat. "We have to tie her up."

Lindsay put a hand to her head. Her face was pale, and from the looks of her, she was about to drop and vomit any second. "I can't be in here anymore," she said. "I'm sorry."

John and Heather watched Lindsay carefully step over Mayor Adams' body. She kept her neck bent, eyes up, not wanting to see a single inch of what lay on the ground. Once past the body, she shuffled quickly out of the locker room.

"Why doesn't he just come inside himself and finish the job?" Heather asked. "Why all the games? What's the point of keeping us all in here?"

The answer clicked with John quickly, which surprised him. If there *was* a Higher Power watching over them, part of that protection came in the form of his brain moving along the paths of equations faster than usual.

"If he keeps us here, he knows where we are," he said. "Keep your friends close, and your enemies closer."

354

"And we're not a threat if he knows where we are."

John looked at her sharply. "We need to find a way out of here. A way that he won't know about."

Heather walked to the sink and stared at herself in the darkened mirror. The light from the lantern didn't do much to illuminate her face, but she could tell she looked like shit. Bags under her eyes, her make-up long gone, dirty sweat stains down her cheeks. She might not be able to see them in the mirror, but she knew they were there.

"Some fucking cop," Heather said to herself in the mirror. "My partner, my friend... God, there was nothing I could do."

John walked up to her and tenderly, quietly, put his hands on her shoulders and turned her around so he could look her straight in the eyes. "You can't blame yourself for that. Blame like that will haunt you forever. I know."

"Then what did you do? How did you get over it? You said yourself you felt it was your fault, so what did you do?! Tell me John, *how did you get over it?!?*"

"I didn't."

Heather pushed him away, turned around again and looked at herself in the mirror. Not being able to face her own eyes, she looked down to the sink. She watched tears fall from her eyes and roll down the drain.

"You're a lot of help, you know that?" Heather said.

"It may not be helpful. But it's realistic. You just have to learn to live with it."

"How?"

"By getting on with things. Doing what you were meant to do. Living the life you think they would have wanted for you," John said.

"Is that what you do?"

"I try. The pain never goes away. Never. But you can keep it at bay. That's the best any of us can do," said John. "Do what you do. Be a cop. Help others. Help us."

Heather couldn't hold back her tears anymore. She didn't fall apart and bawl; that wasn't her style. She gritted her teeth, lips shaking, and felt her eyes fill with tears she didn't know she had. Her hands gripped the sides of the sink tightly, turning her knuckles white. She sucked in a shaky breath and said: "Distraction."

"What?"

Heather let go of the sink to wipe the tears from her eyes and turned around to face John. She was thankful for the darkness for once. "We can use Lindsay as a distraction. Tell her one thing, hope that he hears it through her, then do something entirely different."

"This is, of course, assuming that none of the rest of us are like Jennifer," John pointed out. "Who knows how long he had a hold on her."

The two of them jumped at the sound of footsteps coming from the stairs. John spun around as Heather put her hand to her gun.

"Shit, Jesus guys, it's just me," Gloria said. She looked at Heather, and at the immense sadness that seemed to be emanating from the woman. "What happened?"

"Help him tie up Adams," Heather said to Gloria.

Gloria looked down to the floor where Heather was pointing. Laying there was her former boss and mentor. A small shriek popped out of Gloria's mouth. "What hap-" she started. Then, "What did you do to her?"

She began to move towards Jennifer's body. John grabbed Gloria by the arm, holding her back.

"Don't," he said. "She's one of them."

Gloria let the writer hold her as she stared at the body of Jennifer Adams. "No," Gloria sobbed.

John pulled her closer to him. "I'm sorry. But I need you to be strong now. I need your help tying her up."

"No, I can't," she said. "Why do I have to-"

"Just help me. Heather needs to keep an eye on Lindsay," John said.

Heather put a hand on Gloria's shoulder, a small touch of comfort before turning and heading back up the stairs.

John and Gloria stood over the body of Jennifer Adams as he brought the girl up-to-date in regards to their theory on Lindsay. It seemed to make sense in a weird, maniacal way. Gloria was up for keeping Lindsay in the dark in an effort to find a means of escape from the high school.

They saw no reason to remove the row of lockers from Jennifer — they would do a good job of keeping the mayor in place should she decide to come back. Not willing to put anything past Thomas Manning — he was a lot of things, and one of them was certainly not an idiot — they grabbed handfuls of towels from a nearby basin and proceeded to tie them around Jennifer's wrists, connecting her to the bench.

John tightened his knot. "That oughta do it. If our Mayor wakes up and goes all *Evil Dead* on us, this'll at least buy us some time." John secured the knot around a leg of the bench and tested it for weaknesses, doing his best to ensure it wouldn't come loose.

John stood up, his knees letting out pops of strain. "He's getting stronger."

Gloria tightened the last of her knots and got to her feet herself. "Maybe the more souls he takes, the stronger he gets. Maybe eventually, no matter how innocent the rest of us are, he'll be able to get to us, too."

It finally began to sink in to John that they lived in a New World, now. A world where all the rules had changed. Fuck that. The rules hadn't changed: they were downright *gone*.

John's eyes followed the drip, drip, drip of the blood from Jennifer's mouth to the floor. It created a river of red between the small one-inch square tiles, turning the white caulk that kept them waterproof and connected into a dark red — almost black

— in the low light. The blood moved down a slight slant in the floor, one John wouldn't have noticed if not for the blood traveling down it. It finally found its way to a drain a few feet from them in the middle of the room. John listened, and he heard it. The dead quiet of the school, with no air-conditioning to drown out any ambient noise and the hum of the lights long gone, made the dripping of the blood all that much louder.

The blood was dripping down the drain and landing somewhere.

"Holy shit," he said.

"What?"

"Below the school."

"Care to elaborate?"

"He's blocked us in on all sides and above us. But not *below us*."

"So?"

John looked at her and smiled. "So I think we just found a way out of here."

58.

"Christ on a stick. What hit me?"

Heather and Lindsay turned from their positions on the edge of the bench Richard laid on, near his feet, to face the now conscious doctor. Lindsay jumped up, nearly slipping on the slick wet floor. She stumbled unceremoniously to her husband's side.

"You're awake," she said, stroking his hair.

"It doesn't feel like it," he said, trying to get up. "I'll give you two-thousand dollars to knock me back out."

Heather put out a restraining hand.

Richard obliged, and instead looked down at his right arm, nestled in a sling made of John's blue-striped button-up shirt. His eyes crossed with Heather's as the day's events came back to him.

"Were we attacked by... basketballs?" he asked, sounding as unsure about the question as any sane person would.

"I'm afraid so. You cracked your elbow and tore your shoulder out of its socket," Heather explained.

"It doesn't hurt too bad. My body must still be in shock."

Heather was happy to see that Richard still seemed to have his senses about him. Whether or not he had enough of them left for what lay ahead, she didn't know. She wasn't looking forward to asking this man, a seemingly nice man, that he might have to lie to and deceive his wife.

"My first broken bone. By a basketball." He shut his eyes. "And I always thought it'd be something cool like mountain climbing." With his eyes still closed, Richard leaned his head back. He lay there motionless, slowly breathing in and out, in and out.

Lindsay and Heather worried throughout the pause that Richard was slipping away again into Never-Never Land. He seemed ready to pass out at any second. He surprised (and relieved) them both by turning to Lindsay. "Have you heard the Voice?"

Heather winced at the question.

"No," Lindsay answered. "He's been quiet since we got here."

Richard patted his wife's hand with his good one. "That's good, baby. I'm real glad to hear that."

"But he got to Jennifer," Heather said flatly.

Richard turned back to Heather, startled. "Is she...?"

"She's no longer with us," Heather said.

From the stairway to the girl's locker room,

361

John led Gloria back into the vicinity. Their faces were determined. As if there was a plan of action now, and that the plan wasn't a good one, but the *only* one.

As John walked closer, he saw that the good doctor was awake, and a smile of relief came to the writer's face. "Welcome back."

"Hiya!" Gloria half-screamed, more pleased than anyone with the realization that at least someone else hadn't died in the past ten minutes.

"Hey guys," Richard said, his voice becoming shaky and a little stressed-sounding. Apparently being awake for this long and the task of just sitting up was taking its toll on the man.

John gave Heather a glance, talking to her with his eyes. Reading his expression, which was becoming easier by the minute, she knew what he wanted.

"Lindsay," Heather said, "why don't you and Gloria head into the locker room — the boy's locker room — maybe there's some bottled water in there, something like that."

"And some towels," John added. "I could use some to wipe this shit offa me."

"Yeah ya' could," Heather said with a smile.

Lindsay bent over and kissed Richard on the forehead. She found it drenched with perspiration and hot to the touch of her lips. "I'll be back in a bit, baby," she said as she got to her feet.

"Thank you," he said. "Lindsay."

She stopped half-stride on her way to Gloria. "Yeah?"

"I love you, baby-cakes" he said.

"I love you, too, sweetie-pie" Lindsay replied.

Lindsay spun on her heel and followed Gloria to the boy's locker room. When they were down the stairs and out of sight — and more importantly out of earshot — Richard's smile turned upside down.

"So," he said to John. "Tell me the rest of the bad news."

"I can't say that I like it, but what's to like?" Richard said after hearing John and Heather's idea to use his wife as a distraction against Thomas Manning. Keeping information from her — and feeding her *wrong* information — might be their best and only course of action.

"Or we may be crazy," John said.

"All you need is a jackhammer, and you guys are out scot-free," said Richard.

"I'm not so sure about the *free* part, but we'll definitely be out," Heather said. "I guess the next big question is *how*."

"I'm no architect, but even if we *could* make a hole big enough in the floor, there's bound to be concrete for a foundation," John said.

They couldn't dig. They all knew that. They all also felt as if they were onto something, but that it was just out of their reach. It was like tasting a favorite dish you had loved as a child made by someone other than Mom and knowing an ingredient or two was missing or just plain wrong.

Richard tried to move his arm, stretch it, get

some of the kinks out of it. The pain was starting to come back, so he stopped when it felt like a hundred knives had been pushed into his entire arm, up and down. "Does the school have a basement?"

Heather's breathing halted for a few brief moments. "There's got to be."

Something was still blinking DOES NOT COMPUTE in the back of John's mind. He found the lighter in his hand again, not knowing how long he had been holding it. But there it was, covered in dust and grime and sweat, hiding his initials. He used his Metallica shirt to do a quick cleaning, and the letters re-appeared.

His hands shook, possibly from stress, fright, nervousness, or the ever popular answer of "D": all of the above. The lighter fell out of his hand and *clanked* on the floor. Bending over to pick it up, John found the second part of the equation.

"If there *is* a basement, that means we're not at the base of the school. Maybe the blood ran down the drain not because he's not blocking it, but because it wasn't at the bottom," John said.

"Christ, we could get to the basement only to realize *that* was where he had us cut off," Heather realized.

There was a long silence among the three of them. They had made it to Final Jeopardy, but it looked like none of them had the answer written down in the form of a question to plop down on the monitor.

Richard broke the silence. "Things will not always be this way."

"Excuse me?" Heather asked.

"Things won't always be this way," he repeated. "Something I tell my patients when they can't find a solution, when they can't see a way out of whatever dilemma they're in. Things won't always be great, but they won't always be terrible, either."

"Are you saying we should give up? Just sit around, wait for this guy to show up?" Heather asked.

"Look, you don't know what it's like out there," Richard said. "Whatever's happened out there may not be something you want to be a part of. You may be better off here."

John stood up, staring at his lighter. It had become his source of strength, of hope. He hadn't held onto hope for this long only to have to chuck it in the trash and give up.

He shoved the lighter into his pants pocket. "I'm not giving up. I'm done sitting around, waiting for things to get better. I control my life, not some nut-ball from God-knows-where. We're gettin' out of here, one way or another, and whatever this guy's doin', we're gonna stop him. Things won't always be this way 'cause we're gonna change 'em."

Richard smiled. "Good man."

John looked at him, perplexed.

"You just needed a swift kick in the ass," Richard said. "You can't give up. Ever."

John raised an eyebrow at the psychiatrist. "Do people actually *pay* you for this kind of advice?"

"Most of the time."

John looked to Heather. "You comin' with?"

Gildy's badge rested in Heather's hand. She looked at it much like John had eyeballed his lighter, and he thought she had her talisman ready for the journey, too.

"You'd better fucking believe it," she said, hooking Gildy's badge onto her belt. "This guy's got a good ass-kickin' comin' his way." She turned to Richard. "If we can take him out, maybe his hold on the others will drop."

"And just how do you plan on doing that?" Richard asked.

Heather shrugged. "I haven't the foggiest fucking idea."

John reached out to shake Richard's hand. With his right arm being in the make-shift sling assembled from John's shirt, Richard maneuvered his left hand to shake John's right one.

"I'll want that shirt back."

"It'll be here."

"Thanks," John said.

"Good luck."

John let go of his hand. "Are you sure you're up to this? Lying to your wife, I mean."

Richard closed his eyes. When he opened them again, he looked to the entrance of the boy's locker room, where Gloria and Lindsay were returning from their scavenger hunt. "If he gets a hold on her, she won't be my wife anymore."

"I'm sorry," John said.

"We'll come back for you," Heather said.

"You'd better."

"Just remember one thing, doc," said John.

"What's that?"

"Things won't always be this way."

From the boy's locker room, Gloria and Lindsay had secured five bottles of water, a bottle of aspirin for Richard, and a handful of towels they could use to freshen up with.

Richard swallowed a fistful of the pain relievers while John and Heather kneeled over the pool, using the chlorinated water to wet their towels. The water was cool on their faces and revitalized them both. Within a few minutes, they no longer looked like complete shit.

John glanced behind them. Lindsay was nursing her husband back to health. Gloria gracefully sipped her water, looking as calm as if she were in a restaurant waiting for a waiter to saunter by with a menu and complimentary bread. It dawned on him just how strong this kid was; eating for two and stuck in one of the weirdest situations he could imagine. Food had been scarce in the school, and none of them had had a decent meal in well over a day — yet Gloria seemed full of energy and zeal, ready to take on the world.

"We sure about this?" Heather whispered to John.

"I don't think we have much of a choice."

"I was afraid you'd say that."

367

John dipped his towel in the pool again and let the cold water trickle down his arms. "What do we do after this?"

"What do you mean?"

"Let's say we get out of here. Let's say we find this guy, take him out, kill him, whatever it is we're supposed to do. That won't change anything. We'll still be without power. And who knows what will happen to everybody under his thumb once Thomas Manning is gone," John said.

Heather brought a soaked towel to her head and ran it over her eyes. "One thing at a time, John. I'm not even sure how we can kill this guy, or even if we can. Let's just concentrate on getting out of here, first." She wiped her eyes dry with her fingers. "And don't rinse out your eyes."

John began to laugh as he looked over at Heather's now red and puffy eyelids. "Yeah, I've heard that chlorine burns."

The two stood in unison, dropping their towels on the floor. Heather slicked her hair back, feeling semi-clean for the first time in days. John felt for the lighter in his pocket. It was still there, and for whatever reason, that comforted him.

"How are we playing this?" John asked.

"Follow my lead."

As the two approached the bench, Heather discovered she had no lead for him to follow. Richard, who seemed to have an answer for every occasion at just the right time, suggested the two of them — John and Heather — take a walk to the cafeteria for another food run. He was feeling light-headed, and thought they could all use a snack; there was no telling when their next meal would be.

Lindsay put up no argument. She was pleased as punch to have some alone time with her ailing husband, and promised the three she'd keep an eye on him.

John leaned over Richard's shoulder and whispered. The doctor listened and nodded. John helped him to his feet, and they began to walk towards the boy's locker room.

"Just where do you think you guys are going?" Lindsay asked, getting to her feet.

"Guy stuff," John answered over his shoulder.

Heather lightly seized Lindsay by the elbow and kept her from following them. "Let them go."

Lindsay's eyebrows formed a crude triangle on her forehead as she asked, "This has to do with me, doesn't it?"

"I don't know."

"I can't know what's really going on. Because if I know, *he* knows."

Heather loosened her grip on the woman. Lindsay may have heard the Voice, but she was far from stupid. "I'm sorry."

"No fucking way," Richard said with a tremble in his voice.

"I'm not leaving you here without it."

"Well, you're gonna have to," Richard said, then pushed the gun that John had been holding out to him away.

"You don't know what will happen. You don't know if he'll try and come for her."

Richard leaned against a locker, letting the coolness of the metal sink into his forehead. "If that's the way it goes, so be it."

John held out the gun again. "Don't be stupid."

Richard Stone moved away from the temporary sanctuary of the locker and stared at John. "I'm not going to shoot my wife."

John bowed his head. "If any of those other wackos come back, you'll want some sort of defense. It'll at least buy you some time. It's better to have it and not use it than to not have it and wish you had."

Richard smiled. "*Now* who's the shrink?"

Heather adjusted her holster and once again inspected Gildy's badge — still there, still dirty with blood.

"Why do you keep staring at that?" Lindsay asked.

"Huh?"

"That badge. You're holding onto it like it's a million dollar bill."

Heather straightened it on her belt. "It was my partner's."

"The one that died?"

"Yeah."

"I'm sorry."

Heather stood there motionless, her eyes focused on a tile on the floor. "It's okay."

"Everyone ready?" John asked as he and Richard returned from the locker room.

"As ready as I'll ever be," Gloria answered.

John stared at Gloria with eyes of ice. "You're staying here."

"Why? You guys are just going for some food. I could use the walk, stretch my legs a bit," she said, smiling, knowing that John couldn't put up his real reason for not wanting her to tag along for fear of Lindsay discovering their true plans. But Gloria wanted in on the excursion, John could see it written all over her face.

"Fine," was all he could say.

Lindsay reached for her husband's hand. His eyes were saddened, troubled. She caressed his fingers with her own.

"We'll be back in less than an hour," Heather said. "Anything happens, just scream."

"No worries there," Richard said. "Good luck."

"You, too," John said. He didn't like it, but he had the distinct feeling that would be the last thing he'd ever say to his new friend. He followed Gloria and Heather out of the room, flashing the doctor a quick "peace" sign.

Richard and Lindsay watched the doors close behind the trio. They heard someone (probably John) lock both floor-bolts. Their footsteps moved down the hallway, and soon enough, it was dead quiet again.

Richard turned to Lindsay and gave her a kiss,

371

brushed her hair. He looked into his wife's eyes. They were the same dark green as they were the day they met, although now the whites were overcome by jagged red veins. But they were *her* eyes, and he could tell by losing himself in the blackness of her pupils that Lindsay was still Lindsay.

That could change in the near-future, and he knew it. But for right now it was just Mr. and Mrs. Stone, enjoying an evening (or day — he had lost all track of time since entering the high school) alone together by the pool. The mutilation of his arm didn't seem to matter anymore. All that mattered was that he was allowed another few moments with the woman he had fallen in love with ten years ago.

"How's the arm?" she asked.

"Been better."

Lindsay reached for one of the dry towels stacked on the bench. "You're burning up," she said as she took the three steps to the pool and dipped the towel in the water.

While her back was facing him, Richard reached behind him into his pants and pulled out the gun. Keeping his eyes locked on Lindsay, he shoved the weapon between two of the folded towels still on the bench.

59.

John took the lead, holding the lantern above his head so the others could see. He imagined he looked like an explorer from one of those flicks he loved as a child, taking a deadly journey into King Solomon's mines. There was always a giant spider, a hive of hidden evil local tribesmen, or a lost world of ancient dinosaurs. He was fairly certain there'd be no dinosaurs, but if one or two happened to appear, that would be about par for the course for John's week.

"Did he take it?" Heather asked him.

"Yeah, wasn't too happy about it, either."

"Can you blame him?" Gloria chimed in. "It's not every day your wife jumps off the Looney Tunes bridge and you're told you might have to shoot her."

John halted and turned to face the girl. "Look, I don't know what it was you thought you were pull-

373

ing back there, but you're not coming with us. You stay in the school, out of sight, until we come back."

"The hell I am," Gloria said. "I want outta this place."

"You don't know what's out there," John argued.

"And neither do you. But I know in here there's no chance, nothing to do but wait. Out there — out there at least there's the hope of getting away from this thing."

Heather went to pull John back as he started toward Gloria. He brushed her arm away.

"This is most likely a one way trip," he told her. "We're not getting away from this thing. We're walking right into it."

"Then you'll need all the help you can get," Gloria said as she swept past John and continued down the hallway.

John glanced over at Heather, who simply shrugged. "I'm glad I never any had kids," he said as he turned to follow Gloria.

They hung a right down another hallway, letting the silence from John and Gloria's spat take over. Heather shook her head, not being able to take either one's side. They both had very good points. It was more a matter of who was more stubborn than the other, and in that contest, it looked like John was the clear loser.

"Gloria," John said, breaking the silence. "I don't suppose you know if the school has a basement, do ya'?"

"I didn't build the fucking thing," she answered coyly.

"Look, I'm sorry," John said. "I was just trying to look out for you."

"I appreciate that, but I don't need any looking out for," she said.

She turned them left down another hallway they hadn't been through yet. This one offered no basketballs to swoop down from above and pummel them to death and no crazy dead people.

They passed two doors down the short corridor: a janitor's closet and the teacher's lounge. Confident that neither of those would lead to a basement, they continued forward and came to an open area that John figured to be about a quarter of the size of a football field. Classrooms were more open than closed, separated by office dividers that had been bolted to the floor, creating eight separate "rooms" on either side of them.

Heather peered into the first room, and from the posters on the wall she came to the obvious conclusion that it was a German class. The name *Herr Randill* was engraved into the nameplate that sat on the desk.

"Mr. Randill still works here?" she asked Gloria.

"The man's never gonna die," she said. Then realized the absurdity of her comment — most likely, Herr Randill was either dead or one of the changed by now.

When they came to the end of the rows of divided classrooms, they were presented with an even larger open area. To their left was another set of doors, blocked by whatever black shit the Man in the Dark Coat was using. Before them was a set of giant glass windows — the principal's office. Heather was reminded of an early spelling lesson she had had as a child when she was six, maybe seven. In order to remember the correct spelling of *principal*, their teacher (Mrs. MacMurphy, she couldn't believe she remembered *that*, too) told them, quite simply, "The Prince is your Pal." It had seemed like an idiotic sentiment at the time, but it had worked — almost thirty years later, and she still remembered it.

To their right was, if John's geography of the school was correct, another entrance to the cafeteria. He motioned in that direction. "Cafeteria?"

"Yeah."

"Seems to me if there was a basement, it'd be in the middle of the school. That appears to be the middle," he said.

"What makes you think that?" Gloria asked.

"I don't know. I didn't build the fucking thing," John said with a smile.

Gloria laughed.

"Okay. Let's check it out," Heather said.

The cafeteria was dark, dreary, and all things considered, not a place any of them wanted to hang around for much longer than they needed to. There were too many dark corners, too many shadows, too many tables and chairs and utensils that could come to life. Heather was pretty sure that wouldn't happen without Lindsay around. She hoped they were as blind to Manning now as they had seemed to be before.

Moving through the room, it was Gloria who spotted a door to their far right. It was unmarked, with one simple silver knob.

John put his hand around it, positive it would be locked. He turned it and waited for the *snap-click* of the lock resisting the twist. When the knob silently turned and allowed the door to be opened, John sucked in a breath in surprise.

Maybe someone was watching out for them, after all.

The door swung inwards, and after a brief landing, there were a set of stairs leading down. The light from the lantern couldn't cut through the darkness below. They'd be going in blind. But at least the stairs went in the direction they wanted: down.

"Okay, kids. Anyone who doesn't have a permission slip from their parents should turn around now," John said as he stepped through the doorway. Heather and Gloria followed close behind.

The stairs leading to the basement, fifty of them by Heather's count, ended in a large rectangular room. The dim light made it difficult for her to see into the corners.

Gloria stood between her and John, still in single-file from the walk down the stairs. There seemed to be an unspoken rule between John and the cop that Gloria needed to be protected. Heather didn't know why — Gloria seemed to be handling all of this better than her and John combined — it was just something they felt. She was, after all, soon to be bringing a new life into the world. Or what would be left of it.

Heather's eyes moved to the corner of the room, covered in murkiness. "John."

He looked over to see her nod toward the corner. Once the light from the lantern broke through the darkness, they spotted a metal grate on the floor. It wasn't big, but large enough to fit a person through.

John put the gas lantern on the ground and placed a hand over the grate. "There's a breeze."

"And a smell," Gloria added.

No one had noticed it until Gloria said it, but there was a smell in there, alright. To Heather, it smelled an awful lot like shit.

"The sewer," Heather said as John lifted the grill. It swung open, the hinges creaking and grinding against the metal. He laid it to rest against the wall in front of him. Picking up the lantern again, he looked down into the opening.

"There's a ladder," John said. "She's right. Looks like we found ourselves the sewer."

"At the bottom of a high school? *My* high school?" Gloria asked.

John handed the lantern to Gloria. "Apparently so." He turned himself around and dropped his feet into the hole. Holding himself up with his arms straight, palms on the floor, he looked up at the two women who now towered over him. "If an alligator jumps up and bites my ass, you two should find another way outta here."

They remained silent as John's feet found the top rung of the ladder and he began to climb down. It wasn't long, five seconds at most, when they heard him hit bottom and call up.

"No 'gators. C'mon down."

Gloria passed the lantern to Heather, who waited behind her.

"You gonna be able to make it down okay?" Heather asked.

"If I go down backwards, my back against the ladder, I should be able to, yeah."

Heather watched the girl, this very, very pregnant girl, find her way into a sitting position above the hole that led to the sewer, her legs dangling over the edge.

"Better gimme a push," Gloria said.

Grinning, Heather put the lantern down. With her hands at the small of Gloria's back, she gently pushed her further over the edge. When she felt Gloria drop, her heart raced into her throat.

But the kid only dropped two inches when the heels of her sneakers found the ladder. Heather washed away images of the girl falling into the sewers of Westmont and cracking her head on the damp and shit-covered surface of whatever floor there was down there.

"I'm okay," Gloria said, reassuringly. Evidently she had heard Heather's mild heart attack.

"I can see up your dress," John called from below.

"Nice," Gloria said.

Gloria slowly made her way down, one rung at a time, biting her lower lip the entire way.

When John had called up that Gloria had made it safe and sound, Heather held the lantern above the hole. As she peered down into the short abyss, she saw John standing there, ready to catch the lantern as she dropped it.

She swung around and lowered herself into the sewer. When she was down far enough, she reached up and behind her for the grating. She pulled it down, and it slammed with an echo Richard and Lindsay probably heard.

"Sorry," she said as her feet splashed water and refuse on the cuffs of John's pants. "Sorry about that, too."

"It's okay. I think these jeans have seen their day."

Gloria moved away from the two and leaned against the side wall. Bending over as well as she could, she wretched up the majority of the crackers she had gulped down from the cafeteria. Her vomit landed with a wet *plop*, and John was lucky enough to move his shoes out of the way just in time. Not that it mattered — they were wading in sewage, and a little vomit would probably go unnoticed.

"Okay, this goes down as the grossest two minutes of my life," he said.

Gloria wiped her mouth. "It *really* smells down here."

"Which way?" Heather asked.

There were only two directions to choose from. The three of them had gotten turned around so much, none of them could decide which way was which.

Gloria pointed to her left, down a long cylindrical passage of waste and refuse. "I think Quincy is that way."

"Let's hope you're right," John said. "I'd hate to have to walk all the way *back* through this shit."

With that, the three moved down the sewer corridor, single file with Gloria once again between John and Heather, hopefully on their way towards Quincy Street and a man who had a fondness for trench coats.

Into The Light, Into The Darkness

60.

"Can't be more than two or three miles," Heather said. "If we're moving south, and I think we are, we'll wanna veer west at some point. But without street names, I'm afraid I can't be any more specific than that."

She estimated they had come a third of a mile at most, somewhere below Oakwood Drive which lead to and from the high school. It had taken them thirty minutes to get this far. The stench, a mixture of shit, piss, rat droppings, and God knew what else, was becoming almost unbearable.

"So you're saying eventually we need to surface," John said.

"Yes. To get our bearings."

"Is that such a good idea?" Gloria asked. "I mean, they could still be out there. The changed people."

John took a step, a Reebok submerging itself

into a small pool of liquid. He pulled his foot out with a "yuck," and shook the excess water (and something else) off.

"I don't think so," he said, still shaking his foot. "We've got to be out from under the school by now, and we haven't heard a thing from up there." He pointed up, referencing what might or might not be Oakwood Drive. "I think whatever was happening up there is over."

"But you don't know that, not for sure," Gloria said.

"Would you rather stay down here, see if it takes us to Indiana, maybe?" John said.

"Of course not, but-"

"Look, we're out of the school for a reason," Heather said. "He's still out there and as long as he's out there-"

"I know," Gloria said. "I know."

John moved ahead of them, raising the lantern higher. The light from it began to dim, and he realized there wasn't much gas left in it. It seemed like their hand might be forced sooner than they would like — they certainly couldn't negotiate the sewers in the dark.

John coughed. "If there's no more room in Hell, this place could certainly fill in for it."

Heather laughed. "No kidding."

"What does that mean, anyway?" Gloria asked. "'No more room in Hell'?"

"Well," Heather said, sloshing through the water, "if we take into consideration all the people that have ever been alive, and we're talking, what, billions?"

"Sure," John said. "Billions."

"Billions of people have been born and died. As wonderful as a lot of folks seem to think they are, I'd be willing to bet a vast majority of them end up going to Hell," said Heather. "We've all sinned at some point in our lives."

John covered his nose, trying to avoid the stink that couldn't be avoided. "You would think Hell would be infinite."

"Apparently it's not," Heather said.

John waded through the water and gave up trying to evade the scent of the sewer; it was a lost cause. "You actually believe all this shit."

"I'm agnostic," Heather said. "I believe what I see. And I've seen enough in the past two days to make me give the 'no more room in Hell' theory a shot."

"What about you, kid?" John asked, looking over his shoulder at Gloria. "What's the faithful one's take on all this?"

"We're being tested," she said.

John bowed and shook his head. "Here we go with *this* bullshit now."

Gloria didn't let John's words faze her. "While it makes me wonder why so many people would end up in Hell; there're things called forgiveness, and repentance, and Purgatory, for God's sake. We can atone for our sins — this isn't the first time something like this has happened."

John stopped dead in his tracks. He swung the lantern around and faced Gloria. "Really? I missed class the day they told us about the last time there was a massive power outage and the dead came back to life."

Gloria didn't back down. "I said something *like* this. Not this *exactly*. Pay attention."

John turned back around and picked up the pace again. The water (it was more than that, but in all their minds, it was best to think of it as only water) had gotten deeper. They found themselves ankle-deep in the muck whether they liked it or not.

Gloria continued. "Noah's Ark."

"Excuse me?" John asked.

"Noah's Ark," she repeated. "Deciding that wickedness and sin had run rampant on His earth, God decided to wipe out sin — which meant most of mankind had to go. But not all of his creatures were complete, um..."

"Fuck-ups?" John offered.

"That works," said Gloria. "Not all of his creatures were complete fuck-ups, so he told Noah to build his Ark, and you know the rest of the story."

Heather smiled. "So this is God's version of a wake up call?"

"You could say that."

"You let me know when we need to start stocking up on dogs and giraffes and shit, okay?" John said.

The three walked side-by-side in silence for a bit, each of them letting Gloria's observations and theories sink in. Gloria watched the back of John's head bob up and down with his walk — a kind of odd chicken-walk, now that she noticed it — wondering how someone seemingly so smart and literate could be such a stubborn asshole.

Gloria jerked to her left, lifting her right leg out of the water. She let out a *yelp* and took John's arm in her own.

"I think something just bit me!" she barked.

John looked down without bending (he had no desire to get any closer to the sewage than he already was) and thought he saw a few bubbles pop in the surface of the water.

"Probably just a rat," he said calmly. "Just keep moving. You feel another one, kick it."

"A *rat?!?*" Gloria shouted. "This walk just gets worse and worse."

"It didn't start out all that great," Heather said.

Gloria put a finger up to her mouth, turning to face Heather. "Shh."

"What? I-"

"*Shut up,*" Gloria whispered. She tilted her head to the side, allowing John and Heather to look at one another over her shoulder. They both had question marks in their eyes, and John shrugged.

John was about to tell them to keep it moving when he heard whatever Gloria had heard, too.

The scurrying was faint at first. John thought it sounded like someone filing their nails. Dozens of nails at once. As the scampering got closer, it got louder and began to sound more and more like feet.

Hundreds and hundreds of tiny little feet.

Gloria squinted into the darkness as John lifted the lantern higher, trying to give as much light to the path behind them as he could.

The shadows that the gaslight produced made the sewer look like a disco out of Dr. Seuss' worst nightmare. The clap-clap-clapping grew in volume. Heather narrowed her eyes, and the laser surgery she had three years ago to correct her near-sightedness paid off.

"Rats," she said.

Out of the shadows, across the sides of the walls, and from the water itself, came hundreds, perhaps thousands, of large rats, their fur matted to their skin from the watery sewage.

"I don't think I can kick all those," Gloria said, panic creeping into her voice.

"Let's move," John said.

They broke into a run, as good of a run as they could manage in the underground river. The lantern shook in John's hand, and the light and shadows danced about madly on the walls, making the thousands of rats behind them look like millions. He took a chance and looked behind them again.

The rats were gaining on them.

And somehow, he was sure of it, the little fuckers were *smiling at them.*

Heather spotted a ladder leading to the surface fifty feet ahead of them. A tiny speck of light poked through the ceiling above the ladder; a manhole cover.

"There!" she yelled.

She pushed John and Gloria ahead of her, knocking the lantern out of John's grip. It crashed into the water, and the light quickly faded away.

They reached the ladder, and Heather forced John forward to be the first one up.

"No, Gloria first," he said.

"You first. Then you pull her up. She won't make it on her own," Heather ordered.

John knew she was right, so he climbed up the ladder, two rungs at a time, hoping that he'd be fast enough to avoid having his ankles nibbled on by any of the rats.

John's eyes screamed in pain from the bright light of the afternoon sun. He squinted as he slid the manhole cover to the side. Palms on the ground, he pulled himself up and out of the sewer.

They had wound up across the street from the high school, in the parking lot of the nearby junior high. To his right was the high school itself, although it wasn't a high school anymore.

It was a big black nothing.

It had the shape of the school, the height, and the width, but it was completely covered in blackness and didn't seem to possess any depth whatsoever. He could make out no surface or texture on the building; it was as if the high school had been cut out of existence, leaving an opening to nothingness.

It simply wasn't there.

"Lil' help, please?" Gloria called from below.

Putting the strangeness of what he saw across the street in the back of his mind, John leaned down and grabbed Gloria's hands. He pulled her out of the sewer while Heather pushed from behind. Gloria's feet found the ground, then her eyes found — or didn't find — the high school.

"Jesus," she said. "What *is* that?"

Heather crawled out and stood behind the two. She looked where they looked, to the open space in reality where the high school used to be.

"There's nothing there," Heather said.

"I know. It's hurting my eyes," said John.

John took a quick survey of their immediate surroundings. The parking lot of the junior high, where they now stood, had five empty cars in various parking spots. Across the street and to the left of the high school were houses, and to the right of the high school was an empty baseball field.

"Where *is* everyone?" Gloria said the second it hit John what was missing from the scene: there were no people at all. Anywhere. As far as they could see, the town was deserted.

"They're gone," Heather said. "He took them."

"Where?" Gloria asked.

"Somewhere else." John turned around and faced Blackhawk Drive, just on the other side of the parking lot. "I think we can take Blackhawk to Cass. That'll take us straight across the tracks to Quincy."

Gloria wiped sweat from her face. "Then it's a

quick jog to Manning's place."

Heather pulled her gun, checking to ensure the weapon was loaded, safety off, and ready for action.

John paused before they headed towards the road. There was something else missing, something else a little off about their surroundings.

"There's no noise," he finally figured out. "No birds, no dogs, I don't even hear leaves rustling in the breeze. Fuck that, I don't hear a *breeze*."

Heather and Gloria both listened.

"Holy shit, you're right," Gloria said. "There's nothing."

They all listened for a few more moments, hoping to hear a hungry dog bark for food from somebody's yard or a bird chirp from a nearby treetop. But they got none of that.

"Let's keep moving," John said, continuing en route for Blackhawk Drive.

Gloria moved back to her place beside John, with Heather on her other side so that she was once again cushioned between the two. They walked together to the road and hung a left, aiming themselves towards Cass Avenue.

61.

Lindsay pulled the freshly soaked towel from the pool and returned to her husband, who waited for her on the bench. She lovingly placed it on his forehead while he supported his broken arm with his good one.

"You're really burning up," she said.

Lindsay patted his head with the towel. A bead of pool water mixed with sweat made its way down Richard's cheek. Lindsay caught it before it fell off his chin. She took hold of two of Richard's fingers on the arm that still worked, gripping them tightly. He squeezed back weakly.

"I'm sorry," Lindsay said, barely a whisper.

"For what?"

"For making you come out here. For making you come with me to find my sister," she said, then paused. "Jesus, Amy. I'm never going to see her again, am I?"

"You don't know that."

"I can feel it, Richie."

"Listen," he said. "You saw what was happening just as well as I did. We had to leave Chicago, we had no other choice."

"And now things are so much better, huh?" She was fighting back tears now, and losing. "But you always tell me there's a choice, that we always have a choice, no matter what."

Richard tried to sit up and failed. The combination of the fever, which had come on quick and fierce, and the shock from the pain in his arm — which was returning in a big way — was too much for him.

"Maybe I was wrong," he grunted.

Lindsay surrendered to the tears that wanted out of her ducts. She made no effort to wipe them away. They swam down the contours of her face and collected at the base of her chin, where they then fell to the floor.

"But you're a fucking *psychiatrist*, Richard. I believed you. We always have a choice. You told me we always had a choice." Her bottom lip quivered. She was doing her best to not scream at him, to not slap him, to not fall to the floor and surrender more than just her tears.

Richard was quiet for a few moments. His own personal belief that they had control over their own destiny had been shot to hell over the course of the past two days. He was beginning to wonder if maybe they *never* had a choice, that maybe there was always someone out there, or up there, or down there, pulling the strings.

"I was wrong," he said again.

"But I-"

Lindsay's eyes went blank and she loosened her grip on Richard's fingers. She stared at the wall behind his head.

"Lindsay, baby, what is it?"

After a painful minute of Lindsay sitting there motionless, she finally said: "They're gone."

"Who?"

"The others. John, Gloria, that cop. He knows they're gone," she said.

"The Voice? Thomas Manning?"

She nodded her head.

"I thought he couldn't see them," Richard said.

"He can't. But there are... others, I think, out there. *They* can see them."

Her eyes locked with Richard's, and he got the impression she was staring at his very soul. "You knew," she said. "You knew they were leaving."

Richard moved to sit up again, ignoring the pain that stabbed at every cell in his body. He put his hand on Lindsay's shoulder and gave her his own stare right back.

"You have to ignore that Voice, Lindsay. Don't listen to it. *You can't listen to it.*"

"It's like you said; I might not have a choice."

"We're getting you out of here, we're getting as far away from this place as we can," Richard said.

"I don't think that'd make a difference. And I

don't think we'd make it."

"Why not?" he asked.

Lindsay bowed her head, squinting her eyes closed. Her whole head vibrated from her grinding teeth, the kind of grinding one does when one is in terrible pain.

"Because the Voice is telling me to kill you," she finally said. When she opened her eyes again, they were black. Black as night. "And I don't think I can ignore it this time."

62.

John figured they were now two or three blocks from Cass Avenue. They had yet to see anyone else out on the street. In the middle of the road, Ogden Avenue was riddled with abandoned cars that no longer worked — everything from a Saturn parked in the median to an old red Ford pickup. John thought it just might be the last traffic jam the street would ever see. One that would last forever.

To their right was the parking lot to the local supermarket, Jewel. Like the street, the parking lot was littered with empty cars, making it look like the store was still open and full of customers searching for the perfect fruit salad and the best cereal with the most grain for that early morning bowel movement.

A blue and pink baby carriage was on its side in the grass running perpendicular to the sidewalk, between them and the grocery store. There was no child inside (which John was thankful for — if he had seen a child in there that had died from starvation, he was pretty sure he'd go completely bat-shit insane) and the parents were long gone. He found himself wondering where they had gone; had the Man in the Dark Coat taken them, or had they been spared that unpleasantness and made it out of town?

If they had made it out of town, where did they go? And did it even matter?

John looked over to Gloria, whose eyes were locked on the stroller. A haunted look was on her face. Dark circles had formed under her eyes that made her look ten years older than she actually was. She was probably wondering the same thing John was right now, and what that meant for her own unborn child.

"How ya' holdin' up, sport?" he asked her.

Gloria snapped out of her nightmare. "Oh, just dandy."

"Let's go into the Jewel, stock up," Heather suggested.

"No, I'm fine, we should keep moving," Gloria said.

Heather smiled. "For one, none of us are fine. And for another, we should all eat something."

"Yeah, we wouldn't want to face this guy on empty stomachs," said John. "No tellin' what his hospitality is gonna be like."

Gloria tried to morph her frown into a smile, but it was a futile attempt at best. Her eyes were still glued to the baby carriage, and would probably stay there until she was forced to look away.

John took her by the arm and gently pulled her toward the parking lot. "Come on, you're eating for two. You'll feel better. Trust me."

Gloria managed to move her eyes away from the stroller. She looked at John and realized what he was really saying was *Stop looking at that, ignore the stroller, forget you even saw it.*

Gloria gave in. "I suppose you're right."

It took the strength of both John and Heather to push open the automatic electronic doors. John grunted as the dead motors whined in protest. With her gun drawn, Heather led them into the supermarket.

The stench of rotted food and stale air invaded their lungs. Without the constant refrigeration it desired, all of the fruit in the produce section had gone beyond bad in the summer heat. The smell wasn't as toxic as the one they had discovered in the sewer, but it was still plenty pungent.

The only windows in the building were along the walls facing Ogden Avenue and the few sets of doors spread about. Beyond that, past the cash registers, it was black as night.

John's foot kicked something on the ground. He looked down to watch a tiny MP3 player skirt across the freshly waxed floors and come to a stop in front of the One-Hour Photo.

The floor was covered with other such personal effects from the good people of Westmont. A pair of granny-glasses, lenses half an inch thick. A man's wallet, open to reveal his driver's license (Gary Henderson, 55, organ donor). A child's shoe rested by a bank of gumball machines next to checkout aisle #2.

"Okay, let's stick together. No one goes in back, we stay where there's light," said Heather.

"No argument here," John said.

They walked past the rows of cash registers, passing more and more items from people who seemed to have left the store in a hurry. It quickly became apparent why.

The first sign of violence they saw came in the form of a pool of blood on the conveyor belt of checkout aisle #9. More blood had been scattered across the impulse-buy lane, droplets of the stuff having landed on packs of Hubba-Bubba and Mentos.

Money — also covered in blood — was scattered across one of the bagging stations. Gloria eyed the bills and toed them with a shoe. "Couple hundred bucks," she said. "What the hell happened here?"

"Same thing that happened at the high school," John said.

Heather shook her head. "Except these people didn't have anywhere to hide."

John's stomach tossed and turned. "Suddenly I'm not hungry anymore."

"Me, neither," said Heather.

With the fruit section being a no-go, that left

them with the end caps to each of the ten aisles, and whatever was left in the impulse buy sections that wasn't covered in blood.

John tore open a twelve-pack of Coke and took out three cans, handing one each to Gloria and Heather, keeping one for himself. "We could all probably use the caffeine and sugar."

Gloria took the can, but didn't open it. Instead she held it up, as if she were auditioning for a TV commercial. Her wide eyes shot a stare through John, and he was positive the can would come hurtling at his head any second. *Holy shit, he's gotten to her. I'm gonna die because someone chucked a can of soda at my head.*

Instead, she said: "Coke? Really?"

"What's the problem?" he asked.

"You might as well get me liquored up for all the good this'll do the kid," Gloria answered. To remind him, she pointed at her belly, which was so immense, John was fairly certain there were at least three kids in there.

He took the can of Coke from her and placed it back in the open box. Not that any Jewel clean-up clerk would be running around the corner to make the end-cap tidy, it was just something John did. Civilization hadn't been lost on him. Not yet.

"Sorry, never had kids," was his excuse.

"And so, what, that makes you some sort of idiot?" Gloria scolded.

"Easy there," Heather scolded right back at her.

"I'm just givin' him a hard time, lighten up."

John looked around for a suitable replacement for the soda and walked to the nearest checkout aisle. "You know that video they make you watch in high school, the one where they show that lady giving birth?" he asked as he opened a small refrigerator next to the stacks of blood-covered candy and snatched a bottle of Arrowhead water, which had remained safe from the violence inside the small 'fridge.

"Yeah," Gloria answered. "Didn't do me any good."

"Fucking thing scared me more than an H.P. Lovecraft story."

"H.P. who?"

"Lovecraft. He was a writer. Anyway, that thing gave me nightmares for two solid weeks. Apparently it had the same effect on Tracey, so we never had kids. Never even talked about it."

John handed Gloria the water and caught Heather's amusement-filled glare.

"Thanks," Gloria said. "So you guys never talked about it? Never tried?"

"Oh, we tried. We tried four or five times a week. I just wore a raincoat each time, if you get my meaning."

"Kinda hard not to," Gloria said, now all smiles.

John popped open his can of Coke and downed half of it in one gulp. He walked back to the refrigerator where he had gotten Gloria's water and took out five more, placing them in his backpack.

"As groovy as this place is, can we roll?" Gloria

asked. "I think I'm getting the heebie-jeebies."

Taking no other food other than the five bottles of water John had in his pack — they had all lost their appetites about five minutes ago — they departed the grocery store, not one of them looking back.

They walked through the parking lot in silence. Any sense of hopefulness they had had about their situation was long gone. Not that it had started out as a charming little walk in the park. But where before there was at least a splinter of sunlight breaking through the clouds, there was now nothing but darkness and shadows. What once felt hopeful now felt hopeless.

It wasn't the absence of other people that was getting to them, it was the violence and bloodshed they had seen in the grocery store. Not knowing what had happened, they could each hope that maybe everyone had gotten away, had left town before the changed people took over. But if the evidence in Jewel was any indication, not everyone had gotten away.

And that was worse than not knowing where everyone was.

As they crossed Cass Avenue, Gloria finally spoke up. "So I'm gonna pose a practical question, now."

"Go ahead," said Heather.

"If this guy's all-powerful — I mean, we've see what he can do — just how the hell do we plan on

402

taking him out?"

John looked over to Heather. "Kid's got a point. I hadn't even thought that far ahead. Any bright ideas?"

Heather smiled. "Just one."

The police station was as vacant and bare as the grocery store. It looked like the building had seen its fair share of violence. More blood than before had been wiped across the walls, with the now familiar words "No More Room" written in the red stuff over the captain's desk, within all the cells, and even on the floor.

They walked past what had been Eddie Miller's cell. Looking to her left, Heather got a snapshot of where she had locked up Gildy, then quickly looked away. A snapshot-look was more than enough.

She led John and Gloria into the back to the ammunition parlor. Kneeling down, she slid out the lock box hidden there, underneath the shelves of forms, paperwork, and the occasional magazine. Pulling out her set of keys from a pocket, Heather unlatched the box and pried open the lid.

Inside the box sat the ten cubes of C-4 wrapped in plastic. Heather carefully pulled out five of them — one at a time — and placed them on the floor.

"Is that what I think it is?" Gloria asked.

"C-4," said Heather. "Confiscated it from some kids who got it off the internet. Still waiting for the military boys to come pick it up."

"Lucky for us they never came," Gloria said.

John picked up a block of the stuff to examine it. "Does this stuff work?"

"I think so," Heather said as she locked the box back up and slid it underneath the shelf. "Problem is, it needs a detonator."

John handed her the block of C-4. "Which we don't have."

"Not a proper one, no," Heather said. Then she opened up her backpack and took out a magazine for her Beretta. She slid the bullets out with her thumb and placed them on the floor. Picking up a block of the explosive, she carefully pressed five of the bullets into it.

"C-4 just needs something to set it off, doesn't have to be a big explosion. I figure if we can get this stuff hot enough — or keep shooting it until we hit a bullet — that should be enough," Heather said.

"And then what?" asked Gloria.

Heather held out a completed and ready block of the explosive to John, who carefully put it in his own backpack. "Then we find out if Hell is real or not," he said.

"Wonderful."

Heather grinned as she readied another explosive. "He told you this was a one way trip."

63.

Around the time Heather was pushing the first bullet into the second block of C-4, Lindsay Stone finally snapped. It was quick, sudden, and if he had blinked, Richard would've missed it.

Suddenly the pain in his arm was gone, a relic of the past. He didn't say her name, or ask her what was wrong. He knew. He had known it was coming, it was just a matter of *when.*

He stood up, quickly but not too quickly, and Lindsay's vacant eyes followed him. He stood above her, the pool a few feet behind her. He could've easily given her a good, solid punt and sent her tumbling into the water, but he didn't. He couldn't.

She was still his wife, after all.

"I'm leaving now," he said, not sure why he felt the need to announce his plans. As he side-stepped away from the bench, moving away from Lindsay, she stayed still but kept her eyes on him, like a predator stalking it's prey, just waiting for it to make the wrong move. Her tear ducts were filling, and he could see her lower lip trembling.

She's fighting it. Good God, baby doll, keep it up.

There was still a part of Lindsay Stone, formerly Lindsay Meyer, of Chicago, Illinois, in there somewhere. Richard had the unexpected epiphany that the only way to escape — maybe the only way for *both* of them to escape — was not to run away, but to get in touch with the women he loved still inside the vessel of her body. And like any marriage, any *good* marriage, their relationship had been based primarily on trust.

Richard thought that perhaps reasoning with her wasn't out of the question. He had certainly done enough of it in his thirteen years as a psychiatrist. But he'd never had to do it quite like this. Never with Lindsay, and never with someone that, for lack of a better term, had been possessed by pure evil. No, he couldn't talk to her. If he did, he might not ever leave. He'd break down himself, and no matter what Lindsay turned into or what she did to him, they'd both end up dead. Or worse.

The only way to get through to her was to give her a good ol' dose of "tough love", and show her that he was leaving on his own, he had written her off, and it was time to move on with things

If that wouldn't piss off his wife, he didn't know *what* would.

He could feel the cold stare of her eyes on his back as he turned to face the door. She hadn't moved from her crouching position, not yet. He was pretty sure she would soon, though. Lindsay was strong; the past few days had certainly proven that much. But it had come time for finals, and as much as he loved her and believed in her, he really had no idea if she'd pass or not.

He picked up his left foot and took the first step. The soles of his shoes were damp, and the squeak of the rubber on the linoleum startled him. He wanted to look behind him, but he dared not. He didn't have to. He knew Lindsay was still there. He could sense her moving. She was standing up, getting to her feet, and the air in the room seemed to change. It didn't get colder. Or hotter. It just felt *different*.

As space came between his right foot and the ground, Lindsay attacked. It was a clumsy bash into his spine, her hands trying to frantically find his neck as if she was blind. The two fell to the floor, Richard's bad arm breaking their fall. He heard it *crack* again, and found himself wondering how many times someone could break the same limb without going completely insane.

Despite the new physical pain, Richard was still able to roll over onto his back, moving his wife off of him for a few seconds. He pulled himself forward, sliding on his back toward the exit doors. All he had to do now was get to the door and push open the latch with his good arm.

Richard staggered to his feet and reached for the doors. His hand found the handle, and he pushed it forward.

The door didn't open.

"Your writer buddy locked us in, baby," Lindsay snarled. "Wasn't thinking too far ahead, was he?"

She was back on top of him before he could finish registering what she had said. The top of her head smashed into his chest. He went down fast and hard, his head banging into the linoleum. Lindsay stayed on top of him, straddling him like a horse.

She crawled up his body like a snake, and their faces met. "Can't," she said, then struggled to find another word. "Stop. Can't. Stop."

Richard's legs kicked at the air underneath them, trying to find purchase on the slippery ground. His foot hit the bench. It toppled over, towels flapping to the ground.

A *clunk* followed the soft swish of the towels.

Lindsay was so preoccupied with digging her claws into Richard's neck that she didn't notice the sound of the firearm hitting the floor. Her body threw mild little convulsions as she tried to kill her husband. Her hand tightened, breaking two nails against Richard's left clavicle. She loosened her grip, then tightened it again as she dug deeper into his neck. Tighten, then loosen, as if she couldn't make up her mind if she wanted to go through with it or not.

Using the tip of his shoe, Richard tried to slide the gun toward his good hand. After moving it six inches, he realized that was as far as it was gonna go — his leg simply didn't bend the way he needed it to. He twisted his torso, pulling his head away from Lindsay's, forcing his body into a harsh right angle.

He stretched his good arm out, and his nail grazed the targeting sight of the gun. Lindsay altered tactics and lunged at his neck with an open mouth, vampire-style. Richard swiveled his head out of the way, contorting his body even more.

His hand reached the gun. It was in his grip and at her temple before he knew he had done it.

"Actually, my writer buddy *did* plan ahead," he said.

Lindsay froze and glanced sideways at the weapon, a look on her face that said *you're not really gonna shoot me, are ya'?*

Flipping the gun in his hand and holding it like a hammer, Richard let loose with a powerful blow to the side of Lindsay's skull with the butt of the firearm. Her head spun to the left and a splatter of blood sprayed across the floor. Lindsay looked at the blood, then abruptly brought her attention back to her husband, shaking off the punch from the gun like an annoying itch.

He hit her again, hard as he could. The butt of the gun hit the same mark it had before, and his wife rolled off of him and onto her back beside him. Using the tip of the gun as a quick makeshift crutch, he pushed himself up to his knees.

The screaming of his mangled arm all but forgotten, Richard skidded over to Lindsay. He brought two fingers to her neck and felt for a pulse.

He let out a sigh of relief as he discovered she was still alive. She was out cold, but still breathing.

"Sorry, honey," he said.

He debated whether or not he should leave her there and move to another area of the school, or if he should stay and find a way to tie her up like they had Jennifer, and maybe, just maybe, he could find a way to talk her down. He had no idea how he'd go about that — in all his years of training as a doctor, not once had he come across an article or thesis on how to treat a patient that had gone mad from the possible telepathic powers of an eccentric asshole from the dead.

As he realized that he had no good way of tying up his wife with just his one good arm, he heard something move and rustle about from the girl's locker room. This was quickly followed by the unmistakable sound of metal scraping against concrete.

Jennifer Adams had woken up.

64.

John was the first to feel the eyes on them. He didn't say anything at first; he wanted to keep his words inside until he was sure. No sense in freaking out Heather and Gloria if he was wrong and just being paranoid.

He looked behind them as they passed the small store where John was introduced to comic books. The business had long ago traded its Captain America shield for a Black & Decker drill set and any and every type and size of nail imaginable. But to John, it would always be Lyle's Comics and Books and not George's House of Tools. The business folk of Westmont were keen on naming stores after themselves, which John assumed was either an attempt to lend a feeling of small-town pride, or just plain laziness.

Behind them, the street was as empty as the sky except for the four lanes of dead cars.

411

Heather caught John looking over his shoulder. "What is it?"

"Nothing," said John, turning his head forward.

"It's not nothing," Heather argued.

"She's right. We're being watched," Gloria said.

"Say what?" Heather spat out, her hand going to her gun.

The three slowed their walk, but didn't stop. Something inside each of them — fear of not moving on, fear of whatever was watching them and just waiting for them to stop so it (or they) could jump out and maul them — told them to keep movin'.

"I don't see anything," Heather said.

From the corner of his eye, John saw a shadow move inside George's House of Tools. As soon as he turned to look through the window, the moving silhouette was gone.

"They're inside. In the stores," he said.

"Which one?" asked Heather.

Gloria answered for John. "All of them."

They were one block from the train tracks. Chicago lay one way, Downers Grove the other. On the opposite side of the tracks sat Quincy Avenue and Books Period, Thomas Manning's place of business.

"Keep walking," John said.

"I don't see-"

Heather's next word stuck in her throat as a man and a woman, the first people they'd seen since leaving the high school, walked out of the pharmacy on the corner. They looked normal enough; a husband and wife out for an afternoon stroll for some aspirin and possibly some ice cream for the grand-kids at home.

Then they got closer.

The couple waited for them outside the store. Their clothes were tattered, and it was a good bet these were the same threads they had been wearing when the power went out.

The husband, who was clearly in the latter half of his sixties, held something in his hand, but none of them could make out what it was from where they stood. He didn't have a second hand, and it looked like his right leg was broken in at least three places. The man should not have been able to stand on two feet, but he was.

The wife, who was maybe a decade younger than the husband, wore reading glasses, the chain still around the ear pieces so she wouldn't lose them. They sat crooked on her face — her left ear was missing.

Heather pulled her gun. John silently slid his hand out to hers: *don't do it, you don't need it* his eyes said. Heather's eyes said something else: *Fuck you, pal, the lady's missing an ear and the guy just plain gives me the creeps.*

Out came her gun.

The husband and wife team didn't show any re-action at the sight of the weapon. They just stood there, waiting for the trio, as if this was where the five of them had decided to rendezvous for lunch.

"What do we do?" Gloria asked, her words

barely audible.

"I don't think they're gonna hurt us," John said.

Heather: "Why not?"

"If he wanted to hurt us, if he wanted them to do something to us, he would've done it by now. He's had plenty of opportunities since we got out into the open," John replied.

Heather let her gun fall a few inches to her side. "So what, then?"

"He knows we're out," John said.

They were maybe twenty feet away from the couple when the husband turned and smiled at them. Heather finally got a good look at what he held in his hand and gasped. "Holy shit."

The husband carried what was unmistakably the upper body of a dead infant. He held onto it like it was nothing more than a newspaper, just something he was stuck with holding until he got home and could put it down on a table.

None of them wanted to even think about what happened to the bottom half of the kid.

"Oh-Jesus-shit-fuck-not-me-no-fucking-way-let's-turn-around-and-go-back," Gloria said, her hands going to her belly.

John remained speechless. Although he was positive these two posed no threat, the sight of the dead child certainly wasn't a pick-me-up. He turned to face Gloria and pulled her close to him. He could feel her shaking. Her breath came in short little bursts, and her eyes darted back and forth and down, back and forth and down, between the husband, the wife and the baby.

"We can't go back," he said in a steady, matter-of-fact voice.

"Why the hell not? We just turn around and-"

Gloria twisted out of John's grip and had already taken two steps back toward the high school when she saw why they couldn't go back. Standing in the street and on the sidewalks was the answer to where at least some of the townspeople had gone off to.

By John's count there were twenty-five to thirty people milling about, slowly making their way towards them. But like the husband and the wife, they were unthreatening. They watched the trio, stared at them.

Waited for them.

"Jesus," was all Heather could think of to say.

John scanned the crowd. Leaning against a Subaru hatchback was Pauley, the most intimidating of the group, who still held onto his shotgun. Leaning on either side of him for support where the two teenage girls that Pauley had blasted away in the middle of the street. One of the girls was missing both of her arms. The other girl's torso had been blown wide open, her insides dangling from her belly. The bottom half of her left leg hung onto her knee by a thin strand of tendons.

Flanking either side of the liquor store owner and his girls were Eddie Miller and Malcolm Dwight. They looked no worse for wear than they did before — but that was still plenty bad. Malcolm kept his eyes on Gloria, who looked anywhere but at him. Stephen Adams had an arm draped around Eddie's shoulder, using the kid for support.

John didn't recognize anyone else. There was a businessman who showed no sign of a violent death (although John was positive the guy was far from alive — you didn't hang out with *this* crowd if you were alive and had a choice) a fellow who looked like he might have worked in the hardware store that used to be a comic book store, a hammer in one hand, a chainsaw in the other, and no eyes in his head. A second couple, this one straight from a Target ad except the woman was missing her head and pushed an empty wheelchair behind the man with the hammer and chainsaw.

Their eyes — those that still had them — were dark and black.

Gloria now held onto John's hand. Her grip was tight, her knuckles white. She pointed at two men who stood at the back of the crowd, also in business suits. "Harding and Bryman. Shit, even now they're still inseparable."

Heather turned to her. "You know them?"

"I work with them."

"Not anymore," said John.

Gloria pulled her eyes away from Harding and Bryman when they spotted her and waved. "What do they want?"

"They want to make sure we make it alright," said Heather.

"You know, so we don't get lost," John added.

416

"G-g-reat," Gloria stuttered, slowly turning around, making sure to avert her eyes from the couple with the child.

Pauley broke formation from the group and limped in their direction. The shotgun dangled from his fingers, as if he'd forgotten he had been holding it. Life had been different for him since he fully gave himself over to the man that owned the Voice. He felt more focused, more alive. He no longer had to think — Thomas Manning did all the thinking for him.

Pauley knew his group could very easily take care of John and his friends with no problem and no worries. But that was not what the Man in the Dark Coat wanted. With people as unique as these three — people that he couldn't touch — Thomas wanted the pleasure of killing them the old fashioned way himself.

"No more room," Pauley said to John.

John held his ground. "So I've heard."

As Pauley got closer, they could make out cuts and bruises all across his face, as if he'd been involved in one helluva fight. His skin was pale and seemed to be crusted over with gobs of what looked like rotting flesh.

Heather pulled her gun from its holster as Pauley stopped a few feet from them. John put up a hand: *it's okay, don't shoot him.*

"What is all this, Pauley?" John asked.

Pauley thought about it, his black eyes moving

back and forth in their sockets. "I was wrong, Johnny. What's happening isn't a bad thing. It's a good thing. It's all in my head now, so clear, but so hard to put into words. It's like knowing how gravity works, but not being able to explain it so your kid'll understand.

"We're moving on to the next phase. The old species needs to die out to make room for the new one," Pauley said, then he paused, listening.

John looked from Gloria to Heather — there was no doubt in any of their minds that Pauley was getting a transmission from their friend in the trench coat.

"He wants to see you," Pauley said after a few seconds. Then he nodded in the direction they had been heading, towards Books Period across the train tracks.

John held Gloria's right hand, Heather on the other side, holding her left one. They began walking towards the tracks, and could hear the audience behind them shuffle their feet, following them.

"Well, then," John said. "Let's not keep him waiting any longer."

On the corner of the street to their north, just on the other side of the tracks, another group of escorts waited patiently for them. Like the first group, this crowd looked like a motley bunch that had been to Hell and back. Heather wondered how far away from the truth that was.

None of the citizens of Westmont got closer

than ten feet from the trio. Apparently they respected their personal bubble. Pauley seemed to be the shepherd of his group. The two teenage girls he had shot were his own personal Hounds of Hell. He held his shotgun against the crook of his neck, and John hoped he had used all the shells.

As they crossed the tracks, Gloria first looked left, then right. John caught her looking both ways and smiled. "I don't think there'll be a train comin' for some time."

"Stranger things have happened lately," she replied.

They crossed the tracks, and no locomotive of the Damned came to run them down and finish them off. As they turned the corner onto Quincy Avenue, the second group of escorts met up with the first, forming one big happy shitty looking family. All together, John estimated they had fifty changed people following them now. And having his back to them made him more than a little uneasy.

Three shops up and on the left was Books Period. Out of the three of them, John was ironically the only one who had never been in the store. He enjoyed his time as a silent recluse (his agent commonly referred to him as her Hermit Writer) and had opted to order all his books by mail soon after Tracey died. The Internet had become his best friend when it came time to brush up on some Bradbury or Asimov.

The window to the establishment looked like it

hadn't been cleaned in as long as the store had been there, which according to the tiny plaque on the inside window, was 1921 — the year Westmont had been incorporated into a village. Fake Christmas snow still sat hiding behind the dirt and soot that had crusted over the glass. The wooden door had been gnawed and clawed at by the occasional rat, dog, or stray cat. The paint was chipping and the mail slot at knee-level had been nailed shut.

Gloria looked behind them, back down the block they had just walked. Their guides stood there, obstructing the intersection. John's old buddy Pauley was still on point, a blank, expressionless stare on his face.

"So what are we supposed to do now?" Gloria asked.

John took a glance at Pauley and the fifty others behind him, then back at the door. A yellowed paper sign in the window proclaimed that it was OPEN FOR BUSINESS and to PLEASE COME IN!

"I guess we do some book shopping," John said. His hand reached for the rusted knob and he twisted it. With a squeak and a groan, the knob turned and the door opened. It swung inward on its own momentum, although John thought it might be just a bit more than that.

Sucking in a deep breath, John led the way into Books Period.

*   *   *

The stench of dirt and grime hung heavy in the air. The kind of smell a place gets when the windows haven't been opened in a very, very long time. Light was minimal; the only source came from the grubby window, basking the room in an even filthier haze. Dust covered the books on the display table in front of them.

John picked a book off the table and blew the muck off of it. He wasn't surprised at all to see the title was *Into the Darkness* by John Whitley. Heather looked at the cover over his shoulder.

"Hey, that's your book."

John dropped his novel and brushed the dust off the book next to it. And the one next to that. And the one beneath that.

"All of them are my book," he said, pointing at the covers to those he had cleaned off — revealing a table inundated with copies of his big seller.

Heather let out the breath she hadn't realized she'd been holding. "That can't be very encouraging."

"Guess this explains why it did so well," he said.

"Door's open! Come on in back!" a voice cried from somewhere down the hallway that led from the antique cash register to the back of the store. Gloria jumped at the sudden end of silence by someone other than them.

Heather pulled her gun.

"Walk behind us," Heather told Gloria.

"Fine."

As they made their way past the cash register, John took a quick survey of the books they passed, each and every one of them a paperback copy of his book.

The three moved down a short hallway. They passed framed photos from Westmont's history on either side of them, hanging on the walls. The first paving of Cass Avenue in 1927 was in one. Another had what looked to be one of the first pictures taken of Westmont High School; according to the hand-written date on the bottom, it was snapped in 1972. And a lonely looking picture of the town's first water tower dangled near what they now saw to be the said open door they had been summoned to.

John and Heather stopped just short of the door. Their eyes locked. They both knew that their next few steps would probably change their lives forever. And probably not for the better.

"Come on in, take a load off," the voice said.

So they did.

Thomas Manning sat in a grungy brown leather chair behind an even grungier oak desk. His feet were propped up on the small reception desk, and he looked no more threatening than a simple storeowner on his lunch break. He was finishing a page in a book — it was no shocker that it was John's book — when he looked up and saw the author enter with the two women. He folded a page down to keep his place, shut the book, and tossed it on the desk.

"It's not bad, John. Some of the characters are a

little flat, but I kinda like it. You should write another one," Thomas said.

"Thanks," John replied.

"What do you want from us?" Heather asked.

Thomas smiled. "You're one of those girls that likes to get right down to business, aren't you?"

"How perceptive," she said with a sarcastic twang.

Thomas pushed himself away from the desk, the wheels on the chair squeaking in their hubs. Reaching his full height, a little over six-feet, he towered over the group. He straightened his trench coat, now caked with blood and dirt, and smiled.

"You three came to kill me."

John and the others stood silently, staring at the man.

"I'm really not a bad person," Thomas continued. "Maybe a little misunderstood. I'm just trying to make things better."

"What did you do to all the people?" asked John.

Thomas sighed as he walked around the desk. He stopped at the front of it and leaned against it. He rubbed his five o'clock shadow, thinking. "That's a toughie. I'm not too sure you'd understand."

"Try us," said Heather.

"I had to take them."

"Why?" John asked.

"Because this is the way things go. This is the way things end."

Heather's finger itched on the trigger of her gun. "No more room?"

"You got it," Thomas said. "No more room down there, no more room up here. There're only so many souls that can go around. You... *people* were getting too big for your britches. It's time to wipe the slate clean." He paused, smiling. "It's time to start all over."

John narrowed his eyes. "Then why don't you just be done with it, take *us*, too?"

"Think of it in computer terms — my hardware is not compatible with your systems."

"Why not?" John asked.

"Innocence," Heather said.

Thomas propped himself away from the desk and grinned. "If you're not a sinner, you're not my dinner."

Heather pulled the gun from her holster. "Then it looks like you're not eating."

She fired four quick and succinct shots from her Beretta directly at Thomas Manning's head. His neck snapped back as the bullets entered his forehead.

Heather brought the gun to her side when she realized there were no exit wounds coming out the back of his head, and the most Thomas Manning had moved was an inch. Bringing his head back level, the Man in the Dark Coat locked eyes with the cop as first one, then two, of her bullets came out through the holes they had made. They were soon followed by the second two, which he caught in his hand. Thomas looked at them briefly, then let them fall to the floor with a clatter.

"'It looks like I'm not eating'?" he said with an overly mocking tone. "That's the most piss-pour catch phrase I've heard in all my years."

John leaned over to Heather and whispered. "What are you doing? You knew that wouldn't do any good."

Heather shrugged. "I had to try."

Thomas went on with an offer as if nothing had happened. "Let the world start over, and you can have your own little part of it. If you let me in, if you give yourselves to me, instead of the hell you see all around you, you can have your own little slice of heaven."

"What do you-" John's words choked in his mouth. Standing to his right against the wall was his dead wife.

"Tracey?"

Heather and Gloria followed John's gaze. Nothing was there.

She looked as she had before the car crash, before the windshield had severed her throat and killed her. Her auburn hair was tied back in a strict ponytail, and she wore the same dark blue glamorous dress John had wanted her to wear that night — the one that showed enough but not too much — which draped across her figure as if it were made for her. She even had the same twinkle of happiness for him that had been in her eyes all that night.

John looked from Tracey to the Man in the Dark Coat, then back again to make sure she was still there.

"How are you doing this?" he asked.

"Your wife is closer to my world than your own. If you do what I say, you can be together forever," Thomas said. "I can make it happen. It's what I can offer you."

John was speechless.

"If you go willingly, Tracey will be there."

"And if we don't?" Heather asked for the muted John.

"Ask John," said Thomas.

John watched as Tracey began to slowly shrivel up like her skin was being shrink-wrapped. Her eyes pushed themselves into their sockets, leaving behind two dark and empty voids. Blood streamed down her chin in rivers from her nose. A scar formed around her neck where the windshield had made contact, then opened up, spilling blood onto the wooden floor. Before John could look away, Tracey fell to the ground in a slump, then disappeared.

Heather put a hand on his shoulder. "John, what did you see?"

John ignored her and turned back to Thomas. "She's already dead. You can't do anything to her."

"Quite the contrary. If you give yourself to me, you two can live the clichéd 'happily ever after'. I can arrange that. If you don't, I'll make sure she suffers for the rest of time.

"I can arrange that just as easily."

65.

Her legs were broken, smashed. Her back hurt, but it was a pain she could cope with. What she had trouble dealing with was the fact that it was near impossible for her to move. She couldn't turn herself over, or twist her spine around enough to look down at her legs (which felt like they had the consistency of pudding) but she knew something was holding her flat to the ground. Something big. Something heavy.

After trying to pull herself free, which resulted in nothing more than moving herself and whatever was on top of her a whopping inch, she knew she had to come up with an alternative plan. Her entire life had been spent looking at alternatives, so there was no reason for this situation to be any different. From choosing which flavor of ice cream to buy from Mr. Fatty's Ice Cream Truck to mapping each and every alternate route for consideration when

Cass Avenue had undergone a major face-lift two years ago, alternatives had become a way of life for her.

Her wrists, which were strapped tightly to a nailed-down bench with towels, kept her arms from being useful. She couldn't reach forward with her head to untie them with her teeth — the big heavy thing on top of her was preventing her from doing that.

But she had to get out of here. She knew that. She didn't now how, or even *why*, but she had to move. A Voice was telling her so. It was so powerful, so loud in her head, she didn't even second guess it. She couldn't hear anything else.

She just wanted to obey it.

And it was telling her that time was running out if she ever wanted to be reunited with her husband.

She pulled harder. Either the bench would give, the thing on top of her would move, or her legs just below her knees would snap apart. She didn't care which, as long as she was free.

She heard something rip below her. She didn't feel anything, but she assumed it was the muscles in her legs. Then something down there cracked, and she slid forward another inch. Although she couldn't feel the pain, she could sense that her legs were sliding out from under the object instead of her legs simply sliding off of her body.

When she was able to reach the towel wrapped around her right wrist with her mouth, she chomped her teeth down onto the cloth and pulled. The knot had tightened from all her tugging, and she found it difficult to loosen.

She pulled relentlessly, the veins in her neck bulging with rapidly coursing stress-filled blood. Her incisors began to give. She could feel the roots loosening in their sockets. But she wasn't going to let some shoddy dental work and too much candy and ice cream as a kid be her downfall now.

After five hard yanks on the towel, the knot released itself. She wriggled a hand out of the poorman's handcuff and used her free hand to untie the other. With both arms now liberated, she was able to rotate partially around to look below her.

Crushing her calves — calves she had spent two solid years of toning at Bally's — was a row of lockers. The memory came back in flashes —

— she was talking with someone, a pregnant girl —

— the girl was afraid of her —

— a cop was aiming a gun at her head —

— something creaked behind her —

— a sharp pain shot through her back —

— then all the fucking lights went out.

If her memory was correct, her back should be broken. She shouldn't be able to move at all. But she could, and she wasn't about to look a gift horse in the mouth. Fuck it, she could worry about that miracle later.

Using the bench as a brace, she pushed at the set of lockers on top of her legs with her arms. While pulling her legs out at the same time, she was able to free them from the vice of the metal.

Her legs weren't flattened like Wile E. Coyote's after the Road Runner had a go at him, but they were close to it. Her limbs barely resembled legs anymore; they looked more like a set of pants that had been tossed into the laundry basket with a ground up chicken. Most shocking of all was that they didn't hurt at all. Not a single little bit.

Ignoring their physical appearance, she tried to bend her right knee. Bones cracked. Cartilage moved and squeezed through the joints, sounding like someone mixing a bowl of macaroni and cheese. With some effort, her knee bent and seemed to work just fine. Her Bally's instructor would've been proud.

Her legs worked. She seemed relatively okay. But shouldn't she be dead?

They had said Stephen was dead. Not himself. Not alive. Maybe not dead, either. Someone — or some*thing* — was manipulating the people of Westmont. There was enough of her left in her mind to know that this was a bad thing. Westmont was special to her. She grew up here, and... she had some level of importance. But she couldn't remember what. She had had the memory just a few seconds ago. Something to do with the government. Her memories were fading. It didn't matter. All she could recall now was that people listened to her and looked up to her. But soon that memory was gone, too.

Stephen. Her memory of Stephen was still there.

Focus on that.

She held onto the image of him in her head, as he was before the blackout and not as she last saw him.

She had to find Stephen. She wanted to be with him again.

Putting her palms on the bench behind her, she hoisted herself up to her feet. She was wobbly at first, but with a little stretching, she got used to the new structure of her legs.

She looked to her left at the exit. Her husband was somewhere out there. The Voice was telling her to leave and search for him, and she agreed with it.

With a limp-hobble that was now her new walk, Jennifer Adams, former Mayor of Westmont, made her way toward the exit and the high school swimming pool.

Richard knelt down next to Lindsay, sweat and blood dripping from his forehead. He wiped away a mixture of the fluids from his eyes, trying to keep his wife in focus.

The smack from the butt of the gun had left a small gash just below her ear, and it was already starting to bruise. She had fallen face-first, and he turned her over onto her back. She wasn't dead, so at least he had that going for him.

What he didn't have going for him was mobility. He couldn't pick his wife up even if he wanted to with one arm out of commission, and now that she wasn't attacking him (for the time being) he

431

found it difficult to just leave her there. He hoped that if the others were successful, maybe, just maybe, he'd have his Lindsay back. Maybe Thomas Manning's hold on her would cease.

He hoped.

He had to hope.

It was the only thing keeping him sane at the moment.

"You two have a little marital spat?" a female voice asked him from behind.

Jennifer Adams stood at the entrance to the girl's locker room. Looking at the limbs that used to be her legs made Richard's head hurt — they just didn't look like they could be holding up a body, as if they had multiple joints and no muscles in them whatsoever.

Richard stood, picking up the gun that had fallen next to Lindsay. "You could say that."

Jennifer walked toward him. It was an odd sight, almost comical if not for the fear and death in the woman's eyes. Those eyes, like her legs, just weren't right.

"It's not so bad," she said. "You don't have to make choices anymore. He does it all for you. And when he's finished, it will be paradise. I've seen it."

"That sounds great. Just what is it he needs to finish?"

Jennifer thought about this, still taking limp-hobble steps toward Richard. "Evolution. Out with the old, in with the new."

"So I'm the dinosaur, and you're the caveman,

huh?" Richard said, coy.

Jennifer's face turned into a grin, showing at least five open holes where teeth used to be. Blood poured out of the side of her mouth. "Cave*woman*."

"Right, of course. My bad. Cavewoman."

The former Mayor of Westmont was now ten feet from the psychiatrist. "For those who don't accept the evolution, they need to be taken care of. No more room."

Richard raised the gun to Jennifer's head. "Don't move any closer." He tried to sound threatening and in control, but missed the mark entirely. Instead, his warning came out more like a shaky question than a harsh demand.

Jennifer ignored him. "You have to know this is inevitable," she said. "I'm the Mayor, and I'm asking you as your representative, please consider joining us."

"Fucking politicians."

Richard pulled the trigger. The bullet landed between Jennifer's eyes, surprising Richard as much as her. Having never fired a gun before, he was amazed that he had actually hit what he had been aiming at.

The bullet shot out of the back of Jennifer's head. Bone, flesh and brain-matter sprayed across the floor. Some of it landed in the pool with a *splash*. Bigger pieces, what looked like parts of the back of her skull, hit the floor and bounced away.

She went down backwards, her head slamming into the ground. Richard thought he heard her skull crack, but he couldn't be sure.

He decided he wasn't going to stick around to find out. He had seen enough lately to know that just because someone seemed dead didn't necessarily mean that they *were* dead. In this new twisted world he found himself in, death was not the end. He might not be able to get out of the school, but at least he could get the fuck out of the room.

He couldn't leave Lindsay here, though. Not with whatever Jennifer had become.

Richard stuck the weapon in the back of his pants and grabbed one of the body-length towels that had hidden the gun. He put either end underneath his wife's arms, looped it around the back of her neck. He made a kind of handle for her body, the kind of harness he'd seen in movies and on TV when they needed to rescue someone from drowning in the ocean.

After he grabbed a second towel from the bench and placed it over his shoulders, he began to pull his wife toward the exit. It wasn't easy — in his weakened state she seemed heavier than she should — but it'd have to do.

When they were a few feet from freedom, Richard pulled out the gun again. Taking careful aim, he took three shots at the base of the door. Splinters and shards of metal exploded into the air, and from the other side of the door, he heard the floor-lock ricochet off a wall and skid across the tiles.

He opened the door with his forearm and walked out, dragging his unconscious wife behind him, being careful not to let the door slam shut on Lindsay's feet. When they were both clear of the doorway, he let Lindsay drop slowly to the ground.

Taking the towel off his shoulders, Richard thrust an end through both handles. Using his good arm and some strong teeth, he was able to tie a relatively decent knot. It might not hold for long, but it would at least give them some time.

Now all he had to do was hope the others would be successful so he could have his wife back. He picked up Lindsay's harness again and began walking down the hallway, in search of a good place to hole up until John and the others returned.

66.

Heather Steinman hadn't seen her father since his funeral almost fifteen years ago. She could still see his tuft of hair sticking out of the casket as the minister gave his sermon. The sight of his closed eyes, making him look asleep and not dead, was an image she'd never forget. His skin was pale, and there had been a slight and strange tint of purple to it.

The man in front of her looked nothing like that memory. This version of her father looked the same as he did the day before he had the aneurism. Still coming across like he was in the prime of his life at the age of forty-five, Joseph Steinman gave the impression that he could easily live another forty-five years without batting an eye. The purple tint his skin had had in the casket was gone, replaced by a healthy rosy-red hue. His eyes were open, and he was smiling at her.

"Daddy." It wasn't a question, but it wasn't really a statement, either. She just needed to hear her own voice.

"Hey doll. I've missed you," he said.

"I've missed you, too, Daddy. But-"

"But what?"

"I know this isn't real," she admitted. "I know you're not in this room with me right now." Even though she felt John and Gloria still standing by her side in Thomas Manning's back office, she didn't — she couldn't — look at them.

"I may not be in this room, sugar, but what's waiting for us afterwards is beyond anything you can comprehend," he said. "Heaven truly is a magical place. Like Disneyland, except it's free. You loved Disneyland as a kid. Come with me. Give yourself to this man, and we can be together again."

Heather's eyes watered up, blurring her vision. "And Mom?"

"She's here too, sugar. She's here, too."

Tears dripped out of her eyes and rolled down her cheeks. "But Daddy, Mom killed herself. How... how can she be in Heaven... if she killed herself? Isn't that... isn't that a sin?"

"Not in the heaven we're in. We're in the heaven *he* created," he said, nodding toward Thomas, who smiled. "And in it, anything's possible."

"Daddy, please," Heather said, then her words just stopped. She couldn't go on.

"Come with me, baby-doll. You, me and your mother can all be together again. We can be a happy

437

family again."

"But Daddy," she said, using all her strength to snap out of what she was sure was an illusion created by Thomas Manning, "I *hated* Disneyland."

Joseph Steinman vanished in front of his daughter's eyes, not unlike when Thomas Manning did his own disappearing act. When he was gone, Heather was looking directly into the eyes of Thomas. She shook the cobwebs of the hallucination from her head as John put a hand on her shoulder. She shot lasers at Thomas with her eyes.

"I can give you a life where you're with your family, a life where your mother doesn't kill herself," he said. "A life where your father will never die."

"It wouldn't be real," she argued.

Thomas smirked. "Trust me, you wouldn't know the difference." He turned to Gloria. "But you. What is it *you* want? You haven't lost anything. Yet your face, your eyes, are filled with such sadness."

"You're the smart one, you figure it out," Gloria said. John looked over at her, surprised with her sudden courage. But she was still shaking — whatever had come out of her mouth was the opposite of what was going on inside her head.

"You had a happy childhood. They didn't beat you, they didn't argue with you, and they loved one another so much it made me sick to be in their heads. Until your father met someone else and ran out on you two," he said, watching Gloria begin to crumble at the notion that her parents were now a part of this man's changed people. Heather put a hand on Gloria's other shoulder to give her what strength she could.

"My parents... are dead?"

Thomas answered her with only a silent smile.

Gloria's eyes quickly shot over to John's backpack.

"There's something you haven't told anyone," Thomas said. "Something only *you* know about. If you tell me what it is, maybe I can make it better."

"I highly doubt it," said Gloria. She rested a hand on her belly, feeling the child kick at her fright.

"Your baby," he said.

The words hit Gloria like a bullet. She couldn't hide the fact that he had somehow touched on the very thing she didn't want anyone to know. Everyone has a dark secret, and this was hers.

Thomas moved closer, his smile broadening. "You don't know who the father is, do you?"

Gloria didn't reply, but her eyes quivered and her lips trembled.

"In fact, he's not even in town anymore. No, not he. *They.* Yes, I can see them, now. And that look in your eyes, that's guilt, girl," Thomas said. "You don't know who the father is not because you were promiscuous, but because you were alone. They jumped out at you, and it was over before you even realized it had begun, wasn't it?"

"Shut up," she said.

Thomas moved closer. "And you couldn't tell anyone, could you? No, you felt too guilty. Like it was somehow your fault."

"I said shut up."

"I can give them to you. Yes, I can see it now, the anger in your eyes. It's there, Gloria. I can give them to you, and make everything better."

Heather stepped forward and pulled her gun, bringing the tip of the weapon to Thomas' head. "Why don't we talk about *your* childhood?"

Thomas didn't back away, but merely turned his head to look the cop dead-on. "I didn't have a childhood."

"You were, what, sixteen? Seventeen when your family was killed?" John said, then paused to slip one of the straps from his back pack off a shoulder. "Why did you let him do it?"

"Johnny-boy, whatever are you talking about?" he said.

"I'm not talking to you," John said. "I'm talking to Thomas Manning, the real Thomas Manning, buried deep inside you. That boy you took is still there. Whoever, *whatever*, you are, you took that innocent child and killed his parents. His sister. His family.

"Thomas, why did you let him do it?"

The Man in the Dark Coat moved away from the author. His eyes stared at John with confusion and wonder.

"Tommy," John said, "you can fight him. You don't have to listen to his Voice. Others have fought it off. You can, too."

From down the hallway they heard something hit the ground and the shuffling of feet. Then more and more footsteps, as if the store had just opened up to a mad rush of customers for a super-sale on books.

The Man in the Dark Coat grinned as he stepped away from the desk. "Thomas gave himself to me. Freely. He, like me, was misunderstood. I offered him peace and control if he helped me rid the world of those who didn't understand him. The same peace and control I'm now offering you. He was like you three — different, special, innocent. But once he gave himself to me, nothing was ever the same."

John slid the other strap off his shoulder and let the pack fall to the ground. "You took him. He didn't 'give himself' to you."

Thomas showed his teeth. "Semantics."

Gloria leaned her head out through the door-jamb. Walking towards her was a heavy-set man with a gun, the one John had called Pauley. Behind him were the two girls. And behind them, it looked like everyone else. The store was packed with changed people.

"Oh, shit," she said.

"What?"

John looked down the hallway himself. Pauley was in the lead, and he cocked his shotgun. "Oh, shit," John repeated.

"I didn't want it to go like this. I really thought

441

you'd see things my way, like little Tommy Manning did," the Man in the Dark Coat said. "Maybe I can't touch you because of your innocence, but they can."

"Only if you're around to give out orders," John said as he tossed the backpack full of C-4 at the Man in the Dark Coat's feet. "Do it!" he yelled to Heather.

She squeezed the trigger again and again and again, the bullets pounding into the backpack. On the fifth hit, the bag erupted into flames and exploded, engulfing the man who was once called Thomas Manning in a ferocious ball of fire.

67.

Richard slumped against the blood-soaked wall. The same wall they had blurred past when they had been attacked just after entering the school. The blood had since dried and now resembled a half-assed paint job more than a terror from the living dead. It was hard to believe that had occurred less than five hours ago. To Richard, it felt like five lifetimes ago.

He managed to pull Lindsay's body next to him with a grunt. She hadn't uttered so much as a moan since he had pulled her from the vicinity of the pool. He figured he had either hit her harder than he thought, or something extremely good or extremely bad was going on with the others and the Man in the Dark Coat.

He leaned his back against the wall, letting his head fall against it. Richard Stone had never been a man to give up, and if memory served him correctly, this was the first time in his life when he had thrown in the towel and admitted defeat. In the past five hours, he had lost everything dear to him, and the emotions finally caught up to his heart. No amount of self-analysis could stop the over-powering desire to cry, to let it all out until there were no more tears and no more pain.

He closed his eyes, wondering what the future held. If he and Lindsay even *had* a future. He could see no way out of the high school. Whatever path John, Heather and Gloria had taken was beyond Richard's reckoning.

Opening his eyes, he looked down at his wife again. She looked peaceful. Asleep. He hoped that she wasn't experiencing any of the mental or physical anguish that he was feeling himself. He wanted to join her in her slumber, to be with her wherever she had drifted off to.

Closing his eyes again, Richard waited for sleep to come for him.

68.

The Man in the Dark Coat curled his arms around himself as fire from the backpack cascaded around his body. Apparently the C-4 was older than Heather had thought — or simply no longer worked properly — and only one block had discharged. And it hadn't been much of a discharge, at that. What should have destroyed the entire room instead only bathed their enemy in a six-foot high flame.

His coat now fused to his skin, Thomas Manning peered up at Heather. She could still make out his eyes as his flesh burned. They were red, beaming with hatred and menace. As his skin melted away, Thomas stretched out a hand to reach for her.

To everyone's amazement, his arm extended across the room — a good ten feet — and grabbed Heather by the throat. It was a strange site, breaking all the laws of physics, but their eyes weren't lying to them.

Thomas Manning's hand, now ten feet away from his face, began to crush the cop's windpipe. "If you won't give yourselves to me, then I'll take you the old fashioned way," he growled.

John grabbed Gloria to push her into the hallway. "Go out the back!" he yelled at her, hoping she could find her way to the back door — if there was one — before their escorts came in from the front and did whatever it was the undead did to people.

John's hand slipped off of the girl, and she stood firmly in her place, her feet nailed to the ground. Her eyes stared forward, yet didn't seem to be focused on anything. Just flat and straight ahead, glazed over, as if she were in a catatonic state, hypnotized.

"Kid, *COME ON!*"

But the girl no longer acknowledged John's existence. Her eyes finally unlocked themselves and slowly panned over to where Thomas Manning stood.

The Man in the Dark Coat pulled Heather closer to him, his arm slowly returning to its normal length. He brought the tip of her nose to his own. She could smell the flesh burning, and tried to pull her head back from the heat and disgusting odor. Instead of the fire dying out on his body, it seemed to be growing, to be feeding off of him.

As John tried to grab Gloria again, she finally broke out of her quick little creepy coma and spoke:

"Maybe you can't touch us. But I think I can touch you."

With that her eyes came back to life, but not as they were before. They were brighter, more alive than they had ever been. He couldn't be sure, but John would swear up and down later that her pupils were glowing a bright yellow.

Gloria rose into the air in much the same fashion as the Man in the Dark Coat had. Thomas backed away from her as her feet lifted off the ground. He let his grip on the cop loosen, and Heather fell to the ground in a slump, gasping for air.

A small circle formed behind Thomas' desk. It slowly grew big enough to fit a car through, and the light beyond was tinged yellow. A bright shade of yellow that matched Gloria's new eyes.

Thomas stood in front of his desk, the only thing between him and the portal. His eyes grew red with anger and confusion. It was a look John would never forget.

The Man in the Dark Coat's hair ruffled from an unseen breeze, even though the air in the room was dead calm. His eyebrows turned into an evil M-shape as he glowered at the pregnant woman, who now only looked on with a malevolent smile.

His eyes grew brighter, a vivid red to combat the intense yet calming shade of Gloria's yellow pupils. Veins pulsated in his neck as he took one, then two steps away from the desk. Away from the portal.

And towards Gloria.

The closer he got to her, the more she felt herself being forced back into the wall. She hung there, feet suspended above the ground, slowly being pushed away from Thomas. Fear was sketched all over her face, from the top of her forehead to the bottom of her chin. Underneath that fear, though, was determination. Dead, solid, no-way-in-hell-am-I-gonna-give-up determination.

But no matter how determined she was, Thomas Manning was able to take another step closer to her. Then another.

Gloria squeezed her eyes shut and offered a quiet whisper of strength to herself. "Hail Mary, full of grace, the Lord is with thee. Blessed art thou amongst women, and blessed is the fruit of thy womb Jesus. Holy Mary, Mother of God, pray for us sinners, now and at the hour of our death."

The Man in the Dark Coat traded his frown for a smile. "Whatever it is you think you're doing little girl, best forget it."

Heather took a step past John, an arm on his shoulder to grab his attention. Then she shoved the very scared and very confused writer to the side and moved around Gloria.

Gloria's eyes vibrated in their sockets, threatening to leap out of her head at any moment. She quickly looked over to Heather.

Heather caught the child's stare, and although it lasted no more than half a second (if that) a lifetime of emotions — fear, wonder, betrayal, amusement, anger, and everything in between — passed between them. Heather gave Gloria the slightest of nods, letting her know it'd all be over soon.

"Go back to where you came from," Gloria said. "And don't even think about coming back."

Heather ran full-force toward the Man in the Dark Coat, arms open wide for a tackle. She hit him hard, and the two of them somersaulted on top of the desk, sending papers and Thomas' copy of *Into the Darkness* skidding off the desk and into the portal, where they vanished as a sudden beam of yellow energy crept from the hole and swallowed the best seller.

Heather and Thomas skidded to a stop at the edge of the desk, bringing them a hair's breath from the opening of the gateway. She held the man down, pinning him to the blotter. His arms flailed madly, scattering pens and pencils across the room.

"Heather!" John screamed.

The cop looked back at him. Her eyes said it all: this was goodbye. Then she looked at Gloria and nodded again: she was ready.

They both hoped the other knew what she was doing.

Gloria closed her eyes and the portal slid forward, moving across the floor. The gateway flashed with brilliant yellow arcs of electricity that cascaded across the room. Shadows danced this way and that. The portal gulped up the corner of the desk, half a foot from the Man in the Dark Coat's head. He pushed at Heather, putting a hand around her neck and closing it. He squeezed tighter and tighter and felt something give in her throat.

Heather's eyes rolled into the back of her head. As she was about to pass out, the portal moved in to begin its feast on Thomas' head. The yellow glow swept over the top of his burnt skull like water.

There was no blood. Only what must have been an unbelievable amount of pain as the portal slowly crawled toward the man's eyes.

"This is for Gildy, you prick," Heather grumbled as the opening consumed both of them in one final flash, along with part of the floor and half the desk. Leaving fire in its wake, the gateway shut itself closed with a snap like a television set being turned off.

In the hallway, John heard their escorts fall to the ground in unison. They clumped and dropped on the wooden floor, lifeless. At the same time, Gloria fell to the floor herself. Her limp body hit the ground as fire began to chomp through the room.

John picked her up in both arms. He took a quick peek out the doorway to make sure all the crazy people were still down. When the man who used to be Thomas Manning had left, it seemed so did his hold on these people. But apparently that didn't stop them from being dead.

John stepped over the bodies on the floor, careful not to walk on anyone's hand or neck. He knew it didn't matter — they were nothing but corpses, anyway — but he couldn't stomach the idea of feeling someone's windpipe crack beneath his foot. He passed Pauley and the two girls. Gloria's friend Malcolm, and the Mayor's husband, although he couldn't remember the man's name. All of Westmont had come to the festivities here, one final fire sale at Books Period, and now they all lay crumpled on the floor, as dead as dead got.

John made it to the doorway by the time the fire began to crawl through the hall, cremating the dead bodies as it moved onward. He kicked the door open and stepped outside into the blinding daylight as Thomas Manning's store burned up behind them.

Once they were a safe distance away, John gently placed the still unconscious Gloria down on the sidewalk. He looked back up the block, where Books Period was slowly becoming a smoky shadow of a building. Residents of Westmont were spread throughout the street, finally getting the rest and relaxation that the dead bodies that they had become deserved.

When he looked back down at Gloria, her eyes were open and had returned to their normal shade of green. But the girl looked like she had aged a good twenty years. She winced in pain and grabbed for John's hand, which she squeezed tightly.

"What, what is it?"

She didn't need to answer. A pool of what looked like water had suddenly formed beneath her. John looked around for someone — anyone — that could help. The nearest people lay down the block, and they were all dead, anyway.

John would have to deliver the baby alone.

69.

Richard's eyes were closed when the black substance that had engulfed the school began to slowly ooze away, the ground soaking it up like fresh rain. At first he didn't notice the sunlight shine through the doors and bounce through the school, creating a luminous dance between the beige walls and the red blood. He opened his eyes in time to see the last bit of the stuff slide down the front of the doors and seep into the grass and surrounding concrete.

"Lindsay," he said, nudging his wife to take part in their newfound freedom. She was still out like a dead light bulb, and hadn't seen or heard a thing.

Richard got to his feet and hobbled to the doors. With a weary hand, he pushed on the handle. It didn't budge. They were still trapped in the school, and his recent idea that they would die in the high school seemed like it would come true after all.

Leaning his head against the glass in a moment of despair, his eyes skimmed over the floor-lock, still in its locked position. Bending down, he lifted the tiny steel rod up, unlocking the door, and tried it again.

A cool breeze, unnatural for the mid-west at that time of year, flowed in as the door swung open. Richard let the wind bathe his face and comb his hair. The sweat that had collected on his forehead became cool and refreshing, and for a few seconds, Richard Stone felt like himself again.

He turned around to look at Lindsay. Positive she would be magically waking up from the unconsciousness he had brought to her, he smiled at his wife. But she laid exactly where he had left her, and hadn't moved a bit.

Pulling John's gun from his pants to leave at the crook of the door — no way in hell was he ever gonna let *any* door close behind him again — he moved over to Lindsay. He grabbed the two ends of the towel-harness and pulled her toward the door. Looking back the way he had come, he wondered if Jennifer Adams was slumped down dead and rotting, or was waddling her way in their direction for some good ol' fashioned revenge.

He reached the entrance and hauled Lindsay outside. Once her feet were clear of the doorway, he picked up the gun, closed the door, and used the sidearm as a makeshift lock, stuffing it between the two handles so no one inside could get out. He doubted that it would do much good, but he felt better just having done it.

He softly laid Lindsay on the grass and plopped himself down next to her. Looking up at the sky, he noticed just how quiet it was.

No cars.

No people.

He didn't even hear a bird chirp.

It was the quietest he'd ever heard the world, and for the time being, he enjoyed it.

70.

Luckily for John, the delivery of Gloria Cortez's daughter was over and done with in less than fifteen minutes. He figured that must have been some sort of record.

Recalling the highlights from the video that had scared the shit out of him in high school — now wishing he hadn't closed his eyes so much during it — he remembered the first thing one needed to do was make sure the child's airway was clear. With no water to rinse the newborn off with, John was finding it difficult to decide what to do. Hell, there was no decision to be made. Simply put, John had no fucking clue what to do.

He had nothing to suction the gunk out from the child's mouth, so his best thought was to dig in with his pinky and do the job himself. But before his finger touched the kid's lips, the child began coughing, choking, and he was sure he had done something wrong. The kid had been out in the world for less than five minutes, and John Whitley had already screwed it over.

A fair amount of what looked to John like strawberry jelly exited the baby's mouth. Then she sucked in a breath, coughed once more, and was quiet. The baby looked up at him, expressionless, and blinked. Despite all his misgivings about the miracle of childbirth, the moment took his breath away.

John reached into his back pocket with a free hand and pulled out the switchblade Malcolm had tried to kill him with. With a tiny flick of his wrist, John cut the umbilical cord.

"Is it...?"

John looked down to Gloria, almost forgetting she was even there. He held up her daughter for her to see, the grin of a father on his face.

"You have a daughter, kiddo. And she's just fine."

Her worn and tired face showed a smile, and for a few seconds she looked like the girl he had met two days ago. The bags under her eyes disappeared as the beginnings of a smile came to her face. She reached out with two weak hands, and John gently handed the newborn baby to her mother.

Gloria brought the child to her chest. The baby girl looked up at her mother for the first time, and unless John was imagining things, the infant smiled. He thought he remembered baby's couldn't do that, not at first, but he could've been wrong. He didn't think he was, though. He was pretty sure there was something special about this infant besides being delivered by a hack-writer on a sidewalk.

"She's beautiful," Gloria said.

"Sure is."

Gloria's grin widened, forcing tears to swim out of her eyes.

"What's her name?"

"I don't-" she began, then stopped herself. "Heather."

John smiled back at her, and his most manly attempt to not cry couldn't hold his tears back any longer. "I think she would've like that."

Gloria stroked Heather's bald head as only a mother could. "It's only too bad they'll never get to meet."

"Maybe one day they will," John said.

They stared at one another for a moment, knowing there was more to what had happened in the bookstore, what had happened to Thomas Manning, a man who had had an odd habit of wearing a trench coat in the middle of summer, than had met their eyes.

"John, what happened in there, when he was pulled away, that doorway," Gloria started.

"Yeah. That's quite a trick you pulled outta your ass. We thought that it was him doing that back at the high school-"

"It wasn't me."

"What do you mean?" John asked, but he was pretty sure he already knew.

Gloria didn't have to answer. She simply nodded toward her child.

The purest form of innocence.

They sat in silence for a couple of minutes, taking in, as well as they could at least, the weight of what Heather Cortez might mean for the future. If they even had one.

John broke the silence with the cracking of his knees as he stood up.

"Where are you going?" asked Gloria.

"Well, I figure we can't stay here, and you're in no shape to walk, so I better find us a way to get-" John stopped. "I was gonna say *home*," he continued, "but somehow I don't think that's right."

"Home is where you hang your hat," Gloria said.

"Thanks for the cliché."

"Go get me a wheelchair. I think I saw one of the freaks pushing an empty one," she said.

"I'll check," he said. "I hope you're right, 'cause I ain't carrying you."

"Don't worry, I'm right. And yes, you'd carry me if you had to."

"You're probably right."

71.

Richard watched the sun set from the front lawn of the high school. The black goop that had coated the building and seeped into the ground didn't seem to have an effect on the grass; it was still as bright and green as ever. He hadn't moved in close to two hours, and neither had Lindsay. He checked on her periodically; she was alive, but evidently had suffered some real damage when Thomas Manning had decided to try and take full control over her. Perhaps it was Thomas' demise — if that's what had happened, and with the ease that he was able to leave the high school, he was pretty sure it was — that had caused something in Lindsay's brain to shut down. Richard had seen such catatonic states from patients who had suffered severe mental shock. What she had been through would definitely fall under that category and beyond. He was also afraid that hitting her repeatedly while trying to protect himself had done more damage than he intended. There was simply no telling what she'd be like when she snapped out of it.

Or even *if* she'd snap out of it.

The sound of wheels badly need of some WD-40 thrust him out of his murky thoughts. Shadows had become long and dark on the block, and he couldn't make out who, or what, was coming his way. As they got closer, Richard could see it was a man pushing a wheelchair with someone sitting in it. The man raised up a hand for an out of place wave. The simple everyday gesture looked absurd on the empty sidewalk amidst the silence.

John Whitley pushed Gloria and her child up the sidewalk leading to the high school. Richard smiled at the two, but that felt just as absurd as the wave had looked.

"Hey doc," John said. "Good to see you."

"You, too," he said. "Looks like you lost someone. And gained someone else."

"She saved us all," John said.

"Both of them did," added Gloria.

Gloria gave up her seat in the wheelchair for Lindsay. She had enough strength to walk to the nearby house across the street — the same house, John remembered, where Heather had babysat two kids and played with action figures after school.

The door was unlocked, which was not surprising. Most people had left in a hurry, and it was a solid bet that locking their doors was the last thing on their minds. After a quick search of the home, John and Richard were confident they were alone, and that there were no bodies — dead or alive — to come crawling out of a closet for them.

They laid Lindsay down on a bed in the master bedroom on the second floor. Richard was insanely careful with her, as if she were a fragile piece of hundred-year-old china and the slightest bump would cause her to break into a thousand tiny pieces.

There was still no power, but John was able to whip together three bowls of soup for them, which they ate cold in the darkening kitchen. When they were done, Gloria retired to the adjoining living room to give Heather Cortez her dinner.

John and Richard remained at the kitchen table. They sat in silence, staring through a window looking out on the back yard. The moon hung big and bright in the night sky, and the light from the full moon created shadows in the kitchen.

The shadows on Richard's face deepened as he told John the tale of Jennifer and Lindsay and their escape from the school. After John had recounted the events at Thomas Manning's place of business, they decided that while the immediate danger seemed to be over, they were still up shit creek without the proverbial paddle. There was still not a good enough reason for either of them for the massive power outage. While it might have been true that the Man in the Dark Coat was to blame, it was yet another jump in reality that both men were not eager to take.

"I think we have to accept it," John said.

"You gotta admit, it's a tough pill to swallow."

"I never said it'd be easy," John said. "You think I like thinking one lone goofball was responsible for all this?"

"Maybe it was more than one. Maybe Thomas Manning, or this being that took control of him, was just one of many."

John leaned back in his chair, staring at the doctor. "You sure know how to make a man feel better. I think this is the part where you tell me things won't always be this way."

Richard tried to smile, but it was mediocre at best. His eyes drifted to the floor.

"Will she wake up?"

"I don't know, John. I think so. I hope so. I can't say for sure. This is all a little beyond me."

"Amen to that."

John's hands found their way into his pockets. He pulled out his lighter. John open and closed the Zippo, again and again, deep in thought. Finally, he said, "I'm not staying."

Richard's expression didn't change. He didn't look at all surprised. "Where will you go?"

"I was thinking of heading west. I'd ask you guys to come with me, but this is hardly good traveling time for a newborn," said John.

Richard's eyes moved to the living room. Gloria's back was to them. "Tell me, John. What are you looking for?"

John mulled the question over for a few seconds. "I don't know. Other survivors, maybe. I can't believe we're the only ones. And I can only imagine Westmont isn't gonna be smelling all that good in a day or so," John said. "There's sure to be some diseases floating around when the bodies start to decompose."

"Already thought of that," said Richard. "Tomorrow we'll go to the hospital in Downers Grove. It'll probably be the cleanest environment we'll find nearby. Hopefully there'll at least be some medications there." Richard paused for a moment, sizing up John and his decision. "But you're not really looking for survivors."

"I can't stay here," John said after a full minute of silence. "Everywhere I look, I see Tracey. And when I was able to talk to her again, to really talk to her, whether it was real or not, I felt like my old self. My old *good* self. But now that she's gone again..."

"Running away won't solve anything," Richard said.

"Neither will staying here."

"If you go out there, and I certainly won't try and stop you, not with this arm, you'll be alone. And you don't know what you'll find, or if there even *is* anything to find," Richard said. "But if you come with us to the hospital, join us in Downers Grove, we'll all have a better chance of surviving. Especially Gloria. The kid looks up to you, man. I think it'd break her heart to see you go. Out there, it'll just be you. With us, you'd have friends, a family."

John got to his feet, shoving the Zippo back into his pocket. "I'm gonna turn in."

"At least promise me you'll think about it," Richard said.

"I will."

Richard watched John walk out of the room and up the stairs, where they had found three bedrooms. Richard hoped the man was telling the truth when he said he'd think about it, for his own good.

For *all* their own good.

Sometime the next morning, the sound of John preparing them a breakfast very similar to the previous night's dinner — three cans of Campbell's chicken noodle soup, served room-temperature — woke Richard up. Richard told Gloria about their plan to head to the hospital in the neighboring town, but left out the part about John not coming with. He wanted to put off upsetting her as long as possible.

When they were done with breakfast, John helped Richard place Lindsay into the wheelchair. Her condition hadn't changed. The more time that passed, the less likely her chances of waking seemed. But Richard hoped she would. He supposed that's all any of them really had left anymore: hope.

John pushed Lindsay outside onto the porch, following Richard and Gloria, who had wrapped little Heather in a blanket. Richard moved to take over steering duties of the wheelchair. John brushed his hand away.

"I got it," John said. "You won't be pushing anything for awhile. Not with that arm."

Richard smiled at John and held up his hands: *hey, it's all yours.*

"Which way is Downers Grove?" Gloria asked. "I'm all turned around."

John pointed to the east. "Maybe ten miles that way. We should hit the hospital by sunset." He began pushing the wheelchair out onto the sidewalk. The wheels squeaked in protest, a sound John was getting used to.

"What do you think we'll find there?" Gloria asked.

John and Richard exchanged glances. It wasn't as powerful as the ones he'd shared with Heather, but it was strong enough. The kind of look two people share when they both know there's only one answer to a difficult question.

"Hope," John said. "I think we'll find hope."

THE END

medical

tourism

Indus
Health

LaVergne, TN USA
03 December 2010
207221LV00001B/2/A

9 781432 715656